**Outstanding praise for Mary Burton and her novels!**

## COVER YOUR EYES

"Will keep you up all night reading."
—*The Parkersburg News & Sentinel*

"Burton takes the reader on another of her high-speed
roller-coaster rides."
—BookReporter.com

## YOU'RE NOT SAFE

"Burton once again demonstrates her romantic suspense
chops with this taut novel. Burton plays cat-and-mouse
with the reader through a tight plot, with credible
suspects and romantic spice keeping it real."
—*Publishers Weekly*

"Serial killers, vendettas, tortured souls and romance are
the main ingredients in *You're Not Safe*. Beware! As one
of Burton's main characters might say, she has all kinds
of tricks up her sleeve."
—BookReporter.com

"Mary Burton is one of the best romantic
thriller writers around."
—*The Pilot* (Southern Pines, North Carolina)

"Burton really has a way with plot lines and her delivery
is flawless. *You're Not Safe* carries just the right amount
of suspense, creepiness and romance, that when mixed
together, creates a satisfying mystery with a shocker
of an ending."
—FreshFiction.com

**Please turn the page for more rave reviews!**

# Vulnerable

## MARY BURTON

PINNACLE BOOKS
Kensington Publishing Corp.
www.kensingtonbooks.com

PINNACLE BOOKS are published by

Kensington Publishing Corp.
119 West 40th Street
New York, NY 10018

All Kensington titles, imprints, and distributed lines are available at special quantity discounts for bulk purchases for sales promotions, premiums, fund-raising, educational, or institutional use. Special book excerpts or customized printings can also be created to fit specific needs. For details, write or phone the office of the Kensington sales manager: Kensington Publishing Corp., 119 West 40th Street, New York, NY 10018, attn: Sales Department; phone 1-800-221-2647.

ISBN-13: 978-0-7860-3941-8
ISBN-10: 0-7860-3941-8

First printing: April 2016

10 9 8 7 6 5 4 3 2 1

Printed in the United States of America

First electronic edition: April 2016

ISBN-13: 978-0-7860-3942-5
ISBN-10: 0-7860-3942-6

# PROLOGUE

*Friday, September 29, 6:50 P.M.*
*Nashville, Tennessee*

Elisa pressed up against a tree, her round curves scraping against the bark. Her eyes warmed with heat and longing as if she couldn't believe anyone wanted her with such intensity.

"I can't believe I'm blowing off study group to do this," she breathed. "You make agreeing so easy."

It was easy to trace a calculated hand up Elisa's arm and over breasts that weren't very remarkable. "You're so hot."

As dark sexual sensations sent tension shuddering over Elisa's plain, square face, faint thoughts of reason chased after it, tugging her lips into a frown. "I must be insane to follow a stranger into the woods. A few conversations in the coffee shop don't make us friends."

"Are you really looking for a friend or do you want something hot and dangerous?" A slow, practiced sexy smile always made them forget their worries.

"Hot and dangerous," Elisa breathed.

"You're so beautiful. You have an energy that's so hard to resist."

There were so many Elisas in the world. They were desperate for touch. Desperate for a life with a thrilling excitement that reached beyond work and weighty goals. Desperate to be seen.

Their desperation made them so ripe for the picking. So easy to pluck out of their everyday safe lives. So easy to convince that a walk on the wild side was their chance to create a new incarnation. To believe this was her chance to prove she was cool. Reckless. Could take chances. Be spontaneous.

A kiss at the hollow of Elisa's neck had her moaning and closing her eyes. She was drunk with desire. Her head tipped back against the tree and a brush of a hand over her breasts hardened her nipples into jutting peaks.

"Do you want me to squeeze them?" The warm whisper brushed Elisa's ear. "Do you want me to suck them?"

"Yes." The word exploded free as if she now had no control of her own mind.

"Show me. Show me."

With trembling hands, Elisa reached for the buttons of her shirt and frantically unbuttoned them. In her haste, one button popped and skittered to the ground. She peeled back the folds of her very sensible cotton shirt and revealed a pink lacy bra cupping unremark-able C-cup breasts. A small pink bow frantically clung to the stretch of lace banding under Elisa's cleavage, looking as awkward as she did at her little table in the coffee shop.

"Very nice." Forceful hands pinched a nipple hard enough to make Elisa wince.

Elisa's eyes opened, the pain slicing at the edges of the mindless desire clouding her reason. A whimper tumbled over her lips, but she didn't complain. Her kind never complained or made waves when anyone paid the slightest attention for fear harsh words would chase away what little attention they received.

A gentle kiss on the stinging, reddened nipple nudged away the clouds of worry. "Nice. So hot."

"Really? I'm hot?" A pathetic hope clung to the words as her voice rasped over lips painted a cherry red that made her pale skin look pasty white.

"Yeah. Hot."

Tears moistened muddy brown eyes. "No one has ever said that to me before."

Ah, there it was, the sign that this girl would do whatever was asked of her in this moment because she was so grateful. Long strong fingers rested at the hollow of Elisa's neck as her pulse thrummed a crazed beat.

"You're nervous."

"Yes." She was so blinded with wanting. Her voice melted into a soft moan. Scents of a spicy perfume mingled with the musk of the desire dampening her lace panties.

"You don't have to be nervous."

Elisa lifted her breast, silently begging for more touch. "I can't help it. God, I want this."

Soft, seductive laughter rumbled. "I can smell your fear. Your sex."

She moistened her lips, tasting the cherry flavor of her lip gloss. "You can smell it?"

"Super sexy."

Even white teeth nipped her earlobe and sent a visible shudder through Elisa. "You're wet."

Self-consciousness sent a rush of heat up her face. "I can't help it."

"I can stop if you want."

Energy pulsed. Hummed. The press of fingers to her moist center had Elisa hissing in a breath. Slow circular motions sent the young woman's eyes rolling back in her head as the desire rushed and threatened to knock her over.

The fingers stopped moving in the practiced caress and rose to Elisa's lips, teasing them open until she sucked.

"Don't stop," Elisa said.

"I'm not even close to stopping." Strong hands cupped Elisa's throat and squeezed gently at first.

"Is it going to hurt?" The blurted words stumbled past Elisa's lips before they could be censored.

"Do you doubt me?"

"No. No. I just thought . . ."

A soft chuckle rumbled. "It's okay that this is your first time. You don't need to pretend with me. I like knowing I'm the first."

Elisa searched his face with her moist brown eyes and, finding no hint of judgment or censure, she eased back against the tree.

"I'm going to make you so hot, I'll slide right into you and you'll want all of it."

"I want to feel hot. Sexy. Like the other girls in college."

"You are so much better than those girls. Most of them come from money and have had it all handed to them. You're smart. Different."

"I want to be transformed." Elisa's words rushed past her lips as if she sent a request to the heavens.

"You will be." Again, silken words brushed over Elisa like a caress as the sun hung lower on the horizon, pulling with it the remnants of the day's light. Shadows bathed the woods around them, creeping closer with each second. "It'll be like nothing you've ever experienced before."

Strong fingers gripped tighter around Elisa's neck, sending energy through both the seducer and the seduced. Skin tingled. Thrills grew as the pressure increased. So dangerous. So fun to enjoy such utter control.

Elisa closed her eyes, releasing the reins held most days in a white-knuckled grip. She wanted to be dominated. She wanted to be owned. Mind. Body. And spirit.

When the pressure constricted her airway ever so slightly, the first flickers of doubt sparked. Ah, there it was—the fear, which was far more intoxicating than sex.

"Feels good, doesn't it, baby?" Grinning, the seducer squeezed harder, cutting off all air. The white hot desire blurring Elisa's thoughts cooled as quickly as molten metal plunged into ice water. Common sense elbowed past the dark cravings as she shook her head and raised her hands to the still tightening grip.

"Stop," she croaked.

Pain and fear collided in Elisa, driving more energy and determination into her hold.

"Stop." The word strained to be heard as she dug nails painted a bright purple into ribbons of muscles streaming up powerful forearms.

In these moments, with their bodies joined in such an intimate embrace, their thoughts connected. Elisa, who had so desperately wanted a challenge more phys-

ically thrilling than math problems or debate team practice, wanted now nothing more than to break free and
scurry back to the safety of her little house. She wanted
to breathe. To live.

Malice dimmed all traces of humanity, and opened
the abyss now hungry for fear, pain, and panic. "Fear is
part of the fun, baby. Fear shows us we're alive."

When Elisa's breath caught in her throat and couldn't
pass to her lungs, she struggled with a renewed energy
and then drew up her knee and drove it with a desperate force, into bone and sinew.

Anger rocketed, stole breath and strength, and the
deepening hold slackened. "Fucking bitch!"

Oxygen rushing into her lungs, Elisa gobbled it up
as she raised trembling fingers and shoved back hard.
Her fingers pressed to her bruised neck, she pushed
away from the tree and stumbled forward before right-
ing herself and sprinting toward the narrow path that
cut through the thicket of woods.

"You can't leave yet, Elisa!"

Screaming, she tripped over a root, bit her lip hard,
and nearly tumbled before she caught herself. Lungs
filling and refilling with a wheeze, she hurried faster
and faster down the path toward Percy Warner Park's
main road.

"You won't get away from me, Elisa. I know the
woods too well." Jogging now under the light of the
full moon, it was easy to follow Elisa's panicked footsteps thundering down the path.

"Wondering where the road is Elisa?"

Branches cracked and snapped, fusing with her cries
and prayers. "I know you're wondering where we are
in the park. Let's see, we drove up that main road just

a half hour ago and parked in the lot before I kissed you on those lush lips and led you to the entrance of the woods. Thirty minutes ago excitement and anticipation tingled your skin as you gave me just a peek at those panties and bra you bought just for me."

"Leave me alone! I don't want to do this anymore." She sobbed, sucking in her breath as she raced faster.

"You aren't scared, are you? You know I would never hurt you. This is supposed to be fun for the both of us. I want you so bad, baby."

As night squeezed the last of twilight from the trail, tree branches and briars reached out like specters. Their thoughts rejoined this time as hunter and prey. The roar of a truck engine told them both the road was close. A yelp escaped Elisa's lips as she ran faster. She was calculating the distance to the road. Could she catch the attention of that driver? Would she be saved from the nightmare that had ensnared her?

Elisa could flag down a car and then in a blink she would escape. And the plans would be ruined. That wouldn't work at all.

"Elisa!" Her name sounded as twisted as the dark bent branches. "Elisa! Don't be afraid of me. I don't want to hurt you! I want you, baby."

The woods grew silent, swallowing up the little fawn who was, no doubt, clenching her mouth shut and swallowing her cries.

Ahead, a fallen log lay across the path and to the right its large rotted stump was encircled by a pile of thick branches. Had she burrowed those purple nails into the dirt, clawing and scraping and hoping the earth would swallow her up?

In the center of the path lay a shoe. It belonged to

Elisa. She was close, hiding in the thicket. "Elisa, come out, come out, wherever you are. I won't hurt you, baby. You can run, but you can't hide forever."

A twig broke. Leaves rustled. Another car raced down the road, chased out of the park by the darkness. Time stilled, sharpening all the senses. The hunter noticed the cracked branches beside the freshly trampled path. And then Elisa's soft, soft whimpers echoed in the darkness. The sound led down to a pale foot peeking out from under a log.

Five fast footsteps, and the hunter grabbed her ankle as Elisa dug her fingers into the dirt, fighting to stay burrowed in her hiding spot. The will to live gave her strength.

"I don't want to do this anymore. I want to go home," she screamed.

Fingers bit into her skin, tearing the flesh, yanking her free of her sanctuary. "Got to finish what we started, baby. Got to finish it."

She drew in a breath but fisted fingers smashed against her jaw. She crumpled to the dirt, stunned.

Hoisting her wasn't so difficult nor was it hard to carry her back through the woods to the entrance of a small cave, which had been their ultimate destination since the first day they met.

Elisa fell to the cave's floor with a hard thud. "Please, just let me go. I won't tell."

"I know you won't tell."

# CHAPTER ONE

*Monday, October 2, 1:05 A.M.*

Wrapping her hand around the microphone, the musical notes moved inside of Georgia Morgan's head and heart as she closed her eyes. Her voice caressed the melody of "Blue Velvet" and a hush fell over the thinning crowd in Rudy's, a honky-tonk on South Broadway. She transfixed them all with the smooth melodic words infused with layers of feelings few saw when she wasn't on the stage.

In these moments, Georgia wasn't simply singing but reaching out to her birth mother, Annie, whose single legacy to her only child was her golden voice. There were a few photographs, but no memories of the blond songstress who vanished thirty-two years ago, leaving behind an estranged husband, a secret lover, and a wailing infant.

Georgia gripped the microphone, angling her mouth close as moody emotions entwined the words, sculpting fresh angles and adding layers of dimensions. In her mind, the music became vibrant shades of reds, blues, and greens exploding like fireworks.

Georgia's salute to Annie in no way diminished her love for the Morgans, the clan she joined when she was five days old when her late father, homicide detective Buddy Morgan, carried her away from Annie's bloody cinderblock home. Buddy and his wife, Adele, threaded her easily into their family already bustling with three active boys. They never hid her past. Georgia knew about Annie, understood her roots. She and her family considered her a Morgan. Period.

But when she sang, the music so rooted in her soul took hold, and for a few minutes, Annie came alive, not only for her daughter, but for all those who still remembered her.

The song slowly wound down and the guitarist played the last delicate chords. The room was silent, still gripped by the music. Georgia waited a few more beats and then she opened her eyes. Her vision focused. And she was back.

Georgia settled the microphone in its cradle, and rolled her shoulders, breaking the tension. She shouldn't have stayed so late tonight for the extra set. But the allure of the music had been strong.

As she stepped back from the microphone, the crowd clapped, whooped, and hollered. A few rose to their feet and applauded. She swept her hand toward the grizzled guitarist behind her and smiled as she said into the microphone, "Y'all give a big thanks to Freddie for letting me sit in on his set."

The audience cheered and both Georgia and Freddie stood side by side as the applause settled.

"Nice set, Georgia," Freddie said, as he stuck his pick into the guitar strings. He wore torn jeans, scuffed boots with a hole in the sole, and a faded black T-shirt he'd worn for years. To look at the guy, few would realize he played with some of the best country music artists in Nashville.

She brushed a long thick lock of red hair away from her forehead and tugged at the edges of a black silk top that hugged full breasts and caressed designer jeans that molded her figure. "Thanks, Freddie."

"It's always fun when you sing. Like having Annie back," he rasped. "You should stop by more often."

"You're a charmer, Freddie." She slid her hands into pockets trimmed in rhinestones as she glanced at the metal tip of her red ankle-high cowboy boots. "I could hear the lack of practice in my voice tonight. I was all over the place."

He shook his head, the single gold earring in his left ear catching the light. "A few times I closed my eyes and I could hear your mama. Like she was standing right here."

She winked at the guitarist whom she suspected had been half in love with Annie. When Annie's murder case was reopened two years ago, the media had elevated the singer to the likes of James Dean or Patsy Cline. Beautiful, talented, and stolen from the world before her star could fully rise. Dozens still approached her to share their stories of Annie, who was loved by so many. Georgia always smiled and thanked them.

Freddie patted his flat palm over the inlaid wood of his guitar. "Don't be a stranger. Everyone likes having you here."

Laughter rumbled in her chest as she reached behind an amplifier and grabbed her purse. "Flattery wins my heart every time. But I'm not a singer. Catching bad guys is what charges my batteries. See you, sugar."

Georgia was a forensic technician with the Nashville Police Department. She had been on the job nearly a decade and had proven herself to be detailed and driven. The consummate professional in the courtroom whom defense attorneys could not rattle.

She cut through the crowd, pausing to accept a couple of good wishes. She was never good with receiving compliments or attention, so she smiled, thanked everyone like her parents taught her and kept moving with no real need to strike up a conversation.

She moved up to the bar where KC Kelly, a tall, bald, broad-shouldered man wearing a Hawaiian shirt, polished a set of whiskey glasses fresh from the dishwasher. KC had been her late father's partner in homicide for over twenty-five years. When he retired, he bought Rudy's from the previous owner who had created a place where tourists and locals flocked to hear the up-and-coming talent. When KC took over the honky-tonk, cops initially came to show support for one of their own. Many discovered they liked Rudy's and that KC could really run a bar. And so the tourists, locals, and cops kept returning to the safest South Broadway bar in Nashville.

"Did good tonight, kid," he said. "The crowd loved you." He pushed a fresh glass with ice and diet soda toward her.

She took a long sip. "Thanks for letting me share the stage. The day job has been crazy lately, and I haven't had much time. It was fun."

"So I hear big brother gave you a cold case," KC said.

Big brother was Deke Morgan, who now ran the Nashville Police Homicide Department. He was joined by her other brother, Rick Morgan, who also worked in the same unit. Third brother, Alex, was the outlier. He worked for the Tennessee Bureau of Investigation, or TBI.

"I should be more careful when I ask for extra work." She scooped up a handful of nuts from a bowl on the bar and popped them in her mouth. "It's taken me weeks to read through the files."

"Deke tells me Dalton Marlowe is putting the squeeze on everyone," KC said.

Dalton Marlowe was a very rich man whose son was one of three teens who went into Percy Warner Park five years ago. The students, from an exclusive high school called St. Vincent, went hiking in the southwest Nashville park that covered twenty-six hundred acres of wooded land crisscrossed by a dozen backroad trails, bike paths, and dead end roads. Their plan was to collect data for a science project and return home by dark.

When the teens had not reported in that night, search crews had been dispatched. At the end of the second day, volunteers found one of the kids, Amber Ryder, at the bottom of a ravine. Her arm was badly broken and she suffered a head injury. When she woke up in the hospital the next day, she swore she had no memory of what had happened in the woods. Search crews continued to look for weeks but the two other students, Bethany Reed and Mike Marlowe, were never found.

Mr. Marlowe has been pressing the Missing Persons Unit relentlessly for answers. This year, he again made a sizable donation to the police foundation, a kind of gesture that expects a return. Marlowe was clear that he didn't want to hear any more bullshit theories about his son Mike and Bethany running off like a modern-day Romeo and Juliet.

"So Deke's balls are in a vise with the mayor?" KC asked.

She shrugged. "He's getting a hell of a lot of pressure from City Hall, but it doesn't look like it's fazed him. He hopes to kill two birds with one stone. Give me a cold case that I've been clamoring for and pacify the powers that be. It's a win all the way around."

"I was still on the job then. But because the case was considered a missing persons investigation, homicide never got a crack at it. I think they pulled Buddy in once."

"Well, it's now being investigated as a homicide."

"Too bad your old man and I didn't get a real crack at it."

"I wish you had. So far, I've got eighty hours invested in reading witness statements, search crew reports, interviews, and examining the forensic data."

Dark eyes sharpened as they did when he'd been on a homicide investigation. "What about that kid that survived?"

"Amber Ryder. I tracked down her number through her mother, Tracy. The woman wasn't thrilled to see me or talk, but she gave me a phone number. I've called it a couple of times but so far no return calls."

A tall waitress with dark brown hair signaled KC she had an order. He filled three steins with beer and set them in front of her. As he moved back toward Georgia, he faced the register and punched in the order. "You working the case alone?"

Georgia swirled her drink in the glass. "No, as luck would have it, Deke has assigned Jake Bishop to the case with me."

"He's a solid cop."

"Right."

He shook his head, understanding that stubborn ran as deep in Georgia as it did in her brothers and her late father. "So, what now? You don't want to share?"

"Not that. Jake irritates me."

Amusement tweaked the edges of his lips. "How so?"

She leaned forward. "Started flirting with me in the last year. Hell, I stayed off his radar just fine and then suddenly I'm right in the middle after he caught one of my shows here."

"That so bad?"

She held up a finger as if reading her lists of cons. "He's a cop and I've always made it a policy not to date cops."

"My late wife never had any issues with being married to a cop."

"Well, Deb was a saint and we both know I'm not. I watched Mom do it with Dad and I don't want any part of that."

He pulled a bar rag from his shoulder and wiped up the few peanut shells she'd dropped. "I don't think he's looking to put a ring on your finger."

"No, he's looking for a roll in the hay and I don't need a quickie with a guy that will forget me before his pants are zipped."

KC's laughter rumbled. "Jesus, Georgia, ever thought that you might not be so easy to live with."

She held up her hands in surrender. "No arguments here, KC. Not a one. Which is why I don't need any more cops in my life."

"You got him wrong, kid."

She took a long sip of soda. When she was down to ice, she crunched a few pieces between her teeth. "Don't care. My focus is the case and the case alone."

"Have you found anything the old teams missed?"

"Nothing so far. They didn't leave a stone unturned. And none of those guys gets any criticism from me. Hard to solve a case when you don't have bodies, no suspects, and a witness with no memory."

"You really think you can crack the case after all this time?"

She shrugged. "It's only been five years. Maybe someone knows something and will talk. Maybe Amber Ryder will call me back and tell me she's remembered something."

Skepticism deepened the lines of his face. "Amber always said she never could recall a single detail about what happened in the woods."

She fished through the nuts in the bowl searching for a cashew. "Her testimony was consistent throughout the police files."

"She was a suspect, but her unwavering testimony won over a lot of cops."

She tipped her glass up, drinking until she drained the last bit of liquid. "Could be as simple as she was telling the truth."

"Could be."

Carrie, a tall, thin waitress, wore a tight red Rudy's T-shirt and figure-hugging jeans, placed a drink order with KC. "Georgia, long time no see."

"Looking good, Carrie. How's the baby?"

"Fat and happy. Two months old now."

"Time goes fast." Georgia noticed the dark blue bruise ringing Carrie's forearm. Last she heard from KC, Carrie had broken up with the boyfriend that liked to pepper her with bruises. "You still seeing Hal?"

Carrie turned so the bruise was no longer visible. "Yeah. He loves the baby."

"So much he puts bruises on her mother."

Carrie's skin pinked with embarrassment. "It's not like that. Got this from an accident."

How many times had Georgia had this conversation with Carrie? Too tired to argue, Georgia grabbed a napkin and a pen from behind the bar and scrawled her name and cell phone number on it. "When you and the baby are ready to leave, call me. You can stay at my place."

Carrie shook her head, her eyes wide with panic. "It's not like that. Hal loves me."

"Put the napkin in your pocket. One day you might decide that love doesn't have to hurt like that."

Carrie crushed the napkin, but she tucked it in her jeans pocket before arranging the beers on her tray.

Nodding, Georgia flattened her palms on the bar, wanting to scream at the woman but unwilling to repeat what she had said a dozen times before.

A frowning KC filled the order. "Go on and get those served."

"Sure thing, KC." She offered them both an apologetic smile before she hurried away.

"Damn it," Georgia muttered.

"I know what you're thinking."

A wry grin twisted her lips as she turned from the waitress now smiling at two middle-aged men dressed in flannel and jeans. "And you know it's not legal to track old Hal down and run him over with a car."

"No, it's not." No doubt KC had noticed the bruises and spoken his piece to the waitress.

"Yeah. Too bad."

KC refilled Georgia's glass.

Hard not to see what was coming. "Hal is gonna kill her or that baby one day. It's a matter of time."

"I've talked to her until I'm blue." He rested his big hands gently on the bar.

"I know," she said.

KC shrugged, chasing the fresh tension knotting his shoulders. "So when do you and Bishop start on the case?"

Crunching ice, she thought about the five calls from Bishop now on her voice mail. As she raised her glass to her lips, fatigue crawled up her spine and reminded her she'd not slept in over twenty hours. "Tomorrow. We're meeting with Deke. He's wrapping up another homicide."

KC flipped a white bar towel over his shoulder. "Don't you think you better get some sleep?"

"It would be the logical thing." As Georgia slid off the bar stool, her brain hummed with nervous energy from the performance. A live gig always left her juiced and thinking she could run a marathon. Experience told her that the adrenaline crash would come in about an hour. Just enough time to get home and fall into bed.

Turning to leave, she caught sight of a tall, slim, athletic woman with shoulder-length blond hair and blue eyes. She wore an oversized sweater, jeans, and heeled brown cowboy boots. A backpack slung over her left shoulder, the woman approached Georgia.

She paused. "Can I help you?"

"You're Georgia Morgan?"

"That's right."

"Amber Ryder. You've called me a couple of times."

The name took her by surprise. "Wow, Amber Ryder. Sorry to looked so shocked. I wasn't expecting you out of the blue like this. Or you to be so blond."

Amber tightened her grip around the strap of her backpack. "I changed the hair a couple of years ago. New start."

After the case of the missing teens hit the airways, Amber was besieged with reporters as well as haters who did not believe her story. According to police reports filed, bricks were thrown through her mother's front window and she was harassed and chased several times. Some distrusted her. Some pitied her. But everyone, good or bad, had weighed in with an opinion about Amber Ryder. Finally, forced to drop out of high school, she homeschooled herself until a Good Samaritan offered her a scholarship to the University of Texas and she left Nashville for good.

"How did you find me?" Georgia asked.

"I called the station. They said you were singing tonight."

She wondered who had given out her location to a stranger. Wondered who would get an earful.

"You said you're reopening the case."

Georgia rose off her barstool. "That's right. We're going to be treating the case as a homicide now."

"You found the bodies?"

"Not yet."

Amber nodded toward an empty booth. "Can we sit in one of the booths? I'm starving and could use a meal."

"Yeah, sure." Amber had done more than change her black hair to blond. Gone were the thick bangs and heavy eye makeup that made her pale skin look sallow, the multiple piercings in her left ear, and the half dozen rings on her fingers. Now, natural gold-blond hair and faint traces of mascara accentuated vivid blue eyes and a peaches-and-cream complexion as smooth as a stone.

Georgia caught KC's gaze and noted the raised eyebrow. He was curious as well. Sights set on an empty booth, she led Amber to it and stood waiting until the woman lowered into the seat.

This unexpected meeting had Georgia thumbing through all the questions she wanted to ask Amber. Instead, she raised her hand toward Carrie. "Can I get two menus? Starving."

Carrie grabbed a couple of menus and came toward the table. "Don't you want the regular?"

Burgers, fries, and more soda. She ordered the same thing every single time she ate at Rudy's. "Sure. Amber?"

Amber settled her backpack in the corner of the booth. "I'll have the same."

"Carrie, bring one check," Georgia said.

Amber smiled. "Thanks. Been a day or so since I had a decent meal. I didn't stop much on the drive up from Dallas."

Georgia watched Carrie walk away, noting the bruise on the back of her arm.

Amber tapped her finger on the table. "Who's hitting her?"

Georgia turned back to Amber, feeling protective of Carrie's privacy ignored the question.

"I'm betting a boyfriend or husband. It bothers you."

"This conversation isn't about Carrie."

"You're right. Sorry."

Georgia sat back in her booth and waited until Carrie arrived with their drinks and a basket of rolls. "Thanks, Carrie."

Amber smiled up at her. "Thanks."

"KC says to drink and eat up, ladies. He said you both are too skinny."

As Carrie walked away, Amber unwrapped her straw and placed it carefully in her soda. She reached for a warm roll. She took a bite, her eyes closing for a second as she enjoyed the pure pleasure. "That really hits the spot."

"Good."

Georgia grabbed a piece of roll, tore off a section and bit into it. Soft and warm, it tasted good and filled some of the emptiness in her belly. She'd not really eaten since breakfast. "So you came from Dallas. You been there since you left Nashville."

"Yeah. Earned my degree last summer."

"In four years."

"Summer school helped. I wanted to be done so I could move on and get a real job. No more waiting tables." Amber glanced toward KC and locked gazes with him. She smiled and then looked away. "He's a cop."

"How can you tell?"

"I talked to enough of them."

"He's retired."

Nodding, she said, "I met a lot of cops during the investigation. I don't remember him."

"He's homicide. The case was classified as missing persons."

Frowning, she shook her head. "I spoke to a homicide detective."

Georgia had read in the case files that it had been her father who'd interviewed Amber. "You dealt with Buddy Morgan."

Recognition flickered. "Once, I think. Big, tall, gruff guy. I remember he was nice."

*Nice.* She'd heard her father described a lot of ways but nice had never been one of them. Buddy had been a crack detective, one of the best in the state, but he was tough as nails and single-minded.

As if sensing her thoughts, Amber asked, "Was he your father? Can't be a coincidence that you are a Morgan as well."

"You should be a detective."

Absently, she traced the curved edge of the table. "He told me he had a daughter who was about ten years older than me. That must be you."

"I guess so." Georgia played her cards close, not wanting to give more information than she received. Buddy had taught her that trick. "So why did you come all this way to find me? You could simply have called."

Amber took a bit of bread. "I thought maybe I could help if I came to town. I've tried to move on, but what happened in those woods still dogs me."

As the adrenaline from the stage ebbed, fingers of fatigue now worked on her back and neck and reminded her of the early morning shift waiting for her. "Has any of your memory returned?"

Amber took another bite. "No. And I have tried hypnosis and relaxation techniques, even visualization. Nothing works." She tucked a blond strand behind her ear. "You said in your phone message that you're reviewing all the files associated with the case."

"That's right."

"How much have you read?"

"All of it." She could now boil down dozens of hours of reading into a few lines. "Three teenagers went into the woods and one, you, came out. The other two have not been found yet. You claimed memory loss. The trail went cold."

Amber collected the remaining bits of bread in her hands, watching the crumbs land onto the tabletop. "I had a grade-three concussion. The head injury not only erased the actual day but the days leading up to our trip into the woods. I'm damn lucky to be alive."

Georgia studied the young woman and recalled the facts. "Your head injury was significant. Rescue workers found you at the bottom of a ravine and theorized you hit your head on the rocks at the bottom. Broke your arm. Compound fracture. Some thought you were lying. That you did remember what happened and perhaps were even responsible." She was never good at dancing around tough questions.

"I know. The police questioned me more times than I can remember. They thought if they asked me the same question enough, I'd trip up. But I never did because I told only what I knew, which was the truth." She flattened her palms on the table. "I simply don't remember the woods, and the last memory I had starts three days before we went into the park."

Many a liar had crossed her path while on the job so she wasn't quick to bite on any story. "You have no memory of anything in the woods?"

Amber's voice was steady and unwavering. "No. My hard drive was wiped clean."

"Okay." That didn't mean she believed her, but she wasn't ready to argue the point now.

"I'm glad you've reopened the case. Once and for all, I want to prove that I was also a victim and not some manipulative teenager responsible for what happened to those kids."

The intensity snapping with each quietly spoken word intrigued Georgia more than the words. "Tell me what you do remember."

Hearing the interest in Georgia's voice, Amber relaxed a fraction as if she took comfort that someone might actually believe her. "I remember waking up three days before we had planned our hike at Percy Warner Park."

"We?" She knew but she wanted to hear it from Amber.

"Mike Marlowe and Bethany Reed."

"You were all students at St. Vincent High School.

Bethany was AP/Honors science. You were a solid if not underachieving student, and Mike was the dumb jock. Three unlikely classmates working on a science project."

"Yes."

A wrinkle furrowed in the center of Amber's brow. "The project's focus was ecosystems. Bethany determined that Percy Warner Park would be our ecosystem and we were planning to make extensive observations during that initial visit and then return each week during the fall semester."

Georgia had been a B student in high school and did what she needed to get by. It wasn't until she reached college and took her first forensic class that her fascination with learning kicked into high gear. "Sounds ambitious."

"Bethany pitched the idea to us. She wanted the project to stand out."

"Why did she need you or Mike?"

"She was afraid to go it alone. She had applied to some very prestigious colleges but had blown several interviews. She was painfully shy. She knew I'd go with her because we were friends."

Georgia tried to picture the girl and the nerd as friends. "And Mike?"

"Trying to get his grades up so he could apply to one of the schools here in Tennessee. His dad had a lot of pull in the state and if his grades could be halfway decent, the old man could call in favors."

"What about you?" She knew all the answers but wanted to hear it from Amber.

"My grades were good but not great, and I needed

big scholarship money if I wanted more than living with my mom and working at Blue Note Java."

"The coffee shop."

"Right. The one near the school."

"So the three of you were all motivated."

"I'm not sure how motivated Mike and I were, but we were all desperate for something. Desperation makes strange bedfellows." She threaded her fingers together and rested them on the table. Her nails were neat, trimmed and the cuticles manicured.

"Okay. It's a few days before the hike. What's your last memory?"

"I went by Mike's house to drop off notes from Monday's class. He missed it. Said he was sick but I suspected he was hungover."

"Was he?"

"He liked to drink and he got wasted over the weekend on a road trip for a college football game. That was so typical of Mike."

Georgia shook her head. "My dad would have woken me up and insisted I go to school sick or not. He'd have wanted to teach me a lesson about underage drinking."

"Mike's dad wasn't like that. Dalton, Mr. Marlowe, protected Mike. Covered up his messes. Doted on the boy. If Mike needed an excuse for school, his dad came up with one."

Dalton Marlowe did well as a local corporate attorney, but the real money came through Mike's mother, which Dalton still controlled until Mike was found dead or alive. Mike's mother died when he was fifteen.

"So you gave hungover Mike the notes. That's Tuesday. You three didn't go into the woods until Friday."

"One of the reasons I came by Mike's house was to confirm he wasn't backing out of our project. He did that a lot and I was there to make sure he would hike."

"That's the last time you saw him before the hike?"

"I don't know." She recognized Georgia's word trap. "I have no memory."

Georgia's tone held no hint of apology. "What did Mike say that last day you remembered seeing him?"

"That's the thing. I never saw Mike that day. His father answered the door. I asked to see Mike, but he wouldn't let me. Said Mike was sleeping. So I gave the notes to his dad. His dad appreciated my help and even gave me fifty bucks for my trouble." She crossed her legs and then slowly settled back in the booth.

"That's sounds like a very generous tip for just delivering homework. But it bothered you. Why?"

"I wanted to say no to the tip, but I needed the money. My mom is a cocktail waitress and she never made a lot of money. I spent that fifty bucks on groceries."

Georgia would battle her growing fatigue so she could compare her father's case notes against Amber's comments when she returned home. Buddy had always kept careful notes when he investigated a case. "What do you remember next?"

"I took the money from Mr. Marlowe, bought groceries, and went home. I knocked out my math homework. I stayed in that night and went to bed early. And that's all I remember until I woke up in the hospital. It's unnerving to have no recall, especially for several days. I keep waiting for something to trigger a buried memory."

X-rays and MRIs confirmed the head injury to her

left temporal lobe. "The doctors say memory loss is not uncommon."

"I suppose. It was several weeks before I could think clearly again. Felt like I was in a fog."

KC reappeared with their food and settled hot plates in front of each woman. He looked at Amber. "Loaded extra fries on your plate."

When she smiled up at him, her face lit up. "You're sweet."

KC settled his hand on his hip. "Took me a minute to place you. The hair threw me off."

Amber sat a little straighter, raising her gaze to his. She hesitated as if sizing him up. "And?"

"And nothing," he said. "I didn't work your case and I'm retired now. I'll leave the figuring to Georgia. She's smarter than me by a long shot."

Georgia understood what he was doing. Buddy used to say KC was dumb like a fox. Could make anyone relax. Open up. Tell secrets they never imagined they'd reveal.

Amber reached for her soda and took a sip. "Good. I want this case solved. I'm at your service."

KC scratched behind his ear. "I know you do. Good luck."

Amber picked up a fry but didn't bite it. "I searched you on the Internet after you called me. I wanted to know if you were legit and not some reporter trying to railroad me."

Georgia's name would have popped up more than a few times in association with Annie's murder case. "You get a lot of calls from reporters?"

"I did at the one-year anniversary and then the second. Now that the fifth year is coming up I was expecting more calls."

"Anything threatening?"

She reached for her phone and scrolled through her texts. She read, "'Time you repent, liar. If you thought you escaped, then you are wrong. God knows what you did!'"

"That from the same person?"

"Yeah. But there will be others. I don't know how they find my number but they do."

"Have you had the number traced?"

Amber raised her chin a notch as if this was a normal problem she could handle. "I did a reverse search on the number but nothing came up."

"Has anyone approached you?"

"No. But the change of hair throws most people off. I've not been recognized in person for a couple of years."

"What do you do in Dallas?"

"I'm an account manager in an advertising company. It's entry level, but it's a good job. And the pay is decent."

Everything she said fit.

"I'm glad you're back. Maybe you being here will help solve what happened to Bethany and Mike."

Amber nodded. "Have you contacted Dalton Marlowe yet?"

"He's spoken to the chief of homicide several times, but he and I haven't formally met. I'm sure that will change. He's pressing to see this case solved." Dalton Marlowe was clearly a man accustomed to getting everything he wanted.

"You understand if you fail, he'll do his best to ruin your career."

There were veiled threats according to Deke, but like her brother, she didn't scare so easily when it came to the job. "I'm not planning on failing."

Amber's mood darkened. "Good."

The two ate in silence for a moment before Georgia set her napkin by her plate. She had noticed the dark circles under Amber's eyes. "Do you have a place to stay?"

"I'm in a motel now. When the money runs low, I'll hit my mother up for a place to stay."

"And you have a car?"

"Yes. Don't worry about me. I can take care of myself." Amber balled up her napkin and tossed it beside the half-eaten plate of food.

"I'd like to talk to you again soon. Amber, I'm assuming the cell number I called is still your number."

"It is. And yes. Call me. I'll be here a couple of days. I need to see my mom before I head back to Dallas."

"I'll call you tomorrow."

Amber's gaze met Georgia's and held it. "I'll help in any way I can."

"Thanks. I'm counting on it." She rose as Amber inched out of the booth and stood.

"Thanks for opening this up again. It's time for closure."

"Definitely." Georgia followed Amber to the front door. "Where are you parked?"

"Right out front. I'll be fine."

She stood at the door, watching the woman move down the street and into a mid-sized dark car. When the headlights came on and she pulled out into traffic, Georgia stood there for a long moment watching her drive off.

Earlier fatigue evaporated only to be replaced by a buzzing energy. She moved back to the booth and was greeted by her own half-eaten plate of food.

"Go home," KC said, placing a takeout container on the table.

She looked up, realizing Rudy's had nearly cleared out. "Right."

"You okay?" KC slid into the booth across from her.

"Sure. I'm fine. Amber Ryder is an enigma."

He rested hands on the table. "She's prettier than I remembered."

"She reminds me a little of Annie. Independent. Alone. Living on her terms."

His voice had a gruff sound as if somewhere along the way the tones had been chewed up in a meat grinder. "She's pretty like Annie. But she's not Annie."

"Oh, I know. I'm not harboring any mommy issues."

He grunted. "She's matured. One hell of an attractive woman."

A smile teased the edges of her lips. "Well, look at you ogling a twenty-something."

He smoothed a weathered hand over his bald head. "Just an observation. Bishop know you called her?"

Laughing, she drained the last of her soda watered down from the melting ice. "Didn't realize I needed his permission."

A smile tugged at the edges of his lips. "I thought you were a team."

She shifted, tamping down the irritation that Bishop's name always stirred. "Not a team. Coworkers with a shared goal."

KC boxed up the leftovers of her meal and pushed the carton toward her. "Buddy said Amber's amnesia was convenient as hell. He said if you were gonna go into the woods looking for trouble and found it, then a good dose of not-remembering might be the only plausible excuse given the grade-three concussion. But the boys in missing persons could never trip her up. And with no bodies, homicide didn't participate much in the investigation."

"She said she's glad I'm investigating. Wants me to set the record straight. Wants a clean slate."

His Hawaiian shirt pulled tight against his small paunch as he shifted. "Maybe."

"She's not stupid. She said she still gets threatening texts around the anniversary."

"Not surprising. Lots of crazies in the world."

"Fair enough."

"My one piece of advice: Don't count out Bishop. He's a top cop."

"You should have seen the smug grin on his face when he delivered me the case files."

"There must have been a mountain of files."

"Twenty boxes, packed tight." Each time she considered the task of quitting, she thought about Bishop's smug grin. She'd be damned before admitting defeat.

He pointed a stubby finger at her. "Go home and sleep."

She dug a twenty dollar bill out of her pocket and tossed it on the table. "Right. Home. Sleep."

\* \* \*

Amber parked her car in front of the one-story ranch home in the east end of Nashville. The house was covered in white siding that had long ago grayed and dulled. A broken shutter on the right side clung to the house by one nail and the front porch light dangled, waving back and forth in the slight breeze. The weekly trash was curbside and the dented silver cans overflowed with pizza boxes, Chinese carryout, and empty bottles of rose wine. Her mother, Tracy Ryder, no, Tracy McDaniel now, had done little to fix up the property. How many times had she promised to hire help and see that the place was cleaned up and presentable? How many times had she sworn to lay off the booze? . . .

None of that mattered right now. What mattered was that Amber was in a bind and she needed Tracy's help. Not for the long term, but for the next day or two.

A woman's figure passed in front of the sheer curtains of the front room. Amber recognized her mother's walk, noting she gained a little weight in the last five years. Tracy had always sported a hot figure that had landed her not only Amber's dad, but two husbands before Amber graduated high school. Despite the few extra pounds, Tracy still had the moves to find herself a new man and a new meal ticket.

Sooner or later, she'd have to knock on that front door and let Tracy know she was back in town. Tracy could be a real problem if she didn't handle her right, but Amber wasn't worried. She would manage Tracy just as she had since elementary school.

Amber didn't have the energy tonight to deal with

Tracy. She would stay in the motel a few more days. The last few days had been hectic and talking to Georgia drained her more than she expected. She needed a good drama-free place to sleep. She needed to keep her brain sharp. To think. There was too much at stake now for her to make any kind of mistake. Her phone buzzed, signaling a text. She fished it out of her purse and looked at the display.

*You will soon burn in hell.*

# CHAPTER TWO

***Monday, October 2, 10:00 A.M.***

Homicide Detective Jake Bishop smiled at the determined clip-clop of Georgia's feet moving down the uncarpeted hallway of the homicide department. She always moved as if the demons of hell nipped at her feet. Never relaxed. Never smiling. Buttoned up tight. She was a live wire of determination, drive, and shouldering a need to prove herself.

Today they were scheduled to brief Deke on the Marlowe/Reed case; otherwise, Jake would have taken the day off. The last three days he and his partner, Rick Morgan, had been chasing down a killer who shot two men in east Nashville. It took days to interview witnesses and piece together the fragments of the men's lives. Both, it turned out, were meth dealers unworried about cutting into the business of a rival group. They found the shooter last night shortly after midnight sleeping in the back room of a pool hall. The arrest was textbook and by four a.m. the man was processed and in jail awaiting arraignment. Rick, running on empty, went home for sleep and time alone with his new wife, Jenna, a former Baltimore police officer who was a trained forensic artist. She now freelanced her forensic drawing and sculpting skills to several jurisdictions in the region. Once a missing child herself, she specialized in missing children cases and often charged a very minimal fee to cover expenses. In her spare time, she painted portraits thanks to a growing reputation.

Jake should have packed it in for the day but didn't want to miss the fireworks sure to follow Georgia, who now rushed past his open door toward Deke. Finding his office empty, she emerged frustrated and ducked into Rick's office.

He always liked the way Georgia pinned her red hair up on her head and how the curls wriggled free to form a collection of ringlets at the base of her neck. On a humid day, her hair went into all-out rebellion, as much as the sprinkle of freckles across the bridge of her nose did every time she tried to cover them with makeup. Her neatly tucked shirt tugged at her narrowing waistband as if it also hated being constrained. Every aspect of the woman was in full battle mode.

However, she was always cool, all business, and kept him at arm's distance. That had once suited him fine. There were plenty of women to warm his bed other than her. But six months ago that all changed. He was in Rudy's grabbing a beer when Georgia took center stage. The red curls tumbled around her shoulders and she traded the blue button-down shirt, khakis, and steel-toed boots for a sleek silk top with a V-neck that dipped between her breasts, designer jeans hugging her round hips, and rhinestone studded boots. He took special notice of her as would any man with a pulse in the bar.

KC had leaned forward. "You like? Wait until she sings."

"She can't be that good." He sipped, cold beer sliding over a parched throat.

"She's gonna rock your world."

And she had. He was never so transfixed as he was when Georgia cradled that microphone in her long fingers and sang Faith Hill's "Breathe." Shit. He still got hard when he thought about the moment.

"Deke went to get coffee," Jake called out to Georgia.

Seconds passed and then she stood in his doorway careful not to cross the threshold. "We have a meeting at ten."

He tapped his watch. "Can't wait."

She folded her arms. "You read any of the files?"

"Not many. But I'll get up to speed quickly. Besides," he said grinning and leaning back in his chair, "you'll give me the Cliff Notes, right?"

She closed her eyes for a moment, shaking her head. Before she formed a response, Deke's voice sounded in the hall. Without a word, she turned and vanished into Deke's office.

Figuring this was the meeting on the Marlowe/Reed case, he rose from his desk, straightened his jacket, and ambled toward Deke's office. As he grew closer, he heard Georgia's clipped words sharpening each consonant. She sounded ready to boil over.

"She tracked me down at *Rudy's*." Georgia held a rolled-up stack of papers in her left hand. "Someone here told her I was at Rudy's. Not cool to give out information like that. How do I know someone is not going to cap my ass while I'm onstage with a bright spotlight in my eyes."

"Do you have a name?"

"I tried to ferret it out but no one is talking . . . yet."

"Okay. I'll see what I can find out. What did Amber say?"

Jake leaned on the door frame. "Amber Ryder?"

"She tracked me down at Rudy's last night."

"How did she know to look for you?" Jake asked.

"I called her a while ago."

"And you didn't think to tell me?" Slight annoyance flared. "We're partners on the case, right?"

She sat in one of the two seats angled in front of Deke's desk. "There wasn't much to tell until now, and now I'm telling you all I know."

Instead of sitting, Jake remained standing, feet slightly braced. Her little end run clipped the edges of his good humor. He cut his teeth as a cop on the streets of South Boston before he picked up stakes and moved to Nashville seven years ago. He had learned a few things about Southern niceties and could even employ them when it suited, but when angered, the boy from Southie with the hot temper came out swinging. "Going forward, we work the case as a team. No exceptions."

Blue eyes sharpened. "Sure."

Deke leaned back in his chair. He was tall with broad shoulders that filled the white starched dress shirt with sleeves rolled up to his forearms. A carbon copy of his old man, Jake still found himself doing a double take when he saw Deke glower as well as the old man.

Deke had headed homicide for two years and recently married local defense attorney Rachel Wainwright, who was as bullish on defense as he was prosecution. There'd been a few side bets on how long the two would last.

Unlike Georgia, Deke and his brothers, Rick and Alex, had jet black hair. Deke's had turned more salt and pepper in the last year. He jokingly blamed the gray on his new wife whom he adored.

Deke studied Georgia as he always did—a bit perplexed and annoyed. "Georgia, tell us what she said."

"Like I said, I called her a few weeks ago. I was halfway through the files and took a chance I could quickly catch up with her. She didn't answer."

Deke tapped an index finger on the arm of his chair as he leaned back. "Two missing kids, one found. As you both realize, Dalton Marlowe wants closure and no more delays. It's going to take cooperation to make that happen."

Neither answered, but neither argued with Deke.

"It was a hell of a case," Jake said. "All hands on deck. I've never seen so many man hours dumped into one case."

Georgia wasn't exactly frowning but no smile was in sight either. "We all volunteered for search crews."

"I wish I had a nickel for all the times I walked through Percy Warner Park," he said. "It was fall and one of the warmest on record. We never found a trace of the two other kids."

She folded her arms, openly regarding him. "Did you ever interview Amber during the case? You weren't mentioned in the files."

"I was present while she was interviewed once. She was adamant that she didn't remember what happened in the woods. Her story never varied."

"And you believe her?"

"It was all a little too convenient for me. However, she passed the polygraph test and the body language experts all cleared her. Even the docs said her concussion caused by the fall could have created the amnesia. But I never could swallow it."

"Why?" Georgia challenged. "That's a lot of science backing her up."

That was a trait he liked. She never took anything at face value. She was always pushing, prodding, wanting more until she found the truth. "Never could give you a solid reason."

"Gut instinct?" Her gaze danced just a little with humor.

"Yeah, Dr. Science. My gut. I couldn't boil it down to anything that could be proven in a court of law but the twitch I get around liars was there." Many a cop relied on instinct and the intangibles when they interviewed suspects. Sensing what not to ask was just as important.

Eyes narrowing, a sign she was processing, she turned back to her brother. "As we all agreed, I also pulled the clothes Amber wore at the time of the fall. I reexamined the items a few days ago and collected more samples including hair fibers and a stain. I've sent it all off to the state lab for retesting. No answers yet, but could you lean on the lab?"

Deke shook his head. "You sound like Rachel. She's always pushing for faster, more detailed DNA testing. The lab crews hate the sound of my voice."

She unrolled the papers she was clutching and tried to flatten them out, but they rolled back up as if they too didn't want to take orders. "But they do listen to you."

Deke's newly minted wedding band glinted in the light as he twirled it on his finger. "What do you think you'll find this time?"

"I don't know. But the testing is a little more fine-tuned than even five years ago."

Jake ran his fingers down his Brooks Brother tie, absently making sure it was straight. "They find data now that's so specific, the lab techs don't even know what it means."

Deke's scowl deepened, accentuating the lines around his mouth and his eyes.

"You better than anyone, Detective Bishop, under-stand the value of fresh eyes," he said. "This case is worth a second look. And with Amber now back in town, we might have a shot at solving it."

"That case got thousands of looks five years ago. But Dalton Marlowe has political juice and it's coming to a head." Jake didn't like being boxed into a corner but he understood better than anyone the power of a grieving overprotective parent with influence. "Five years. Tests change. People change their stories. It's still worth a look."

"How much time have you invested in the case files so far, Georgia?" Deke asked.

"Eighty hours," she said. "All my spare time in the last few weeks. The sooner I get any test results back on DNA, the sooner I can develop new leads. I'm not on anyone's priority list so it will take months."

Deke's chair squeaked as he leaned forward. "You're preaching to the choir. I'll rattle the cages."

"Thanks." Her grin was sweet and friendly and Jake guessed she used that same smile a thousand times since she was a tiny girl. She was expert at wrapping her big brothers around her little finger.

"That case was full of dead ends." Jake liked the smile, but refused to be manipulated by it.

"Don't you want to know what happened to those kids?" Georgia's voice rose an octave.

"Sure. And I'll give the case one hundred percent. But the search and investigation back in the day was pretty damn extensive." Truth was he liked the idea of giving this case a second look. Two kids remained missing. His argument now was based solely on pissing Georgia off. He could dish out as well as he took from her.

"It's a start," she said.

"Retesting forensic evidence is a small but integral piece of the puzzle. Most cases are solved by a detective's legwork." Jake shook his head. "If this case is cracked, it'll be because someone is now willing to talk."

She was too professional to roll her eyes, but for him, she did anyway with a shit-eating smirk.

Jake shook his head as he looked directly at her. "You, Georgia, aren't always nice to people. You're about as subtle as a crowbar."

A nod of acknowledgment lobbed his way. "I'm nice to some people."

Deke laughed, but quickly caught himself and sobered his expression. "Your heart is in the right place, but you can be so direct that you put people off."

She glared as if daring his smile to reappear. "I can't help it if they have thin skins."

Jake shook his head. "I'll do the talking."

"Bishop's right, Georgia," Deke said before she could rebut. "You'll have to do more than read case files and retest DNA. Bishop excels at the interviews. Did you make a witness list while you were reading the case files?"

As much as she wanted to work this case alone she was smart enough to realize it would take them both. "I did. I also have a ten-page synopsis."

"Perfect." Deke rose. "You two work out the details and make something happen. Now get out of my office."

In the hallway, she drew in a steadying breath. "How can you interview people if you haven't read the files?"

"Get me your list and the synopsis and I'll be up to speed enough to get the ball rolling."

"You and Rick went nonstop for the last three days. Don't you need a day off?"

Hearing a challenge, his white teeth bared into a mirthless smile. "I always have some gas in the tank."

Her eyes sparked as if a thousand arguments crowded her mind, but she silenced them, fearing releasing one would toss the lid off Pandora's box. "Sure."

"Sounds like a plan," Bishop said, clapping his hands together.

Georgia's frown deepened, but she didn't complain. To her credit, she put the case before her feelings. She forced a smile, but it reminded him of someone who'd bitten into a lemon. "Detective Bishop."

Jake watched her walk down the hall, tapping the roll of papers on her side. His gaze skittered briefly over her lovely backside that made regulation khakis look good before returning to Deke's office.

"Top of my interview list is Amber Ryder," he said from Deke's doorway. "Interesting that she showed up instead of calling Georgia. From what I remember, she swore she'd never return to Nashville."

"Yeah, talk to Amber, but take Georgia with you. She's damn good at what she does, and I trust her instincts."

"Between the two of us we just might solve this one."

"I'm counting on it."

Jake left Deke's office and made his way down to the forensic offices where he found Georgia inventorying and restocking a crime scene kit. "Hey, partner."

She stood in front of a clear fingerprint fuming chamber where a cup rested in the center. "We're not partners."

He couldn't resist. "Deke wants us to talk to Amber Ryder."

She opened a white packet of fingerprint developer, which was basically superglue, hung it in the chamber, and closed it. The packet would release dense fumes that would attach to the oil left behind by the fingerprints.

"When can you set up an interview with Amber?" He picked up a clear plastic jar filled with graphite that was also used to lift fingerprints.

"I can call her now."

"She came to you on your turf. Invaded your space," he said. "Next time we meet on our turf."

"Here at the station?"

"Not yet. Pick a restaurant. A place where the food isn't good."

"There's a diner in East Nashville. Smilie's. Awful food."

"I know the place. Smells like bleach half the time. It'll work."

She took the graphite jar from him. "Why?"

"This is our case. We're in control. Not Amber." He winked at her, his annoyance fading. Lately, he always got a little juiced when she was close. "I'm good at what I do, Georgia."

She jabbed, "I've no doubt."

"When this is all over, we should get dinner." He imagined himself tossing a ball in the air and swinging, aiming for the fences.

"You're not getting in my pants."

Feigning hurt, he dropped his voice a notch. "One mention of dinner and your mind heads straight to the gutter. A guy like me has standards, too."

She turned her attention back to a dozen paper bags tagged as evidence. "Go away."

Annoyed she could segregate him so easily from her life, Jake slid his hand into his pocket and fingered the small pocketknife he always carried. "Send me the case notes. Set the meeting up for tomorrow. Early."

"Done."

"You're a peach, Morgan."

Frustration rumbled in her chest. "Why are you still here?"


Dalton Marlowe stood in front of the large picture window of his penthouse condominium overlooking downtown Nashville. From up here the lights on Broadway blinked distantly and brightly and reminded him of sparkling gems. He liked looking down on Broadway's loud and bustling honky-tonks, which ran from the banks of the Cumberland River eight blocks west. From this vantage, he didn't have to deal with the tourists and beggars who often crowded the streets. He liked the distance his money afforded him.

He raised a glass of bourbon to his lips and sipped, savoring the burn in his throat. Today was a day he'd have avoided if at all possible, but no matter how much money he made or how big he grew his business, there was no stopping the calendar.

Today was October second. In a little over a week his son would celebrate his twenty-third birthday. He tried to imagine what Mike would look like these days. He was a tall and muscular teen, but his face was round with enough baby fat to remind Dalton that his kid was still just that—a kid. Five years since Mike had hiked into the woods with those two other kids. Five years since his son vanished and his life fell into limbo.

From the moment he woke up on that day five years ago, he sensed trouble. Mike was hungover and in a foul mood. He skipped school the day before. It was the second time that week and Dalton had been annoyed as hell.

"When are you gonna get your shit together, Mike?" he shouted as the boy had cradled his head in his hands. "Keep this crap up and you're going to get kicked off the football team."

"Jesus, Dad, do you have to shout so much? I'm the f-ing star. I'm not gonna get kicked off as long as I keep throwing passes for TDs."

"Don't assume you got a lock on life. With me behind you, it might take you longer to fuck up your life, but keep at it, and you'll find a way."

"Dad, *stop* talking. My head is pounding."

Dalton was frustrated and angry, because it sickened him to see so much promise get flushed down the toilet. He slammed a few doors and left his son asleep in his room. He went into the office and spent the better part of the day seething and thinking of ways to jerk a knot in that kid for his own good.

And then he came home to silence. He didn't panic at first. Hell, he was relieved to have a drink and eat his dinner in peace. At midnight, his anger simmered again and by two in the morning he decided to cut Mike off from his allowance. And then before dawn, worry tightened his gut. It wasn't the first time the kid had stayed out all night but that night brought a persistent worry that chewed at him relentlessly.

The next morning he received a call from Emma Reed. Her daughter Bethany had been on the science trip with Mike. Her voice was steeped with stress and worry when she told him that Bethany had not come home either. His annoyance gave way to enough worry that he started calling around. When he found out Amber Ryder was one of the three kids on the trip, his blood boiled. Mike was forbidden to see her, and yet, the kid went behind his father's back. Knowing Amber Ryder was in the mix ramped up worry tenfold.

He called the cops, who dispatched officers to the park immediately. The first forty-eight hours were full of hope that the kids would be found. Percy Warner Park was a couple thousand acres and getting lost would be easy to do. The weather wasn't bitterly cold, so he suspected the kids would be uncomfortable but would survive.

When search patrols found Amber, he and Emma were hopeful. But then Amber insisted she did not remember. Hope cracked and then crumbled with each passing day.

And now the fifth anniversary loomed.

Five years without his boy. Five long years. He never thought he'd miss the arguments, the piles of dirty laundry, and the thud of Mike's size thirteen feet. But he missed it all. He ached.

He kept tabs on Amber for the last five years, putting detectives on her, thinking she'd make a mistake. Confess her sins to someone. But she never had. She always maintained she did not remember. She went about her life as if none of this happened.

Life. Mike and Bethany remained missing. They weren't living their lives as God had intended. But Amber was, and she was back in town.

"You'll pay for all this, you little bitch."


That evening, Georgia stopped at the Chinese takeout restaurant just after nine and ordered stir fried vegetables, sauce on the side, and two egg rolls. Climbing the steps to her apartment, she realized how little time she spent there. No doubt, if not for this case, she'd have opted to work or sing. Every candle could only take so much burning and hers was just about extinguished.

She kicked her front door closed and set down the bag. Turning, she flipped the two dead bolts and then slid the chain in place. She'd upgraded all three of the locks when she moved in, knowing it was likely against the rental company's policy, but figured it was easier to ask for forgiveness than permission.

She kicked off her shoes and pulled the rubber band from her hair, letting the red curls tumble over her shoulders. Her apartment was small, not more than seven hundred square feet with a living area, small dining space, and a galley kitchen. The furnishings in the den were nice but incomplete. When she first moved into the apartment, she was excited and ready to make it her own. She received approval to put up wallpaper on an accent wall and choose paints for her bedroom and bathroom. However, she discovered after painting one wall she did not have the patience for decorating. She could collect fingerprints for hours but putting a roller in paint and then to the wall was mind numbing. No wonder painters drank.

And so the paint cans were sealed up and the unopened rolls of wallpaper still leaned against the wall.

The furniture, straight from the factory showroom, created more of a department store feel than a designed, chic space. Feng Shui it wasn't. But her one saving grace was the dozens of framed family pictures featuring her brothers, her parents, and even an old publicity still of her birth mother, Annie.

She set the food in the small kitchen and moved to her bedroom where she changed into an oversized Titans T-shirt and a blue pair of workout shorts that dated back to college.

Grabbing a plastic fork from the takeout bag, she didn't bother with a plate as she moved straight to the small couch and sat down Indian style. She grabbed the remote and flipped on the cooking channel. Whenever her brothers caught her watching a cooking show they laughed. Her cooking skills fell far short of her mother's culinary talents and though her brothers always smiled when they ate her cooking, she never missed the hesitations and grimaces. Why couldn't she be more like her mother? Why did she always choose singing in a smoky honky-tonk over decorating or cooking? Why wasn't she patient or even-tempered?

She stabbed a plump piece of shrimp. "Sorry, Mom. I'm trying, but I don't ever think I'll be you."

Georgia popped the shrimp in her mouth. She ate in silence for a few minutes and watched Bobby Flay battle it out with an amateur cook for bragging rights. Growing restless, she switched the channel to the country music channel. With her appetite satisfied, she brewed a strong cup of coffee and reached for one of the last file boxes. She had read through the box's content once before, but she wanted to be ready for her meeting tomorrow with Amber and Jake, which she confirmed hours ago by phone when Amber finally returned her call. Jake had his files. Tomorrow was set.

Flipping off the lid, she reached for the first slightly yellowed file and opened it. Though her father's reports were typewritten, Buddy never missed a chance to double back and write more notes in the margin. Dark bold handwriting punctuated with question marks filled the edges of his interview assessment of Amber Ryder. "Consistent. Unwavering. Credible?"

In the body of his report, Buddy stated that the seventeen-year-old was "openly upset that she can't remember." He noted she cried often and asked if there were drugs available or hypnosis, anything to make her remember. She appeared desperate to find her friends. She couldn't remember how she fell. Her last memory had stretched back to days before the fateful hike.

All this was consistent with the story she told Georgia yesterday.

Georgia sat back knowing the process of recreating a cold case took time. Her eighty-plus hours had given her a basic overview of the case so that she could discuss it, but so far nothing jumped out at her as a new development. Her hope was that the DNA retesting would also shed more light.

This case had a pull. It had sunk its claws into her; she would stick with it until she figured out what had happened to those missing kids.


Candlelight flickered from a few small half-melted candles. Light danced on the walls of the small cave and Elisa's pale lifeless body lay prone, hands crossed over her chest. The space was so small one could not stand up straight for fear of scraping the rocky ceiling.

In the moments before life had left Elisa, their minds were painfully close. They were one. They shared the same desires, the same fears.

Letting go of her was harder than imagined. Maybe it was because a shared resemblance to Bethany stirred too many memories.

"You look so happy now. No more worries about who is the smartest."

The cave's cool temperatures would keep her safe, intact for several days. Even now, other than the stiffness of her limbs and the pulling around her mouth, she looked alive, her eyes partly open, staring sightlessly. She looked almost as if she could rise up and beg for more affection.

But a kiss to those lips found only coldness. Her chest did not rise and fall. Her spirit had left.

In the distance the wind cut through the trees. It would be dawn soon. As tempting as it was to linger, it was time to say good-bye. She'd been dead three days and soon the cops would be looking for Elisa and this area would be ground zero.

The blue ribbon of bruises around Elisa's neck hugged the pale skin like jewelry. "I won't ever forget you. We are together in my heart. Like the others." A glance toward the back of the cave found a narrow entrance walled up five years ago with neatly stacked stone. Dangling from one of the jagged rocks on the right was a gold pendant and chain that glistened in the soft candlelight. For five years it hung here undiscovered and untouched.

"I know you miss me, too. Don't think I forgot. I remember it all. In fact, I think about you every day. Of all the people in town, I know you especially are glad I'm back."

# CHAPTER THREE

*Tuesday, October 3, 7:00 A.M.*

"Damn it!" Joey ran through the park, his fingers wrapped around the dog leash, searching the woods for his golden retriever, Cooper. Experience told him not to let the dog off the leash. But as Joey and Cooper moved deeper into the woods, the animal pulled more and more, wanting to run. And so Joey, feeling for the dog, let him go.

The dog never looked back and took off like a bat out of hell into the woods. In the distance, the dog barked, his cry high and desperate, the sure sign he was on the trail of a squirrel or rabbit. Joey peered into the thicket. "Cooper, come here!"

The dog yelped and barked but showed no signs of returning. Checking his watch and knowing he only had an hour to shower and get to work, he moved into the thicket, cursing as the branches pulled and tugged at his jacket. "Shit, I know better than to turn that dog loose."

Joey picked up his pace, cutting through the woods until he came to a small clearing. He spotted the dog's full golden tail wagging as he poked his head into a grouping of rocks. Cooper pawed at the rocks, sending a few tumbling. Maybe a nest of rabbits, he thought. Cooper barked louder.

Hoping the dog would remain distracted, Joey hurried and quickly grabbed hold of its red collar. He pulled hard to free the dog's head from the small opening. When he did, Cooper looked at him, wagging his tail as if he'd found the mother lode.

Joey clicked the leash onto the collar. "Remedial training for you, pal."

Cooper strained at the leash as he lunged again for the hole.

Curious, Joey rubbed the dog on the head and peered past him into the dark hole. A few inches closer and he was struck by the smell. "Something sure died in there."

Cooper pawed at the rocks, barking to be released.

Joey fished his cell out of his back pocket, turned on the flashlight app, and cast it in the opening. The first time he looked, the dog nudged him from behind almost knocking him over. Joey pushed the dog aside and peered into the darkness.

His light bounced off jagged rocks, a dirt floor, and then . . . a bare foot, a leg, and a woman's torso.

"Holy shit!" Joey shouted backing up as fast as his feet would carry him. In his haste, he dropped the leash, giving Cooper free rein to burrow into the hole again.

Joey quickly grappled for the leash and pulled the dog out of the hole. When the foul scent from the hole hit his nose again, the bagel he ate an hour ago twisted into a hard knot.

Hands shaking, he dialed 911. Cooper barked louder. When the operator answered, he sucked in a breath as he now dragged the hell-bent dog from the cave. "I'm in Percy Warner Park. And I think I just found a dead body."

Jake Bishop arrived at the forensic lab with two hot cups of coffee. He drank his black and he knew Georgia drank hers with cream and two sugars. He wasn't foolish enough to think a coffee peace offering would sweeten her mood, but the much-needed jolt of caffeine would take the edge off her customary morning bad humor.

He found her in deep thought sitting at her desk in the corner of the lab slumped over her files. She pulled up her hair and had already stuck a couple of pencils into the topknot. The look appealed in a hot, school-teacher kind of way.

He set the coffee beside her. "Thanks for the synopsis and list of witnesses. Very detailed. After Amber, I want to talk to Tim Taylor, Mike's best friend. And Mike's father and the teachers at his school as well."

She reached for the coffee, sipped and nodded. "Thank you. Why Tim?"

"Here to serve, Ms. Morgan." He hesitated, enjoying his coffee before he answered. "Tim spent a lot of time with Mike. If anyone knew if the kid were into something that got him killed, Tim would know."

"Okay." She glanced up at him, her eyes narrowing with suspicion. "You're smiling. Why?"

He sipped again, letting the question skitter past. "What did you find in the files last night? Anything new?"

"How do you know I reviewed them?"

Laughter rumbled in his chest. He set the cup down. "Right. You took the night off and did what, washed your hair or had some *me* time?"

"Funny."

"You're a Morgan and Morgans work. So what did you find?"

A frustrated shake of her head released a curl that she had tucked behind her ear. "I'm not sure I found anything. Much of what I reread were Buddy's notes about Amber."

Buddy Morgan. Hell of a cop and a man who two years after his death still cast a long shadow. "And what did he tell you about her?"

"The kid must have been interviewed dozens of times. Homicide cops, missing person cops, psychologists, and prosecutors. Buddy, like all the others, made her go over her story from beginning to end."

"And?"

She took several more sips. "She never varied. Not once. She was adamant that she couldn't remember what happened."

"And Buddy believed her?"

"He could find no reason not to believe her. She never wavered, never gave them any reason to doubt her."

"Maybe she's a good liar."

"Or maybe she's telling the truth. Maybe she was a kid who went into the woods and something terrible happened and she escaped only to be roasted by her rescuers."

Georgia Morgan could be a hardass on the job. He witnessed her going toe-to-toe with cops who violated her crime scene. She didn't care whom she pissed off or irritated when it came to protecting evidence. But when it came to the injured, she might not gush or show much emotion, but deep feelings simmered under that thick skin.

For some reason, she might have a blind side for Amber. "So what is it about Amber Ryder that's gotten under your skin?"

The frown deepened and she rose from her chair. "She's not under my skin."

"Right. What is it?"

She shoved out a sigh, shaking her head as she paced. "She seemed a little lost to me, that's all."

"And what does that have to do with anything?"

"I don't know. There's something vulnerable about her."

"Please don't tell me you have a gut feeling about her."

She grimaced. "No. Not exactly."

"Don't be ashamed of it. Instinct is powerful." But it was always important to verify those intangible feelings with facts. Hard evidence earned convictions.

He continued. "I'm worried there's something we haven't explored with Amber. The sooner we talk to her, the better. If anyone's story might have changed in the last five years, it would be hers."

"Why do you say that?" Georgia asked.

"She might not remember the story she told back then. Or," he said with a nod to her, "some of the memories might have returned."

"You think she's making it all up?"

"I didn't say that."

"You don't have to. It's written all over you."

Now she believed she could read him. "I never

question you when it comes to forensic data and science. Hands down, you're one of the best. But when it comes to people, you're in my backyard."

"You're sure about that?"

"I am. And any self-respecting detective wouldn't take anyone else at their word when it came to a key witness. What time are we meeting her?"

"In a half hour."

"Not much of a heads up."

"If you can't make it, I'll take care of it."

"Nice try. I'll drive."

She hesitated as if she wondered if this was an issue worth battling.

He laughed. "Think you can tolerate surrendering control of the wheel?"

She studied him, her eyes narrowing. "Let's go."


When Jake and Georgia arrived at the diner, it was eight in the morning. The tiny restaurant on the side of I-40 smelled of greasy fried eggs, overdone pancakes, and bacon a little too extra crispy. Behind the packed counter stood three short-order cooks who faced a hot grill, each flipping and preparing meals with precision and speed.

Georgia's stomach grew unsettled as she smelled the strong scents of grease and bleach. Tightening her hand on a backpack that served as purse and go-bag equipped with a camera and a few basic necessities she always carried, she realized a few nuked leftover veggies for breakfast would have to hold her.

She approached the hostess, digging deep for a smile. "Table for three."

The hostess studied her seating chart and shook her head. "It's a half hour wait."

"Half hour? Who sits for a half hour eating breakfast?"

Jake moved toward the hostess, a tall leggy blonde with ample perky breasts, a bright smile, and red manicured nails. He glanced at her name badge and smiled. "Cassie, I don't suppose we could get a table for three."

Cassie moistened red lips while counting out three menus. "I can get you a table, doll."

He winked. "You're the best."

Annoyance stabbed at Georgia. Did the man ever throttle it back?

Jake glanced past her out the picture window and nodded. "My guess is that blonde walking toward the door is her."

Georgia turned to see Amber. She wore jeans, an oversized gray top, and cowboy boots. Her blond hair was swept into a ponytail that caught the sunlight, and she moved with a self-confident ease.

"Amber," she said. "Glad you could make it."

Amber tightened her fingers around the strap of her purse, nodding as she approached. "Thanks for taking a look at the case."

"Detective Bishop would also like to talk to you."

"Sure. I'll talk to whomever you say."

His gaze sharpened and the easy friendliness faded. He might have been joking seconds ago, but he was all business now.

"I'm Detective Jake Bishop. You must be Amber Ryder."

She raised her chin a notch as little bits of tension worked their way through her body. "Detective."

The three moved through the diner, following the hostess who seated them and gave each a laminated menu. As tempted as Georgia was to eat something, this meeting was business, not pleasure. She ordered coffee and a bagel. Jake asked for coffee, black. At first, Amber ordered only coffee, but when Jake insisted she eat, she added on pancakes.

When the coffees arrived, Jake sat back in his seat. The sharpened angles of his face softened and his posture relaxed. Anyone glancing at him now could easily imagine they were just three friends sitting down for a coffee and talking about the weather.

Jake grinned, his demeanor relaxed. "Georgia tells me you've been going to school in Dallas. Graduated?"

"At the end of last summer." She sipped her coffee.

"And working, too, I hear?"

"An account manager in an advertising company."

"That sounds exciting," he said scratching the side of his head. "Have you been back to Nashville since you left five years ago?"

"No. I don't think I'd have returned if Georgia hadn't called."

Jake turned his cup so that the handle faced right. He picked it up and sipped. "You still keep tabs on the case?"

"At first, I checked online a lot. It was kind of an obsession. Those missing kids were friends of mine. I'll never forget them. But life does move on, and I started checking less and less." She swiped away a small blond ringlet from her eyes.

"No one else has contacted you?"

"I received texts. I told Georgia about the old ones and showed her the latest. For whatever reason, some people attached themselves to the case and contact me as if we know each other."

"Seems all the more reason to steer clear of Nashville."

"I couldn't stay away. If I can help find my friends then I will." She fished her phone from her purse and scrolled through messages. "I received another text last night. I didn't recognize the number, but I think my arrival has been noticed."

"What did the text say?" Jake asked.

Amber turned her phone so he could see the message. It read: *You should be with Bethany and Mike.*

Jake frowned. "Have any idea what that means?"

"No, but it gave me the creeps," Amber said. "There were plenty of people that didn't believe my story, including Dalton Marlowe. I was harassed a lot. Amazing how unkind people can be. The constant harassment was a big part of the reason I left."

"Do you recognize this number?"

"No."

Jake tapped his finger on the table by the phone. "Do you mind?"

Amber shrugged. "No."

He picked up the phone and hit redial. The phone rang five times but no one answered, and no voice mail picked up. He set the phone back down on the table between them.

She glanced at the display. "I called it back a couple of times, but no one answered. I even searched it on the Internet, but I couldn't figure out who owned the number."

"I'll search it."

Amber shook her head. "I thought five years was enough time. People would forget and leave me the hell alone."

"It was a high-profile crime. And some people never move on."

Jake sat back and waited as if he had all the time in the world. Georgia had seen him do this before when interviewing a suspect. Patient and easygoing, he rarely raised his voice with an interviewee and had a way of drawing them closer as if they could trust him. Sly as a fox, as her dad used to say.

The waitress, a brunette with a petite, full build, arrived with their order, setting a big pile of pancakes in front of Amber and the bagel in front of Georgia. She smiled at Jake as she reached for a coffeepot and warmed up his cup. "I'm sure I can get you something, hon."

Jake grinned. "Thanks, but I've got to watch my weight or I'm gonna lose my boyish figure."

The waitress laughed, her cheeks blushing as she tucked a curl behind her ear. Did the man enchant every woman? "Baby, you look just fine to me."

He winked. "You're a doll."

"You call me if you need anything, you hear? The name's Tammy."

Jake sipped his coffee, winking. "Sure will, Tammy."

Irritated, Georgia kept her gaze on her plate.

"Do you have any memories of anyone else in the woods?" Jake asked. "Was someone watching you? Following you?"

"I don't remember seeing or hearing anyone that day or any of the days I remember before the park. And before you ask, there was nothing that caught my attention, that struck me as odd in the weeks leading up to the trip."

"You know my questions before I ask 'em," Jake said.

She traced the edges of her fork handle. "I was interviewed by so many cops after all this happened, I feel as if I can almost guess your next question."

Jake's grin didn't quite reach his eyes. "We can be a bit on the predictable side."

She shook her head, cutting into the pancake with the side of her fork and raising it. "I didn't mean that as an insult. It's just that there's a pattern of thought. After a while, I began to anticipate what was next."

"Have you been back to the park since that day you were found in the woods?" Jake asked.

She hesitated, and set the fork back down on the plate. "I went back with the cops a couple of times but never alone."

"Would you consider going back now? Ms. Morgan and I would come along."

Amber tapped an unpolished nail against the side of her coffee cup. "Yeah, I'd go back. I don't think it'll help much. But sure, I'll give it a try."

"When do you want to go?" Jake asked.

"I can go now. All I need to do is hit the restroom."

Jake sipped his coffee. "There's no rush. Tell me about how it was attending St. Vincent."

A small shift in posture suggested resentment. "It was a school for rich kids. I never fit in and it didn't help that I could kick their butts academically."

"Kids can be shitty," Jake said.

"They were," Amber said, grinning. "Weren't you a little shitty as a kid?"

Jake grinned. "I was an altar boy. A regular saint."

Georgia bit into her bagel, refusing to take the bait in front of Amber. "I could see that."

"I bet you can," he said. His phone buzzed and he glanced at the display. "How did you afford a school like St. Vincent? Pretty pricy."

"Scholarship. The guidance counselor at my middle school found it and told me. I didn't really care, but she knew it was a good thing for me. She always believed in me."

"Your grades were average," Jake said.

"I had a great opportunity, but didn't have the sense to see it. It was foolish."

"How so?"

"Kids from my world don't get lucky breaks like I got."

Jake's phone buzzed again and he glanced down at the display, frowning. "Ladies, finish up while I take this call from my boss."

When Jake left, Amber loaded her fork with pancakes. "He's homicide, I'm assuming?"

"Correct. And his boss, Deke Morgan, is head of the Nashville Homicide Department, and also my brother. He's the one that gave me the go-ahead to look into this case."

"You're lucky to have a brother. I always wanted one." After Amber swallowed her bite, she cut another slice. "Deke must be an older brother?"

"Older by ten years."

"How many Morgans are there?"

"Four. Three boys and me."

Amber shrugged as if shooing away something that bothered her. "I was an only child. I always wondered what it would be like to have a brother."

Georgia glanced out the diner window to see Jake standing on the sidewalk, phone to his ear. His broad shoulders filled an expertly tailored suit jacket that tapered to a narrow waist. He paced as he talked.

"You and Detective Bishop are friends?" Amber asked.

Georgia realized she'd been caught staring. "Not exactly friends. But he's a great cop."

Amber's gaze searched. "You don't like it when other women flirt with him."

Georgia stiffened. "Why do you say that?"

"You tense. It's very slight, but I see it. I guess it's something all women notice about each other."

"You've read me all wrong. There's nothing between us."

Amber smiled. "But he wants something more. I saw it when he looked at you."

"I doubt it."

Jake returned to the diner, his expression dark. "Amber, Georgia and I need to respond to a crime scene. Can you find your way home?"

"Sure. I'll be fine."

He tossed twenty bucks on the table. "Take your time and enjoy your meal. We'll be back with you soon."

"Yeah, sure. Okay."

Georgia collected her backpack and followed Jake outside. "What's that about?"

"A hiker and his dog found a body at Percy Warner Park. Likely a young girl placed in a cave."

A chill rolled over Georgia's skin. "Is there an identification yet?"

He opened her car door. "No. But the uniforms on the scene want us there ASAP."

She slid into the car, glanced back at the diner and found Amber in her booth nodding to them with a slight smile. As Jake settled behind the wheel, she asked, "What do you think about Amber?"

"Jury's still out."

# CHAPTER FOUR

*Tuesday, October 3, 10:00 A.M.*

A dozen marked police cars with lights flashing and a forensic van greeted Jake and Georgia when they arrived at the park.

The entrance to the northern path was blocked with yellow crime scene tape and a uniformed officer stood guard. Jake extended his hand. "How's it going, Randy?"

Randy was mid-sized with a thick chest and muscled arms. "Right now, not much to say. Guy and his dog found a body and called us. Forensic techs just got here and until the body is processed there isn't much to report."

"How far up the trail?" Jake asked.

"About a half mile. Fairly easy hiking."

Georgia glanced toward the forensic van, half tempted to jump in. "Is Brad Holcombe here?"

"Yeah," Randy said. "He's about twenty minutes ahead of you."

Brad Holcombe worked the Forensic Department with Georgia and had joined the team about five years ago. In his early thirties, he was tall, trim, and sported a mop of blond hair. She considered him one of the best in the field and he was as meticulous as she. "Great."

Randy held up the tape and the two ducked under it and headed up the trail. The morning remained crisp, but bright skies suggested the sun would warm the air to another unseasonably warm day. Early into October, it was always a mixed bag with weather more often turning warm as cold. By November, it would stay colder but, for now, bright days like this remained possible.

She thought back to the last few days' temperatures, and her mind immediately turned to accelerated decomposition rates. Whatever they were going to find would not be pretty.

Jake recognized the smell of human death the instant they rounded the corner and came upon the collection of cops. The stench, in his mind, was dense, wet, and sickeningly sweet. It always tightened his belly and sent his muscles bracing. Oddly, most of the bodies he dealt with in homicide were fresh. There were lots of nasty things to experience around the murdered victim, but usually not the smell.

"Damn."

Georgia moved past him to Brad. "What do you have?"

"I've only shined a light into the cave, but I can see the body of a dead woman."

Jake moved forward and studied the narrow opening. "Brad, can I borrow your light?"

"Sure."

Jake clicked on the light and shined it in the cave. Putrid air wafted out of the opening and smacked his senses. The smell, simply the breakdown of chemicals in the body, told him death had occurred at least twenty-four hours to ninety-six hours ago. He would become accustomed to the smell, but his clothes would reek and his dry cleaner would cuss and charge him double.

The light bounced off the low-lying rock ceiling down onto the outline of a body. No missing it was a dead woman. By the looks, she'd been young.

Georgia switched on her own light and crouched close. Her shoulder brushed his and he caught the faint scent of soap clinging to her skin. This would be the last nice smell for hours. "Are you aware of any missing women?"

He nodded. There was a BOLO—a Be On The Lookout—that had come across his desk late last night. "Missing teenager. Brown hair. Nineteen. She's not been seen for a few days. Roommate reported her missing. Parents were traveling, but are back in town."

Georgia leaned closer to the opening. "She fits the description."

Jake rose, handed the light back to Brad and dusted his hands. "Yeah." He pulled out his phone and pulled up his text messages. "Her name is Elisa Spence. She's a sophomore in college." Not every BOLO stuck with him, but when it came to a young person, he never forgot.

"Looks like it's time for Brad and me to do our thing."

He rubbed the back of his neck, staring at the narrow opening. "I don't envy your work."

She shrugged as if this were a walk in the park. "Are you kidding? I live for this kind of thing."

With a camera dangling from her neck, Georgia and Brad stood at the entrance of the cave. While she snapped pictures, Brad sketched the scene, marking distances and the general layout. Detail at this stage of the game was critical. Both knew very well that one day they could be sitting in a courtroom justifying every iota to the judge, jury, and attorneys.

Rick, Georgia's older brother and Jake's partner, had also arrived on the scene. Rick had come up through the canine unit and he and his canine, Tracker, had had an impressive record. The two had been on a routine traffic stop when the car's driver had fired on Rick, hitting him in the hip. As the driver approached Rick with gun drawn, Rick was able to press the door release button on his vehicle, freeing Tracker. The dog lunged at the driver as the second shot was fired. The canine was hit, but the shooter was startled, giving Rick enough time to fire the kill shot. Both Rick and Tracker had recovered, but neither was certified to return to patrol duty. Rick transferred to homicide and Tracker ended up with Rick's new wife, Jenna.

After Georgia snapped over fifty pictures of the area, she signaled uniformed officers to remove the stones still blocking the cave's entrance. Slowly, the jagged entrance grew wider and wider, sending waves of death rolling out of the darkness like a black thundercloud.

Moving closer, Georgia took more pictures of the cave entrance, the flash offering quick glimpses into the darkness. Each burst of light illuminated the body, which she now knew lay on its back, hands positioned neatly over her heart. She was fully dressed but her blouse, though it had been straightened, appeared torn at the sleeve and the collar.

She heard the rumble of rocks sliding down the hill and turned to see Jake and Rick. Both men's expressions were dark.

Jake had removed his jacket and tie and had rolled up his sleeves. "Looks like you're about to go into the cave."

When he was all business, she could deal with him. She even liked him. They talked about decomposition rates, blood splatter, and stippling. No innuendo. No messing around. Safe. "I'm headed in now."

She held up her camera so the detective could see the crime scene images on her viewfinder. "As you can see, the body is positioned in the middle of the cave. She's fully dressed with the face covered. The cave is about seven feet deep and four feet high. Doesn't appear to be any other access to the cave, but I won't know until I get inside."

"As soon as we can make an identification," Rick said, "we need to notify her parents."

"Sure. I'll move as quickly as I can," she said.

She set her camera aside and donned a Tyvek suit as well as a small headlight, which she snapped on. Without another word, she crouched and began crawling into the cave.

Her heart beat a little faster and beads of sweat formed on her face. She never relaxed in tight spaces. A stupid kind of fear. She was perfectly safe but her body always recoiled when the job required her to squirm into a tiny space. She'd been under the crawl spaces of homes, in small basement rooms, and low attic spaces. She should have been used to this kind of thing after a decade on the job. But she never made peace with it.

She moved forward, her shoulders stooped and she turned toward the entrance. "Brad, I need my camera."

"Right here," he said handing it to her.

The body was bloated with decomposition gasses and in several places the victim's skin had split, allowing bodily fluids to puddle around her body. This close, she could see the white button-down had subtle blue stripes. The right sleeve was ripped and the arm bloodied, suggesting the injury happened before she died. Her skirt was khaki and her shoes, or rather shoe, was a blue loafer. The shoe on her right foot was missing, revealing small white toes painted a vivid purple that matched the color of her fingernails. The funky color didn't quite jibe with the overall preppy look, and Georgia wondered if the girl had harbored a risky side that might very well have gotten her killed. Her right and left hands where crossed over her heart and her face was turned to the side.

She snapped more images and then allowed her gaze to skim the girl's face. Death and time had ravaged what must have been a full and bright face into a very pale, drawn expression. Her lips were slightly apart.

*Snap. Snap. Snap.*

The victim wore simple gold earrings and a pearl necklace. Both looked as if they were expensive. Under the necklace, a dark purple band of bruises circled a thin white neck. This girl had been strangled, but it would take the medical examiner to determine if that had been the cause of death. She rose up above the body as much as the jagged low ceiling would allow.

*Snap. Snap. Snap.*

Peeking out from the white button-down was a pink, sleek lacy bra, another hint that this girl had harbored secrets.

A class ring encircled the victim's right pinky and as Georgia leaned in close, she discovered it was a newly minted college ring. So damn young.

Her gaze trailed around the body as she searched for anything that might have belonged to the victim. She noted piles of leaves and rocks and along the rock wall several puddles of wax, remnants of candles burned down to the wick.

On her knees, she passed through something wet and she glanced back to see decomposition fluid on her jumpsuit.

"It just doesn't get any lovelier than this," she grumbled. A sharp rock on the cave's floor cut into her palms and strained the protection of her latex gloves.

Beyond the body, the cave narrowed like the neck of a bottle. She tucked the camera into a pocket of her jumpsuit and crawled past the body toward the narrowing space closed off by a pile of neatly piled rocks. The arrangement was too defined to be natural and was reminiscent of the rocks piled in the primary cave's entrance.

"How's it look?" Brad asked.

"Dark. Very, very dark."

"You okay?"

"I'm doing just swell. You know I live for this." Her

nose itched and she rubbed it with her forearm. As she shifted to the right, she hit her elbow against a jagged rock. Pain shot up her arm and she muttered a curse. Every move had to be deliberate to ensure no evidence was damaged.

The narrow light of her headlamp caught a wink of metal as she stared up at the rocks. When she leaned closer, she realized there was a pendant hanging from a chain dangling from the rocks. She snapped a picture of the pendant and then glanced in her viewfinder and blew up the image. The pendant was engraved with two scripted letters: BR.

Shit. Bethany Reed.

The death scent mingled with the musty wet mossy smells that belonged in caves. She glanced at the ceiling, praying the bats and hairy critters hiding in the darkness would scurry out of her path. Hating the space, she kept her focus on what she did best: cataloging facts.

She photographed the pendant several more times and then the rocks stacked at the back of the cave. As she set the stones aside a second, smaller area appeared. "What the hell is this place?"

Shinning her light into the second space, she could see it narrowed so much that once in she would not be able to turn around. The only way out of here was to back out so if something furry charged, she would have to choke back a godawful scream or suffer the jokes of the cops.

She cleared more rocks so that she could move forward into the second chamber.

Her left hand settled on something hard, brittle and

narrow. She dropped her gaze, her headlight catching the object.

It was a bone. Human.

Jake stood at the cave's entrance, listening as Georgia burrowed deeper into the darkness. He admired her guts. He was street tough, but this scene put him on edge.

Feet braced, he tapped his index finger against the butt of his gun. "Brad, I don't hear her moving. What's going on in there?"

Brad, kneeling at the mouth of the cave, glanced back at Jake as if to caution patience. But when he took a good look at Jake, he silenced his comments and leaned into the mouth of the cave. "Georgia, what's going on?"

For a moment, she did not answer and the silence fueled Jake's concern.

"She's fine," Brad said. "She'll holler if she needs help."

"I understand that." A blunt tone sharpened the edges of each word.

Rick shifted his stance. "Give her a few more seconds."

Jake's lips flattened into a grim line. "Brad. Yell in there again."

"Georgia!" Brad hollered. "What's your status?"

Jake was quickly losing patience. He'd give her five more seconds and then he'd head inside. One. Two. Three.

"I'm alive." Her strong voice echoed out from the depths of the cave. The camera flashed a dozen more times. "It's a bitch turning around in here. I'm on the way out."

He freed some of the tension banding his shoulders. "She's taking a hell of a lot of pictures."

"She won't miss anything," Rick said.

Finally, he saw her booted, muddied feet appear at the entrance. Next, a very nice bottom, also covered in dirt and sludge, a narrow waist, shoulders, and that crop of red hair pulled into a topknot.

She straightened and rolled her shoulders as she turned. She wiped a curl from her face with the back of her hand. "Female, approximately twenty years old. Nicely dressed. My guess is that she was strangled, but that's the medical examiner's call. She's well into the decomposition process and given the cool weather and fifty or sixty degree temperature in the cave, she's been in there three or four days."

"You were in there a while," Jake said.

"I searched around the body. I found three candles burned down into puddles of wax, but nothing else. And I spotted a pile of rocks in the back of the cave. They're too neatly arranged to be natural so I removed a few. Behind the first chamber there's a longer, narrower tunnel that cuts deeper into the hill. That's what took me so long."

"You get stuck?" Rick asked.

She shot him an annoyed look. "No. Are you saying I have a big ass?"

"Not at all."

She drew in a breath. "In the second chamber I found bones."

"Human?" Jake asked.

She reached inside the front pocket of her jumpsuit

and pulled out her camera. She scrolled back through pictures and handed it to Jake. Rick moved forward and the two studied the image. "You tell me. Looks like a human femur to me."

"How many sets?" Jake asked.

"One that I saw, but I won't know until I get back into the cave and really look," she said.

"There is no chance that two killers would find the same hiding spot?" Rick asked.

"Whoever hid the body in the exterior chamber had already hid a victim in the back section of the cave," Jake said.

Georgia pushed the back button on the viewfinder until the image of a gold pendant and chain appeared. "Found that dangling from one of the rocks blocking the back chamber. Look closely at the pendant. It's engraved with the initials BR."

Both detectives studied the image. "Bethany Reed," Rick said.

"You'd think the hounds would have picked up the scent five years ago," Jake said. "Jesus, there must have been two hundred people canvassing the park."

"That back chamber is tucked away and the entrance was covered with rocks," Georgia said. "If the killer spread a little lye on the body, that would have masked the scent. But before I can think about excavating the second site, I've got to deal with our Jane Doe."

Rick removed a small notebook from the breast pocket of his suit jacket and flipped it open. "Elisa Spence, age nineteen, was reported missing on Sunday by her roommate. Five foot four, one hundred and fifty pounds, muddy brown hair."

"That fits the description of the victim," Georgia said. "She does appear to be missing a shoe. Blue loafer. Bottom of her foot is torn up pretty good." She pulled in a deep breath, as if needing the scent of fresh clean air to chase away the death. "Let me stock up and get back inside. I'll need to bag her hands and find a way to wrap the body so that we don't lose evidence dragging her out of the cave."

Jake shouldn't care about Georgia going back into the cave. This was her job. She'd been knee deep in all kinds of nastiness. But it did bother him. He hated the idea of her returning to that dark stone grave.

Expressing his concern would belittle her. She was a professional and regardless of how she felt about the horrendous task, she would do it.

She moved to the truck and, stripping off her gloves, grabbed a water, and drank. Rolling her head from side to side, she gathered the supplies she'd need in the cave. She didn't complain. Didn't bitch. Didn't decide to pawn off the work on Brad. But he saw the deep set lines in her forehead and the strain behind her eyes.

Jake decided the kindest thing he could do was send her in just a little angry and dreaming of landing a punch on his square jaw.

Grinning Satan's smile, Jake said, "When you get back in the cave, try not to scare the bats, Georgia."

# CHAPTER FIVE

*Tuesday, October 3, 6:00 P.M.*

Georgia lost track of the time. The artificial lights that had chased the darkness also dulled the lines between night and day. Only one technician could fit in at a time, so she and Brad alternated one-hour shifts. She began by searching the area around the body, shifting through the cool damp soil for anything a killer might have left behind. Other than the wax there was nothing. It seemed she barely searched a few square feet when Brad would shout in to her.

When Brad yelled, "Time," she glanced out the cave's entrance and could see the glow of floodlights hauled into the remote location by uniformed officers. "I'll be out in a minute. I've a few more details before I'm at a stopping point."

"That's what you said twenty minutes ago."

"It takes time," she snapped, rolling her head from side to side. "I'm not rushing this."

A layman would have expected the body to be stiff but this hardening of the body, rigor mortis, happened in the first two to four hours post death. After about six hours, the chemical reaction that triggered the rigor mortis ebbed, the muscles slackened and became flaccid again. Now at least forty-eight hours post death the limbs were malleable. The medical examiner would have to measure the body's liver temperature to determine a more accurate time of death.

Georgia sat cross-legged as she lifted the victim's cold and badly swollen hand. Though the cuticles had receded, she could see that in life the victim kept them neatly filed and painted with a faint sheen of purple nail polish that still caught the light. Carefully, Georgia inspected the fingernails, crusted with dirt, searching for any sign that the victim might have scratched her attacker. Knowing the medical examiner would do scrapings under the fingernails, she covered both hands with paper bags. Porous, the paper allowed air to circulate so that moisture didn't form and destroy any DNA that might be present.

"Let's hope you scratched the hell out of him. Maybe together, we can put this asshole away."

When both hands and feet were bagged, she gently rolled the body on its side. Pushing up the shirt, she noted a purplish discoloration darkening the backside of the girl's legs and arms. Called stippling, the color change was caused by blood settling or pooling in the body's lowest point when the heart stopped pumping. Forensic technicians used stippling patterns to determine if the body had been moved or repositioned. If there'd been stippling on the front of the body, she'd have known the girl lay face down for a time before being placed on her back. In this case, the stippling ran the back length of the girl's body. This suggested the girl was positioned here at the time of death

"How's it going in there?" Brad asked. He dropped his voice a notch. "Got some mighty testy detectives out here pacing around."

"Why should I care? Do they have another party to go to?"

He shook his head slowly with conviction. "If I ask them that now, I'll be taking my life into my own hands."

Neither detective scared or intimidated her and she found their annoyance almost amusing, considering she was knee deep in death. She rolled her head from side to side, feeling a small pop in the stiff vertebrae. "She's almost ready to move. Go ahead and send in the body bag."

"Jake Bishop also wants to see the cave and the scene before you move her."

"Tell him to suit up. I'll give him the grand tour."

Georgia did her best to consider dead bodies as evidence to be studied. But when the victim was young, as this girl had been, it wasn't difficult to not look beyond the ravages of death and see a sweet young girl brutally robbed of her life.

A heaviness settled in her chest and, for a moment, she didn't move as she sat quietly by the girl, her gloved hand resting on the lifeless arm. As she sat, she glanced over at the three waxy puddles that had illuminated the cave. Why the candles? Had the killer used it to light up his little cave of horrors? Tears burned in the back of her throat. "I swear, I'll find out who did this."

"Talking to yourself?" Jake asked.

"I talk to dead people," she said. "Didn't you know that?"

"Can I come in?"

"Make yourself at home." She sat back on her haunches and moved back to make room for him.

He'd put on a Tyvek suit, gloves, and booties. Moving with practiced care, he crawled into the cave and squatted in the few feet on the other side of the body. He studied the body, his scowl deepening with disgust. "Jesus, the smell in here. You okay?"

"Never better." She shoved back a stray lock of hair from her eyes with the back of her hand.

He inspected the details of the body and then took in the candles and the necklace and pendant dangling from the rock. "How the hell did he find this place?"

"I didn't know caves like this existed in the area. Whoever was here knew the area well."

"Three kids on a science expedition, maybe?"

She shook her head. "The kids parked and entered on the opposite side of the park. They were never supposed to be close to this section."

He looked at the thin line of bruises ringing the victim's neck as well as the collection of other marks. "He didn't strangle her the first time he laid hands on her."

"A choking game?"

"Maybe."

He raised the victim's bagged hand. "Are there signs she tried to get away?"

"That's what it looks like. The other shoe is out there somewhere."

"I'll call in the scent dogs and see if they can find it."

For a moment, both sat in silence, each lost in their own thoughts.

"Her face is turned to the side," Jake said. "The killer or killers didn't want her looking at him."

"Is that some kind of dominance thing?"

"That and anger."

"We've got a real gem of a killer this time."

"You need anything from me?" Jake asked.

What could he do for her now? Nothing. But it was nice he asked. "Have Brad send in the body bag."

"Consider it done." He winked at her and then slowly retraced his path out of the cave.

"I've got the bag," Brad shouted.

She blinked and turned, breaking her long stare. "Great, hand it in."

Jake stripped off his Tyvek suit, gloves, and booties the instant he left the cave. The smell would cling to him and be in his airways for days.

"She hates tight spaces," Rick said.

Hell, Jake was in that damn tomb less than ten minutes and wouldn't forget it for a long time. He knew this was a hard scene and the tight proximity to the body was clearly taking its toll. "Why?"

Rick slid his hands into his pockets. "I'll deny it, if you ever tell her I told you."

That tweaked a small smile. "Your baby sister scare you?"

Rick chuckled. "Damn right. And if you had any sense you would fear her, too."

Jake had witnessed her temper in full force when a young uniformed cop had trampled her crime scene and another time when she was singing and a guy from the audience at Rudy's got too familiar with another female singer. Georgia Morgan, defender of the defenseless, whether they be dead or alive.

"I'll never tell," Jake said.

Rick shook his head. "You heard the story about Dad finding Georgia at a homicide scene?"

"Yeah. Hell, it was all over the Internet when Annie's case was reopened." He pictured the infant lying in her crib, crying with panic and fear. Just feet away, the cops found the walls splattered with blood, but there was no sign of Georgia's birth mother, Annie Rivers Dawson. Every cop in the city had been put on alert, until a body later identified as Annie's was found in a remote section of woods off I-40.

"Dad always thought her quirk for tight spaces went back to the day Annie was attacked. Annie's sister found Georgia and immediately took her out of the crib and covered her face snugly with a blanket. When Dad arrived, Georgia was red faced and screaming. He took her away from the scene right away. She was only five days old, but kids absorb more than anyone can ever say. I can't imagine what it would have been like to hear your mother's screams and then have your aunt nearly suffocate you."

"She ever talk about it?"

"Georgia never talks about anything. She keeps it all bottled up. More and more since that defense attorney dug into Annie's case and it all hit the news two years ago. I've tried to talk to her but she brushes it off."

Jake glanced toward the cave entrance and watched as Brad and another officer gently pulled the body bag out of the cave. "So we have a killer who has at least two and possibly three kills to his credit."

"Yeah." He spat out the word as if it were distasteful.

"Right. Well, it's our turn to get a crack at this guy. We'll start with the most recent victim. Fingerprints or dental records should tell us pretty quickly if she's Elisa Spence."

"Georgia said this victim was wearing an onyx college ring and a pink sweater."

"That fits the description given by Elisa's roommate. As soon as we have a fingerprint identification, we can hit the streets."

"Roger that." Rick rubbed the back of his neck with his hand. Several other technicians from the medical examiner's office lifted the bag onto a waiting lightweight stretcher used in rugged terrain.

Jake watched the opening of the cave, waiting for Georgia. When she appeared, her face was pale and her mouth a thin grim line.

Georgia slowly stood and pressed her hand into the base of her back, but a glance toward Jake dared him to make any wisecracks. "I'll have a report in a minute."

"No rush."

Rick, however, was no longer able to hide his concern. He moved across the rocky terrain, his gait uneven and laid his hand on her shoulder. "You look like shit."

She glowered but didn't shove his hand away. "Love you, too, bro."

"Get something to drink. Get off your feet."

"I'm headed in that direction now."

She moved out of the area marked by yellow crime scene tape and stripped off her black gloves. She tucked them in her pocket and pushed back a lock of hair with the back of her hand. Grabbing a bottle of water from a forensic cooler, she twisted off the top and drank liberally.

Jake and Rick followed, stopping feet from her.

"Might want to stay back. I reek. It's going to take a few showers to get this smell off me and these clothes are headed to the incinerator." She glanced at Jake and held open her arms. "Want a hug?"

He took a half step toward her. "That a dare?"

She dropped her arms. "You're no fun. I thought you'd run from the smell."

"Running's not my style."

She held his gaze a moment as if rooting for the real meaning and then closed her eyes and focused on drinking more water.

A breeze rustled through the trees catching the detectives downwind. Jake and Rick got a whiff of her scent.

"You weren't kidding," Rick said.

Georgia raised a brow. "That keen eye for detail . . . you should be a detective."

Jake gave her time to finish her bottle and eat a handful of crackers. "See anything that the killer might have left behind?"

"I found three candles. They had melted into a puddle of wax."

Jake's jaw tightened. "She was fully dressed, but do you think she was raped?"

"Yes."

The cave was the killer's special hiding place that no one had found in the last five years. How many times had the killer returned to this spot to gaze at the cave's entrance? Had he been a friend or acquaintance of Elisa's, or had she simply been his type, at the wrong place at the wrong time?

"We'll start with Elisa Spence's parents. Once we have an identification, we can easily move forward. Can you tell anything about the older body at this point?" Jake asked.

"No. It's going to take hours to process the scene."

"You need to eat," Rick said.

"I'll be lucky to stomach crackers at this point."

"Just be sure to eat," he said.

She glared at her brother. If it had been Jake asking the questions, she'd have tuned him out. "Understood."

Jake and Rick left her standing by the cave entrance, watching as Brad prepared to enter the cave. At Jake's car, he slid behind the wheel while Rick settled in the passenger seat. "Did you have Tracker when you searched five years ago?"

"Yeah, but he's not a scent dog. Strictly apprehension."

"Tracker would have liked these woods."

"He misses the work. But his hip is now arthritic. He was curled up on the couch with Jenna when I got the call today and I like the idea of him looking out for her. Makes the long evenings away easier knowing he's on the job, even if he can't run as well."

"I'm surprised he let you out of the house." Seeing the dog in action was impressive. Once Rick reached for his badge and gun from the home safe, the dog tripped a switch and was all business.

"Jenna bribed him with a piece of steak left over from dinner."

"That worked?"

"Not really. But I let Jenna believe it did."

Tracker had not been thrilled about Rick's marriage and the insertion of another person in his life. The fact that the canine was guarding Jenna showed signs of progress.

Rick shook his head. "Tracker and I were a mean lean team until I got married. She's made us a little soft."

"That a complaint?"

"No, not at all. He's warming up to her charm and good cooking."

Jake's phone buzzed, signaling a text. He had called in to the missing person's detective on the Spence case and requested a picture. "Picture of Elisa Spence."

Jake compared the photo Georgia took to Elisa's picture. Despite decomposition, it was apparently a match. "We need to talk to her parents."

"You need a shower first."

"Right."


After a shower and change of clothes at headquarters, the detectives drove to Franklin, Tennessee, a suburb twenty miles west of Nashville. In a much older neighborhood, they found the small well-kept home located at the end of a gravel driveway.

The Spences' one-story house had a half dozen windows all lit up as if everyone in the house was up and waiting for Elisa to come home. There wasn't a leaf on the neatly raked lawn and all the flowerbeds had recently been filled with yellow pansies. They parked in the driveway and climbed the brick steps to a black lacquered front door.

Jake drew in a breath, straightened his tie, and rang

the bell. Immediately, footsteps sounded in the hallway and the door opened to an older couple who looked to be in their mid-sixties.

"Mr. and Mrs. Spence?" Jake asked, as he held up his badge.

"Yes," Mr. Spence said. He had thinning white hair and wore thick glasses that accented red-rimmed eyes. His cotton shirt was badly wrinkled and not tucked into his dark pants. The man looked like he hadn't slept in days.

"I'm Mrs. Spence," the woman said. She had shoulder-length gray hair cut into a pageboy style and wore a simple black cotton dress. "Are you here about Elisa?"

"Yes, ma'am. I'm Detective Jake Bishop and this is my partner, Rick Morgan. We're with the Nashville Police Department. May we come in?"

Both Spences stepped aside, their expressions deepening with each passing second.

"Did you find Elisa?" Mr. Spence asked.

"Is there somewhere we can sit?" Jake asked. Eight years ago he'd been visited by the Boston police making the death announcement that his fiancée was hit by a drunk driver. The shock of the news had been a punch to the gut. After the initial stab of pain, next came confusion, disbelief, and then blinding anger. When he'd learned the driver was the youngest son of an Irish mob boss, Jake found the guy and beat the living shit out of him. He would have killed him if his brothers hadn't restrained him.

"I don't want to sit," Mrs. Spence said. "Sitting won't change a thing. Is our baby girl alive or dead?"

"The girl we found is dead and we believe it's Elisa."

Mrs. Spence's face dropped to her hands and she wept soul-wrenching sobs. Her husband stood tall, his arm wrapped around his wife's shoulders. "Are you sure it's not a mistake?"

"We've compared pictures you gave the missing persons department to the woman we found. It appears to be a match."

The old man's shoulders stooped. "So it could be a mistake?"

"I don't want to give you false hope. Clothes, hair color, height, and weight are all a match. I'm sorry."

Mr. Spence raised his chin as if he were a boxer in the ring who took a hard upper right. "I want to see our child. I won't believe it until I see it."

"She's at the medical examiner's office. She'll be under the care of Dr. Miriam Heller," Jake said. "I'll give you Dr. Heller's number."

"When can we—" His voice broke. "When can we see her?"

"I'll arrange it so you can go in tonight."

The old man nodded as his wife buried her face in her palms.

Times like this were sensitive, but questions needed to be asked. A killer needed to be caught. "Do you know of anyone that would want to hurt your daughter?"

He shook his head. "No. No one. Elisa was sweet and nice. The perfect daughter. She was a hardworking girl who had a brilliant future." Tears of utter desolation fell down his cheek. "None of this makes sense."

Mrs. Spence raised her eyes. Through the sadness burned a determination. "Talk to her roommate. Girls away at school change. Here, she was a sweet girl, but I know she was growing up. Experimenting. If anyone knew what was happening, her roommate, Cheryl Milton, will. I know her address but don't remember her phone number."

Elisa Spence and her roommate, Cheryl Milton, lived near the university campus in a small one-story house. Made of brick, the mid-century modern house had a large bay window, now curtained off, and a small porch that led to a front door positioned left of the window. The yard was small, but neatly cut. The house was dark, as if no one were home.

As Jake parked, he checked his watch. "It's after nine."

"Doesn't look like anyone is home."

"No other way to find out than to knock." As he reached for the car door handle, he cocked his head toward Rick. "What do you have on Cheryl Milton?"

"According to missing persons, she's twenty-one. She and Elisa are both biology majors. Both in the honor society. No arrest record or complaints on Milton or Spence."

Out of the car, Jake and Rick moved to the front door and rang the bell. When he didn't get an immediate response, he pounded hard on the door. "Cheryl Milton, this is Detective Jake Bishop with the Nashville Police Department." He waited a beat, his hand poised to knock again when he saw a light click on inside the house. Seconds later, footsteps followed. By the sound, the house's occupant had walked to the front door but was making no move to open it.

Jake removed his badge from his pocket and held it up toward the picture window. "Ms. Milton, have a look out the window and you will see I'm here with my partner, Detective Rick Morgan. We have questions about Elisa."

The curtains fluttered and a small opening appeared at the edge. Jake couldn't see the occupant but sensed the scrutiny. Both detectives waited, badges held high. After a pause, the curtains fluttered closed and footsteps moved toward the door. Chains were pulled free of locks and the door opened.

Standing in the doorway was a short, heavyset blond woman with a round face and large blue eyes. A sprinkle of freckles peppered her face. She wore a large Vanderbilt sweatshirt that rippled around her full frame, faded jeans, and flip-flops. Her gaze settled on the badges before she nodded. "I'm Cheryl Milton. Have you found Elisa?"

"Can we speak?" Jake asked. He carefully tucked his badge back in his breast pocket.

"Is she all right? Did she say where she's been?" Her accent was Southern but not Middle Tennessee.

If he had to guess, he'd bet the Carolinas. "We need your help with a few questions?"

A wrinkle furrowed her brow. "This isn't good news, is it?"

"Ma'am, may we speak inside?"

Nodding, she opened the door and stepped aside. The living room was small but neatly furnished with

Scandinavian furniture. There was a low sleek red couch that didn't look a bit comfortable, a couple of black chairs, and a black-striped rug under a glass coffee table complete with a stack of design magazines.

"Please have a seat." Cheryl pointed to the black chairs. She took the end of the couch. "Can I get you something to drink?"

"No, thank you," Jake said. On the walls were several large black-and-white photos that were too abstract for him to pinpoint the exact subject matter. "You were the one that reported Elisa Spence missing?"

"I was." She moved to tuck her legs under her and then, as if realizing that was too informal, settled her feet on the ground and laid her hands on her jeans. "The last time I saw her was four days ago. Friday."

Jake pulled a notebook from his breast pocket. The timeline fit with Georgia's estimations. "Where did you see Elisa last?"

"We were at the coffee shop Blue Note Java on Maple Avenue. We met there a lot to have coffee and just talk about school." She leaned forward, her fingers gripping her knees so tightly that her knuckles whitened. "What happened to Elisa?"

"That's what we're still trying to figure out," Rick said.

"Where is she?"

No cop enjoyed making a death notice. Jake tugged at the edge of his jacket, suddenly feeling constrained. "We believe she was murdered."

For a moment, Cheryl blinked as if a bucket of cold water had been splashed on her head. She waited a beat as if wondering, as if expecting them to recant. When they didn't, she leaned forward and threaded her hands together. "Are you sure? She's the nicest person I know."

"We're almost certain. You gave a very good description to missing persons which we were able to match against the woman we found."

Color drained from her face, leaving her white and drawn. "Why would anyone want to kill Elisa? Who would do this?"

"That's what we're trying to find out."

Tears glistened in her eyes. Two fat tears trickled down her cheeks and she quickly wiped them away. "This is a bad dream. We were supposed to drive to Knoxville on Thursday. She had a job interview for a midwinter break internship. She was so excited and asked me to ride along for moral support. We were going to hit the outlets while we were there."

"You said you two were close?"

"Like sisters," she said, shaking her head. "We were matched as roommates our freshman year and really hit it off. We spend time together over the holidays and summers." A sigh shuddered. "Her parents must be devastated."

"They are," Rick said.

"Did she date anyone?" Jake asked.

"She had dates with a few guys last year, but nothing that went beyond a first date. She was really picky about guys and always found something wrong with them."

"She reject anyone lately?"

"No. Honestly, she was cute in her own way but most guys didn't think she was all that hot."

"Was there anyone bothering or following Elisa? She might have cut someone off in traffic or gotten into a spat in the grocery store line. It doesn't always take a lot to catch the attention of a killer," Jake said.

With a trembling hand she tucked a curl behind her ear. "No. No one. Like I said, everyone liked her. Guys might not have wanted to date her but she was everyone's friend."

Maybe the killer didn't have a beef with her. Maybe it wasn't personal for the killer. Maybe it had been sport. "Can we see her room?"

"Sure." She rose, moving slowly toward a small hallway that led to two rooms separated by a bathroom.

Cheryl opened the bedroom door and clicked on the light. "The other detectives asked me if she kept any kind of diary or journal but I said no. She wasn't really the introspective type."

"These were the detectives from missing persons?"

"Yes. Thompson and Levy, I think."

"I know them," Jake said.

His focus moved past Cheryl to Elisa's room. A bedroom could tell him a lot about a person. It was the inner sanctum for most, their secrets held closely were generally found here.

Elisa slept in a twin bed placed against the wall. Covered in a pink-and-blue quilt with a collection of fluffy pillows, it was neatly made, the seam lines crisp and clean. In front of the bed was a square white shag rug and to the right a small desk with a lamp, a blotter centered directly in the middle, a Titans coffee mug filled with sharpened pencils, and a stack of thick textbooks. "I don't see a computer."

"She always had that with her," Cheryl said. "She carried a black backpack that had her initials ES embossed on the back."

Neither the backpack nor the laptop had been found at the crime scene. "She looks as if she were very neat."

"She had a thing about order. Said an unmade bed drove her crazy. As soon as she got up in the morning, she made her bed. Even before she went to the bathroom she made her bed. I'm not so neat as her."

"The living room also looked neat as a pin."

She folded her arms over her chest and tipped her head back to keep more tears from spilling. "I've been keeping it extra neat. Making an effort to straighten and vacuum so when she came home it would be clean like she likes it."

"As I understand it, you didn't report her missing until Sunday."

"She texted me on Friday. Said she was going to see her parents."

"You think that was odd?" Rick asked.

"No. She's close to home and her mom has been after her to visit.

"We were supposed to see a movie on Sunday. When I called her that morning, she didn't pick up. I started asking friends if they'd seen her. No one had, so I called her mom. They hadn't seen her in a couple of weeks. That's when I got scared. When all of us got scared."

"What's Elisa's cell phone number?"

Cheryl rattled off the number, which Jake wrote down. He'd have the number searched immediately and see if it could be pinged off a cell tower.

Jake moved to a tall chest of drawers painted an off white. On top were a mirror and a collection of lipsticks. Several were a pale pink and one or two were clear glosses but there was one tube that was a bright red. The label on the end dubbed it "Siren Red." There was also a bottle of purple nail polish. It matched the color worn by the victim.

He set the lipstick back down and opened the top drawer. To his surprise he found a collection of very lacy and sexy undergarments. "How did she dress?"

"She liked khakis and sweaters. Very preppy."

He noted the black thongs and sheer bras. "And these belong to her?"

Cheryl peeked in the drawer. Her face blossomed into a bright red. "She just bought those a week ago. She said she liked the way they made her feel. I was sure she had a thing for a guy, but she said no."

"And you believed her?"

"Like I said, I never saw a guy around here or with her. My guess is she had a crush on someone and was working out a fantasy."

"She do that a lot?"

"She liked guys. But as I said, she wasn't exactly the sexy type. I figured it was a phase and whoever she had a secret crush on would pass."

"No odd behavior?"

"No. None. She was a solid science student, but she was young and she didn't want to feel like a grandma before her time."

"So she slipped on the undergarments to make her feel sexy and attractive for some guy who might not even know she existed?"

She swiped away a tear with the back of her hand. "That would be my guess. And you know, a lot of young girls wear undergarments like that."

"What else did she do to make herself feel young and pretty?" Rick asked as he closed the door.

"She liked to drink and party like any other woman her age. Not a lot, mind you, but once in a while."

"What about drugs?" Jake had seen straight-laced kids like Elisa do stupid things to get noticed. All thought they'd take a quick walk on the wild side only to discover that the wild side came with fun and also its share of risk and danger. Crossing the line always had a price.

"She smoked a little pot but none of the hard stuff. She understood moderation. She wasn't like an addict or anything. She just had fun once in a while."

"You left her in the coffee shop on Friday?" The question came from Rick who stood by a sheer curtained window. He wasn't looking at her but outside toward the trees and the cars parked on the street.

"Yeah. She was working on a presentation for this week and wanted to finish polishing it."

Jake moved to the small closet. He opened the door and found a collection of conservative skirts, pants, and button-down shirts. Several pairs of worn brown loafers lined the bottom of the closet.

He pulled on latex gloves. "Mind if I have a look in her closet?"

She bit her top lip and shivered. "No, go ahead."

He pushed aside the clothes and discovered way in the back a sleek black dress. Judging by the length, it would have hit the average woman several inches above the knee. "This hers?"

"Yes. I have a similar one."

"I don't see shoes to match."

"I borrowed them. They're still in my closet if you want me to get them."

"No, that's okay for now." He glanced at his near empty notepad. "There was no one that was bothering her? No one that she liked or talked about? No one paying attention in any way."

"I mean, she mentioned she saw a cute guy at the coffee shop last week. He said hi. She said hi. But that was the end of it as far as I know."

"What's the name of the coffee shop again?" Jake asked.

"Blue Note Java. It's in the West End on Maple Avenue."

Jake circled Blue Note Java in his notes. Amber had worked at the café five years ago. He tucked the notebook back in his breast pocket and then pulled out a business card. "If you think of anything else, will you call me?"

She accepted the card, flicking the edge with her index finger. "Sure. Of course."

He felt for Cheryl. She called in a missing person's report likely thinking her friend would be found alive and well. "Do you mind if we have a look around while we're here?"

"No. Take as much time as you need. I'll be in the living room if you have questions."

Jake and Rick nodded as she turned and left the room. Both stood in the center of the girl's room, canvassing everything. Four days ago, the woman lying dead in that cave had been in this room, full of hopes and dreams. She'd been laughing. Maybe crying. Studying. Alive. And now gone.

Rick moved toward the desk and opened the center drawer where he found her checkbook, banking statements, pens, gum, a single earring, and paperclips. All things that belonged in a desk drawer. Lifting the banking statements, he scanned the list of her most recent transactions. "She spends most of her money at the campus bookstore, the grocery, and Blue Note Java. Judging by the list of expenses charged to Blue Note Java, I'd say it was her home away from home."

"I've not been there," Jake said.

"Neither have I." Rick closed the drawer and moved to the neatly made bed. He knelt down and pushed up the quilt so that he could see under the bed. He found one storage box and a neatly vacuumed floor. Pulling out the box, he found it layered with a collection of summer clothes. Again, nothing out of the ordinary. In fact, a complete search of the room revealed nothing that didn't fit the profile of a hardworking, very intelligent young woman. Well, nothing except the undergarments.

"Let's visit Blue Note Java and see if they remember Elisa," Rick said.

They arrived at the coffee shop fifteen minutes later, and after circling the block, found a parking spot close to the entrance. The front had a large picture window reminiscent of an old bakery or perhaps a butcher shop. The words *Blue Note Java* were painted in a vibrant blue arched over the window's center, and below it the image of a coffee cup filled with steaming musical notes dangled. Lining the bottom of the window was a flowerbox filled with red geraniums that had begun to drop their petals.

Inside the shop, long industrial lights cast a warm glow on walls painted a faint yellow and wide-paneled hardwood floor. On the far wall of the shop stood a coffee and pastry bar and in front of it a couple dozen tables that could seat three or four people each. Nearly every table was filled with young students, some huddled close in conversation and others chatting and laughing.

"Place is hopping," Rick said.

He glanced at the store hours painted on the door. "Sign says they're open until midnight."

Jake and Rick pushed open the door, the bells above it jingling. The instant they entered, the scents of coffee and cinnamon swirled around them as the hum of conversation dimmed. Jake and Rick were plainclothes officers, but both looked like cops. Dark suits could have tipped everyone off or it could have been a combination of swagger mixed with assessing gazes always searching for threats or counting exits. The silence confirmed they would now be the official topic of conversation.

Reaching for his badge, Jake moved up to the register where a young girl stood. She had coal black hair, a firebrand tattoo on her right arm, and wore a purple shapeless dress that sparkled a little when she moved. Her shorn nails were painted black and a ring glistened from each of her index fingers and thumbs. She looked up at Jake, mild surprise registering in her hazel eyes as she studied his badge and smiled. "Five-O. What can I do for ya?"

He grinned, liking the girl's familiarity. "My name

is Detective Jake Bishop and this is my partner, Detective Rick Morgan."

"I'm Cleo."

Slowly, he tucked the badge back in his breast pocket and then dug out his phone. He pulled up the picture of Elisa that missing persons had sent him. "Cleo, can you do me a favor and tell me if you've seen this gal before in Blue Note Java."

For an instant she simply stared at him, a bit stunned, before she bought her focus to the picture. "Yeah, that's Elisa Spence. She comes in here all the time. I heard she was missing or something. Her roommate, Cheryl, was here looking for her midday Sunday and then I heard cops came by on Monday."

"How often would you say Elisa Spence comes in here?" Rick asked.

"Almost every day. But I didn't work Sunday evening or Monday so I can't say for sure." Cleo turned to a large billboard covered with flyers and reached for one featuring Elisa's smiling face. At the bottom was a phone number he recognized as Nashville Police Missing Person's Department. "Is she okay?"

"When's the last time you saw her?"

"I think it was last Friday. She was in here working on a paper."

"Was she by herself the entire time?" Rick asked.

"Elisa mostly kept to herself. Sometimes her roommate would stop and study with her. Last week she was putting the finishing touches on a big paper that was due this week."

"She's a good student?"

"She is solid but she liked being around the really smart students. This whole place is full of people who are Einstein smart. I couldn't tell you what most of them are studying. Me, I just went to high school."

Jake shook his head. "Don't sell yourself short, Cleo. I bet you never forget a face."

She fingered the gold hoop hanging from her right ear. "I'm good with faces. And names. Pays to remember people when you work for tips."

"So most of your customers are regulars?"

She considered the question. "Yeah. I'd say eighty to ninety percent are regulars. Like I said, I remember almost everyone's name."

Someone Elisa knew could have killed her. In fact, most women were killed by an acquaintance. "Anyone pay any close attention to Elisa lately?"

"No. Not really. She kept to herself most of the time."

"Most of the time," Jake repeated.

"Well, she did talk to this guy about a week ago. I only noticed because he was way out of her league in the looks department."

"What did he look like?"

"Tall, lean, muscular build. He had long dark hair that skimmed his shoulders and a beard. And he wore faded jeans and a dark T-shirt—a bit scruffy. Very sexy. And he had a guitar."

"So he made an impression on you?"

"I know handsome when I see it. And this dude was handsome. Me and the other girl working the counter that day were a little shocked when he took his cup and sat next to Elisa's table. He started talking to her and at first she didn't look up as if she thought he was talking to someone else. When she realized he seemed to be into her, she blushed. It was cute. And a little creepy."

"Why creepy?"

"Please. A guy like that doesn't hang out with a girl like Elisa unless he wants something. Money, help with a project. He wanted something, but I'd bet sex was at the bottom of his list."

An espresso machine hissed as another employee steamed milk and then blended in three shots of black coffee. "Did they leave together?"

"No. But I saw her punching a number into her phone. I'm guessing it was his number. They could have hooked up later somewhere else." She held up a ringed finger. "Like I said, the scene didn't fit. Elisa's more likely to win a science contest than a date with a hot guy."

"Has this guy been back to the coffee shop?" Jake asked.

"No, haven't seen him. That seemed to be the only time he came in here while I was working."

"Right." Jake closed his notebook and tucked it in his breast pocket.

Rick handed the clerk his card. "Cleo, would you be willing to talk to a forensic artist so we could develop an image of this guy?"

"Yeah, sure. Kinda cool. Very *CSI*."

"When do you get off work?"

She glanced toward the wall behind her at a large round clock with a coffeepot painted in the center. "About an hour."

"And you could talk to the artist tonight?"

"Sure."

Rick texted a message and within seconds received an answer back. "The artist will be here at the end of your shift. Her name is Jenna Morgan."

"What, is she like your sister?"

"Wife."

"All in the family."

Jake shook his head. "You've no idea."

Cleo's expression sobered. "Are you any closer to finding Elisa?"

Jake allowed a sigh to leak out. "We found her. But the news isn't good."

# CHAPTER SIX

*Tuesday, October 3, 11:00 P.M.*

Georgia and Brad alternated shifts. The scent of death had faded slightly with the removal of Elisa's body, but strong hints lingered in the cavern like a dark oppressive cloud. Lights from exterior floodlights mingled with several small portable lights placed around the interior chamber.

She bagged the pendant and then she and Brad slowly removed the remaining stones around the smaller entrance to widen the opening, letting more light stream inside and chase away the darkness. When they set aside the last stone, she got her first good look at the second body. It was laid out, arms crossed over the chest. The empty sockets of the skull stared sightlessly up and the jaw slacked open almost as if it were laughing at a dark joke.

She swept her light over the bones to the darkened corners until the beam unexpectedly settled on a second set of remains. This skeleton wasn't lying flat but had crumbled into a heap as if at the time of death the victim had been sitting. To the right lay a .22 pistol.

She sat back on her haunches, studying the scene. Had this been some kind of murder/suicide? She glanced back at the opening and the rocks she'd piled to the side. Could they have been stacked from inside the chamber from a murder/suicide or had someone killed these two and walled up the inner cave? The BR pendant hung to the right of the opening so it could have been hung before the wall was closed.

She searched around the bones into all the shadowed crevices of the second chamber, confirming this cave was a dead end and there were no other bodies. "What the hell happened here?"

"Did you say something?" Brad asked.

She rubbed her forehead using the back of her hand. "Brad, we've got two bodies in here."

Silence crackled. "Can you tell if they're male or female?"

Georgia examined the skull in the bone pile in the corner. It appeared large with a wide brow ridge, indicating male. The skull attached to the other body was smaller with a narrow brow. "Looks like we have one of each."

"Understood." Resignation weighed down the word. "Let's get to it. It's going to be longer than I thought."

She focused on the female because it was closest to the opening. This one would have to be processed and removed first.

The low ceiling forced her to work sitting cross-legged or on her hands and knees. The skeleton was laid out in the center of the chamber with the hands positioned over the chest like Elisa Spence. The clothes had all but deteriorated from the body except for traces of what looked to have been the snaps or a zipper of denim jeans. The victim had also been wearing tennis shoes with rubber bottoms that remained partially intact.

The bones weren't green, or new, but were stripped of flesh and dry. She guessed the victim had died at least three to five years ago. Bethany and Mike had vanished five years ago.

The girl the cops and countless volunteers all searched so hard to find might now be finally coming home, and parents trapped in a terrible limbo would have some closure. As heart breaking as it was, at least there would be some closure. "What happened to you, Bethany? How did you end up here for so, so long?"

She spent nearly an hour photographing the chamber and making sketches that she might one day have to refer back to in court.

When Brad moved to the mouth of the front chamber and called her name she was startled at the sound of another living voice. "Are you about ready to move the second body?"

"Yes. I've photographed it all, sketched everything I've seen and bagged anything that might have been attached to the body at one point. Once the bones are removed, I'll sweep the area one last time."

"I've got the flat board as you requested."

"Great." Since she couldn't stand and excavate under the bones, she planned to shimmy a body board under the bones and hopefully keep the skeleton intact as much as possible. Once they had the bones on the board, they could slide the board into the body bag. She also hoped this method would preserve the soil under the bones which might very well contain evidence that had settled into the dirt.

Georgia blew out a breath and wiped sweat from her brow while trying to maintain a measured pace that would soon get her out of the cave. For a moment, her chest tightened and her heart kicked up a notch. Closing her eyes, she took a half dozen deep breaths. The lights in the cave had heated the chamber and thickened the air, which left her a little nauseous.

Brad fed in the board and slowly worked the edge under the bones. She shimmied the board back and forth, scooping up a bit of dirt as she wedged the hard edge under the bones. The dirt was packed tight and digging into it took more muscle than she imagined. Cursing under her breath, she kept pushing until the edge eased under the female skeleton's leg bones, rib cage, and head. Bones shifted and moved slightly as she kept working the board farther and farther under the remains. When she finally reached the other side, sweat rolled down her back and she was breathless.

"You okay?" Brad asked.

Her laugh held no hints of humor. "Never better. How about you?"

"I could think of a few things I'd rather be doing now?"

She grinned. "Just a few?"

"Maybe a couple of dozen."

She sat back on her heels and wiped her brow again. "I think the body is ready to go. I'll slide out the board toward you."

The pendant suggested they had a female victim. The bones confirmed it. "Dr. Heller might prove me wrong, but I'm certain the victim was a woman."

"More evidence to suggest it's Bethany."

"If I had to bet, yeah."

She didn't have to remind him to go slowly or to treat the remains carefully. She and Brad had worked together for five years now and she trusted his attention to detail.

When the second body was gone, the chamber felt suddenly empty, even lighter, as if removing the bones had uncorked the bottle and freed the trapped spirits. "Time to go home, Bethany."

Georgia studied the ground where the bones had lain. She took more pictures before reaching for a small soil sifter. Carefully, she sifted through the dirt, searching for any trace evidence.

Unlike witness statements, evidence was slower to yield its story, but it didn't lie either. It would easily be weeks, perhaps months, before all the evidence would be processed. But when it did speak, she was determined there'd be no contamination, and its voice would be clear and decisive.

With the first of the pair out of the cave, she turned to the second set of remains and began the process all over again.

It was close to one in the morning when she crawled out of the cave and watched as the bagged remains of both victims were carried up the hill. There were representatives from the medical examiner's office waiting to carry the body bags out of the woods where they would be loaded into a transport vehicle and taken directly to the medical examiner's office.

Her knees and back groaned as she straightened. A check of her watch told her she'd been at this more than twelve hours. She unzipped her Tyvek suit and peeled it off. A cool breeze blew across her sweat-soaked shirt plastered to her skin. A shiver chased the warmth out of her body.

"Had enough for one night?" Jake Bishop's Boston accent cut through the air, snatching her attention away from the darkness. He handed her a water bottle, which she readily accepted.

She cracked open the bottle cap. "What brings you out here on this lovely night?"

He had showered and changed into a clean shirt and suit. The faint scent of his aftershave wafted toward her. No doubt he showered at the station. Homicide cops often went nonstop in the first forty-eight to seventy-two hours of an investigation. Though it took time to sort through all the evidence, they understood that critical witness statements needed to be gathered as quickly as possible.

Under Georgia's gaze, he slid his fingers down the gig line, the center seam of his shirt, to his belt buckle as if checking its accuracy.

"It's straight." She gulped down water. "It's always straight."

Dark eyes lightened with laughter. "Jealous?"

"Not really." She held out her arms. "Not when I'm feeling so fetching today."

"It works for me."

The heat under the words warmed her cheeks, tipping her to the defensive. "Why are you here?"

"Just checking in to see how my crime scene is progressing."

"It's our crime scene." She drank from the bottle, savoring the cool liquid.

"Sure." He handed her a packet of crackers. "I met

with Elisa Spence's parents. They've gone by the medical examiner's office, and according to Dr. Heller, positively identified their daughter."

She shoved out a breath. "Damn."

"Yeah." Both stood in silence for a moment as the weight of the day settled. Finally, Jake cleared his throat. "So what did you find inside?"

As she peeled away the wrapper, she detailed her findings in the catalog of facts. "Follow me to the truck. There are a few things I'd like to show you."

"Don't tease me."

Any other cop who'd made that joke would have earned a laugh. However, Jake's idea of a joke unsettled her. "So not funny."

"That the best you got?"

"Afraid so." Too tired to fire back, she kept walking, putting one foot in front of the other. She only slept an hour or two last night and the nonstop day had drained what little reserves she had mustered this morning.

She opened the back of the evidence truck and rooted through the plastic bags which all held the evidence she had collected from the scene. At this point, she had an unnamed killer who had presented her with a giant puzzle with hundreds of pieces in need of sorting before she could create a cohesive forensic picture for the detectives.

"To begin with, there were two victims in the back chamber." She detailed her findings and then from her collected evidence, she found a bag with the remnants of candle wax.

Jake held up the bag to the floodlight and studied

the dark ring. "What do you make of it? Looks like a wax."

She rolled her head from side to side wincing as the stiff muscles protested. "Just like I found in the outer chamber. Whoever this guy is, he likes to light a candle while he's in the cave with his victims."

"He likes seeing his victims suffer. Can't tell if he killed them here or placed them here."

"Yeah, he's a real peach." She raised the bottle to her lips, draining the last of it.

"Three out of three bodies have been found," Jake said. "But we still can't confirm if we have Bethany and Mike."

"I think we do, but Dr. Heller will make the final call," Georgia said.

"And no sign of anything belonging to Mike in the cave?"

"Unless you count the gun next to the body. It appears the serial number has been filed off. Still, ask Marlowe if he's missing a gun. Might get lucky."

"I can let Bethany's family know we found the pendant?"

"Sure. It might mean something to her mother."

"I'm sure it will."

She grabbed another water bottle from the truck and twisted off the top. "So what did you find out about the first victim?"

"Nothing jumping out yet. Rick's going through surveillance data from a local coffee shop now. According to her roommate, it was Elisa Spence's home away from home."

"I have a few hangouts like that." She liked being lost in a crowd. She felt safer and more protected when she was surrounded by the chatter and laughter of strangers, lights, and the sense that she was not alone.

Again, she rubbed her neck, soothing tight muscles and frayed nerves. Like it or not, she had to go to her apartment soon and get some sleep. If she kept going with little or no rest, she'd drop right where she stood.

"You look like you're dead on your feet," Jake said.

Georgia refocused her gaze, realizing she'd allowed the veil to drop for a split second. She grinned as she raised the water bottle to her lips. "Just need more water; otherwise, I'm fine. I've a few more hours here and then I'll head home and get a good night's sleep."

"When was the last time you really slept?"

"Last night was hit or miss, but I'm used to it."

"Used to it? What's that mean?"

She'd heard things about Jake Bishop in the few years they'd worked together. Arrogant. Brash. A charmer. Temper when pushed. Hell of a detective who read people damn well.

Now she was trying to keep her act together as the Amazing Mindreading Kreskin studied her. "Direct those eyes elsewhere. I'm not into any kind of deep Q&A right now. I have to wrap up this scene."

"You always get a little pissy when you're tired."

"Bite me."

"I've hit one of your nerves." His voice deepened with a smoky tone.

She looked around her to see who was in earshot. The last thing she needed was someone picking up on this conversation and spreading rumors that somehow they were more than associates.

"Go away," she said. "And lose the grin."

He did a bad job of smothering his smile. "Anything else I can do?"

"I'll collect the evidence and process it and you catch yourself a bad guy."

His jaw tightened and released, drawing her attention to his closely cropped beard. Neat and well-trimmed, she suspected it was soft to the touch. She wondered what it felt like if he were nestled behind her in bed.

Soft. To. The. Touch. God, what the hell was wrong with her? Jake Bishop. Detective Pain-in-the-Ass. She would rather stumble into the beds of a million different guys than his. "Maybe you're right. Maybe I do need sleep."

Amber Ryder rolled to her left side, trying to get comfortable on the lumpy motel bed. She glanced at the clock. Three thirty-three. Halfway to hell, she noted, as she sat up and clicked on a light.

She moved to the plastic-lined curtains. The cheap feel of the curtain fabric had her counting the minutes until she bolted out of this dump.

A peek outside revealed a dark night sky and a full moon. She loved the nights but hated it when the sun rose. Even as a kid, she kicked and cried when her mother woke her up and made her dress for school. She never felt like herself until about three in the afternoon when her internal body clock kicked into high gear. As an adult, the only time she saw the sunrise was after a long night out.

After peeing, she set up the coffeemaker in the room

and switched it on. Soon, water gurgled and hissed. Her conversation yesterday with the detectives was disappointing to say the least. She had expected to learn more behind Georgia's motivation for reopening the case. Was new interest in the case based on new evidence or had Dalton Marlowe finally paid off the right person to reopen it? She guessed the latter.

Remembering yesterday's breakfast, she considered Detective Jake Bishop. He had a relaxed manner and yet his eyes were cold and unrelenting. The guy wasn't dumb like so many of the cops she dealt with five years ago. If he had been in charge of the search then, she wondered if the outcome would have been the same.

Georgia Morgan was just as dedicated as Bishop. She was wound tighter, but was clearly one of those obsessively dedicated professionals. The two together were an impressive combination.

A knock at her motel room sent a ripple of tension through her body. "Who is it?"

"It's the manager. Your three days are up. If you want to stay longer, you're gonna have to pay."

Combing her fingers through her long blond hair, she considered her options. She could spend one more night here, but that meant dipping into the last of this week's paycheck. Another would hit her account in a few days, but until then, she had to make do.

"I'm leaving." She slipped her feet into her shoes and stood. "I'll be out in five minutes."

"Five minutes is all you get. I have to get the maid inside and have her flip the room."

"Does she have a flamethrower?" She glanced at the industrial gray carpet covered with stains, the brown veneer dresser and nightstand dinged with scratches and dents from years of use. The television looked like it dated back to the Stone Age.

"What?"

The place deserved to be burned to the ground. "Never mind. I'll be gone in ten minutes." She stretched and then moved quickly to the bathroom to wash up. A glance in the mirror, and she spent several minutes touching up her eye makeup and lipstick.

"Time to deal with Nashville." She tossed one last look at herself before she grabbed her purse and bag and headed out of the room with her coffee. Even in the shitty light of this dump, she looked good. The morning air smelled fresh and sweet, a nice change from the musty motel room. As she loaded her small roller suitcase in the car, she glanced toward the motel office and saw the manager staring at her as he leaned against the brick wall and smoked a cigarette. Smoke trailed past squinting eyes.

"Ass," she muttered as she dumped her bag in the backseat. "Someone should burn this place to the ground."

The drive to her mother's small house in East Nashville took less than ten minutes and when she pulled into the driveway an invisible fist clenched her heart. When she left for college she swore she'd never return to this dump. She had such big dreams when she grabbed her scholarship to the University of Texas, expecting by now to be married to a rich boy.

Shit. Rich boy. For a time she had plenty of them so hot to fuck her they would do anything she asked. Anything.

Amber made her way slowly up to the front door.

Through the door she heard the voices from the television. That didn't mean her mother was awake or home.
That damn television was always blaring because her
mother so hated the silence. She knocked on the door
with the flat of her hand. At first, her only response
was the sound of a commercial about dog food, but
then she heard the scrape of a chair and she imagined
her mother pushing herself up. Footsteps padded. A
chain scraped against the door and it opened. Staring at
her through the screen door was her mother, a petite
woman with gray-blond hair, faded blue eyes that had
once been as vivid as sapphires. The lines around her
mouth and eyes had deepened, but her face still possessed hints of the beauty that Amber had once envied.

"Hey, Mom," she said.

An unspoken smugness narrowed her eyes and she
nodded. "So, you're back."

"Yes."

"Never thought I'd see you again."

Amber tightened her hand on her purse strap. The
taste of crow was far more bitter than she imagined. "I
said some pretty harsh things when I left."

Her mother folded her arms over her chest, accentuating the wrinkled cleavage in the V-neck of her sweater.
"You had a lot of mouth on you. But then, the world
dumped a lot of trouble on your shoulders and mine.
They were tough times."

"I was hoping I could stay here for a few days."

"Sure. You can stay. But why are you back, Amber?
You being here is only going to stir up trouble."

"I'm not the one that stirred the trouble. Dalton reopened the past, not me."

"I been watching the television. I saw that the cops found the bodies up at the park."

Amber cocked her head. There'd been no mention when she shut off the television at one a.m. "What bodies?"

"Bodies found in Percy Warner Park. One they think is that missing girl, but no cop is talking about the other two. Reporter thinks it's Bethany and Mike."

"Bethany and Mike?" The frown lines in her smooth face deepened. "After all this time, they've been found?"

"Well, that's what the reporters are saying. No one really knows. Reporters stir all kinds of shit up for headlines."

"Damn."

Tracy raised a bony finger and swiped away a brittle strand of bleached blond hair. "Ain't that some shit?"

"Yeah." She ticked through the trouble that would soon swirl around her now. "Where did they find them?"

"In a cave in the park. You'd think with all the people looking so many years ago that someone would have found them."

"You'd think."

Tracy took Amber's bag. "Come on inside. You look like you could sit."

"Thanks." Her mother smelled of cigarette smoke and cheap perfume. She recalled the image of Detective Bishop on the phone outside the diner and the way he stared at Georgia as he spoke. He'd found out then about the bodies. "Mom, I'm almost out of money."

She sighed and set the bag beside a tall stack of

magazines. "We've had our differences, but you're my baby girl. You can stay here as long as you want."

Amber glanced around her mother's house that was as it had been when she was a kid. Beer. More cigarettes. Stale Chinese food. Air freshener. Her life had done a one-eighty and she was back where she started five years ago. And she hated it.

Her mother opened her arms. "Give Mama a hug, baby girl."

Amber lowered her purse to the floor and stepped into her mother's arms. As her mother's thin arms tightened around her, she carefully raised her hands to pat her mother on the back as her mind drifted to the bodies found in the park. "Thank you, Mama."

# CHAPTER SEVEN

*Wednesday, October 4, 11:00 A.M.*

Georgia made it back to her apartment just after two in the morning. So damn exhausted, she stripped her clothes and shoved them in a green trash bag, which she set on her balcony. Straight to the shower, she turned on the hot tap, and stepped under it, letting the hot water wash away the chill, dirt, and the smells of the crime scene. She scrubbed until her skin was pink as the grime swirled down the drain. Falling into bed minutes later, she slept like the dead until ten in the morning.

Now as she walked through the door of the forensic lab, a cup of coffee in hand and her mind sharp, she was ready to work. The sleep had always left her energized better than any amount of coffee. At times like this, she promised herself that the next time she would sleep like a normal person.

Right. Who was she kidding? With her crazy life, sleep was a low priority.

Brad had showered and shaved, and judging by the number of paper coffee cups on his desk, he had arrived hours ago. He stood in front of a large examination table. On top of it was a red sweater spread arms wide. The garment had the old musty smell of the evidence room.

"I'm sorry," she said. "I didn't mean to sleep so late."

He glanced up, noted her relaxed demeanor and smiled. "It's nice to see the color back in your face."

"Nice not to feel as if I have five pounds of sand in each eye." She sipped her coffee. "So what case is that sweater from?"

"It's from a rape in the East End. I collected it last week but haven't had the chance yet to test it."

She remembered the case. Seventeen-year-old girl walking home from work was dragged into an alley, beaten and raped. So far, her attacker remained on the loose.

"The media has gotten hold of the Percy Warner Park case. They are calling every half hour trying to find out if the old and new cases are linked."

She didn't listen to the news much. Half the time it upset her, and the other half made her angry when reporters spouted misleading junk science. "Don't bother to take the calls. None of them wants to hear it can take months to assemble all the physical evidence. They all think we can process the scenes in an hour and have DNA in twenty minutes just like the TV show."

He laughed. "The word from the top is no one talks to the media. Deke has summoned Jake and Rick, and they're headed this way now for a meeting."

"That should be fun."

"I hear the retests you did on Amber Ryder's old

clothes have been bumped to the top of the priority list."

"Good." The discovery of the bodies, along with a push from Deke, accomplished that miracle. She fished her phone out of her purse and glanced at the display. Six missed calls. Scrolling through, she identified four as local media. "Looks like the reporters have me on their radar."

"Isn't this what you wanted? Shining a light on cold cases?"

"Be careful what you wish for, right?"

"You know you love it."

"Maybe a little," she said with a hint of satisfaction. She set her cup and purse down on her desk and moved toward a box of latex gloves.

"Our pal Detective Bishop called at five in the morning to tell me the medical examiner's office would be delivering Elisa Spence's clothes before noon and they needed them to be processed ASAP. The articles arrived about five minutes ago."

"I understand Jake and Rick talked to the parents, and they made the formal ID at the medical examiner's office."

When she imagined Rick and Jake making the death notice, she pictured Rick doing the talking. He possessed that soft Boy Scout vibe that put people at ease, whereas Jake was more like a charming jackhammer.

"Did you get any sleep at all last night?" she asked as Brad arched his back and tried to stretch out the stiffness.

"A few hours. I'm surprised Bishop didn't call you."

She set her coffee cup down, moving toward the table where he worked. "He did. My phone's been off until a few seconds ago."

Georgia donned plastic gloves before unpacking the paper bags of Elisa Spence's clothes sent over by the medical examiner's office. Paper bags allowed air to flow in and out whereas plastic bags created an airtight seal that allowed for the buildup of heat and mold. Both could destroy any kind of biological evidence within hours.

She laid out the garments on a light table. There was a white bloodstained shirt, a khaki skirt, a shoe, and lacy undergarments.

"Leave no stone unturned," he said copying Jake's Boston accent.

She laughed. "You sound like him."

"Seriously, that guy can be pushy as hell."

"He can't help it," she said, grinning. "I think he was born with a stick up his ass."

Brad laughed, glancing toward the door as if he were afraid Jake would appear. "I never said that."

"That's because you're afraid of him."

He straightened his shoulders. "Not afraid, exactly. Just damn leery. Never know when he'll throw the switch."

"Take his best shot." When it came to Jake, she was always snapping back and pushing away.

Pushing him from her thoughts, she focused on the white striped button-down shirt, taking extra care to tug any wrinkles on the arms or front panel. She clicked on a light suspended from a retractable arm and shone it on the material. She would go over the shirt, combing the fibers and threads for any loose materials that could be tested for DNA.

Killers always thought they were clever, but like she had said before, they all left something behind for her to find. It might be barely noticeable, but it was there.

She moved up and down the shirt, plucking several dark hairs with tweezers and then bagging and tagging them. She collected blood samples from the torn right sleeve and from the collar of the shirt. Once she reviewed every inch of the shirt a second time, she turned off the white light and grabbed a black light. Clicking it on, she scanned the shirt, searching for stains, including blood, semen, or urine. As she raised the bottom hem of the shirt, she spotted a faint stain glowing under the black light.

"Hey, now," she muttered. "Where did you come from?" She carefully clipped away part of the fabric and dropped it in a test tube. "Thought you were so clever, didn't you."

"Did you say something?" Brad asked.

"Found a stain."

He raised his head. "Good."

Georgia scraped dirt from the bottom of Elisa's shoe, plucked hair fibers from her skirt and documented two more stains.

She studied the shoe Elisa had worn into the woods. It was simple but expensive. Checking the label on her skirt and shirt, Georgia noted the moderately priced labels.

"The bodies in the back chamber look like a murder/suicide," Brad said.

"I'd have bought it, if not for the newest victim. No

way a second killer would have found that cave. No way."

Likely little forensic data remained on the bones, but it only took a little to connect killer to victim.

Jake and Rick arrived at the medical examiner's office in late afternoon. Jake showed his badge to the receptionist behind the thick glass panel and, leaning into the microphone, said, "Dr. Heller is expecting us."

"I'll buzz her," the tall, thin woman said.

Rick reached into the breast pocket of his jacket and removed a folded piece of white paper. "Jenna swung by the coffee shop and talked to Cleo and spent a couple of hours with her drawing a composite. She thinks the likeness she drew is a fair representation given Cleo's memory isn't as sharp as she hoped."

Jake studied the precise sketch of a bearded man. "He looks like a country-western star. But they all look alike to me."

"That's what I said. Cleo does have a thing for the country singers, according to Jenna. She talked about them a lot over the few hours Jenna spent with Cleo."

Jake tapped the edge of the paper with his finger. "I appreciate her doing the work. Every bit helps."

"Killers are creatures of habit," Rick said. "Maybe his habit is Blue Note Java."

"Very possible." His phone buzzed and he checked the display. Dalton Marlowe's name flashed. He sent the call to voice mail. He'd call him back as soon as he had more concrete answers.

The side door buzzed open and Dr. Miriam Heller appeared. She wore loose fitting green scrubs that moved easily with her as her long legs ate up the distance. Originally from the Northeast, she settled in Nashville four years ago and had established herself as a top-notch pathologist. Armed with a dry humor, Dr. Heller not only interacted well with the cops but also was known for her compassion when dealing with the families of the dead.

Jake smoothed his hand over his tie. "Dr. H. So we meet again."

"We've got to stop meeting like this, gentlemen." She nodded to Rick and smiled. "How are Jenna and Tracker?"

"Doing great. Thanks."

"Maybe sometime we can all meet for a beer," she said. "We can figure out if we can have a conversation that doesn't involve death."

Jake shrugged. "So what do you want to talk about while we're having this beer, Dr. H.? You don't strike me as a football or country music fan."

"You might be surprised." She turned and punched numbers into the keypad that unlocked the side door. They followed, allowing the door to close behind them.

Jake lowered his voice a notch. "Thanks for coming in last night and meeting with Mr. and Mrs. Spence."

"I've seen their kind of pain so many times in this office, but it never gets easier. Seeing their daughter was a shock but they handled it the best they could."

She moved down the hallway and then pushed open the doors to the large exam room. "Go ahead and gown up and I'll meet you in the autopsy room."

As Dr. Heller vanished through swinging doors, Jake and Rick reached for gowns.

"Have you spoken to the Spences this morning?" Rick asked.

"I talked to Mr. Spence a half hour ago," Jake said. "They're anxious to reclaim their daughter's body and have her cremated."

"I don't blame them. Got to be hell for them."

"Yeah."

Within minutes, both had stripped off their suit jackets and slipped on green gowns and donned latex gloves. When they entered exam room one, Dr. Heller stood at the head of the exam table that held the sheet-clad body of Elisa Spence.

Dr. Heller slid on glasses and tied her dark hair back in a tight ponytail. She pulled on latex gloves and then adjusted the powerful light that was suspended above the exam table. As she stood over the body, her face showed a grim determination.

Her assistant, Debbie, a brunette with freckles and a round unsmiling face, stood next to her. Debbie's body was rounder, softer, and made Dr. Heller, who'd traded smoking for obsessive running, all the more stark. Debbie uncovered the tray containing the instruments.

Dr. Heller moved to the body's feet and uncovered them. Decomposition had discolored the soles and shrunk the skin around the toes' cuticles, giving the impression that the nails had grown. The doctor turned the ankle so that the heel was in plain view. "She has fresh blisters and abrasions. I took a look at her remaining shoe before I sent it to the lab and noted it was older, well worn. I wouldn't think the shoes would have worn blisters unless she'd been on her feet a long time.

There are also scratches on her upper arm that suggest she ran into something abrasive like a tree."

Jake rested his hands on his belt. "Like someone was chasing her through heavy brush?"

"That would be my guess. Her shoes created the blisters and the branches scratched her face." Dr. Heller arched a brow. "One could assume she lost her other shoe while she running."

"Scent dogs are combing the brush, but so far have not found it," Rick said.

She moved to the head of the table and uncovered the girl's face, also darkened and drawn from death. Her lips were pale, bloodless, and more scratches raked across the left side of her face. A purple ligature mark ringed the skin around her neck like a Victorian choker. "The scratches on her cheekbones are also consistent with running through the woods." She lifted the head and turned it to the right, exposing the flesh under the left ear. "What does that look like to you?"

Jake leaned in to study the blue-purple marks. "Looks like bruises."

"She's got matching sets on the other side. The shape is consistent with fingers. Because they're in slightly different positions, it appears whoever strangled her put hands on her neck several times."

"Strangled her but didn't kill her," Jake said.

"That's right. I've seen bodies marked like this before. They often indicate a choking game."

Rick pointed to the narrow ribbon of bruises around her neck. "That's a ligature mark if I'm not mistaken?"

"It is. She died from asphyxiation. The other marks might have been enough to make her pass out but not sufficient to cause death."

Jake flexed his fingers. "So this started as a game?"

Absently, Dr. Heller laid a hand on the victim's shoulder. "Smart girls can make stupid choices sometimes. And she might have gone into the woods thinking it was going to be fun when the killer had a different plan all along."

"Shit," Jake muttered, thinking about the cave and the candle that had burned through. The killer had not simply dragged her to the cave and killed her, he kept her there for hours and toyed with her. "Any older bruises that might suggest she tried this kind of thing before?"

"No, also no signs of drug abuse. This could have been her first foray into this kind of sexual play."

"According to her roommate she was smart," Rick said. "But she did like to party."

Dr. Heller raised the victim's right hand and fanned the pale fingers painted in purple chipped at the fingertips. "Debbie found dirt under her nails as if she'd been digging. Maybe she got away and tried to hide. Also embedded in the dirt under her nails, I found skin, so I did scrapings. We've processed and sent it off for DNA testing. Looks like she was able to scratch him perhaps a couple of times."

"Hopefully, she marked him up good," Rick said.

"Be interesting to know if our killer is in a DNA database."

"Wouldn't that be nice." DNA in a database wasn't a given. If this guy had never been arrested, it was very possible law enforcement possessed no record of him.

Jake studied the facial features discolored with decomposition. She'd not been a beautiful woman, but remembering the pictures in her room she had a spark in her eyes and a dimple in her cheek. She was some-one's child. "I hope she gouged the hell out of this guy."

Dr. Heller carefully closed the fingers and laid the hand gently down. She didn't hide the satisfaction when she said, "I'd say she put up a good fight."

"She was found in a remote part of Percy Warner Park," Jake said. "Did he grab her and take her there?"

"I don't think so. I think she went willingly. I found lubricant in the front pocket of her skirt."

"Lubricant?" Jake tapped his finger. "So she follows him to the park thinking it'll be fun and games and then he, what? Strangles her. She panics. Scratches him. Takes off running until he finally catches her and, really pissed at this point, drags her back to the cave to torture her."

"At some point she was penetrated," Dr. Heller said. "Judging by the vaginal bruising, my guess, it was not consensual. However, no traces of semen."

"The killer likely used a condom," Rick said.

"Or," Dr. Heller said, "he used something else to penetrate her other than himself."

Jake muttered a curse.

"If he knew about the cave, he was familiar with the park," Rick said. "Fact, I'd say he knows it intimately."

"Makes sense," Jake said.

"How was she found?" Dr. Heller asked.

"Guy walking his dog. The dog was running free and found the cave. But judging by the smell, it was a matter of time before someone found her." He rubbed his forehead. "Anything else you can tell us about her?"

Rick shifted as he did when his hip bothered him.

"Dr. H., anything you can tell us about the bones of the other two victims?"

"I've an assistant arranging the bones so they can be photographed. As Georgia suggested, one body is female and the other male. Judging by the length of the femur bone, I'd say the female stood about five foot five and the male at six feet."

"That would be consistent with the descriptions of Bethany Reed and Mike Marlowe."

"I've not had a chance to really study the bones in great detail, but I have taken dental x-rays of the teeth. I've requested X-rays from Bethany Reed's dentist so I can compare."

"Any thoughts on cause of death?" Jake asked.

The method of murder often left indicators on the bones. A knick from a knife. A dent in the skull from blunt force trauma. A hole from a bullet. A break in a pelvis that had once been very vascular. A snap of the small horseshoe-shaped bone at the base of the neck called the hyoid. However, sometimes the manner of death wasn't recorded on the bones, in which case, the medical examiner would begin more extensive testing.

She folded her arms, shaking her head. "The female's skull appears to have a hairline fracture in the back. I don't think that injury was enough to kill her, but certainly enough to stun her. I'll get a better idea when I dig into the examination. The male however has a hole to his right temple. He appears to have been shot in the head."

"He shot himself?"

"That, I don't know yet. I need to analyze the entrance and exit holes more carefully."

Impatience nipped at Jake. "Great. Call me as soon as you've got anything here."

"Of course." Dr. Heller adjusted her protective goggles and pulled back the sheet, exposing Elisa Spence's body. Jake shifted, doing his best to remain objective and view the body before him as evidence and not as a person.

Rick cleared his throat and grimaced slightly.

Dr. Heller selected a scalpel from the instrument tray and made a Y-incision in the chest. After she peeled back the flesh, she reached for bone cutters to open the sternum. The two detectives stood and watched as she began the process of autopsying Elisa Spence.

By the time they left the exam room, they had confirmed that Elisa Spence was healthy and fit, had maintained a good weight, strong bones with no breaks, and no signs of drug use with a needle. Despite clean living, she'd died hard, in a manner no one deserved.

The detectives stripped off their gowns and made their way down the elevator and out the front door. The air was warm, the afternoon sun brilliant in the western sky. These kinds of details rarely got past Jake, especially if he were fresh from an autopsy. "Life is so fucking fragile, so fleeting," he said. "And yet everyone thinks they're owed tomorrow."

Rick shook his head. "What makes a girl who's smart and has such a bright future go into the woods with a near stranger? So damn stupid."

Jake shook his head as he reached for dark sunglasses in his breast pocket. "Sex always trumps smart."

Rick drew in a deep breath and shifted his weight as if working tension out of his body. "How could anyone be so starved for attention?"

Teenagers mostly don't think beyond the moment. Didn't stop. Didn't consider. Jake wished the hell they did, but they didn't. He reached for his cell and checked his messages. None from Georgia, but that wasn't a surprise. "You didn't do anything stupid when you were that age?"

"Yeah. I did plenty. So did Deke and Alex. Hell, Alex almost got himself killed falling off Miller Falls. But luck was with us."

"What was Georgia like as a teenager?"

"Much like she is now. Demanding. Hardworking. She loved Mom and was closest to her of all us kids. She also took it the hardest when Mom died."

He'd heard once from Buddy about how Georgia had suffered when her mother died after a long battle with cancer. The old man, who'd been a rock for so many years, also looked broken and lost when he spoke about his late wife. "You Morgans are one hell of a tight-knit group."

Rick cocked his head as he slid the phone back into his pocket. "Buddy and Mom made sure of that."

Jake shoved his hand in his pocket, his fingers absently turning the pocketknife over and over. "I want to put out a BOLO on the guy who met Elisa in the coffee shop. We'll use Jenna's drawing."

"Good."

"Scruffy guy with a beard and jeans in Nashville. Hell, you can't swing a dead cat without hitting a guy like that in this town."

Rick arched a brow, a smile teasing the edges of his lips. "Said by the guy with the beard."

He rubbed the neat whiskers on his chin. "My beard

is always neatly trimmed and never a bird's nest like this character's."

"How long have you had that damn thing?"

"Twelve years."

"Why grow it?"

Jake had grown the beard long ago for a woman who liked them. She was thrilled when he told her it was just for her. And later, after she was gone, well, he couldn't bring himself to shave it off. He scratched his chin, never stopping to wonder what Georgia thought of it. "Fashion statement."

The detectives moved toward the car. Jake slid behind the wheel while Rick rode shotgun. He fired up the engine, glanced in the rearview mirror, and backed up. "I've read up on Mike Marlowe in a few of the old files, but I want to track down some of the people who knew him. The kid had a hot temper and was considered a bully by many."

"Best place to start is with his old man, Dalton Marlowe. He's champing at the bit for a visit."

# CHAPTER EIGHT

*Wednesday, October 4, 5:00 P.M.*

Jake and Rick pulled into the exclusive gated community located ten miles north of Nashville. They drove down the freshly paved road peppered with manicured flowerbeds and well pruned trees towering over them.

"So how did Marlowe make his money?" Jake asked, as he drove down a long private drive.

"Started off in law, then real estate and from there bought up distressed homes, then flipped them. The guy did fairly well. Didn't set the world on fire, but had the great fortune to marry a rich woman."

Jake pulled into a circular drive and parked in front of a brick home that had to be ten thousand square feet. They stepped out, pausing to take in the long staircase that led to massive dark oak front doors.

"He also has a penthouse in the city center," Rick said.

"The wife was loaded?" Jake said.

"Yeah. He couldn't have touched this kind of community on his own."

"Mike Marlowe, kid with the silver spoon," Jake said. "Think he could be alive and also our killer?" He thought about the hours of interviews Amber gave to the cops. "Amber always defended him in her interviews. Were they sleeping together?"

"Several cops asked her the same questions multiple times," Rick said. "She said no."

"And you believe that?" Jake asked.

"I've no idea. I've not spent enough time to get a read on her. She sure as hell looks like she couldn't hurt a fly, but that's not what makes her dangerous."

"If Mike Marlowe killed Bethany and Amber saw it, she might have become hysterical and run. She doesn't look where she's going and falls. He thinks she's dead and his life would be spent in a cage, so he returns to the cave, walls it up, and shoots himself."

"Maybe," Rick said.

"Dalton won't be ready to hear that his kid was a killer," Jake said.

"I only report the facts." Rick shifted his hand, nudging the handle of his gun as he stared up the staircase.

"Let's see what Daddy has to say," Jake said.

Rick followed Jake up the stairs and resisted the urge to button his jacket as the doorbell echoed inside the house. Marlowe had met with Deke, but this would be their first meeting. Jake pulled his badge from his breast pocket, as steady footsteps clicked in the hallway and the door opened to a short round woman dressed in a black dress and white apron. She wore her gray hair back in a tight ponytail.

"I'm Detective Jake Bishop and this is my partner, Rick Morgan. We're here to see Mr. Dalton Marlowe."

A frown deepened the lines at the corners of her dark eyes. "Come in. I'll let him know you're here."

They waited in the marble tiled foyer surrounded by modern paintings featuring bold, striking colors. A curved staircase hugged the wall and led up to a landing that wound along a hallway of closed doors. From the ceiling, a large chandelier made of dozens of crystal teardrops hovered above them. Not one stick of furniture cost less than his annual salary.

Before either detective could comment, hard determined steps marched toward them from deep within the house. The door to the parlor on their right swung open.

Dalton Marlowe was tall and slim with a fit build. He wore black dress pants, a white shirt opened at the collar with sleeves rolled up his forearms, and polished loafers. Short gray hair, brushed back, accentuated a face with chiseled angles and lines etched deeply around the mouth and across the forehead.

"It's about time I got an update. I've called the station a dozen times since the news started reporting this morning. How the hell did they get the scoop before me?"

Jake bristled a fraction, reminding himself to smile. Always smart to play nice with the big boys with political juice until the gloves had to come off. "I'm Detective Bishop and this is my partner, Detective Morgan. We'd like to talk to you about Mike."

Frown lines deepened. "What about Mike?"

"Bones were found in a cave today at Percy Warner Park."

"I heard the reports. I don't care about an unnamed girl. I care about my son."

"Is there somewhere we can sit and talk?" Jake did not want to have this conversation in the hallway.

A shadow passed over Dalton's eyes as if he braced for their conversation. He nodded toward the side door and headed toward it without extending an invitation to follow. Jake, never one to be easily put off, followed, figuring if the old man had an issue, he could say so. Rick followed in step.

They moved down a long hallway painted a creamy white and carpeted with a rich, plush light tan rug. Hanging from the walls were a collection of black-and-white photos. One quick glance told Jake they featured Mike. As a small boy at Halloween. As a young football player. With his father on a tropical beach. In Paris. All images of Mike and his father. No pictures of any woman who looked as if she could be his mother.

Marlowe pushed open pocket doors and moved into a large library. The centerpiece of the room was a tall stone fireplace surrounded by bookshelves filled with leather-bound books, various trophies, and more pictures of Mike and his father.

Marlowe moved to a side bar displaying crystal decanters filled with a host of liquors. He removed the top on one and poured the nutty brown liquid into a tumbler. He drained it in one swallow.

Jake removed his notebook from his breast pocket. "We discovered the remains of two females and one male in Percy Warner Park. One female died a couple of days ago, but the second female and the male were found in a back chamber of the cave. They've been dead at least five years."

The man's sallow face paled. "Is it Mike?"

"We haven't identified the bones of either victim yet, but expect to within the next twenty-four hours. We have your son's dental records on file for comparison."

"Jesus H. Christ." Marlowe refilled his glass and tossed the soothing liquid down in one shot.

"Can you tell us about your son?" Jake asked, as he reached in his breast pocket for a pen. "Was there any hint of trouble before he vanished five years ago?"

"I told all this to the police countless times five years ago. Can't you read a fucking file?"

Jake clicked the pen a couple of times. "Doesn't hurt to go over it one more time with your help."

Marlowe raised his glass, his index finger pointing at Jake. "You're not even sure the body is Mike's. This could be a mistake."

"Possibly, but not likely. The skeletal remains suggest a male in his late teens who stood about six feet. That fits Mike's description."

Marlowe's jaw clenched. "Mike was a popular kid. Not the smartest, but one hell of a football player."

"No one made any threats against him?"

"No, none that I'm aware of. He was an eighteen-year-old boy. He wasn't under my thumb all the time and boys will be boys. If Mike really fucked up, I heard about it and could clean it up."

"Was he friends with Bethany Reed?"

"No. She was a mousy kid like her mother. Smart. Useful when he needed tutoring, but overall, forgettable."

Jake watched Marlowe closely. "What about Amber Ryder?"

The man's face thinned into a contemptuous frown as if he tasted something foul. "She was trouble. If there's anyone that you should be chasing, it's her. That bitch remembered what happened in the woods."

"The doctors corroborate her claim of amnesia as possible given her head injury," Jake said.

"She's smart, conniving, and trouble. Don't believe her." He refilled his glass, but this time took only a small sip. "She's in Dallas. I can give you her address if you need it."

"You know where she is?" Jake asked.

"I've kept tabs on her for five years, waiting for her to make a mistake."

"So you didn't know she was back in Nashville?" Rick asked.

Dalton's faced hardened with hatred. "I did not. How long?"

"Arrived on Monday."

Dalton moved to a large picture window and stared out over the green landscape. His body stilled as if the weight of the news settled on his shoulders.

"Was Mike ever depressed?" Jake asked.

Marlowe didn't face him for a long moment before he turned. "Is this some kind of fishing expedition? Why would you come into my home and ask me about my son's mental health when you know Amber Ryder

is here? Anybody ask her why she returned to Nashville?"

"One of the folks on our team called her. She was a
prime witness in the case five years ago and it made
sense to re-interview her. She states she is here to help."

Dalton laughed, but the sound held no hint of humor.
"Right. Amber is here to help. Did she tell you her
memory has miraculously returned?"

"She still has no memories of those days," Jake
said.

"Where is she? I want to see her."

"Not now."

"You're not going to tell me what to do."

Like hell. The old man might have opened the case,
but now that it was wide open it belonged to Jake. He
might have his own doubts about Amber, but until he
had solid proof, they stayed within his team. "We wanted
your take on Mike."

"Why?"

Tension snaked up Jake's spine as he stared at the
older man. Whatever slack he wanted to cut this guy
had thinned rapidly. "Sir? About Mike?"

Dalton shook his head and then downed the remains
of what was in his glass. "Christ, the cops were all over
that park five years ago. I can't tell you how many times
I've driven through since then myself. Hell, I even
hired people to comb those woods."

"This is a small cave with two chambers. It could
have been easily missed. And the older bodies were
in the back chamber."

"Shit."

"What can you tell us about Mike?"

The old man's eyes sharpened as he set down his glass. "He was a great kid. The best a father could ever ask for."

"Mike got into some trouble when he was fifteen. He vandalized several cars in the school parking lot," Jake said.

Marlowe frowned. "He was a good kid. But even good kids sometimes do stupid things. I paid for all the damage."

"Your son wasn't depressed?"

"Hell no, he was not depressed. I resent you asking the question."

He ignored the man's bluster. "I also read an interview of a teacher who said Mike could be disruptive."

"He was a boy. A high-energy, athletic boy who did dumb things. I never denied that. But he was a good kid until Amber got under his skin."

"They were dating?"

Marlowe shook his head. "Fucking would be a better description."

Jake studied the hard lines of Marlowe's face. "Someone is sending her threatening texts."

He looked amused. "Threatening texts?"

"That's right," Rick said. "She received several while in Dallas."

A mirthless laugh rumbled in his chest. "And you think I might have been the one to do that?"

The man's disdain for Amber was clear. "Why don't you like her?" Jake asked.

He rested his hands around the empty glass. "She's a liar and a manipulator. Other than that, I have no opinion of her one way or the other."

Jake shifted tactics. "Your wife passed away when Mike was a freshman in high school."

"You seem to know so much about my family. Why don't you tell me?"

Tension thumped the back of Jake's skull like an annoying flick of a finger. "I'm asking you, sir."

Lips flattened into a rigid line. "Susan was never a strong woman and she struggled for most of our marriage with many illnesses. However, she did love Mike. He was her whole life. About three years before he vanished she was diagnosed with cancer. It killed her."

"She came from a wealthy family?"

"She did." He shook his head. "And just in case you're wondering, when she passed, her family money went into a trust for Mike. He was slated to inherit next week as a matter of fact. He would have been twenty-three in just a few days."

"How much money was in the trust?"

"Millions."

"And if Mike were dead?"

Frown lines deepened. "I pray every day he's not."

"But if he were dead or declared dead, what would happen to the money?"

A muscle tensed and released in his jaw. "Then the money would go to me. Mike has no other living relatives."

"Make you a really rich man," Rick said.

"I don't like what you're insinuating," Marlowe growled.

Jake's phone buzzed on his hip and he glanced at the number. Dr. Heller. "I need to take this."

Marlowe's jaw tightened and released. "Sure. Why not? Take as long as you want."

Jake moved into the hallway and dialed back the doctor's number. It rang twice before she picked up.

"Detective," Dr. Heller said. "I have dental X-rays on my desk."

"And?"

"And, I can say for certain that the female is Bethany Reed and the male is Mike Marlowe."

A ray of light streaming through a skylight cut across the foyer's tiled floor. "You're sure?"

"Bethany had two front teeth replaced when she was twelve. She wrecked her bike and flew over the handlebars. She went headfirst and struck the curb with the side of her face. Broke two teeth and ended up with a bridge. That is an identical match to the skull. Mike had a distinct pattern of fillings in his mouth and had a right molar pulled after it was fractured during a hard tackle."

Jake dropped his voice a notch as tension climbed up his back and clamped around the back of his head. "Okay, doc. When you have more information, please feed it to me."

"I have preliminary information that I want to confirm before I share. I should have more to tell you tomorrow."

"Understood." Jake pocketed the phone and returned to the room where Rick was talking to Mr. Marlowe. "That was the medical examiner's office."

Marlowe's bravado wavered and he appeared to age two decades in two seconds. "And?"

"We found the body of your son, Mike."

\*   \*   \*

As Jake and Rick sat in the living room of Bethany Reed's mother, Jake put aside his distaste for Dalton Marlowe, reminding himself that grief dragged out the worst of emotions. He understood firsthand that it could drive anyone to do just about anything.

Now, he focused on the grieving eyes of the woman before him. There were many parts of the job that were not easy but this was the worst.

Mrs. Reed was a short and plump woman and, though age had pulled the edges of her eyes down, her hair remained an unnatural shade of dark brown. She sat on the green silk couch of a living room decorated in Colonial style next to a portrait of her husband and wept. Her thin shoulders looked fragile and broken as she leaned forward, a tissue clutched in her hands.

"And you're certain it's Bethany?" Mrs. Reed asked.

"Yes, ma'am. Her dental records are an exact match." Jake avoided as many details of the crime scene as he could manage.

"I'm glad my husband has passed now. I miss him, but I know now he's with our Bethany. They have each other."

"Yes, ma'am."

"How did you find her?"

"Another body was found in the park."

"I heard about that on the news today."

He shifted, and tugged his jacket forward. "Bethany was found close by in a back chamber of the cave." He reached for his cell and pulled up the picture of the pendant. "We found this near her."

With trembling hands, she took the phone and studied the picture. Tears welled in her eyes. "I gave this to her when she turned sixteen. She wore it all the time."

"We also found a body next to Bethany's. It's Mike."

Tears spilled down her face. "Ah, no. Poor Dalton. He must be absolutely devastated. He hung the moon on that boy."

"Yes, ma'am."

She balled her hands into tiny fists. "How did she die?"

He wanted to keep several details of the case quiet until he had a little more time. As much as he wanted to tell Mrs. Reed, he said only, "We're still running tests. But as soon as I know, I'll tell you."

She raised a trembling chin. "Thank you."

"I'm not sure if you're aware, but Amber Ryder is back in Nashville."

The older woman's eyes brightened with an odd happiness he did not expect. "How's Amber doing? Last time, the police had just about everyone in this town put that poor girl through the wringer."

"She's doing fine. What do you know about Amber?" Jake asked.

She knitted long, pale fingers together and settled them in her lap. "She was smart as a whip. Not as smart as Bethany, but smart. She helped Bethany from time to time with the kids at school. Bethany was smart in so many ways, but her social skills were lacking." She glanced down at her hands. Carefully, she unfurled her fingers and stretched them out. Pink manicured nails glistened in the soft light. "Amber was such a great kid. My Bethany was a great kid."

"Amber was hoping to get scholarship money to attend college."

"She had applied to several Texas schools and the

counselor said she had a very good chance. She was very excited."

"It sounds like you knew her well."

"She was in my house all the time. She was my Bethany's friend and needed an adult female to nurture her. I know her mother loved her. But she had her own issues, so I was happy to look after her."

"How did she and Amber become friends? From what you said, they don't strike me as a likely pair."

"Bethany needed someone to show her how to be a teenager. How to fit into a school like St. Vincent. It's one thing to be given money to attend, another to navigate the waters. Amber needed a family to look out for her. It was natural for me to fold her into our family." A ragged breath caught in her throat. "Amber was always so polite and nice when she was here. I used to joke that she was too skinny. And I was always feeding her. Every time she was here she said thank you. Not all kids are that polite, but she was." Dark eyes filled with fresh tears. "After all this time, it's still Amber looking out for Bethany."

"Yes, ma'am."

Mrs. Reed shook her head. "I know she wasn't popular after what happened in the woods, but my husband and I never lost sight of the fact that she was just a child herself. We both think if she came from a different side of town, she'd have been treated better."

"Yes, ma'am."

"You said she's in town. Where is she now?" Mrs. Reed asked. "She's not staying with her mother?"

"Why would her mother be a problem?" Jake asked.

"Tracy's not a bad woman, but as I suggested, she

found motherhood constrictive. If she were more attuned to Amber, that girl could have had such a different life. Amber Ryder was smart enough to do anything she wanted, but Tracy didn't care much."

"Was there anyone that could have wanted to hurt the girls or Mike?"

"I've had five years to think about that, and I have the same answer I did then." She raised her watery gaze to Jake. "I don't know of anyone who would hurt her."

# CHAPTER NINE

*Wednesday, October 4, 11:15 P.M.*

When Jake parked in front of the small bar in the west end of Nashville, his third coffee consumed, his second wind kicked into play and chased away the fatigue that burrowed into his skull. Juiced like this, he could keep going most of the night.

The bar where Tracy Ryder worked was housed in what had been a one-story home with a large front porch, tin roof, and floor-to-ceiling windows. Small round tables with their patrons crowded the porch and main room inside.

He got out of his car, jangling his keys in his hand as he followed the small slate path to the front steps. Guitar music blended with a rusty male voice and the hum of a dozen conversations. He shrugged his shoulders, easing his right elbow back until it butted against his gun.

A few patrons on the front porch stopped in mid conversation to glance his way as if they understood this call was business and not pleasure.

His dark hair, slicked back, accentuated his square

face and the beard covered his strong chin. Cowboy boots didn't quite offset the crisp white shirt, the dark tie, or the swagger practiced by every boy on the streets of South Boston. Most didn't know which side of the law he preferred until he showed his badge.

Let 'em wonder.

Boots thudding hard on the pocked pine floor, he pushed through the front-screened door. In the corner to his right sat a guitar player, his gaze focused on his callused fingers plucking out-of-tune guitar strings. The guy, a younger version of Willie Nelson, tied back his long hair with a piece of rawhide and wore his beard thick and scraggly. Though his jeans looked tattered, Jake would bet there was a fancy designer label on the waistband.

Jake paused, as the singer crooned and found himself listening for sharp notes or dropped keys. He never paid close attention to the honky-tonk musicians until he first heard Georgia sing. Onstage, her guard relaxed and she leaned into the mic greedily, even desperately, smiling as if she knew a very important secret. She poured heart and soul into the melody and when she reached for the high notes, everyone in the room noticed.

A short blond gal with cutoff jeans, a peasant top barely covering full breasts, pink hoop earrings, and red cowboy boots stopped as he scanned the room. She balanced a tray holding four beers, grinning as her pale blue eyes studied him. "Can I help you, doll? You're looking a little lost to me."

"I'm looking for Tracy Ryder."

The waitress shook her head slowly. "She's not your type."

He grinned. "And how would you know what my type is?"

She winked. "I can read people, sugar. I can spot couples who are made for each other in a heartbeat. I can also call it when a couple isn't meant to be."

"And Tracy and I don't have the magic?"

"No, sugar." She moistened her glossy lips. "But I think you and I might be able to make some real special magic."

He leaned toward her a fraction with a slight smile. "That so?"

"Yeah." Her eyes narrowed as she caught her bottom lip in her teeth. "Where are you from, baby? Got to be up north. New York?"

"Close, but not quite. Boston. I'm a Southie."

Her gaze cataloged him. "Yeah, you're not a Southern boy."

"That's a bad thing?" Even seven years in Nashville had not upgraded his outlier status.

"Not at all. We welcome all kinds in Nashville, especially your type."

"Good to know." He liked this woman. A year ago he'd have taken her to his bed. Now, he found himself comparing her to a particular redhead and found her lacking. "And Tracy is where?"

She moistened her lips as she pulled a pen from her pocket and scrawled her number with a heart on a napkin, which she handed to him. "Out back. Having a smoke."

Grinning, he carefully folded the napkin. "Thanks, doll."

"You gonna call me?"

One or two words would seal the deal. Still, he shook his head. "Not tonight, doll."

"Doesn't have to be tonight, sugar."

He made a show of tucking the napkin in his pocket. "Maybe some other time."

He wove through the crowded room and pushed through the swinging doors leading to a kitchen filled with the scents of fried chicken, hush puppies, and sweet potato pie. Out the screened back door, he surveyed a parking lot filled with cars. He spotted a woman standing over by a tall oak tree, leaning and drawing heavily on a cigarette. Reed thin and short, her bejeweled jeans hugged her narrow hips. Blond shoulder-length hair was fashioned into a shag and heavy dark blue eye makeup accentuated crow's feet. She looked like an older, harder version of Amber.

He moved slowly and easily, wanting this to be a nice friendly conversation. He did not want to stir the pot . . . yet.

"Ms. Ryder?"

Whereas Amber had the healthful glow of youth, too many cigarettes and too much booze had leached away Tracy's vitality, leaving her looking brittle.

She raised the cigarette to her lips and puffed. "That's right. What do you want?"

He held up his badge. "Detective Jake Bishop. I'm with the Nashville Police Department."

She stared at the large full moon in the sky and then took another pull on her cigarette. Slowly, she let out the smoke, allowing it to curl around her. "This about Amber?"

"Yes, ma'am."

"I heard you found a body at the park. You coming to blame that one on my girl, too?"

"No, ma'am. But I am looking into the disappearance of Bethany Reed and Mike Marlowe."

Tracy studied the tip of her cigarette. "Amber was dead on her feet when she arrived at my house this morning. She's been staying in a motel and ran low on money so she came back here to her mama."

"I didn't realize she left the motel."

"She was gonna tell that lady cop, but she drifted off and slept most of the day away. I'm glad she came home to me. I've missed her." She took another drag and released more smoke. "She in some kind of trouble or are you just poking around an old case?"

"It's a little bit more than poking around old files. We found two other bodies at the park. Looks like one is Bethany Reed and the other is Mike Marlowe. That discovery puts Amber right back in the middle of it all."

She flicked her cigarette, watching the ash fall to the pavement. "Shit, so this is gonna be a replay of the last time. At least those kids have been found. At least those parents will have some kind of closure."

He studied her face, which was highlighted by the overhead parking lot floodlight. "What can you tell me about that time? What were Bethany and Mike like?"

"Bethany, I only met once. She was a nice enough girl. Mousy. Not much personality, if you ask me, God rest her soul. Amber liked spending time at her house. Hard to believe those two clicked. I always thought Amber hung out at the Reeds' house because that Reed woman doted on her. Mrs. Reed liked the way Amber paid attention to Bethany. I don't think Bethany had many friends."

"Why do you think Bethany and Amber got on so well?"

"Hard to say why they clicked." She ran her tongue over her teeth, picking at a piece of tobacco left from her cigarette.

"And Mike?"

A frown deepened the lines around her mouth. "I only met him a couple of times. Amber didn't talk much about him." She dropped her cigarette and crushed it into the ground with the tip of her black cowboy boot. "I didn't like Mike."

"Why not?"

"Self-centered. Privileged prick who thought because of his mama's money he could do whatever he wanted. His daddy was the same way. Acted like money made him better than everyone."

"Mike spend a lot of time with Amber?"

"No. I mean they knew each other but they didn't hang out a lot, well, at least around me. Teenage girls don't like to stick around the house much, and she was always on the go."

"How did those three hook up for that last hike into the woods?"

"It was Bethany's idea." Her gaze softened as if she were drifting to the past. "She was the organizer. The rah-rah kind of gal who wanted to organize the best science project ever. She asked Amber because she liked her. Knowing Mike, he finagled his way onto their team because his grades were so weak. His daddy fixed as much as he could, but you couldn't help noticing that that boy had a chip missing."

"A chip missing."

"He was smart enough, but he never really had a set of balls."

"Did Amber ever talk to you about what happened in the woods?"

She shook her head. "She didn't remember a thing. In the months she was with me after her return, she never gave me a whiff that she remembered anything. And there were times I tried to trick her to see if she were lying. She never gave me any reason to doubt. Not once."

"A lot of people didn't believe her."

"Oh, I know it. A fair share of folks thought she was a liar. She tried to go back to school and finish out her senior year, but those kids at that school made life hell for her. Finally, she gave up and finished her schooling up at home. Taught herself those last couple of months."

"And then she took off for college."

She fingered a tassel on her silver belt. "I never blamed her. She needed a fresh start. She needed to get away from all this. Hell, I'm almost glad she never did remember. Terrible things must have happened that day in the woods."

"Why didn't you leave Nashville?"

A sad smile lifted one corner of her mouth. "Where would I go? I'm not smart like Amber. Or young. And my last husband's illness ate up all the money. You can't teach an old dog new tricks."

"Has she spoken to you about the past since her return?"

"We haven't talked about it. Frankly, my head is still spinning with the idea of her returning and those kids being found."

"Anybody threaten you after those kids went missing?"

She latched on to anger as if it had been a lifeline. "Sure, we had trouble. Someone threw a brick through our front window, and I found a dead cat on the front lawn. That was a real treat. And there were notes."

"What kind of notes?"

"They mostly called Amber a liar and a murderer. There were some that thought she killed those two kids." She shook her head. "Can you imagine that? She's five feet five inches tall and a hundred and twenty pounds soaking wet and they figure her for a killer. Maybe she could have taken Bethany if she got in a lucky shot, but Mike outweighed her by a hundred pounds."

Dr. Heller theorized Bethany might have been stabbed based on slash marks on the bones. Bethany had stood five inches taller than Amber, so if Bethany were standing when she'd been stabbed, Amber couldn't have done it, given the angle of the cut in the bone. That also left Mike, a large beefy football player who couldn't have been taken by Amber unless she had help or was armed.

Forensic evidence aside, he understood a motivated killer could do things that defied the interpretations of the evidence. "Have you had much contact with her in the last five years?"

"Some. I went to see her at school once. She looked happy. Had a boyfriend. And we exchanged a few phone calls. I sent her money when I could."

"And since she took her job?"

"She's a grown woman. She's got her life." She reached in her pocket for her pack of cigarettes. A flick of the lighter and she lit another. She inhaled deeply, allowing the smoke to trickle out of her nose. "I worry more about me paying my bills. Now that she's back, this crap from the past is gonna stir trouble and cost me my job."

He rested his hand on his belt. "Is Amber worried?"

"I don't know. She never was the kind to show it. Always kept her emotions locked up tight."

"Did she spend any time with her father?"

Tracy laughed. "He was never in the picture. It was always just me and Amber." A very faint smile teased the edges of her thin lips. "We were the Dynamic Duo."

"How'd she get into a school like St. Vincent?"

"She's smart. She set her sights on the school. I told her not to dream so big, but she did. Somehow she found a way to do the impossible."

"I understand she received a scholarship."

"I didn't ask where the money was coming from. As long as it wasn't costing me, I didn't care."

"How did it go for her at St. Vincent?"

"How do you think? She was the outsider. Kids can be cruel. But she was smart and tough, so she stuck it out. Rich folks can smell poor a mile away."

"It had to have been tough."

"I know it was. Like I said, Amber doesn't say much when she's upset. But she got that glint in her eye and I knew she'd be okay."

"What glint?"

"The one that said she'd get her way, no matter what, in the end."

The light table in the forensic lab glowed as Georgia draped Elisa Spence's skirt over it. She had processed the shirt, shoe, and undergarments but still needed to examine the skirt. Moving slowly and carefully, she spread the material wide and adjusted the hem until it was straight. Touching the items of the dead, especially one so young, always took more effort and concentration. Sometimes it was as if the dead reached out from the grave and begged her to find their killer. *Help me. Help me.* The words whispered close, brushing her ear as she studied the simple skirt.

Less than a week ago, Elisa had awoken and slipped on this skirt. Had she been distracted, worried, excited as she fastened each button? Had her thoughts been to the future? Georgia lifted the hem with a gloved hand and closed her eyes. She took deep, even breaths.

*Elisa had been excited. The day held secrets. Unspoken thrills.*

When Georgia opened her eyes, she pulled down the magnifying glass suspended from above, and with tweezers in hand, began to study the fabric with precise detail. Centimeter by centimeter she combed, searching for hairs or fibers that had clung to the fabric. No one entered a room or left without leaving some trace evidence. No one.

She was midway up the front of the skirt when she spotted several dark hairs. They could be Elisa's. A roommate. A friend. A killer.

Carefully, she bagged the hair fiber and continued her search. By the time she finished examining the material, seven hair fibers were bagged for testing. All black, coarse, and long.

"So who were you excited about seeing?" she whispered as she rose from the stool and stretched out her back.

She reached for a blue light and held it over the fabric, searching for stains. On the bottom edge of the skirt's front, she spotted a small stain. She photographed it and then took scrapings, which she placed on a slide. She packaged the item up for the state lab where the DNA testing would be conducted.

By the time Georgia processed the skirt, it was around midnight. Her back ached and, though she had had a solid eight hours of sleep last night, she was exhausted. Time to leave. She shrugged on her jacket and reached for her purse. Quickly she dug out her cell and checked the display. Two missed calls. From Jake.

Georgia squeezed the bridge of her nose. She did not need to deal with Jake now. She did not need to maintain her guard or remain sharp. "Leave me alone."

The sound of determined footsteps had her looking up as she stretched the strained muscles of her neck.

Jake Bishop entered the lab.

Just great.

From that first night he had stood front and center while she sang, she noticed him more than she should. The cut of his beard on his square jaw. The slight tilt of his head and the swagger that mirrored an all-star athlete ready to play the game of his life. She noticed.

She stood up straighter, pushing a stray curl from her eyes. "So what brings you to the dungeon?"

He moved into the room, vibrant, hurricane force energy swirling. "Came to see how the forensic testing is going on the Spence case."

"Micromanaging, detective?"

A slight, pirate's smile. "Always. You getting ready to leave?"

No matter how hard or cutting, she never told a white

lie to soften the truth. "I just finished processing Elisa's clothes."

"Find anything?"

Soft scents of a spicy cologne swirled. "More hair strands. It's dark and could be hers. DNA testing will tell me if any of it matters."

"That's gonna be a few weeks if we're lucky. More likely, months."

"Yeah." She did her best not to stare into eyes that noticed and cataloged every detail. "I hear you made a couple of death notices today."

"Doesn't matter if it's five years or one week. Never gets easier."

The light table glowed, deepening the lines around his mouth. "Any idea who texted Amber?"

His jaw tensed. "I had the number traced. It was a burner. Untraceable."

Jake slid his hand into his pocket, rattling his keys. "You look rough."

She glanced toward a stainless-steel refrigerator and caught a glimpse of a pale face spotted with freckles and haloed in wisps of red curls. She wondered if she should laugh or cry at her reflection. "It's my natural state. Fatigue and I are good friends."

"I'm getting a burger. Come with me."

No hint of a request at the end of each sentence. Just an order. A little less tired and she'd have called him on it. He wasn't the boss of her. But right now she liked not having a choice. Leave. Go. Eat. Simple. "Sure. Why not? Let me just close up the lab."

He straightened his shoulders a fraction as if her answer surprised him.

She grinned. "You were expecting an argument?"

A smile quirked the edge of his lips. "I had a list of comebacks for your no."

"That would be a long list. I say no a lot."

"Why is that?" he asked with genuine interest.

"I've always been a tough case. Just ask any of my brothers."

"That I know. Why?" He opened the door as she moved through it.

"I've always felt a little out of control so I compensate by trying to control the world around me."

"That your therapist talking?"

She stiffened a fraction. "You know about that?"

"Heard Rick talking to you once on the phone. No one else knows."

"Good, because I've been paying out of pocket in cash. I hate the idea of going, let alone anyone knowing."

"Secret's safe." He punched the elevator button.

She couldn't quite meet his gaze, knowing he was absorbing every little detail. "Thanks."

The doors opened and they stepped into the empty cab. When the doors closed, he stood silently for a moment.

"Georgia, why are you not sleeping lately?"

Deep concern vibrated in the shadows of his voice and for the first time in a couple of years, she said, "It's the way I'm wired. When I have a case on my desk that's complicated, I don't sleep so well until it's untangled."

"Ever thought about quitting the job?"

"Hell, no. I'm not finished catching bad guys."

"You're not gonna catch many more bad guys if

you drop from exhaustion. At the rate you're going, I see you gray haired and meaner than ever."

"Thanks."

"Calling it like it is."

"I'm not dropping. And I'm not ready for the trash heap just yet."

He punched the lobby button hard, as if he were trying to drive it into the wall. "No, not yet."

The door opened to the bustle of people. No matter the time of day, this place never really was quiet. Their conversation tabled for now, they crossed the lobby and walked through the front door. Down Third Street they both gravitated to an all-night diner that catered to cops and their around-the-clock schedules. Soon, the two were seated at a booth in the back of the dining room. Jake took the seat facing the door and Georgia slid in across from him.

A waitress came up to their table with menus and a couple cups of coffee. She served enough cops to know coffee was a mainstay and when both declined menus and placed their order without looking, she didn't bat an eye. Like many cops, they'd been here enough to know the offerings backward and forward. Late nights like this, Georgia always went for pancakes. Jake ordered the burger and fries.

"They do coffee well. I can forgive a lot but not bad coffee."

She smiled as she mixed two sugars and cream into hers. "Amen."

"So why pancakes this late at night?"

"I love breakfast, and I never have time for a good breakfast until late at night. And last I checked, there's no hard and fast rules about when it can be eaten."

He raised the cup to his lips. "I make killer pan-cakes."

She let the subtle invitation pass. "I didn't realize you cooked."

"I'm very good at it."

She traced the rim of her stoneware cup with her finger. "My cooking sends my brothers into a panic. They pretend it's good, but I know they hate it."

"I've heard."

She glanced up, half smiling, half frowning. "Hey now!"

"I've tasted some of your cooking, Georgia. Your brothers are saints."

She laughed, not sure why his cutting honesty amused her. Aware that others in the diner had noticed them, and that cops gossiped, she leaned forward. "It's edible."

"No, it sucks."

Truth was she didn't like to cook. "I only started after my mother died because Mom's cooking was a unifying force in our family. Dinnertime was always special in the Morgan house. I guess I want to hang on to that."

"The Morgans are a really tight clan. I don't think you have to worry about holding them together."

"I suppose." She circled the rim of her cup with her finger. "You and Rick seem to be getting along better," she said.

Rick never complained when Jake first joined homicide, but she saw the tension between the two. Jake had made no secret that he believed Rick's pro-motion to detective was directly linked to his relation-ship to Deke. Morgans might look out for Morgans, but Rick proved to all he was a hell of a detective.

He offered only a hint of surprise. "He's my partner. Why wouldn't we?"

"It doesn't take a genius to see you two didn't click right away."

"Call it a rough start. Like I said, you Morgans are tight. And not the easiest people to get to know."

She shrugged. "I'm tough, but my brothers are okay."

"Don't kid yourself. You four run like a pack."

She smiled, liking the idea of being a part of the pack. "So Rick has finally proven himself?"

Jake laughed, but it was a hard-edged sound. "You don't mince words, do you?"

She shrugged. "The pot calling the kettle black?"

He sipped his coffee. "Rick's one hell of a cop. Saved my life."

"Really?" She studied him, waiting for a punchline or quip. When none came, she said, "He never said anything to me."

He shrugged. "It was year before last. We were on a call. I'd have taken a bullet in the back if Tracker hadn't started barking and your brother reacted."

"He never mentioned it." The work Rick and Jake did was so dangerous. They all accepted the risks, but whenever she thought about losing one of her brothers, or even Jake for that matter, it was a punch in the gut.

"What, no dig or comment? Come on, Georgia, you're losing your touch."

"Am I that mean?"

"As a snake, baby. As a snake."

That startled another laugh. God bless Jake Bishop. He never coddled her or treated her like fragile china as her brothers had since she was a baby. "I never pretend to be something that I'm not."

He paused, his cup inches from his lips. "You're correct."

She sat back in the booth, laying both palms on the table. "Let's talk about something fun. Who're you dating these days?"

He set his cup down with a deliberate slowness. "Who says I am?"

"You're always dating someone, Jake Bishop. Always." The guy's reputation was legendary.

"I've been on a dating diet lately," he said as he raised his cup back up to his lips. "I'll get back in the saddle soon."

"Last I heard, you were dating a woman named Christy, or was it Susie in administration? Tall, buxom, and blond from what I remember."

"Yes, to Christy last year. And Susie and I are friends."

"What about Sharon in personnel?"

He tugged on his cuff. "She's old news."

"Did your lover boy reputation go south?" Her tone teased, but she didn't exactly like the idea of his dating around.

"I closed the little black book a while ago. I'm telling you, I'm a reformed man."

She laughed. "So you headed to the priesthood?"

"No. Definitely not."

She cleared her throat, doing a one-eighty in another direction. "So what's the story of you moving to Nashville? You showed up here seven years ago and it was clear you didn't like the place or wanted to be here."

"That obvious?"

"Very."

"Let's say I outgrew Boston. Time for a change."

"Translation: a chick broke your heart?"

He studied her for a long beat. "Something like that."

"Why pick Nashville?"

"Laid out a map of the United States, closed my eyes and pointed my finger. It landed on Nashville."

"Really?"

"As good a place as any."

The waitress showed up with a large plate of pancakes and another platter with a burger and a massive pile of fries. Georgia was grateful for the food and something to do with her mouth other than talk. God, she needed to stop talking.

"I'm starving," she said reaching for her fork and knife wrapped in a paper napkin.

"You don't eat enough."

"I had a cheese stick on the way into work."

Jake reached for the mustard on the table and dolloped a big blob beside the fries. He dunked a fry into the mustard and ate it in one bite.

"Mustard on fries," she said. "A dead giveaway you're not from the South."

"And here I thought it was my accent and the way I dressed."

She laughed. "There is that." She poured a liberal amount of syrup over her pancakes and cut out a large wedge. She held it up, savoring the scent before she ate it. For several moments, neither talked.

Eating settled her nerves a fraction and by the time she'd had her second cup of coffee, she felt a little more like herself. She thought that if she had to define what she was these days, she couldn't exactly put her finger on it.

"So what did you find out about Elisa Spence?" She turned the conversation to the homicide, sensing it was the safest territory for them.

Nodding, he wiped his mouth with his napkin and then balled it up and tossed it on his plate. "I'm still digging, but my gut tells me she was a good kid, straight arrow, but for some reason got a wild hair and decided to take a walk on the dark side."

"The dark side?"

"I think she met a man. From what I've heard, a good-looking guy. And he was a charmer. He talked her into something and then I think he killed her."

"You learned all that in so little time?"

He winked. "I move fast."

When the forensic data came back from the lab, she'd bet much of it would back up what he'd found out today. But the data took weeks and sometimes months to analyze, whereas a fast-moving detective worked his magic in hours, days at most. "I'll say."

"Her financials don't show any strange expenses except for some expensive lingerie she purchased about six days ago. Whoever killed her hasn't been using her credit card."

"The undergarments were sent over from the medical examiner's office. I'll admit they didn't jibe with her clothes."

"She wasn't expecting to see this guy last week, but hoping. That would fit with what the clerk at the coffee shop said."

"The cave at Percy Warner Park proves this guy is from Nashville and knows the city well."

"Agreed. He's a local."

"Any hits on the BOLO?"

"Not so far. But he's gonna be good at hiding. He's been doing it for five years."

"What's the allure of bookish, quiet girls?"

"Who knows? Guys like that have all kinds of dark quirks that drive them. The girls might have reminded him of a sister or cousin or a girl who was mean to him. Maybe she was smarter and made him feel stupid. We won't know until we find him."

He leaned back in his seat and shook his head. "We need to talk to Amber Ryder again. This guy must have known her and the others."

"In the case files, the cops made mention of Tim Taylor. He was Mike's best friend. Have you talked to him yet?"

"He's first on the list in the morning."

She tucked a curl behind her ear. "I want to be with you when you talk to Tim and Amber."

He shook his head. "I don't hover over your shoulder when you're collecting evidence, and you can't tag along with me."

"I want to."

He slowly shook his head. "Who said you're entitled to everything you want?"

"Not everything, just this."

"No."

Her frown deepening, she stared out the window onto the street. Outside a soft rain began to fall. "Very irritating, Bishop. You're disappointing me."

He smiled. "Why is this case so important to you? I know you aren't afraid of Dalton Marlowe."

"All my cases are important."

"But . . ."

For a moment she didn't speak as she considered a lie and then rejected it. "Three kids went into the woods. Lives were lost, families tortured. Someone can't just destroy lives and get away with it."

"All the more reason for you to stick to the science."

She leaned forward, her gaze sparking with challenge. "But you're biased against Amber. I see it."

He scratched the underside of his chin. "You think you know me that well?"

Challenge weaved around the words. "I know you well enough."

"No, baby, you haven't scratched the surface."

"That's hardly true."

A smile quirked the edges of his lips but he dropped his voice a notch. "You know me at work." He paused. "But you don't know me."

# CHAPTER TEN

*Thursday, October 5, 8:00 A.M.*

Jake pushed through the door to the science department at Vanderbilt, and with Elisa Spence's advisor's name in hand, headed to the second floor and found room 122. A knock on the door earned him a brusque "Enter."

He rolled his head from side to side, wondering if Georgia had slept as poorly as he had last night. She went home after they left the diner, but he returned to work to review surveillance tapes from several of the shops around Blue Note Java. So far, no sign of Elisa or her new guy.

Dinner last night was nice. First time they had shared anything real. Whether it would last or she'd retreat back into her shell was anybody's guess. What was it with his attraction to Georgia? He could have anyone he wanted and he wanted the one ready to bust his balls all the time.

Jake found a lean, gray-haired man leaning over a desk piled high with papers, books, and journals. Light sneaked around a tall window behind him, catching countless dust particles in dozens of thin beams. The walls were lined with bookshelves crammed as full as the desk in front of him. The room smelled of Ben Gay.

"Professor Robbins?"

The man nodded but didn't glance up as squinting eyes continued to stare at his research papers covered with cracker crumbs and coffee stains.

"I'm Detective Jake Bishop. I'm here to talk to you about Elisa Spence."

The downcast gray head shook. "I haven't seen Elisa in a few days. I can't help you."

News of her murder would have spread by now, if not from her roommate, then from the girl in the coffee shop. He waited until the professor looked up. "Did you know Elisa was dead?"

"What?" His head shook as he pulled off his glasses and pinched the bridge of his nose. "What do you mean, dead?!"

"Really? You haven't heard?"

He raised his head, returned to his nose the thick glasses that magnified dark eyes. "No, I haven't heard. I've been working."

"No one has called you?"

"I've been working from home for a few days. People call and text me all the time, but I rarely answer. I don't have time for calls." He laid a wrinkled, arthritic hand on the desk as he rose up on unsteady legs.

Rick noticed the cane to the man's right. "She was killed. We think over the weekend."

"My God." The words rushed out breathlessly. "How?"

Jake ignored the question. "When was the last time you saw her?"

"Last Thursday."

"Did you notice anything different about her?"

"She was distracted. She wasn't concentrating on her work. Are you sure you haven't made a mistake?"

"Very. Why was she distracted?"

"I can't say. But I can tell you she was acting like a silly girl. Very unlike her. She's very sensible. That's what I always appreciated about Elisa. She was no-nonsense. She did her work. And on Thursday in walked a flighty girl. I knew she had met a boy. It's always a boy."

"Did she say anything about this boy?"

"Not to me, but I heard her in the hallway talking to someone on her phone." He shook his head and his gaze drifted as if his thoughts had been tugged away.

"Professor, did you hear what she was saying to this person while she was on the phone?"

Professor Robbins blinked and met Jake's gaze. "She was talking about playing a game. She said she wasn't any good at games but that she would try."

"What kind of game?"

"I don't know. A lot of the kids in this department are big gamers." He frowned. "But I don't think it was that kind of game. Her voice got soft and low, but I think it had to do with sex."

"Why do you say that?"

"Elisa is, was a smart woman. She works hard and most boys her age don't appreciate that. One finally looks at her and it's inevitable that she would be flat-tered. I told her to be careful before and she would always laugh and tell me not to worry. But I knew it was a matter of time. She is—was too trusting."

Copies of her cell phone records should be on Jake's desk later today. "That's the last time you saw her?"

Old eyes narrowed. "They were going to meet, but I don't know where."

"Percy Warner Park?"

"I don't know."

"Did she mention a name?"

"If she did, I didn't catch it." Heavy gray brows slumped.

"There's nothing else you can remember?"

"No. No. I'm sorry."

Frustrations like this were part of the process. Most interviews gave him bits and pieces of the truth that he had to string together like beads on a necklace. He dug his card from his breast pocket and handed it to the old man. "Thank you."

The old man studied the card. "You never told me how she died."

"She was strangled."

His face creased. "Who would do such a thing?"

"That's what we're trying to find out."

"Her parents travel a great deal. They like to go off the grid in the wilderness. They're often gone for weeks at a time."

"We've spoken to them."

He moved out from behind his desk and motioned for Jake to follow. The old man walked down the hallway, his posture bent but his gaze burning with purpose. He stopped at an office door at the end of the hallway and opened the door without knocking. A young man glanced up from a computer screen, his look of annoyance fading with he saw Dr. Robbins. "Yes, sir."

Faded jeans hugged a lean waist and long legs. A Titans T-shirt stretched tightly across his chest. Dark hair skimmed wide shoulders. He was a good-looking guy, much like the man described by the clerk at Blue Note Java.

"This is Detective Jake Bishop. Detective, this is Ray Downs. He's my teaching assistant. He and Elisa were good friends." The old man glanced at the younger. "Elisa Spence was killed this past weekend."

Ray shifted his stance and moved out from behind his desk. "I heard this morning. I was camping for a couple of days and was out of touch with the news until a few hours ago."

"Why didn't you tell me when you arrived this morning?" Dr. Robbins demanded.

"You had a Do-Not-Disturb on your door, sir. The last time I knocked when the sign was up you threatened to fire me."

The old man rested a gnarled fist on his hip. "Not for news like this."

The young man's face flushed with frustration. "I knew you'd be out sooner than later. I was planning to tell you."

Dr. Robbins waved a wrinkled, bent hand in the air as if shooing his words like a pesky fly. "Tell the detective all you know about Elisa."

The younger man slid a hand into his pocket, his gaze flickering between Jake and the floor. "She was nice. A sweet girl. Always wanted others to be happy. I hear she was strangled. Is that true?"

"Yes." Jake flipped to a new page in his notebook.

After gathering Ray's contact information, he asked, "Was she dating anyone?"

"No. Elisa was all about her work. She was putting the finishing touches on her senior thesis."

Dr. Robbins shook his head. "I heard her talking to someone on the phone. Her voice sounded all girlie and soft. Who was that? You seem to know everything that goes on here."

Ray shifted his stance. "She wasn't dating anyone, but she did meet a guy a week or two ago that she said was hot. I thought she was making it up. I couldn't see her with a hot guy." He glanced at the professor to gauge his reaction. "She was hoping to hook up with him."

The professor shook his head, regret chasing his words as he whispered, "Such a foolish girl."

"What do you know about the guy?" Jake asked.

"From what she said, he just arrived in town. Said he wanted to make music." Ray shook his head. "Everyone wants to make music in this town, and I laughed when she told me. I half expected her to laugh with me but she didn't. She said he was really talented. She heard him sing and play the guitar."

"Where was this?" Jake asked.

"She met him at the café, but went to hear him sing on Broadway. You know how singers just find a spot and start singing for tips. That's what this guy was doing. Playing for tips when she met him. She thought he was amazing."

"Do you know anything else about this guy?" Jake pressed.

"I snapped a photo of the two of them when I was at the coffee shop." He reached in his back pocket and fished out his phone. Scrolling through several pictures, he handed the phone to Jake. "She asked me to because she was kinda proud of his attention."

The image featured a smiling young girl standing next to a tall guy with long dark hair. A black beard covered the lower half of his face and dark sunglasses shielded his eyes. He wore a plain dark T-shirt and his left ear was pierced at least twice.

"Can you send me this photo?"

"Yeah, sure." Ray took the phone and as Jake rattled off his phone number, the younger man typed the numbers into his phone. A whooshing sound rushed between them as Ray tucked the phone in his back pocket.

"This guy got a name?" Jake asked as he checked his phone for the image.

"Scott. But I didn't catch a last name. I can tell you I didn't like the guy. He was nice to Elisa, but she was also paying his tab at the coffee shop. She had a big heart, and he picked right up on it. Did he kill her?"

"We don't know. I'm chasing as many leads as I can."

"What about DNA and stuff? Don't you have DNA? I thought that kind of thing caught bad guys."

"Not quite the magic bullet everyone thinks it is."

"I thought when you had a match that was it."

"Some tests are dead-on matches but enough results land in the gray zone between yes and no. We've processed the scene, but it will take time to get the DNA back."

"What about fingerprints?" Professor Robbins asked.

"We're analyzing everything as we get it."

"Shit," Ray said. "I thought you guys had all this equipment to catch the bad guys. What the hell?"

Jake smiled, unwilling to explain that interviews cracked cases faster than forensic testing. "We're working on it. Do you know if this guy was staying around here?"

"I don't know. I was hoping to catch up with Elisa today and ask her. I looked for her this morning and then heard the news."

Professor Robbins raised a hand. "She had a small cubby space if you'd like to look at it."

"I would."

"Ray, show him to the study cubbies."

"Sure, professor."

Jake and Ray left Professor Robbins standing in the hallway staring after them as they made their way to the elevators. Ray punched the bottom floor button and soon the two were in a windowless section of the building. Crowded in the corner was a collection of cubbies. Ray took him to Elisa's space.

Books neatly stacked lined the back of the cubicle. There were pictures of a smiling Elisa with her roommate as well as two older people whom he recognized as her parents. In one image, grand mountains reached up to a dark cloudy sky. Also on the table were neatly sharpened pencils, a pack of gum, a clean red coffee cup, and a pack of matches and notepad both from the Palmer Motel.

"Did she smoke?" Jake asked. Dr. Heller had said her lungs were clean.

"No."

Jake flipped open the matches. The inside flap was blank with some missing matches. But on the notepad he noticed indentation from writing made on the previous page now missing. He picked up one of the pencils and shadowed over the blank page of the notepad. The pencil darkened the page while highlighting words indented from the last page. The name Scott, circled several times, appeared along with "Palmer Motel."

"Damn," Ray said.

"Not high-tech forensic work, but effective. She say anything else about this guy?"

The kid glanced back to make sure Dr. Robbins wasn't close. "She said the guy was into kinky stuff."

"Kinky stuff?"

"They'd not tried anything yet, but she said it all sounded exciting. I've never seen her so giddy."

"What did he suggest they do?"

"He was into strangulation."

"And you didn't think to call the cops about that?"

His gaze dropped before meeting his again. "I thought about it. Wanted to, but just wasn't sure how to go about it."

Jake allowed the flash of anger to chill before he held up his phone. "Not only takes pictures but it makes phone calls."

The sun had burned off the morning chill when Jake arrived at the Palmer Motel. It was a seedy one-story motel with two dozen rooms strung together like a collection of little boxes. He parked in front of the office, which wasn't more than a cinderblock box outfitted with a counter and a cigarette and soda machines. The young guy standing behind the counter was of medium build with short dark hair and a neatly trimmed mustache. His shirt was clean and starched and his jeans looked new.

Before Jake could pull his badge, the counter guy asked, "Cop, right?"

Jake nodded. "That's right. And you are?"

"Barry McGraw. Day manager. I'm in school and working here lets me study while I get paid. Not much happens. Mostly, I make sure no one rips off cigarettes or sodas."

Jake fished the matches out of his pocket. "Barry, I found these matches at a crime scene. Trying to link them to a suspect."

Barry's eyes widened. "Sure. Who arc you looking for?"

He unfolded the sketch Jenna had drawn. "Seen this guy around?"

"Sure. That's Scott Murphy. Room 18."

"He's there now?"

"I haven't seen him since I started my shift a few hours ago. But I can open his room for you if you like. Boss always said if the cops show, give 'em what they want."

"Let's have a look."

Key in hand, Barry led Jake to the room, but as he readied to knock, Jake shook his head. "Give me the key. You step back."

"Yeah, sure. Right. What if he's waiting for you, right?"

"Exactly." Jake knocked hard on the door, careful to stand just off to the side, his hand on his gun. When he heard nothing, he banged again. "Mr. Murphy, this is Detective Jake Bishop with the Nashville Police Department."

The manager stood to the right of the detective, hovering close to the wall. "Like I said, I haven't seen him come back yet."

Jake always entered a room assuming a loaded gun waited for him on the other side of the door. "Are there any other windows or doors connected to the room?"

"None. Just cinderblock walls." Barry glanced around as if he expected trouble. "You gonna go in there?"

Jake reached for his cell and dialed. "As soon as backup arrives."

"Right. Makes sense. He could have a gun."

"Would you do me a favor and return to your office and wait for the police to arrive? Safer that way."

Barry shoved out a breath. "Yeah, sure. But can I watch from my office window?"

"I'd get behind the counter."

"Right." Barry hesitated, then catching Jake's gaze, tugged the edge of his shirt over his belly, turned and walked back to his office.

Within seconds, a patrol car pulled up in front of the door, lights flashing. The officer, tall, lean, and very young, reminded Jake of himself when he had first moved to Nashville. He'd been twenty-eight when he opted to give Nashville a chance. Had he looked that young?

The officer got out, and with a nod to Jake, moved to the other side of the door. A second patrol car arrived and took position at the curb.

Carefully, Jake unlocked the door and pushed it open, still angled to the side. When he heard nothing, he flipped on the light and glanced to the left. Seeing nothing, he allowed his gaze to sweep above him and then immediately behind the door. Momentarily satisfied, he moved toward the bed, and while the officer covered him, he glanced underneath the mattress.

"Clear," he said. The officer moved past him to the bathroom and announced it, too, was clear.

The officer did a second sweep of the room before moving back toward the threshold. Jake thanked him and slowly holstered his weapon. He pulled on latex gloves as he stood in the center of the room. The thick stale air closed in around him. On a dresser next to the television stood a stack of pizza boxes and an ashtray filled with cigarette butts. Rumpled sheets clumped in the middle of the double bed and on the nightstand sat a half bottle of whiskey and several scattered un-opened condoms.

An old guitar covered with stickers leaned against the wall. Hard to live in Nashville or hang out with Georgia Morgan and not learn something about gui-tars. This one appeared to be a low-end model. Georgia would know more than he, but he guessed the sound wouldn't have been great. But he doubted Elisa cared about acoustics as long as the player was a good-looking guy who paid attention to her.

A shadow appeared at the door and Jake turned to see Rick. "Heard you called for backup. Find any-thing?"

"Our man Scott Murphy liked his pizza and booze. He fancied himself some kind of musician. It's been a few hours since the manager has seen him."

"There was a brief mention of a person of interest in this case on the midday news. Media used Jenna's sketch," he said. "Our guy could have heard something and bolted."

"Or he's out hunting again. He left his guitar behind. That's what caught Elisa's imagination."

"Maybe he has a few lures he uses to catch a girl's attention."

"Maybe."

Jake rested his hands on his hips, his elbow brushing his gun holster, before moving toward a closet filled with a pile of dirty clothes. He rummaged under the clothes and found a worn black backpack. Carefully, he lifted it so that Rick could get a good look.

"Elisa Spence's backpack?"

Jake unzipped the bag and pulled out a laptop covered in flower stickers and a single shoe that matched the one found on Elisa's body. He opened the computer and powered it up. He selected a word document and the first he opened had Elisa Spence's name at the top. "Call in the forensic team and have them sweep the room. Maybe we'll get lucky and pull prints off something." DNA would be collected and tested, but like he said earlier, getting DNA results would take too long for him. Scott Murphy, or whoever the hell he was, could be long gone before they had solid results. Boots on the ground would catch this monster.

He found several rumpled receipts on the floor. One was for burgers. Another was from a drug store where he bought bandages, antibiotic ointment, and candy. The last for rope from a hardware store. "We need to check each store and see if they had surveillance cameras rolling at the time of his purchase." He'd learned firsthand after knocking on shop doors for surveillance footage that many stores didn't have cameras. And if there was a camera in place, there was no guarantee it was hooked up. These days, with the economy tightening, expenses got cut, and that included surveillance cameras.

Jake arrived at the downtown offices of Walter, Owen & Davis, a Nashville law firm that specialized in entertainment law. He had traced Tim Taylor, Mike's best friend at St. Vincent, to this firm where he worked as a law clerk while attending law school at Vanderbilt.

He stepped out of the sleek elevator and approached the receptionist, a slim petite blonde with green eyes the color of emeralds. She wore a blue silk blouse and a black pencil skirt. A strand of pearls dangled around her neck. She was as sleek as the office.

She smiled up at him. "Can I help you?"

"I called earlier. I'm Jake Bishop with Nashville Homicide. I'm here to see Tim Taylor."

"Right. Tim. Let me buzz him." Manicured hands picked up the phone and she pressed several numbers before an extension buzzed. "Detective Bishop. Of course." She hung up. "He'll be right out."

"Thank you."

She rose, running her hands over her narrow hips.

"I'm Alexandra Jones. Call me Alexandra."

He nodded.

"I've been trying to guess why homicide would want to talk to Tim. He's about the most mild-mannered guy you'd ever want to know." Her smile widened. "But isn't that what they say about all the serial killers?"

"I wouldn't know. And my questions for him are very routine."

"I heard about that girl they found in the park? You working that case?"

"I am."

"Terrible. Such a young girl."

"Yes, ma'am."

Footsteps sounded in the hall and a tall young man wearing a dark suit, white shirt, and red tie approached Jake. His hair was cut short and neatly parted.

"Detective Bishop. I'm Tim Taylor."

Jake shook his hand wondering if Tim looked all that young or if he was just getting older. Second time today. Hell, maybe he was losing a step. "Thank you for seeing me. Is there a place where we can talk in private?"

Tim glanced toward Miss Jones who stared boldly at them. "Sure. There's a small conference room."

Jake followed Tim to a small paneled room furnished with an oval oak table surrounded by eight leather chairs.

Tim reached for the phone. "Would you like coffee? My assistant can bring it."

"No, thank you."

Tim sat at the head of the table and Jake sat in a chair angled to his right and ran his hand down his tie as he crossed his legs. "I'm here to talk about Mike Marlowe."

"I figured as much. I must have talked to ten cops after he vanished. Mr. Marlowe took me out for drinks a few weeks ago to talk about Mike."

"What did he want to talk about?"

"Same old thing. First, we talked about how great Mike was on the football field."

"He was the quarterback and you were the receiver."

"Exactly. Then he asked if I ever thought about Mike and was there anything that I remembered that might help find him."

"What was your response?"

"Frankly, I don't think about Mike. Occasionally a reporter will call, but I don't even take those calls anymore. I don't see the point in dredging up the past."

"What do you think happened to Mike?"

Tim leaned forward, tapping an index finger lightly on the table. "I think he pissed someone off."

"Enough to kill him?"

"Yeah. He was a bully. And he could be a real dick. Don't get me wrong, I loved playing ball with the guy and we partied more than a few times. His old man's money made him a spoiled brat."

"You tell that to Marlowe?"

"I tried once but he didn't want to hear it. Death has done Mike's reputation a favor. All the people that hated his ass in school were the first to light candles at his vigil. They were the first to go after Amber."

"Why did they go after Amber?"

He rubbed the back of his neck. "I think mostly because it was easy. She really couldn't defend herself. Sadly, if she'd been the one to die in the woods there wouldn't have been as big a fuss made. She was a nobody."

"Marlowe doesn't like her."

"Hates her guts is more like it. Once, after Mike vanished, he nearly drove her off the road with his car. He'd have done it if a cop hadn't seen what was happening and stopped. Marlowe found a way to smooth it over so the charges never got filed."

"What did you think about Amber?"

"Smokin' hot. Freaky chick. Liked the guys and drove them nuts."

"She slept around?"

"She did her share. We all knew she was working her way up the food chain, determined to land with the rich guy . . . Mike."

"And she got him."

"Hook, line, and sinker. He used to talk about her in the locker room. Said she was a freak in bed."

Locker room talk about a girl wasn't his idea of reliable. Oversexed teenaged boys exaggerated. "Did you ever sleep with her?"

His face paled. "No. Not that I didn't want to or would have said no, but she was with Mike."

"What do you remember best about her?"

"One time at lunch break junior year, we were sitting outside and Mike was harassing Bethany. The girl looked ready to cry. Amber appears and gives Mike a piece of her mind and then puts her arm around Bethany and tells her not to worry."

"Mike ever talk to you about the field trip into the woods."

He shook his head. "He didn't want to do it. Thought science was for pussies. But he needed the grade to get his old man off his back and not take his fat allowance away. They fought tooth and nail over the money. Mike kept saying it was his and Marlowe reminded him he didn't get a dime until he was twenty-three."

"Did you know Amber is back in town?"

He shifted as if he'd been jabbed. "I didn't know that. Is that why you're here? Did she remember something?"

"She says she's not remembered a thing. I'm here because we found Bethany and Mike's remains in the park. They've been dead five years."

"Shit."

Jake let the comment sit there and waited for Tim to make a move.

Again, the finger tapped on the table. "You know Mike hired someone to take his SATs for him."

"I didn't know that. Who did he hire?"

"Bethany."

"How do you know this?"

"He got drunk and talked." The phone buzzed and Tim picked it up. "Right thanks." He hung up. "I've got to get back. We're getting briefs ready for a case."

As the two rose, Jake pulled out a card. "We'll talk again, Mr. Taylor. I'm not going away." He held out a card. "Call me if you think of anything."

Tim had to reach out to get the card. "I will."

Miss Jones asked Jake if he needed anything else as he was leaving. He smiled and kept walking. He hated lawyers.


Georgia arrived at the medical examiner's office just after four. It wasn't customary for techs to attend an autopsy. That was the jurisdiction of the medical examiner, but she wanted to be present when Dr. Heller provided a detailed analysis of Bethany Reed and Mike Marlowe's bones found in the cave. As she moved toward the glass partition separating the lobby from the receptionist, she heard, "Georgia."

She turned to see Deke standing by the wall, leaning, his phone in hand scrolling through e-mails. "Look what the cat dragged in."

A smile traced his lips as he pushed off from the wall and moved toward her, his strides long and purposeful. "Doesn't surprise me to find you here."

"Don't tell me you want in on the analysis? That's a lot of science and technical stuff and you're all about following the interviews."

"Even an old dog can learn a trick or two."

"I think of the science end of this case as mine."

"Yours?"

"Sure." Every time she looked at Deke she saw their father Buddy and felt as if she needed to justify herself. "If not for me opening the cold case, none of us would be here."

"True. True enough." He raised an index finger, just like Buddy used to, pointing to her as if he'd just remembered an important detail. "Alex called me last night. Leah's finalizing the details of their Christmas wedding."

Brother Alex, TBI agent, was a man of few emotions and often came across as unfeeling. What few realized was that his emotions ran bone deep for his job, his family, and now his fiancée, Leah. She was a veterinarian who was bright and vibrant. When Georgia saw her with Alex, it was easy to assume Leah's life had been charmed. A closer look revealed scars, sliced into her by an ex-husband, and now so carefully hidden with special makeup.

"Right. I have to get by for the last fitting of my bridesmaid dress. I keep putting that off."

Deke shifted. "Right. Well, she wants to know if you're bringing a date."

"A date?" Color rushed her cheeks as she stared at the brother so like her father and thought about Jake, not expecting some kind of commitment. "No. No date. Wearing a bridesmaid dress is traumatic enough."

He looked at her as if he picked up the shift in her vibration. "You sure? No plus one?"

"Very." She cleared her throat, needing to run for the cover of work details. "Where's Rick?"

"He was at the Palmer Motel searching a room belonging to Scott Murphy. They found Elisa's backpack in the room."

"Really?" Adrenaline surged through her muscles. She lived for moments like this. "Any sight of this Murphy guy?"

"No. He's gone and officers on scene are waiting for the forensic team."

She glanced at her phone. "I've not received a text yet. I should be on the scene."

"Last I checked, you're not the only one in the department." He shifted, standing between her and the elevator. "Scott Murphy fits Jenna's sketch, so he's using the image and going door to door in the motel."

She tapped an impatient finger on her belt. "You said this Scott Murphy guy vanished."

"He can run, but he can't hide from me for long." He slid the phone in his pocket. "I'm very sure your buddies in the lab will lift all kinds of good DNA."

She checked her watch. "Four o'clock. I bet Brad got that text. He was hoping to get out of the office on time today."

"Join the club."

The doors opened and Dr. Heller appeared. Georgia

liked the pathologist, who moved with a quiet efficiency that she found calming. If Georgia had to classify herself she'd be a tornado. Dr. Heller was smooth calm waters. Jake, well, he was an earthquake. He turned everything upside down.

"Looks like a party today," Dr. Heller said. "I'm flattered you could join me."

They followed her up to the exam room and each donned gowns and gloves before joining Dr. Heller in a tiled exam room. In the center of the room lay two sets of skeletal remains. Bones, darkened to a muddy brown by time and the damp cave were laid out in anatomical order side by side. One glance at the smaller set of bones with the wide pelvis and delicate brow line confirmed what she had suspected in the cave. The bones were female. The other set was markedly larger and clearly those of a male.

Her gaze settled on the empty spot that should have held the right femur bone of the female. "We bagged everything in that cave."

Dr. Heller, her athletic frame now swallowed by a green gown, nodded as she linked gloved fingers together. "I don't see signs of trauma on the adjoining bones. No saw or ax marks to suggest that the killer dismembered the body. But there are small gnaw marks at the end of the femur. My guess is an animal burrowed in from some small crevice in the cave and chewed on the body."

Georgia grimaced, trying not to picture a wild animal defiling the remains of Bethany Reed. "Do you know how she died?"

"It's as I expected. She was stabbed." She lifted a

rib bone that would have rested near the heart. "See the slash mark here? That's a knife mark. Someone drove a knife from above her into her chest."

"That someone would likely be taller," Georgia said. "Like Mike."

"Sure, but that's assuming she was standing when she was stabbed." Dr. Heller shrugged. "She was also struck very hard on the back right scapula and the back of her skull. The blows would not have been enough to kill her, but would have knocked her to her knees." She raised the triangular-shaped scapula bone and pointed to weblike fractures.

"She fell to her knees first," Georgia said as she tried to visualize the last moments of Bethany's life.

"Maybe," Dr. Heller replied. "It would have been an incredibly painful blow."

"What was she hit with?" Deke asked.

"Hard to say exactly." She pointed to the center of the fractures. "The contact area is tight and circular. Perhaps a hammer or a palm-sized rock."

"And then the killer moved in front of her and drove a knife in her chest," Georgia said.

"That would be my guess," Dr. Heller said. "We've photographed the bones and have examined them, and I won't need to hold onto them much longer. Mrs. Reed and Mr. Marlowe are anxious to take custody of the remains so that they can hold funeral services."

"When will you release the bones?" Deke asked.

"In a day or two. I released Elisa Spence's remains to her parents a couple of hours ago. They're planning on cremation and no ceremony, but it's my understanding that Mrs. Reed is planning a funeral and I don't know Marlowe's plans yet."

Georgia understood the pain of burying a parent but thankfully not a child. "Those families have suffered enough."

Deke shook his head. "They've got some closure. That counts for a lot."

"That's not enough. I want their killer more than ever now."

A grin tugged the edges of his mouth. "You sound like Buddy."

"Really?"

"More every day."

"Thanks. I think." As she stared at the large bones, she visualized the file photographs of the tall young man with broad shoulders and a square jaw. "What's Mike's story?"

"He was shot in the head just above the left temporal lobe as you suspected. No other wounds or damage to the body."

"I searched the cave floor and found the bullet lodged in the dirt."

Dr. Heller lifted the skull and moved to a side counter where she picked up a long narrow rod. She inserted the rod into the hole in the temple and out the one at the back of the skull. "This is the trajectory of the bullet." She held a pointed finger as if it were the barrel of a gun to the temple. "The slight downward trajectory suggests it was fired at close range. He would have died instantly."

"An execution," Deke said.

"I would have bought the murder/suicide angle if not for the Spence body," Georgia said.

"Agreed."

"I'm running ballistics on the bullet. I've done my best to pull up the serial number on the gun but no luck."

"Let Bishop break the news to Marlowe about the manner of death. I don't know who the hell killed those kids, but right now everyone is a suspect, even Marlowe."

"Understood."

"Any remains of clothes found with the bodies?"

"Zippers. The rest rotted away. The zippers are from standard jeans that could be purchased in any box store."

"And the necklace was dangling from the rocks, correct?" Dr. Heller asked.

"Yes. I'm still trying to figure that one," Georgia said. "Damn thing's hanging there almost like a grave marker for Bethany." Georgia couldn't imagine the terror the girls endured in their last moments. "Deke, have you fed the details into ViCAP yet?"

ViCAP, an FBI national database stood for the Violent Criminal Apprehension Program. The system was not as perfect as many on the outside thought. Not all jurisdictions across the country entered data into the system. Many of the smaller municipalities were short on funds and manpower

Deke shook his head. "I'm holding off until I have a few more details. Fingerprints from the motel would be a big help."

"There will be dozens, and we'll have to sift through what's found." Impatience nipped at her as she thought about the shifting and digging it would take to find a fingerprint match.

"I have uniforms canvassing the area around the coffee shop with the picture Jenna drew," Deke said. "A few people think they saw him but no one has any specific details. The guy knows how to blend."

"We need to sift through the fingerprints in that motel room. We'll focus on the ones on the remote, any food or drink containers, and door handles."

"They found a guitar."

"Perfect."

"I can input a fingerprint into the databases and we're more likely to get a hit from that than eyewitness testimony."

Georgia studied the collection of dark brittle bones. "What set him off?"

"Who the hell knows," Deke said.


The fresh voice mails sat unanswered in Amber's phone from several reporters and a couple of guys she'd met in a bar her first night in town. The reporters were an annoyance and of no use to her and the men, though they had been entertaining for a few hours, now irritated her.

As the television commercial featuring dog food flashed, she muted the television. She was watching for any news reports on the girl, Elisa Spence. She was found dead in Percy Warner Park and very likely the reason Jake and Georgia had left so quickly from the diner.

Finding the Spence girl also explained why she didn't hear back from Georgia and Jake, even though they were so eager to reopen the missing persons cases on Bethany and Mike.

As her mother turned on the shower in the back bathroom, she rose and moved toward the kitchen. Her mother had arrived home fifteen minutes ago and promised to talk as soon as she washed the stench of the bar out of her hair. Once her mother finished her shower, she would say a word or two to Amber, but it would be less than a half hour before she fell into bed, exhausted.

Her mother's ritual had not changed in the last five years, leaving Amber to believe the stench most likely came from a strange man as much as the bar. When the sun was down, her mother loved men. When it was up, she hated them.

Amber dug a Mason jar from the cabinet and filled it with tap water. As she drank and stared out the back kitchen window into the barren backyard, the irony of the moment struck hard. For all her plans of making it big and getting rich, she'd come full circle. She was back in her mother's house and still wanting more and wondering why her mother could not get her shit together.

She finished her water and then turned to the grocery bag her mother had deposited on the counter. She had brought home a few cans of soup, crackers, and milk. Though the thought of the milk made Amber's stomach turn, soup appealed to her. She pulled the lid off the can, found a big mug and dumped it inside. She punched in two minutes on the microwave, put the soup inside, and hit start.

Her phone buzzed and she pulled it from her back pocket to glance at the display. She swore and sent the call to voice mail.

He stood outside, his slim muscled body pressed against the bark of an old oak tree. He watched as Amber passed in front of the window, the T-shirt and jeans molding her supple body.

The last five years had not changed her. She looked just as she had in high school. Small, petite, she always had a way about her that made him want to protect her when he wasn't fucking her.

He pressed his forehead against the rough bark and gently rocked back and forth. He wanted to see her again. Touch her. Hold her. Be inside her. Life was always more vivid and jazzed when he was with her. What had she called them once? Bonnie and Clyde.

He dug his cell from his pocket and dialed her number. As her phone rang, her head turned and she picked up the phone. For a long moment she stared at the display and he thought she might pick it up. But then she hit silent as her mother appeared in view.

Amber turned from the window, as if he did not exist. Almost like she knew he was out here, watching her.

Pressing the phone to his head, he needed her. He wanted Amber so much.

Be patient. Be patient. She promised they would be together soon. Very soon.

# CHAPTER ELEVEN

***Thursday, October 5, 9:00 P.M.***

Overhead lights of the Nashville Police Department's parking lot hummed as Georgia crossed to her car. She left Deke at the medical examiner's office hours ago and returned to her lab where she spent several hours processing a robbery scene. As she cut across the lot she could only think about food. She was starving.

"Georgia!"

She turned at the sound as a tall, lean man stepped from the shadows. He wore a dark blue shirt from a local garage that skimmed his muscled biceps and chest. His black beard was thick and his dark hair tied back.

She looked around the lot, irritated she'd not paid more attention to her surroundings before she walked out of the building. "Can I help you?"

"I'm Hal West. Carrie's boyfriend."

She reached in her purse, thumbing the canister of mace she always carried. "Right. The guy that likes to put bruises on the mother of his child. How the hell are you, Hal?"

He held up a crumpled napkin. "I found this in her purse. When I asked her what it was about she got real jumpy. Mind telling me what my girl is doing with your number?"

Jamming her thumb under the safety on the mace, she hoped this jerk stepped closer. "I told her that when she's tired of being your punching bag to call me." She was outmuscled, but knew if she showed any kind of fear he would take the offensive. "When she wises up, I'll see to it she leaves you for good."

"Fuck you." He ripped the napkin and threw it on the ground. "You got no business in my life."

She pulled her phone from her back pocket and hit the 911 speed dial icon. "You got no business beating on a woman half your size, pal. Let's see how badass you are when the cops show up in less than a minute."

He advanced a step, his fists clenched. In the distance she heard sirens and knew valuable seconds would separate her from the cops being able to stop real trouble.

"Is there a problem here?" The deep male voice belonged to Jake Bishop.

Georgia looked past Hal to see Jake standing outside the circle's edge of light. His feet were braced, his hand rested on his gun as if hoping.

Hal's gaze remained locked on Georgia. "I'm having a conversation with the lady. She's glad to see me."

Georgia shook her head. "Detective Bishop, I've told Hal here the cops are on the way."

"What's the issue, Hal?"

Hal stared at Georgia, grinding his teeth as if he were chewing on a bit. "Nothing. I got no problem."

"He hurt you in any way," Jake asked Georgia.

"Nope."

"Threats?"

"Nothing to charge him with." There would be no holding Hal tonight, but that didn't mean the trouble was over.

A marked squad car raced into the lot and stopped, catching the trio in the headlights. An officer got out of the car. "What's the trouble?"

Hal shook his head. "No trouble."

"Then leave," Jake ordered.

Hal flexed his fists, but he turned and moved along the line of parked cars until he reached a beat-up truck. He got behind the wheel, fired up the engine, and peeled out of the lot.

Georgia looked at the officer, allowing herself to release the breath she'd been holding. "Thanks for the quick call."

"We're set," Jake said.

The officer nodded, got in his squad car and left, leaving them alone.

"How long has this been going on?" Jake asked.

"That's the first time I met Hal. But I know his girl-friend. Hal likes to knock her around and I offered her a place to stay if she ever wised up and left his ass."

He faced her, the light from the streetlight cutting across his face. "Did he do anything to threaten you in any way?"

"No. This is the first." She pressed trembling fingers to her forehead. "But I'm sure it won't be the last."

His hand rested near his weapon, the ring on his finger tapping against the grip of the gun. "Shit, you've got to be more careful."

"Yeah, I know. I'm sure if he wasn't pissed off when he arrived, he was when he left."

"Don't take this lightly, Georgia. I've seen stalkers before. Hell, ask your brother Alex what it's like to deal with a stalker. His fiancée, Leah, went through hell and back with her stalker."

"He's all bluster. He's used to backing down. But you're right. I'll be more careful, but I am worried about Carrie." She dialed a new number on her phone and listened until she landed in Carrie's voice mail. She detailed what had happened and told her to be careful. She also repeated her phone number and offer for a place to stay.

"Shit. You're taking this too lightly."

"What are you doing here?"

"Taking a break. I've been reviewing tapes since I left Scott Murphy's motel room. Figured you were working and decided to stop by."

"Why are you so nice to me?"

"I don't know. You sure don't deserve it, yet."

Good. He was annoyed. At least the evening wasn't a total loss. "Any more leads on the guy who was spending time with Elisa?"

He studied her an extra moment as if sensing the tangle of emotions. "Not yet."

"Brad tells me the motel room was filled with prints."

He flashed one of his smartass smiles. "You forensic folks are the turtle in this race."

Talk of work soothed some of the chaos. "Slow and steady wins the race."

"You keep telling yourself that when I cross the finish line with my suspect."

"My evidence will keep him behind bars."

"It'll help, but I could do without."

That prompted a laugh. "You're so sure of yourself."

"I'm sure I know how to chase a trail and catch bad guys."

She understood what he was doing. Grating on her last nerve to make her feel better. Words rose up in her and caught in her throat. "Thanks for showing up when you did."

He offered a slight nod of the head. "You can count on me, Georgia. I've got your back."

"You do," she whispered.

A heavy silence settled between them. In the distance she heard people talking, knew others from the station were approaching their own cars. She tightened her hand on her keys.

He leaned closer, his body eating up a little more of the wedge of space between them. "I'm not kidding, Georgia. Don't underestimate Hal or think he'll forget about you."

"I won't."

Finally, he stepped back and allowed her to open her car door and sit. Silent, Jake stood steady as she closed her door and turned over the engine. In the rearview mirror she watched as he stood in the parking lot staring in her direction. She watched until she turned the corner and he vanished from sight.

* * *

Georgia wasn't sure how long her eyes had been closed when her cell rang. She sat up on her couch, dropping the television channel selector as she twisted around and searched for her phone. She glanced toward the television and the muted infomercial that displayed some kind of kitchen gadget that could peel and dice.

She found her cell between the cushions of her couch and accepted the call without bothering to look at the number. She wasn't on call tonight, but that didn't mean she couldn't be called in to a rape or homicide scene.

"Hello." Her voice sounded like sandpaper, forcing her to clear her throat. "Hello."

"Georgia Morgan?" The feminine voice sounded small and charged with fear.

"That's me. Who is this?"

"It's Amber Ryder." She hissed in a breath and then slowly released it.

"What's happening?" Georgia stood, dusting cracker crumbs from her shirt. She'd not intended to fall asleep on the couch when she'd switched on the romantic comedy. However, she'd dozed almost immediately and at this moment couldn't have told you a thing about the plot.

"I've been mugged."

She rubbed her eyes. "Where are you?"

"I'm at a convenience store."

"What happened?"

"I was inside buying beer and I walked to get in my car when a guy showed up out of nowhere. He tried to take my purse, but I fought back. He shoved me to the curb."

"Are you hurt?"

"I'm bruised up. And I've a cut on my forehead that's going to need stitches."

Georgia blinked the fatigue from her eyes, trying to clear her thoughts. "What do you need?"

"Can you take me to the hospital? I know you don't know me that well, but I just don't know who else to call."

Georgia blinked the fatigue from her eyes. "Yeah, sure. Give me the address."

Amber rattled off her location. "I'll come get you. Just sit tight."

Georgia hurried into her small kitchen and set a K-Cup into the coffeemaker. While it gurgled, she washed her face in the kitchen sink, tucked her shirt into her jeans, and finger-combed her hair before tying it in a ponytail. A few minutes later, coffee in hand, Georgia was backing out of her parking space at her apartment complex. It was two-forty a.m.

The roads were empty except for the occasional delivery truck and marked police car. The drive to the East Nashville address took only twenty minutes. When she pulled up in front of the convenience station, there was no sign of Amber. Parking, with the engine still running, she surveyed the lot, studying the shadows. She thought about Hal stepping out, grabbing her, luring her into a trap.

Her hand on her phone, she unrolled her window. "Amber!"

Seconds later, Amber slowly walked out of the shadows, a fistful of napkins pressed to her bloody forehead. She hurried around to the passenger side of the car.

Georgia unlocked the door long enough for her to get in before relocking it. She turned on the dome light and looked at Amber, blood soaking the napkins and oozing down the side of her cheeks. "Who did this to you?"

"I don't know. He came out of nowhere."

"Did you call the cops?"

"No. I don't want to deal with cops right now. Please. I don't need an interrogation."

"They're here to protect you."

Amber winced as she pressed the wound harder to staunch the flow. "I can't deal with them now."

"Okay. Let's get you to the emergency room." Georgia put the car in drive and pulled out of the parking lot.

Amber laid her head back against the seat and drew in a steadying breath. "This is not how I pictured my return to Nashville."

"Have you received any other texts?"

"A few calls and hang-ups but no texts."

"Who's calling?"

"I didn't recognize the number."

She pulled the napkin from her head and grimaced at the sight of the blood. "It was stupid of me to go out so late, but I was craving a beer."

Georgia frowned as the stoplight turned yellow. She punched the gas and slid through the intersection as the light turned red. "Where's your mother?"

"Working, I think. Or maybe she's off her shift now and gone out with friends for a drink. That's her favorite part of the day, or at least it was when I was in high school." She grimaced as she pressed the napkin back on the wound.

Amber turned a little toward Georgia, her face half shadowed in the darkness. "I heard about that poor girl on the news. I'm guessing that's why you and the detective had to leave so quickly."

"We've been meaning to get back to you but there's been no time." She shoved out a breath. "You'll hear this soon from someone, but we found Bethany and Mike's bodies."

She rolled the window down to get some fresh air. "I heard on the news they found something at the park. How did you find them?"

"The murdered girl was in a cave. Bethany and Mike were behind her in another chamber."

She pressed a hand to her temple. "I don't understand. Why would all three bodies be together?"

"That's what we're trying to figure out."

Tears tightened her throat. "My God, after all this time. We finally know where they are. How did they die?"

"We've not released that yet. Still doing tests."

"My God," she whispered again as she stared out the window at the rushing lights. "Mrs. Reed will be devastated. And Mr. Marlowe was very dedicated to Mike. His son was his world. He'll not rest until he finds out what happened. I didn't like the guy, but he doesn't deserve this. No one does."

Georgia tightened her grip on the wheel. "We want to talk to you again."

"Of course." She shook her head. "God, after all this time and they were right here."

Amber moaned softly as more pain seemed to

course through her head. When it appeared to pass, she was pale and her clear eyes murky.

Georgia, sensing Amber's condition was worsening, drove faster, even running a red light until she spotted the hospital ahead. Pulling into the parking spot reserved for emergency, she ran around the front of the car and helped Amber stagger to her feet.

The two women made their way across the lot, and by the time they reached the emergency door entrance, Georgia was able to flag down an orderly and get Amber into a wheelchair.

The next half hour centered on getting Amber into an ER room, changed into a gown, and seeing that her paperwork was filled out. Georgia was relieved when Amber removed an insurance card from her wallet.

A nurse examined Amber and determined she would need a dozen stitches. "That's a nasty gash. How did you get it?"

"I was mugged. As I was running away, I was shoved and hit the curb. Cut my forehead, I think the blood scared the guy away."

Frowning, the nurse nodded. "Let's get you numbed up and then sutured. I'm also going to ask the doctor to check in on you because you might have a concussion. Have you ever had a head injury before?"

"I had a bad fall five years ago and suffered a grade-three concussion."

"Okay, the doctor might order an MRI."

Amber closed her eyes. "Sure. Fine."

The nurse returned within a few minutes with a supply tray. She numbed the wound and then stitched up the gash. A doctor appeared and ordered an MRI and she was then wheeled away.

Georgia made her way to a breakroom and poured herself a cup of coffee. She checked her phone and discovered she had a few missed calls. At the top of the list was Jake Bishop. This time, she dialed his number.

"Where are you? You haven't answered your phone in hours," he said.

"Amber was mugged. She split her head open and needed stitches. I drove her to the hospital."

"Why did she call you?"

She shoved a stray curl from her eyes. "She didn't have anyone else."

"She's staying with her mother," he countered. "Nine-one-one works."

"Mom is MIA and Amber was afraid the rescue crew would call the cops, and she doesn't want to deal with more cops."

"Is that really smart, Georgia? Amber is part of an active investigation."

"Shit, Jake. She didn't have anyone." She walked down the hallway out of the breakroom toward the sliding glass doors. The sun hovered at the lip of the horizon ready to rise and leaking pinks and reds into the waning night sky. "I couldn't exactly tell her to take a cab."

"Why not?"

She sipped her coffee, which tasted bitter. "Because I'm a nice person, remember?"

"You're a soft touch, Georgia."

A shiver climbed up her spine. She had the sense someone was watching her, and on reflex, hesitated as she scanned the lot. She saw no one.

"Are you there?"

"Yeah, I'm here."

"When does Amber leave?"

"They're talking about admitting her. Once I know, I'll leave." Her stomach grumbled, reminding her she'd not eaten a decent meal in a while. "So, why are you in such a rush to talk to me?"

"Just checking in."

"Why?"

"I'm asking myself that question right now. Mainly, I wanted to make sure Hal didn't return."

She turned and moved back into the hospital, taking comfort from the bright lights and the hum of conversation. "Aw, that's sweet. How did it go with the surveillance tapes?"

Silence and then a frustrated sigh. "I think we spotted our guy on surveillance tape buying rope eight days ago. But he kept his head ducked and his face turned as if he expected cameras."

"Smart guy."

"I'm smarter."

He stood outside the hospital waiting for the nurse to leave Amber's room. He thought about the gash in her head and all the blood that had streamed down her face when he'd seen her fall. She'd cried out in pain but had kept her cool. He was glad she only required some stitches. At one point, he feared all the blood loss would kill her.

When he saw the redheaded cop leave just after sunrise, he knew Amber was stable and resting. He reached for his phone, needing to call Amber. He dialed her number, but she didn't answer.

He shoved the cell in his pocket, debating about

whether he could sneak inside and visit her just for a moment. He wouldn't stay long, he couldn't.

Moving inside the double doors he was nearly to the elevator when he saw the uniformed cop standing guard. Shit. He needed to stay out of sight. And when Amber got out of the hospital he would find her. One way or another, they would be together. She owed him that much after all he'd done for her.

# CHAPTER TWELVE

*Friday, October 6, 9:00 A.M.*

When Jake arrived at the Marlowe residence, a truck was parked at the top of the driveway. The sign on the side read PIPER LANDSCAPING. Two gardeners armed with rakes were collecting the leaves that had fallen over the last couple of days while a third bagged a neat pile.

Jake hurried up the steps and rang the bell. Footsteps sounded and the door opened to the housekeeper who had answered the door the other day for him. Calmly, she escorted him into the study and promised to get Mr. Marlowe right away. He paced the floor, his hands in his pockets as he thought about what he was going to say to Marlowe. He did not like the man, but the news he had to deliver would cut in a very cruel way. No one deserved that kind of pain.

"Detective Bishop," Marlowe said from the door.

Jake turned to find Marlowe dressed in black slacks, a black turtle neck, and loafers. He wore a large silver watch on his wrist and his salt-and-pepper hair, neatly brushed back, accentuated lines that looked deeper than they had just days ago.

"You have news for me?" Marlowe asked.

"Yes, sir. I spoke to the medical examiner."

"She wouldn't give me details about my son's death. She said it had to come from you. Part of the investigation."

"Yes, sir. We're keeping a tight control on the news we release."

"I am his father."

"Yes, sir. That's why I'm here to give you a report."

This time Marlowe didn't walk to the sideboard and fill a glass with bourbon. Instead, he stood tall and rigid. "How did my boy die?"

"There was a single gunshot wound to his head behind the left temple."

"Shot. In the head." Marlowe crossed the room and sat on the plush leather sofa. He leaned forward and buried his face in his hands. He sat, breathing in and out as he struggled to control the pain from this latest one-two punch.

Finally, Marlowe drew in a breath and rose. "How did Bethany die?"

"She was stabbed."

"Jesus." He shook his head. "Do you have any idea who shot my boy?"

Jake cleared his throat, his gaze unwavering. "We're theorizing that he shot himself."

Dark eyes flared. "That's bullshit. My boy wouldn't kill himself. He had everything to live for."

"He was found in a rear chamber of the cave next to Bethany's body. The cave was walled up. The scene was staged to look like a murder/suicide."

"No!" He pointed a finger at Jake. "My boy didn't kill that girl and then himself. That is just wrong."

"I agree. The original scene was staged that way, but with the discovery of the latest victim, we realize we're dealing with a killer."

"Where the hell is Amber in all this? That bitch could have killed them both and made it look like a murder/suicide."

"Why would she do something like that?"

Marlowe stiffened. "The girl is not what she seems."

"How so?"

He shook his head. "She's beautiful. Charming. Smart."

"And?"

He hesitated, as if choosing his words carefully. "She's a manipulator. She likes to hurt people."

"She sustained a very nasty fall in the woods that day. Grade-three concussion and a fracture of the arm. The evidence suggests that she saw something horrible and started running and fell."

"And you think that horrible thing absolves her of the death of Mike and Bethany?"

"She could have been running for her life that day. She might have seen something terrible in those woods. She was attacked just last night."

"Really?"

"Where were you?"

"Here." He shook his head. "Do not be fooled by her, detective. You want a killer, go after her."

Jake flexed his fingers. "This investigation is still very much open and I have more people to interview. The reason I stopped by today was to deliver this information in person. I will get to the bottom of this, but I need to go."

Marlowe's jaw set in a hard line. "Don't hurt my boy any more, detective. You've been warned."

Jake turned, moving toward the front door. The sound of the older man's weeping leaked out from the study and followed him out the front door.

Jake drove straight to St. Vincent after his visit with Marlowe. As he got out of his car and climbed the steps, his eyes itched from fatigue and too many hours of staring at a computer screen last night. Even the caffeine was losing its punch. Still, it had been worth it. He spotted Elisa on surveillance camera, which was mounted in a shoe store and shot through the main display window. Elisa paused in front of the window to admire a pair of heels. Closer inspection revealed a fuzzy image of their suspect across the street, stopping to stare at her. That had been this past Wednesday, September 27.

Jake parked in front of the school, pausing to stare at the white columns and the neatly manicured lawn void of a stray stick or leaf. A collection of tall planters held vibrant yellow flowers with ivy cascading over the sides. Gilded letters spelled out ST. VINCENT on a sign attached to two stone columns surrounded by a thick bed of ivy. This was your typical school for rich kids.

Amber had been one of the few exceptions, earning a scholarship from the business community at the age of sixteen by wowing school officials with PSAT scores and an essay. Her scores, along with the public relations they would milk from offering scholarships to disadvantaged kids, were a win-win for both sides.

He climbed the wide marble stairs, wondering what it would have been like for a kid like Amber to come here. Despite her intelligence, she was pegged an outsider from day one. Making friends would have been a challenge. Hell, he was twenty-eight when he moved to Nashville and found himself on the outside trying to crack the police department culture that heavily favored locals. Standing on the outside looking in was not an enviable position to be in, but he was up to the challenge. For all his life he was the guy from the neighborhood. The guy who knew everyone. The guy that naturally maneuvered the ins and outs of the town. Cops respected him. Even the guys in the mob had a measure of respect for him because they knew he always did what he promised. He was discrete.

But that had been in Boston. In Nashville, no matter how long he lived here, he'd always be the abrasive carpetbagger from up north. But as much as he disliked his outcast status, it was better than the memories and the sense of loss he had felt back home.

He didn't pretend to understand the mind of a teen girl, but he could guess she'd have wanted to fit into the crowd. To blend. Mix. Blend. Isn't that what all teens really wanted? Acceptance.

He pushed through the large, polished lacquered double doors that fed into a black-and-white tiled entryway. He heard the distant hum of conversations as he studied a large trophy case filled with glittering gold and silver cups. Tennis. Soccer. Football. You name the sport and some student had won an award.

He was a baseball guy. Had played it nonstop as a

kid. He tried out and made the high school team, but he
blew his chances of playing when he got into a pissing
match with the coach after complaining about his lack
of playing time. He argued he was one of the best hit-
ters on the team and that the old man always gave pref-
erence to a couple of senior players. Jake's teenage
brain didn't know how to put the brakes on his mouth or
his temper. He said if he could not play, he would quit.
The old man didn't argue and Jake sat on the bench for
the remaining games. By the end of the season, he
made good on his challenge. Stupid.

Jake turned from the trophy case, wondering if his
life would be any different if he'd had better control of
his temper. Though he sometimes looked back with
more than one or two regrets, he was old enough now
to accept that sometimes life delivered a shit sandwich
and expected you to eat it. All of it.

He moved down the hallway toward a set of doors
marked OFFICE and went inside. Sitting in a bank of
chairs were a couple of boys. Collars askew, both had
dirt stains on pressed white shirts. Yeah, you could
dress a rich teen boy up, but that didn't mean they were
any less boneheaded than a poor kid.

Jake pulled his badge from his belt and caught the
attention of a tall, sour-faced woman standing behind
the counter. She was filling out a tardy slip for a young
girl with braids and wearing a plaid skirt and a white
shirt. The girl politely thanked the woman, and grabbing the note, turned to leave. She glanced quickly at
Jake, stopped, stared for a beat or two and then hurried
on her way. A homicide detective fit as well in a posh
school as did Amber five years ago.

The woman behind the counter was in her late fifties.

She tied her gray wavy hair back in a short ponytail and perched thick glasses on a wide-set nose. A white shirt drained what little color she had from her pale face.

"May I help you?" Her gaze flickered to his badge as she looked more intrigued than worried.

"Detective Jake Bishop. I'm with the Nashville Homicide Department. I have an appointment with Principal Byrd."

She stacked the pile of pink slips until the edges were again sharp and neat. "I'll get him. Please wait a minute."

"Thanks."

Jake tucked his badge back on his belt and turned toward a bulletin board covered with notices about a fall dance, yearbook pictures, and football games. As he shifted, he noticed the two scuffed-up boys staring at him. He didn't smile, instead choosing to stare until they looked away. "Keep your nose clean. You don't want me showing up at your door."

The boys sat straighter, blanching, as Jake turned to the sound of footsteps and the sound of his name. "Detective Bishop."

The principal, Dave Byrd, was a tall lean man with dark hair. He wore dark pants, a white shirt, and a sweater vest that didn't quite hide the belly paunch. Late thirties, he moved easily as he extended a hand to Jake.

Jake admired the man's firm handshake. "Thanks for seeing me."

"Sure. Come on back to my office." The principal turned to the boys. "Patrick and Ryan. Go back to your classrooms. No more trouble."

"Yes, sir."

As the principal closed the door to his office he grinned. "They're good boys, but they got into a scuffle at assembly this morning. Uncharacteristic enough that I've decided not to call their parents, though I've not told them."

Jake ran his fingers along his tie, making sure it was straight. "In my day, fights boiled down to pride or a girl."

"That hasn't changed a bit. A cute girl can make smart boys lose whatever common sense they've managed to scrape together."

Jake took a seat while scanning the room's wood paneled walls covered with a few fancy-looking diplomas and pictures of the principal at various stages of his career. Jake earned his college degree going to school at night and weekends in Boston. The first to earn a degree in his family, he framed the diploma in a nice cherry frame with special acid free matting. It was a keeper and hung in the second bedroom of his house that was set up as a den. He often paused to look at it because it reminded him he was one stubborn bastard.

"I pulled the records of Amber Ryder, Bethany Reed, and Mike Marlowe. I've spent the last hour reading through them to familiarize myself with their time at the school. I've been here only a year, so I never knew any of them. I did locate a faculty member who was here during that time and she's available to speak to you. She should be here any minute."

Jake sat back, resting his ankle on his knee. "That's great. So did anything jump out at you when you read the files?"

"Amber was the smartest of the three by far. As I mentioned on the phone, her test results were off the charts. She did fairly well in classes, low As and a few high Bs, but all her teachers believed she could have done better. She didn't fully apply herself." He flipped a page. "She was on the chess team. She did well enough to lead the school to the semifinals."

"She didn't win?"

"Close. Her coach thought she could have won it, but she made a few strategic mistakes at the end that cost her the match."

"If I had a nickel for every time I heard that as a teenager."

"Getting kids to focus and see the big picture is a constant struggle."

"Did she get into trouble?"

"No. She was never a discipline problem, or at least, she wasn't caught."

"Why do you say that?"

He leaned forward, threading his fingers together. "The smart ones rarely get caught."

"Did she do anything to raise a red flag?"

"There's nothing in her file." He flipped through the pages.

"What about the other kids?"

"Bethany was a model student. No trouble. Good grades. No clubs. She kept to herself. Her interview skills needed work. In fact, she was denied early admission to a few colleges because she did so poorly on the interview."

"I understand she and Amber were friends."

"That, I don't know. And Mike played football. Mike did get himself into some trouble his junior year. It involved a prank. He brought a couple dozen chickens to school and released them at lunchtime. Caused quite a stir. Teachers still talk about it today. According to the file, his father came by the school and paid for all the damages. He also made a sizable contribution to the school shortly after. No charges were filed."

"No record to get in the way of his college entrance chances."

"None. He was also the star quarterback on the football team. Led the school to a couple of big victories his junior year. He played only four games his senior year before he disappeared." The principal shook his head. "We're all still processing what you told me on the phone this morning."

The principal's phone buzzed and he picked it up. "Great. Send her in." Hanging up, he rose. "That's Mrs. Garfield. She teaches English and knew all three kids. She might be of help."

"Excellent." Jake rose as the door opened to a woman in her early forties. Short black hair, sturdy build, and a skirt and jacket created the impression of a corporate executive rather than a private school teacher.

She held out a manicured hand as the principal made the introductions. "We're all so sorry to hear about the grim discovery. What can I do to help?"

"Gathering background on the victims right now," Jake said. "If you can, tell me what you know about Amber, Mike, and Bethany." He indicated for her to take the seat next to his and when she did, the men took their seats.

She folded her arms. "They were about as different as three kids could be. I was surprised when the science teacher told me they were working together. They were an unlikely group."

"Why's that?" Jake asked.

"To put it bluntly, you had a scholarship kid, a nerd, and a jock. Most kids at this age stay in their cliques."

"What can you tell me about Amber?"

"She was from a different world as far as these kids were concerned. Those who have big money live in a different world than the average person. We wear school uniforms at St. Vincent, but a glance at the jewelry, backpacks, shoes, watches, or the cars they drive tells everyone who has what and how much. A pecking order. Though some of the students might have liked her, none really accepted her."

"What did you think about Amber?"

"I liked her," Mrs. Garfield said, crossing her legs. "She wanted to be accepted, even if it appeared she didn't seem to care. It mattered a lot to her. A lot."

"Did she date anyone?" Jake asked.

"She dated quite a few boys. She was growing into a striking young woman, and she liked the attention she received from them. It empowered her. I cautioned her once about being careful, but she laughed and said she knew exactly what she was doing."

"What about Mike Marlowe? They hook up?"

"I saw them a couple of times. Kissing." She plucked a stray string from her hem. "I hear she's back in town."

"She was mugged last night. Apparently, someone jumped her and she struck her head hard against a curb. She needed a dozen stitches, but she'll survive."

Mrs. Garfield's gaze softened with sadness. "Does anyone know she's back? There were many who didn't appreciate her being the lone survivor."

"I'm not sure who she's told. She's staying with her mother. What about Mike? Those two hang out besides the kissing?"

"Not in school from what I could see. But I heard students talking about seeing Amber and Mike together around town."

"Why not hang out at school?"

"I don't know."

"Mike was a leader in the school?"

"Mike was a jock but not a leader. His father wanted the world to think he was smart and going places, but I wasn't so sure. Short temper, mediocre intelligence, and a poor work ethic."

"What about the kids' parents? Know any of them?"

"I met Mike's father once and worked with his mother on several committees. Mrs. Marlowe was dead by Mike's freshman year."

Jake rummaged through the facts he'd absorbed from Georgia's synopsis. "Cancer, from what I understand."

She hesitated. "She did have cancer, but I thought it was the fall."

"What fall?" There was no mention of a fall anywhere. Jake would have remembered that detail.

"As I understand it, her medications made her dizzy and she fell down a flight of stairs in their home. She didn't die immediately, but the trauma weakened her. She passed a week later. Mike was really rattled about it and understandably missed two weeks of school."

"What else can you tell me about Mrs. Marlowe?"

"A lovely woman. Not very attractive in the classic sense but she made the best of what she had."

No surprise that Marlowe might have married his

wife for her money. It certainly wasn't against the law. "So, we have three unlikely kids headed into the park to do a science project. These kids have anyone that didn't like them enough to track them into the woods?"

"Mike made a few enemies," she said. "He was a bully. Bethany went unnoticed, by and large. And there were plenty that didn't like Amber because she wasn't one of them." She adjusted her glasses. "But it's one thing to not like someone, quite another to kill."

"Mike had a very good friend, Tim Taylor. What do you remember about him?"

"Tim was always quite the charmer. He could sweet talk his way out of any situation." She adjusted her glasses. "I always knew he was manipulating me when he asked for an extension on a project, but he was so sweet and likable that I didn't mind."

"He date anyone?"

"He had a girlfriend or two but nothing serious."

"He and Amber get along?"

"I don't know about that. I see a lot in the classroom, but not everything."

"What did you think of Amber's story after she was found in the woods?" Jake asked.

"I believed her," she said without hesitation. "She was basically a good kid, and in time would have found her way to a successful life. She didn't ask for this trouble. It found her. When it became clear returning to school would not work for her, I offered to help her with her studies at home."

"How'd she do?"

"Great. Ten percent of our students don't need teachers because they're so smart. She was one of the ten percent."

"You don't think she could have killed Bethany or Mike?"

She shook her head, her lips flattening into a grim line. "The cops asked me that question several times five years ago, and my answer remains the same. Amber did not kill those kids. She was poor, not evil."

# CHAPTER THIRTEEN

*Friday, October 6, 2:00 P.M.*

For observation purposes, Amber rested in her hospital bed, her head and shoulder aching from the fall. She shifted her weight, searching for a more comfortable position.

The doctor determined she had a mild concussion and nurses were ordered to monitor her vitals. She drifted in and out of sleep. Time drifted and the past and present blurred. One minute  she was dreaming of the woods. Heart pumping, laughing, she was quizzing Bethany about the names of plants in the woods, as they hiked the long path in Percy Warner Park. Mike was teasing them both, tossing leaves at them and complaining about how slowly they walked. Amber, Mike, and Bethany had no worries.

The dream shifted, the laughter silenced, and the lightness of the day seemed to dim.

She and Mike were alone, hidden by a cluster of trees. Bethany had wandered off to collect samples. Amber flashed a sly grin and slowly dropped to her knees in front of Mike. His eyes darkened with desire as she reached for his belt and slowly unbuckled it.

As she reached for his erection, he threaded his fingers through her hair and sucked in a breath as her mouth wrapped around the tip of his penis.

Footsteps sounded in the woods, followed by the rustle of leaves and the snap of twigs. A shadow darkened over them but Mike, his eyes closed and his senses rattled, didn't notice. And then the tip of a gun barrel pressed against Mike's temple. The gun fired. Blood dripped down the side of his face. His body collapsed and he fell to the ground like a ragdoll.

"Mike!" Amber yelled clutching the sheets of her hospital bed and staring at the pale specter of Mike. Sweat moistened her brow and her hands trembled as she tried to shake off the confusion. "I didn't mean it."

"You selfish bitch," he whispered, as he leaned toward her. "Why the fuck did you do it?"

"Go away! Leave me alone. You're dead!"

Amber started awake, her heart racing as her gaze darted around the hospital room. Sweat dripped from her forehead. Shadows danced on the walls, bathing it all in darkness. Seconds passed before clarity pushed through the haze to take control of her mind. She was in the hospital. Safe. She raised her fingers to her temple and felt the smooth bandage on her head.

She reached for the saline IV in her arm and yanked it free, fearing suddenly that it was laced with drugs designed to rob her of the control so very necessary for her survival.

She had to get out of here. Had to get free.

A door opened and a figure appeared in the sliver of

light now flooding the dimly lit room. Amber teetered between panic and relief. Who was there? Had they heard her talking in her sleep?

A nurse in scrubs stepped from the shadows. A name badge pinned to her pocket read JULIA and a stethoscope was draped around her neck. She moved into the room and inspected the IV's injection point in Amber's arm. "Ms. Ryder, are you all right? Why did you pull your IV out?"

"It makes my brain fuzzy." She ran a shaking hand through her hair. "I feel too out of control."

"The IV doesn't make you fuzzy. It's just saline. You have a head injury. That's why you're confused. If you stay hydrated, you'll feel better." The nurse frowned at the trickle of blood streaming down Amber's arm.

"I don't want any more."

"You took a nasty fall. Your head has to be pounding." Julia fumbled in her front pocket for a fresh Band-Aid and opened it. Carefully, she placed it over the hole left by the IV needle.

Amber drew her arm back, curling it up. "I don't care about hydration. I don't want anything else."

The nurse rolled up the IV tube. "You look upset. Are you okay?"

"I think I had a dream."

"I heard you fussing and carrying on as I came down the hallway." The nurse reached for Amber's slim wrist and pressed her first two fingers against a racing pulse. "Your heart's beating a mile a minute."

In the dream, the last five years had vanished and she found herself back in the woods. Mike stood before her, half naked and wanting, his eyes glazed with pleasure when she stroked him. "I usually don't dream. It's not like me to freak out."

The nurse inspected the spot where the IV had been. The vein was bruised and marked where Amber's fingernails had scraped the skin. "An assault can be very traumatic. Things just kind of short circuit for a bit."

She moistened dry lips. "Can I have some water? Please."

"Sure you can." The nurse moved to the bedside table and poured a cup from a plastic pitcher marked with the name RYDER.

Amber accepted the water and gratefully drank. Cool liquid soothed her parched throat and eased the anxiety stalking her in the dream. Realizing the nurse was watching her, she offered a tentative and embarrassed smile. "Sorry to cause such a fuss."

"Honey, that's why I'm here. Don't you worry about it." She took the cup back. "Do you want some more?"

"No, I'm fine. Thank you." She relaxed back against the pillows, willing her racing thoughts to calm. Mike was not alive. He was dead, his body reduced to bones. "Did I say anything while I was dreaming?"

"You were shouting at Mike. You told him to leave you alone."

She twisted the hospital band around her slim wrist. "I said the name Mike? You're sure?"

"Very sure." She tugged the sheet up so that it covered Amber's chest. "It was on the news today about those two other children. To be found dead after all this time. So sad."

Aware of the woman's curious gaze, she offered a relaxed, if not apologetic, smile. "The police are hoping that I'll remember what happened in the woods. Maybe my memory is coming back."

The nurse patted Amber on the arm. "The brain heals at its own pace. Never know when you'll have a breakthrough."

"Let's hope."

Even now, as she tried to recall the dream, it faded farther and farther out of reach into the mist. "Did I say anything else other than Mike?"

"You didn't say anything else about Mike, but I could hear the panic in your voice. You were definitely afraid." She leaned in a fraction. "Were you afraid of Mike?"

Amber met her gaze, seeing the interest and curiosity. She dragged a trembling hand through her hair. "We were friends in high school. I was never afraid of him in school. But I don't know about that day."

Brown eyes deepened with concern. "Well, you sure were afraid of him in this dream. Terrified is a better word."

She drew back, making herself look small. "Mike wouldn't have hurt me. He was my friend."

"You sure sounded afraid of him."

"Maybe it was just a dream. Maybe it didn't mean anything." She steadied her smile. "What time is it?"

"Oh, it's after lunchtime. A little after two.

"I slept the morning away?"

"Very natural you'd sleep, honey."

Amber liked the way the nurse called her honey. She felt just a little nurtured and loved.

"I think that redheaded gal that brought you in said she called your mama."

"Georgia Morgan."

"That's right. She's a tough gal. Wouldn't leave until she knew you were taken care of."

"Yeah. She really came through for me last night. I'd like to call her."

A brow arched. "Right now we're having quiet hours. No calls in or out until three."

"Why can't I call her?"

"You can in a little bit. We have this time to make sure our patients rest. But as soon as it's three, I'll let you call out."

Amber had always found the world irritating. This policy made no sense to her. But right now it was better to accept this small inconvenience. "Okay."

"Now, let me get you a fresh IV. You're skin and bone and it wouldn't hurt for you to have another bag."

"No drugs."

"No drugs. I'll be back. Can I get you a pudding cup or fruit?"

"A pudding cup would be nice. Thank you."

She barely closed her eyes when she heard her door open. Thinking it was the nurse, she didn't bother to look until an odd sensation tingled at the back of her skull. Slowly, she opened her eyes.

Standing at the base of her bed was Dalton Marlowe. His hands fisted at his side, his sour face was pulled tight in a frown.

Instead of being afraid, she found herself studying him. The last five years had aged him. The dark hair was now more salt than pepper and the lines around his mouth and eyes had deepened. He had put on just a little weight and his once trim face had softened. He still dressed impeccably. His shirt was starched, Windsor knot tie, and a hand-tailored dark suit.

She pushed herself up into a sitting position, refusing to straighten her open gown that showed a sliver of her breast. "*Mr*. Marlowe."

He tapped his thumb against his thigh. "I heard you were back in town, but I didn't quite believe it."

Brushing back a strand of hair, her face remained blank with no hint of reaction. "What did you use to say about me? I'm a bad penny that just keeps showing up? Well, here I am again." She shifted, showing more of her breast.

The expensive cologne swirled around him just as it had five years ago. "Why are you back?"

Instead of answering his question, she said, "The cops called me. They opened this can of worms."

"A call for information is not a reason to come seven hundred miles. You're here for your own agenda."

She lifted her chin a fraction to prove to him she wasn't street trash to be ignored. "Did you hear I was mugged?"

"You sure it was random? You made a lot of enemies in this town."

"And very intimate friends, too. Did you send someone to rough me up so I would leave town? A stunt like that would be your style. You always liked it rough."

His cheeks flushed slightly under his salon tan as he tapped an impatient finger against the smooth, Italian leather belt. "You've come back to taunt us, haven't you? You became bored, didn't you? Real life was too dull, so you came back to Nashville to stir things up until your own demented desires are satisfied."

Something inside her bristled. From the first day he laid eyes on her, he thought of her as trash. Funny how marrying money could make a man forget humble roots. "Did you also hear I've been receiving threatening texts? Did you send those as well?"

Eyes narrowed. "If there were threats, you made them up."

"The threats were real. But I'm not going to argue with you. I've moved on with my life. I'm happy. Places like Nashville and people like you no longer bring me happiness. I was doing fine until the texts began to arrive and then that cop called."

Her voice seemed to buzz past him like annoying flies. "The cops will figure you out," he said. "They'll put it all together. There won't be a lie standing at the end."

She studied the man's face, searching for even the slightest hint of softness. There was a time when she wanted him to like her. How many times did she help his simpleton son with his homework hoping to have this man toss her a kind word? If he could have accepted her, then so would the others.

But he never tossed her anything. He ignored her as if she weren't deserving of his attention. He and all the kids at that damn private high school didn't want her in their world. None of them really wanted her beyond her status as either a poster child for the disadvantaged, her SAT scores or her stunning looks. *Take your crumbs, Amber. Be grateful we're allowing you in our world. Mind your manners or we'll toss you back onto the East Nashville heap where we found you.*

Amber was better than all of them. They knew it, but they would never admit it.

Suddenly, she felt very weary. This was an old fight that no longer interested her. She had other plans. The people in the isolated world of the rich didn't matter.

"There is nothing to figure out, Mr. Marlowe. I came back to help the cops solve this case and maybe figure out who's sending me threatening texts. At least now you know what happened to Mike."

He flinched as if she had struck him. "What the hell did you do to my boy in those damned woods?"

She smiled innocently. "I didn't do anything. I was a victim."

"You've been a predator since the day you walked into our lives."

She studied the tension radiating from his attractive gray eyes. It felt good to know she could still unnerve him. "People might have a different take on all this if they knew more about our relationship."

He swallowed as if his throat were raw. "You are sick."

Ah, was that a bit of panic in his voice? "Perhaps, but I see you as the pretender. Your control of your late wife's money is all that separates you from me. Tell me, what happens to the money now that we know Mike can't inherit it? Isn't there some kind of charitable trust? Or did you get your attorneys to break it?"

Another wince on his angled face told her that her words cut him. "The cops are going to keep digging," Amber said. "You'll see to that. But if you press them to dig too deep, there's no telling what you'll find."

He gritted his teeth. "You know what happened to Mike, don't you? He hung on every one of your words. Mike followed you like a puppy . . . worshipped that fucking body of yours."

She moistened her lips, pulling back her shoulders so that her breasts strained against her hospital gown. "I don't know what happened to Mike, Mr. Marlowe.

My last memory of him is days before we went into the woods. Know what we were doing?"

"I don't care."

"Fucking," she whispered. "We were fucking."

"You're a cancer. A goddamned cancer."

"Mike and I were close. I loved him." She met his gaze as she took a moment to study him. "He was so sweet to me. We could talk. Never argued. We shared so many secrets. Some were even about you."

Marlowe's jaw tightened. "You ever tell him about us?"

She touched her fingertips to her lips as if she remembered one of Mike's kisses. "Friends don't keep secrets. They share everything."

He leaned toward her and she suspected he would punch her in the face if he could get away with it. Amber fed on his anger and frustration.

"Who do you think killed Bethany and Mike?" she asked.

Fingers clenched into fists.

Her gaze held his in an iron grip. "You had a good reason to kill Bethany."

His head cocked as if assessing an opponent in a boxing ring. "Why the hell would I want to hurt that damn geek kid, she was harmless."

"Mike needed the grades to stay on the football team. You and I both know he cheated and we both know Bethany helped him cheat. Without football, he'd have lost any shot at anything but a second-tier college. All your plans for him would have been ruined."

He tugged at a gold cufflink monogrammed with an M. "After five years of hell, none of that really matters."

"When Bethany was alive, she was big trouble for you and Mike. She was going to tell unless Mike got her into his inner circle of friends."

The veins in his neck rose like corded strips of rawhide as he struggled to corral his words. "You're twisting things, just like you always did."

"I'm not twisting anything. You hated Bethany. I know that." Her words raked over his nerves.

"I didn't even know her."

"Oh, you knew Bethany Reed. She was a mousy little thing. She was so much like your weak little wife who threw herself down the stairs so she could get away from you."

He glanced toward the door and when he was sure it was closed he said, "If there is anyone I ever wanted to kill, it was you."

The words jabbed and sliced. "It would be like you to find new ways to torture me. Sending texts. Stirring up the past when you knew I'd gotten on with my life. I know you missed me."

"You're a cruel young woman."

She leaned forward a fraction. "You left out beautiful, *Mr.* Marlowe."

"You're a bitch."

She laughed, knowing she was a burr under his skin. "Get out of my room, or I'm calling security."

He studied her a moment and then, as always, considered the bigger picture. He did not need to be escorted out of the hospital room. His image was still his pride and joy, his fragile mantle of success. "This isn't over."

"I hope not. I'd like to see you again."

                              *   *   *

Georgia waved to the nurses as she approached Amber's room where she spotted a plump older woman hovering by the door. Her dress was plain and simple and her brown shoes sensible. She held a vase filled with sunflowers.

The woman raised her hand to knock on Amber's partially opened door, hesitated, and then turned to leave.

"Can I help you?" Georgia asked.

The woman glanced at her. "No, I'm fine."

"Are you here to see Amber Ryder?"

The woman's eyes sparked with knowing and Georgia recognized the woman from her photos in her cold case files. She was Emma Reed, Bethany's mother. "I wanted to see her. Talk to her. But now I think this might not be a good time."

"You're Mrs. Reed, aren't you? Bethany's mother."

Dark eyes watered. "Yes. How did you know?"

"I'm Georgia Morgan. I work in the Forensic Department with the Nashville Police Department." *I found your daughter.* "I'm working her case."

She reached out and took Georgia's hand, choking back tears. "You're the one who found her, aren't you?"

"Yes." She always treaded carefully with the victim's family.

Mrs. Reed's fingers tightened on the vase. "Thank you for helping to bring my daughter home. Knowing is terrible, but not knowing is unbearable. At least I know she's with her father now and at peace."

She flipped through an invisible rolodex of nice words, wishing she had better people skills like Jake.

Damn, how did he make people feel like he cared? "I'm sorry for your loss."

Mrs. Reed shook her head. "I clung to hope for a long, long time. And then, after my husband died, I just stopped. It's been years since I expected good news."

Georgia rummaged for more words that would ease this moment but realized saying nothing was better. "You should go in and see Amber. She'd like to see you. She said you were kind to her."

Dull eyes brightened. "She said that? I always liked her. She was a true friend to Bethany. Not everyone saw Bethany the same way. She was an awkward girl who liked books and microscopes better than makeup and boys. But Amber showed her respect and compassion."

Before entering, Mrs. Reed hesitated. "I heard she was mugged."

"Yes. A dozen stitches to her head, but she'll be fine. No lasting damage from the fall."

"Do you think it was random? There were plenty of people that didn't like her."

"I don't know. It all happened so fast. She didn't get a good look at the guy."

Her grip tightened on Georgia's arm. "Sweetheart, you're going in, too? It's been so long for Amber and me, it might be best if we had someone else in the room to smooth the waters."

"Sure, I'll come inside."

"Thank you." She released her grip and the breath she was holding. "I almost lost my nerve and left without seeing her."

As they turned to the door, a man pushed out of

Amber's room. Tall with salt-and-pepper hair, his anger was etched deeply into his face.

"Dalton," Mrs. Reed said.

Hearing his name, the man stopped. "Emma. What are you doing here?"

"I came to see Amber."

He glanced toward the bright yellow flowers, blooming brightly as small sunbursts. "Those are for her?"

"They are." She straightened her shoulders as if she mentally dug in her heels. Puzzled, she searched for the cause of Dalton's anger.

"You always defended her," he said. "I never understood what you saw in her."

Mrs. Reed gently shook her head. "She was a young girl caught in a bad situation. None of what happened was her fault."

He shoved his hand in his pocket and rattled his change. "You always were an optimist, weren't you, Emma?"

"Not really, Dalton." Her tone had turned imperious, as if she wanted to remind him he'd not come from their world. "I see more than most realize."

Eyes narrowing, he leaned toward her a fraction as if wanting to remind her of his rise to his current status. "Well, at least you have your answers now. At least you know where to find Bethany."

"And you have yours."

"Not even close."

"Dalton, we need to talk about the arrangements for our children. I thought maybe we could honor them in a memorial service together."

He glanced back toward Amber's door. "I'm not so sure."

"I know how hard this is, Dalton. I know. Think about what I'm offering, and we'll talk later."

He drew in a deep breath and released it. "I can't discuss this now."

Georgia watched the man stalk off, her attention immediately turning to Emma. "He really doesn't like Amber."

"He never did. He never said anything in front of me, of course, but I caught the way he used to look at her." Distaste wrinkled her face.

"Was it sexual?" Georgia asked.

"Yes. His attention struck me as lurid and creepy. It was no secret that Dalton played around and liked to look at the young pretty girls. His wife was a lovely woman but not beautiful like Amber."

"You said he was drawn to her at first. Did something change?"

"Yes. I don't know the specifics, but it did as quickly as you'd shut off a light. Perhaps it had to do with his wife dying after her fall. Whatever happened between Dalton and Amber, it wasn't good. At that last football game a week before they all . . . left us . . . I saw Dalton glaring at Amber. He looked at her as if she revolted him."

"Why would she revolt him?"

"I've no idea. I asked Bethany once, but she seemed surprised by the question." Mention of her daughter's name doused her annoyance with sadness. "Bethany was an idealist. It never would have occurred to her that someone like Dalton would want to sleep with a friend of hers."

Older men had affairs with high school girls. Dalton wouldn't have been the first. And a girl like Amber, desperate for acceptance, might have mistaken lust for understanding and love. "Let's go check on Amber."

Mrs. Reed nodded, producing a smile that didn't quite touch her eyes. "Sure. But you go first. I just need one more quick second to collect myself."

"You're coming in, right?"

She smiled. "Of course, dear."

"Don't run off."

"I won't."

Georgia pushed into the room and found Amber in her bed, sitting straight up, her fists balled so tightly her knuckles were white. "Everything all right?"

Amber's gaze locked on Georgia as she seemed to take a mental hold of herself, releasing her anger with a breath. She unfurled her fingers and straightened her hospital gown. "I'm fine."

"I saw Dalton Marlowe outside," Georgia said. "He looked upset. What happened?"

Amber leaned back against the pillows, her pale skin a close match to the pillow's shade. "It's the same old thing. He's blaming me for Mike's problems."

"What kind of problems?" Georgia asked.

As she sighed, it seemed the fire dimmed with her breath. "He always thought I was bad for Mike."

"How so? Did you two date?"

"Sorta. Mike and I messed around a little, but he wanted more than I was willing to give. I stayed friends with Mike, but Mr. Marlowe continued to assume I was a gold digger."

"I thought the money passed to Mike's dad," Georgia said.

"Sure, that was true at first, but the assets pass to Mike on his twenty-third birthday."

"That had to sting," Georgia said.

Amber's expression remained neutral. "They didn't have a happy marriage. She was a controlling woman who got her own way no matter the cost. Her dying was almost a relief to Mike and Dalton."

"Did anything happen the day she fell down the stairs?"

"Like what?"

"A fight, maybe between Mrs. Marlowe and her husband or son?"

"Those three were always fighting. Either one could have given her a shove in a moment of anger." She shook her head. "That sounds awful. Mr. Marlowe is cold but he doesn't have the stomach for murder."

There was a soft knock at the door and Mrs. Reed appeared. "Amber."

Amber studied Mrs. Reed and then her eyes filled with tears. She sat forward and stretched out her hand. "Mrs. Reed, I'm so sorry."

Mrs. Reed came to her, set the flowers on the nightstand, and hugged the young girl. Both women wept as they clung to each other.

"I'm so glad you're back in town," Mrs. Reed said as she pulled back and wiped tears from her cheeks. "Makes sense Bethany would be found as soon as you returned. She loved being with you so much."

Amber dabbed red-rimmed eyes with trembling fingertips. "I'm so sorry. She's really gone now."

"Honey, I know this has been hard for you." She leaned forward and gently wiped Amber's tears. "And now you're all grown up. That's so hard to believe."

Amber's eyes again filled with tears. "Bethany was

my best friend. Not a day goes by that I don't think about her."

Mrs. Reed stood very still for a moment and then hugged Amber close. "Honey, that's so sweet. You don't know what that means to me."

Georgia stepped back, realizing that it was best if she left. "I'm going to leave the two of you alone."

Amber shook her head. "You don't have to leave."

"No, that's okay. I just wanted to make sure you weren't alone, and I see now you're going to be fine. Do you have a ride home from the hospital?"

"Not yet," Amber said. "I think my car is still parked at that convenience store."

"If you give me the keys," Georgia said, "I can move it back to your mom's."

"You don't have to do that," Amber said.

Mrs. Reed held up a hand. "I can take care of the car. It's the least I can do."

Amber squeezed Mrs. Reed's hand.

"Where are you going after you leave here?" Mrs. Reed asked.

"Home to Mom, I guess. She should be by anytime now to see me."

Mrs. Reed shook her head. "Is your mother up to helping you? With a head injury, you can't be too careful."

Amber shook her head. "I don't need much from her. Just a week or so until I can get back to Texas."

Mrs. Reed frowned. "That's a very long drive, honey. Is it even safe for you to do that? How about you come home with me? It'll give us a chance to spend some time together."

"You would do that?" Amber's voice broke under the weight of emotion.

"Of course I would. I mean, that is, if your mother doesn't mind."

Amber shook her head, her pressed lips suggesting unvoiced disappointment. "She won't mind."

Mrs. Reed took Amber's hand in hers. "Then it's settled, you can stay with me. It's been a long time since I've had another person in the house."

Georgia cleared her throat. In her job, she witnessed the darker side of life. Rarely did she see kindness. "It's settled. You now have a place to go."

Amber squeezed Mrs. Reed's hand. "For the first time in a couple of days, I feel as if a weight has been lifted. And yet I feel guilty. You have so much heartache right now."

Mrs. Reed kissed Amber on the cheek. "You're the best medicine. You represent life, and I can't think of anything better than having you stay with me."

# CHAPTER FOURTEEN

***Saturday, October 7, 10:00 P.M.***

Saturday night at Rudy's was always crowded and tonight was no exception. People stood two deep at the bar and each of the round tables and booths were full. KC moved behind the bar filling drink orders, directing waitresses and cooks, joking with the customers with an ease that suggested he'd been doing this all his life.

Georgia wore tight jeans, an ivory lace blouse that skimmed her hips, and black high-heeled shoes that added three inches to her height. As she stood offstage, she listened to the young singer, Natalie, croon five back-to-back fast-paced melodies that kept the crowd, made up mostly of cops tonight clapping their hands and ordering drinks.

The main door opened carrying with it a cool breeze and she looked over to see Rick and Jenna. Her brother had changed into a V-neck sweater and jeans. Combed back dark hair could have made him look intimidating if not for the easy smile. His good humor was directly linked to the lovely dark-haired bride standing at his side. She caught Rick and Jenna's attention and both waved.

She liked having family in the audience. It always relaxed her and reminded her that no matter how nervous she might be before she stepped onstage, they had her back.

The clink of glass had her turning to Carrie, who carried a tray completely filled with empty beer bottles. As the singer's set concluded, Carrie approached Georgia.

"Hal told me he came to see you. He was pissed more than usual but I got him to calm down. I can take care of myself and the baby."

She scanned the young waitress for more bruises. She spotted a dark purple ring around her right wrist. He'd grabbed her and wrenched her arm. "He's still hurting you. Why stay?"

Carrie shook her head, dismissing Georgia's logic. "He's having a rough go of it. He lost his job and he's worried about taking care of me and the baby. He doesn't like it that I have to work."

"Where's the baby, Carrie?"

"She's with my neighbor. She's okay."

"My offer still stands for a place to stay, Carrie. You don't have to live this way. Think about the baby."

A stick-thin man with a handlebar mustache held up an empty glass to get Carrie's attention. She grinned broadly at him. "Be right there, sugar." The spotlight overhead caught the bruise across her cheekbone, covered almost completely with makeup.

Georgia shoved back a mouthful of anger.

Carrie turned back to Georgia. "I got to get back to work, but thank you."

"You can thank me by moving out."

"I can't leave Hal now."

Georgia drew in a breath, realizing her message was not being received. Again, she worried how violent Hal would have to be for Carrie to take a stand. She watched the waitress hold her tray high as she angled her slim body through the crowd.

"And now, we got a special treat tonight." The voice came from the stage and she turned to see Freddie grinning at the crowd. "Little Miss Georgia Morgan is here tonight."

The crowd began to clap, forcing her to push aside worry. She smiled as she stepped up onstage and nestled close to the microphone. "How ya'll doing tonight?"

The audience hollered and her grin broadened. The front door opened and she glanced over to find Jake Bishop entering. He wore a dark suit and a white shirt. He wasn't wearing a tie but she suspected he had removed it and tucked it in his pocket. With three active murder investigations on his desk, she knew this break for both Jake and Rick would be short-lived.

Jake glanced in her direction, nodded, and moved to the bar to speak to KC. The two exchanged words and KC laughed, reaching for an iced bar glass and filling it with soda. Jake accepted it and raised it to his lips.

"Georgia," a woman shouted from the crowd. "Sing 'Breathe'!"

Her attention grabbed, she shifted her focus to the

audience. "If that's what you want, I'll sing it. I'm here to make ya'll happy."

The crowd clapped with excitement as she turned to Freddie. "That work for you, sugar?"

"It sure does."

And so he began the song, gently strumming the guitar strings and setting the tempo. She moistened her lips and leaned close to the microphone, closing her eyes as she began to sing.

The tempo built and the crowd grew silent. When she reached the first chorus, the crowd cheered and she felt their energy rush through her as she hit a high note and then dropped her voice to a near whisper. And so it went, her riding the tune up and down, imagining bright vivid colors, and feeling the longing of wanting a man that squeezed her heart until her eyes moistened with tears. For a dozen beats of her heart, the walls dropped and she was exposed. Naked.

When she finished, the bar exploded with applause, everyone jumping to their feet. She smiled, tipping her head back. The next few songs were fast and upbeat and she rolled through them while enjoying the emotional roller coaster.

By the time she finished her set, she acknowledged Freddie, thanked everyone, and then headed to the bar where KC handed her a diet soda. She drank, willing her heart to slow and her nerves to settle.

"That was hot, Morgan," Jake said as he nestled in the spot beside her at the bar.

Her heartbeat kicked up a notch. She raised her glass to her lips. "Thanks, detective."

"So whom were you thinking about when you were singing that song?"

"Ah, it was you, baby," she said with a grin. "It's always you."

He tossed back his head and laughed. "Looks like I won the bet with KC."

"What bet was that?"

"I said you were singing to me. Singing is your way of telling the world how hot you are for me?"

She shook her head, grinning. "It's all about the J, right?"

"Hey, I can't help it. I know you want me. I'm just waiting for you to realize it, but you'll come around."

"You keep telling yourself that, cowboy. Keep telling yourself." She drained the last of her soda. "Aren't you working tonight?"

"I'm taking a few hours. I need the break to clear my head."

"I hear Amber's on the mend."

"She's been avoiding me. Says her headache won't go away." He set the nearly full stein down. "But she underestimates me if she thinks I'm giving up."

"You are a dog on a bone."

His eyes darkened. "When you're in my sights, I don't stop until I get what I want."

Electricity surged inside her. "Good to know."

He grabbed a handful of nuts. "As much as I'd like to stay and chat, I can't."

A surprise jolt of disappointment zapped her gut, but she covered with a wide smile. "Who's the lucky girl?"

"You don't know her." He winked and popped a nut in his mouth. "See you in the salt mines on Monday."

She held up her glass filled with melting ice. "You bet."

He turned and left the bar, leaving her annoyed and deflated, something that never happened when she just stepped off the stage. "He just played me, ass."

KC refilled her glass. "So what's got you all sour faced?"

"Jake Bishop. That guy can really piss me off."

KC laughed. "Really, you hide it so well."

"Hush up."

"He's a hell of a guy, Georgia."

"He's a hound dog. Always looking for the next woman to bed. I bet a mob of angry husbands and boyfriends chased him out of Boston."

KC's expression sobered. "You really don't know why he left Boston?"

"No. Should I?"

He pulled the bar rag from his shoulder. "He was engaged to be married. Fiancée's car was hit by a drunk driver who left the scene. She was killed. Jake was Boston PD then, but that didn't stop him from finding the guy and beating the hell out of him. He would have killed the guy if his brother hadn't pull him off."

"Damn."

"That's only half of it. The hit and run driver was a mob boss's son, but the boss told Jake the boy deserved the beating. But touch him again and he wouldn't spare Jake's life or the lives of his family. Jake knew if he stayed in Boston he'd see this prick again and would kill him, so he did what was best for all and left town."

"Wow." It was no secret that Jake had a temper and kept it on a short leash.

"Cut the guy some slack. It's clear he's got the hots for you."

She held up her glass for a refill. "It will pass."

"Oh, it sure as shit won't. Guy could not take his eyes off you while you were singing. Completely mesmerized."

Amber's stitches itched but her headache had passed and she was feeling much better. Especially now that she was staying at the Reeds' house. She could get used to a soft bed, fancy food, and a view of the lake behind the house, which she enjoyed while sipping morning coffee. This was the kind of life she deserved. This was the kind of life she wanted.

Mrs. Reed had gone to bed at nine but Amber couldn't sleep. As the minutes ticked by, she became more and more restless, realizing her return to Nashville was not going as planned.

# CHAPTER FIFTEEN

*Tuesday, October 10, 11:00 A.M.*

The medical examiner released the remains of Bethany Reed and Mike Marlowe on a rainy Sunday afternoon. Jake visited Marlowe again and convinced him to hold the services together. A combined service might be too much for the killer to resist. By Monday, Mrs. Reed finalized plans for the funeral, which would honor both children. Mr. Marlowe's only input had been the venue, which he insisted be held in the stadium-sized Baptist church near St. Vincent.

During the time leading up to the funeral, Georgia filled her days to overflowing. She visited Amber at the Reed house and found her doing well. She continued to review the files, searching for something that might break the case. As tempted as she was to call the lab every day for DNA results, she resisted. She even made time for lunch with her sisters-in-law for the final, somewhat torturous, fittings of their bridesmaids' dresses.

Now as Georgia walked into the police department

in high heels and a black dress, she thought about Jake and wondered about his weekend date. Which lovely woman had he chosen to take out or warm his bed? The unexpected thought jabbed her like an elbow to the ribs.

At Rick's request, she arrived at the homicide offices early so that she could drive to the funeral with Jake and him. When she entered Rick's office, Jake was there standing next to a bookcase fiddling with an old baseball that dated back to Rick's high school days.

Jake wore a dark suit, crisp white shirt, and a black tie. Broad shoulders, a straight-backed posture and the flawless suit held her gaze for a beat longer than it really should.

Seeing him now, she freely acknowledged to herself that she missed the irritating and smartass questions. Wanting him was not smart.

"Georgia," Rick said rising. "Like the dress."

Jake set the baseball down and turned toward her. A hint of a smile crossed his lips. "Clean up nice, Morgan."

Annoyance mingled with pleasure. "Thanks. Feels weird wearing a dress, and I'm fairly sure these heels were designed by a sadist."

Jake's gaze slid up and down the ribbon of muscle in her calf. He said nothing, but his look telegraphed a need to touch.

Rick reached for his gun from his desk drawer and holstered it. "Is Amber coming to the funeral?"

Georgia shook off thoughts of Jake touching her calves with his weathered hands. "She is."

Rick pulled his suit jacket from his desk chair and

shrugged it on. "Is it really smart for her to be staying with Mrs. Reed?"

"I don't think so, but Mrs. Reed enjoys doting on her."

Jake tugged the front folds of his jacket in place and adjusted his tie. "Let's get this show on the road."

She shifted, her hand at her side fingering the soft fabric of her dress. As the elevator doors dinged open, Rick's cell phone buzzed. He glanced down, shaking his head. "It's Jenna. Let me take this. I'll meet you downstairs."

Jake blocked the door open with his arm. "Sure. Take all the time you need."

As Georgia moved past Jake, the heat of his body rushed out to touch her. The two stepped into the empty elevator and the door closed behind them.

He punched the elevator button. "You look sexy as hell. Gonna be hard to forget those heels the next time I see you in steel-toed boots."

She tugged on her dress. "Take a picture. These heels are about to be retired."

"Too bad."

As the elevator doors closed, his energy magnified in the small space. She glanced at her reflection in the scuffed stainless-steel door. Her red hair skimmed the tops of her shoulders and curled up slightly. She had taken the time to wash and blow-dry her hair this morning, something she rarely did. However, despite her efforts the rain had grabbed ahold of the strands and twirled them sideways into tighter curls. Damn. She wanted to make a good impression at the funeral, but the truth was she wanted to please Jake.

"How was the date?" she asked.

"Fun. You have a good weekend?"

Chinese food. A very sad attempt at running a mile. Binge watching a comedy series. "Awesome."

He glanced at her, his gaze searching, intense. "Singing again soon?"

"Who knows? The day job's got most of my time this week." She thought about him standing at the bar as she began her set. "Why'd you stop by Rudy's the other night?"

"KC wanted to run something past me. Nothing special."

She thought about what KC had told her about Jake's fiancée. Of all the backstories she might have expected, that was the last. It added a dimension to the guy she didn't expect. She admired him for starting over. Easy to give in to a bad temper, but much harder to walk away from a fight to protect those you love.

The doors opened to the lobby and a group of officers talking. Jake waited until Georgia stepped off. A few minutes later, Rick strode out of the other bank of elevators. He glanced at them both as he tucked his phone back in the holster on his belt. "We need to get moving if we want to be there early."

Jake opened Georgia's car door, causing her to stop, surprised. "Something about heels, Morgan. Reminds me you're a woman."

Maybe she wouldn't retire the heels. "Thanks."

Georgia slid into the backseat, adjusting her dress, wiggling toes inside shoes that pinched. Rick and Jake both sat up front.

"So you boys actually think the killer will show at the funeral?" she asked.

Rick adjusted his rearview mirror and pulled into traffic as rain began to drizzle onto the windshield. "With all this media attention, I wouldn't doubt it."

Jake turned slightly in his seat so she could see his profile as he talked. "I'm betting the killer is there. He'll want to revel in the damage he's done."

"Do you think there's also an element of grief?" she asked. "I've seen murderers weep with remorse after they've killed someone in anger."

"Sure, it's possible," Jake said. "I've been thinking about how the bodies were laid out in the cave. Both Elisa and Bethany's bodies were carefully arranged. Hands crossed over the chest. Elisa's face was covered. Bethany's pendant hanging on the rocks to memorialize. All signs of regret."

"Mike didn't kill Elisa," she said.

"No, he didn't," Jake said.

"That leaves Amber. Or there was a fourth person in the woods the day the teens were attacked."

"Maybe," Jake said. "It's anybody's guess at this point."

"You said Mrs. Reed dotes on Amber," Rick said glancing at her in the rearview mirror. "I don't see why she's reaching out to Amber."

Georgia leaned forward in her seat. "She's a link to her daughter. Hard to let go of something like that. And in her mind, Amber's return to Nashville and the discovery of the bodies are somehow connected. Almost as if Bethany's spirit reached out to Amber."

"That's a load of crap." Rick's hands tightened on the steering wheel.

"Grief does strange things to people," she said. When she looked up, Jake's gaze caught hers in the mirror before she looked out the window to concentrate on the light drizzle of rain dripping down the glass.

They arrived at the church nearly thirty minutes before the ceremony, but the large parking lot was already filling. Lines of people carrying umbrellas were moving down the sidewalk to the large double wooden front doors where the minister stood and greeted people. Several news crews took up position under a tent so that they could film the mourners as they arrived.

Georgia dug an umbrella out of her purse and opened it when she stepped outside the car. Rain pattered steadily as Rick took the umbrella and held it high so it covered Georgia as they moved toward the front doors of the church. They stopped to greet the minister, who stood under an overhang, unmindful of the rain dripping behind him.

The minister caught sight of Jake's badge on his belt as he shook his hand. "I'm glad law enforcement could be here. It's my greatest hope that you catch the person who took those two precious lives from us."

Jake raised a brow while buttoning his jacket. "We're here to observe so, if you don't mind, please don't mention our presence."

"Of course."

Rick shook off the umbrella and closed it before they moved inside. Georgia slid her sunglasses into her battered brown purse, wishing she'd swapped it for something nicer. "Good luck blending, guys You two look like the *Men in Black* duo."

Rick adjusted his jacket. "Bishop, where do you shop in this city? Everything about you screams *somewhere else*."

"The cowboy boots don't help me assimilate?" Jake quipped.

She glanced at the black polished boots. "It's beyond me how you can get such a shine on cowboy boots. They're supposed to be a little scuffed. Drugstore cowboy."

"I don't wear scuffed boots," Jake said.

Rick shook his head. "And we rest out case. Let's find an out of the way spot where we three don't stick out."

Georgia slid into the back pew first and then Jake followed. Rick took the aisle seat.

This close to Jake, his strong energy mingled with the faint scent of his aftershave. She'd always kidded him about the aftershave at crime scenes. But really, she'd appreciated the touch. A bit of humanity in some of the worst places.

If he'd not lost his fiancée and he'd not made the decision to move here, she'd never have known him. She was glad he could tease her out of an occasional foul mood. Georgia knew she could be a pain in the ass, a fact few, including her brothers, called her out on. But Jake did. And that was okay.

"Amber Ryder is here," Jake said.

Georgia leaned forward a fraction and caught sight of the young woman walking into the church with Mrs. Reed. She was wearing a slim fitting black dress that looked new and expensive and designer black shoes. Her hair had been cut and styled into a sleek curtain of hair that draped her shoulders and covered the small flesh-colored bandage on her forehead. Her nails were manicured, painted a vibrant red. All the pampering, she guessed, was Mrs. Reed's doing.

Seconds later, Dalton Marlowe entered the church. Dressed in a hand-tailored black suit, he moved with a stiff-backed posture. Several people stopped to shake his hand and share their condolences. He spoke to all, his demeanor oddly warm.

He approached the front pew where Mrs. Reed sat with Amber to her right. Dalton looked down the row at Amber who smiled serenely up at him. He hesitated and then, as if aware that the eyes of the church and community were upon him, took the seat beside her. She leaned her head toward him, speaking softly. He did not talk or nod his head.

"He's wound up," Jake said, trailing her line of sight.

"I didn't think he wanted to hold a joint funeral."

"I called him. Suggested we might find the killer if the funerals were held together."

"His hatred feels like overkill to me," she said. "She has no power over him now that Mike is dead. He doesn't have to worry about her getting knocked up with a Baby Marlowe and sharing holidays for the next several decades."

"He reminds me of a jilted lover," Jake said.

"Really?"

Jake tugged his shirt cuff and leaned closer to her, dropping his voice so only she could hear. "There are rumors that the two were an item for a brief time."

"Mrs. Reed hinted at a relationship between them." She shook her head. "She could be his daughter. The age difference has to be thirty years."

"And your point is?" Jake asked.

"You've got to be kidding?"

"I'm not defending the guy. But just because there's snow on the roof doesn't mean the boiler isn't firing."

"Okay. Let's say they were lovers," she whispered. "She ditches the old man and goes for the son. That would sting the pride of a man like Marlowe."

"In spades. And he's not forgotten it." Jake tugged at his cuffs again. "Amber Ryder surprises me at every turn. I never know what to expect with her. One day she's a waif and the next a vixen."

Both he and Rick scanned the crowds, looking for anyone that stood out. Anyone that lingered on the fringes or looked nervous. Even a bit elated or satisfied by the scene they had created.

"He keeps an apartment in town," Georgia said. "Maybe the doorman might remember something."

"Good detective work. I'll follow up." Jake inclined his head toward a tall, neatly dressed young man who found a seat several seats in front of them. "That's Tim Taylor. He and Mike were best friends."

"I read about him. He planned to tag along with the three other kids, but at the last minute had to cancel. His mother got sick."

"He's second-year law and clerking in a downtown firm."

She watched Tim and noticed he glanced several times toward the front pew where Mrs. Reed, Marlowe, and Amber sat. A lot of people were looking at the trio, but his demeanor projected an intensity matched by few.

By the time attendants closed the back doors a half hour later, the place had filled to standing room only. When the minister took his place at the front of the church and began the service, the congregation was silent. Many of the attendees looked as if they were in their mid-twenties and clearly must have been contemporaries of Bethany and Mike. Half of Nashville had shown up in big numbers to mourn the girl that had no friends and the high school jock.

As the organist's rendition of "Amazing Grace" began, the slow procession of two caskets commenced. One was large and made of mahogany with shining brass handles, whereas the other was smaller, made of cherry with silver handles. Both were draped with a blanket of white roses.

Jake rubbed his chin, his dark eyes burning with contempt reserved for the bastard that did this.

She found herself wondering what kind of funeral he had held for his fiancée. Had the church been packed? No doubt it must have been. Her death had been senseless. A tragedy.

Was it possible to take comfort in knowing a loved one had never known what had hit her, that her last minutes had not been terrifying, as a killer squeezed life from body and soul?

As if he read her thoughts, Jake glanced down at her, his jaw clenched, his gaze narrowed. Their eyes held just for a moment before he lifted them back to the minister.

Jake, Rick, and Georgia sat in their car afterward watching as the congregation emptied out of the church. First out were the children's parents and Amber. As they all stood by the minister, Mrs. Reed reached out and hugged Marlowe and he in kind wrapped his arms around her and hugged her back. When Mrs. Reed pulled back, Amber leaned over and put her arms around Marlowe. The gesture appeared normal. One person reaching out to another in grief. But Marlowe's body stiffened at her touch and he made no move to touch her any more than necessary. She was slow to release him, as if she sensed her touch was torturous.

On the church stairs, Amber and Mrs. Reed exchanged words while holding hands. Their smiles had a sad, lost quality and it was clear the older woman had a genuine affection for Amber, who kissed her on the cheek before they descended the stairs and slipped into a black limo.

"Marlowe's doing a hell of a job hiding his anger," Jake said. "If he were alone with her now, I think he'd beat the hell out of her."

"She knows he hates her," Georgia said. "She has to know. So why does she push his buttons in plain view when he can't react without making a scene?"

"Time to find out what the hell is going on between those two."

# CHAPTER SIXTEEN

*Tuesday, October 10, 1:00 P.M.*

As they drove across town, Jake's phone buzzed with a text. "Interesting."

"What?" Georgia pulled her stare from the raindrops sliding down the passenger-side window. The rain had a way of bringing down her mood. Never quite knew why.

"I entered the dates of the Reed case into ViCAP. I also referenced what we had on the Spence case as well."

"And?" Rick asked.

"According to Deke's text, we have a hit from the Austin Police Department. There was a murder in Texas very similar two years ago. Girl fits almost the exact description of our victims, Elisa and Bethany."

A bitter smile curved the edges of her lips. "*Our?*"

Jake shrugged. "We're in this together to win it, Morgan."

She studied him a beat, as if trying to decipher what he meant. "I want this case solved."

"Join the club." Rick shifted, something he did when

sitting too long stressed the hip grazed by a perp's bullet a couple of years ago. "Deke is back at the office?"

"Yeah, and he's got files to share on the Texas case." Jake tucked his phone back in his breast pocket.

"Good," Georgia said, rubbing her hands together. "I'm not in the mood for sitting at home today. Always better to work."

Rick tapped his finger against the steering wheel. "Are you ever going to slow down and take a breath?"

"What do you mean?" she asked.

"You're either at work or at Rudy's."

Jake's attention zeroed in on the question and her answer.

"I was home on Sunday, if you must know, but I like to work. What's the big deal?"

"How about some balance in your life?" Rick challenged.

She waved her hand, brushing aside reasons for worry. "Balance, for me? *Please.* There's no middle setting for me."

Rick studied her as he would a crime scene that wasn't giving up its secrets fast enough. "And . . ."

"And nothing, Rick. I'm fine. Really and truly fine. Just your garden variety workaholic."

His fingers tightened on the steering wheel, suggesting his dissatisfaction. He was aware that Jake was paying very close attention to their conversation.

They arrived at the station and Rick gingerly got out of the car. "I'm going to stroll to stretch out my hip. See you two inside."

"Sure," Georgia said. She would have pressed him about the hip if they'd been alone.

This time, as Jake opened her door and she stood, he

asked in a voice only loud enough for her to hear, "Hot or cold? That's the best you got? Really?"

She glanced toward her brother who was now on his cell as he paced. "Like you have room to talk?"

He shut the car door and yawned, sending her a message that he was tiring of her. "That about sums it up."

"Maybe one day I'll take a tropical vacation, just to prove I can slow down. White sand and blue waters. Even have a few mojitos with funny umbrellas sticking out of a big glass. That might do the trick."

He didn't speak for a long moment before he said, "I can recommend a nice little beach in the Caribbean. Blue waters and drinks with little umbrellas might not be the absolute fix but it does help."

She laughed. "I can't picture you holding a drink with an umbrella."

"I did. Once. Too sweet. I switched right back to beer." A slight smile tugged his lips, but his eyes burned with unspoken emotion. "I can picture us on a tropical beach. You in a bikini."

For a split second she allowed the not-so-bad image to play in her mind before she elbowed it aside. "Dream on."

"Always."

She paused as he opened the door for her. Waving to the officer behind the duty desk, they crossed to the elevators and rode to the fifth floor before making their way to Deke's office.

"How was the funeral?" Looking up from a report, he leaned back in his chair. Taking his glasses off, he rubbed the bridge of his nose.

"Both Amber and Dalton were there. There's some bad history between them," Jake said.

"Why don't we talk about the Texas case," Georgia said. "How's that victim similar to Elisa and Bethany?"

Deke reached for his glasses and a yellow legal pad covered in scrawled notes.

"So when did you start wearing those?" Georgia quipped.

Deke glanced over the rim of the glasses. "Not happy about them, Georgia. Don't poke the bear."

She laughed, unable to resist adding, "Kinda makes you look even more like Dad."

He growled for effect, taking the remark as a compliment. But then, he glanced at Jake, daring him to say something.

Jake held up his hands. "I know baby sister gets away with saying things I'd get shot for."

Deke nodded. "Damn right."

She laughed. "What does Rachel think about them?"

A faint grin proudly arched across his face. "She thinks I look like a professor."

"Well, then, it can't be all bad," she said.

Tossing her another annoyed glance, he settled the glasses on his face. She had to admit, they gave him a distinguished air. "I'll give you this. You're definitely a hipper version of Dad."

Deke cleared his throat, ignoring her. "The girl in Texas was named Anne Smith and her body was found two years ago. She was nineteen years old, a sophomore in college and top of her class. She'd been missing for three weeks and the autopsy confirmed she'd been strangled and then stabbed close to the time of her abduction. Her body was found in a wooded area near a small town in the hill country." He pulled a copy of Anne's driver's license from the Telex and handed it to Jake. He studied it and gave it to Georgia.

"She looks like Elisa and Bethany," Georgia said.

"The description of her school record is almost identical to the Nashville victims."

"The killer doesn't like smart women," Georgia noted.

"It may be their intelligence," Jake pointed out. "They have a similar look. But it could be something else entirely. Maybe they're weak and easy to control."

"Any suspects?"

"There was a person of interest in the case," Deke said. "He's not been identified but was picked up by a surveillance camera near the shop where Anne Smith was last seen. The picture taken of him is grainy, but he doesn't fit the description of the man seen hanging around Elisa's coffee shop."

Jake looked at the picture, holding it low enough so Georgia could see. "No. He sorta looks like the sketch Jenna drew of Scott Murphy, but it's hard to tell. The coffee shop waitress in Nashville thought he was a wannabe musician. Carried a guitar, she said."

"Anyone can get a guitar," Georgia said. "Cheap ones are a dime a dozen in this town.

"Chicks eat that sensitive crap up," Jake said.

Georgia shook her head. "We do?"

"What? It's true. I bet this guy opened with the song 'Feelings.'"

"That's crap," she said. "Elisa probably didn't get much male attention and then this good-looking guy befriends her. Basically, low hanging fruit."

\* \* \*

Jake parked at the top of a circular driveway in front of the tall brick home that belonged to Dalton Marlowe. Marlowe kept a place in the city but according to his assistant was here today working from home.

The rain had stopped, leaving a sheen of moisture clinging to the driveway and lawn. Jake climbed the stairs, tugging his jacket forward over his gun. He rang the bell which echoed inside the home.

A young maid answered the door and, when he showed her his badge, she escorted him to the study. A thick Oriental rug warmed the floor in front of a six-foot fireplace. Four overstuffed club chairs nestled close in the center of the room around a large round coffee table.

"Detective."

Dalton Marlowe stood on the threshold of the double doors. He wore suit pants, a white shirt with sleeves rolled up his forearms, and a red tie that now hung loose. "I saw you at the funeral. It was well attended. Any thoughts?"

"You have my condolences."

"I don't want your condolences. I want you to find a way to prove Amber killed my son."

"I hear you visited Amber in the hospital."

Gray eyes narrowed. "She tell you that?"

"You bumped into one of my people on your way out."

"The redhead with Mrs. Reed?"

"That's right."

He moved to an antique sideboard that displayed a collection of crystal decanters filled with all shades of liquor. He filled a glass and held it up to Jake in offering. When Jake refused, Marlowe replaced the crystal stopper in the decanter and took a long drink. "So is that why you came here, to ask me about my visit to Amber?"

"Yes. I've heard a few rumors about you two."

Absently, he rubbed his finger over the finely cut crystal as he studied Jake. "People gossip. Doesn't mean it's true."

"Were you having an affair with her?"

His face paled and his mouth hardened as if he'd bit into something foul. "Who told you that?"

"Was it true?"

He pressed the glass to his temple, and for a second, closed his eyes. "My wife was sick for a long time. Caring for someone who's dying is a lonely place. It's draining."

"Is that a yes or a no?"

"Yes, I slept with her. Three or four times."

"Did it have anything to do with the scholarship she received from the business community so that she could attend St. Vincent?"

"Yes. I funded the scholarship so she could attend. I didn't need anyone knowing that I slept with an underage girl. If that information leaked, it would have put added strain on my wife."

"And then she hooked up with Mike."

"Yes. But it had nothing to do with my son. She's smart. She's damn smart, and she always has an agenda. *Cunning* would sum her up."

"You know anything about the texts she's received?"

He shook his head as he drank. "I'd bet you she sent them to herself."

"Why did you visit her in the hospital?"

"Figured it would be hard for her to dodge, plus her guard would be down. I've always said she knew more than she was saying." He sipped his whiskey. "But as always, she was on her game. She killed my son and Bethany. I don't know how she did it, but she did."

"Why?"

"To punish me. She hates me."

"Because?"

He tapped an index finger on the side of the glass. "She had her eye set on this house, this life. She fancied herself as more important than her current status. I didn't want the drama so I ended it. She became furious and vindictive. She threatened to tell everyone about the affair."

"And that's when you came up with the money."

"It's one of the oldest stories in the world. Older man falls for younger woman and he pays dearly for his sins."

"You think it was a sin that you slept with Amber."

He hesitated. "I know it."

Jake reached in his pocket and pulled out the telex picture of the Texas man. "I'd like you to have a look at this picture and see if you recognize him."

"Who is this guy?"

He held the picture close to his chest, sensing he had the man's attention. "Someone that hit our radar. The image is not very good but it should be enough to give you an idea."

Marlowe took the picture and glanced at it. For a moment he stared before he set down his glass and moved to a drawer and pulled out reading glasses. He studied the picture closely. "I don't know this man. Why should I care?"

"Two years ago, in Austin, he was involved in a case similar to Bethany's and Elisa's and Mike's."

Marlowe flicked the edges of the photo. "Amber lives in Texas."

"It's a big state and Austin and Dallas aren't close. It's a big leap without more evidence."

"If this case has any connection to the Nashville cases, I'll bet my fortune she's involved."


Amber knocked on the apartment door, smiling as she fingered a large gold hoop earring. It had been a long day for Mrs. Reed so she had gone to bed early. Amber however, was juiced with energy and unable to sit still, let alone sleep.

She tightened her hand on her purse strap as she waited. Seconds passed and her annoyance grew. He better be home, she mused. Restless, she took a step when the light clicked on and the front door snapped open.

Tim Taylor stood there in the light, wearing only a sleeveless T-shirt and sweatpants. A gold chain dangled around his neck and his hand was behind his back. She guessed it was curled around a gun. Tim always liked his guns.

"Amber." Surprise frayed the edge of her name. "Where the hell have you been?"

She moistened her lips and pouted. "Ah, did I wake you up?"

"Yeah, you did."

"Sorry. I know it's late." She pressed her hand at the

base of her neck and then slowly trailed it down to her breast. "Are you up for a little fun?"

Tim cleared his throat. "What are you doing here?"

She met his assessing gaze. "I missed you. Seeing you today got me to thinking about the things I'd rather be doing. Is that a sin to want you while I'm at my two friends' funeral?"

A muscle twitched on the side of his jaw.

She stared at his handsome face and lips. She felt the wanting buzzing around him. "Don't be mad. Let me make it up to you now."

"Just like that?"

She caught her bottom lip between her teeth. "Or I could leave and you could keep following me around, lurking in the shadows."

He grabbed her hand and pulled her through the doorway. Closing the door hard, he put his gun in the entry table drawer. She lowered her purse to the floor, savoring the look of the muscles rippling over his back. He always had a knack for making her forget; if not forever, for a little while.

He turned, caught her sizing him up, and pushed her against the door, pinning her arms above her head. His dark hair was rumpled and beard stubble covered his square jaw.

Should she tease him and make him suffer for hesitating moments ago, or go down on him right here in the hallway?

He watched, waiting for the signal from her, and released her arms. He'd always been good at instruction. Following orders. She took his face in her hands, savoring the feel of his warm skin. She pulled him toward hers and slowly kissed him.

He leaned into the kiss, cupping his hand at the base of her neck and pushing his tongue into her mouth as if he were half starved. His other hand glided up under her silk blouse past her narrow waist. He cupped her full breast, teasing the hard nipple with his fingertips as he deepened the kiss.

Her heartbeat skipped and then rattled faster in her chest as she grew moist. Ah, this was what she needed. She reached for the waistband of his sweats and slipped her hand inside, softly stroking his hard erection. He moaned her name as he broke the kiss and pushed up her shirt so he could suck her breast.

Closing her eyes, sensation overtook her. She was aware of his other hand unbuttoning her jeans and pushing them down just as she had once taught him. His hand moved inside her panties, but instead of touching her center, he teased the edges of her curls.

"I do the teasing, not you," she whispered as she bit his earlobe and tugged.

As instructed, he began to rub her and she arched into him. She kicked off her heels, squirmed out of her pants, and stepped out.

This time when she kissed him, she rubbed her half-naked body against his erection until she knew it throbbed. Swearing, he jerked down his sweats and hiking up one of her legs, pushed hard into her. She cupped his buttocks as he thrust inside her with a frenzy that excited her. She could feel him climaxing. He wanted release and soon would beg for it.

"Not yet, lover," she said. "Me first."

"I hate it when you do this."

"You love it."

She held off on her own orgasm, knowing as he

drove into her with growing need, he was suffering. Finally, she found her release and closed her eyes.

His body remained taut like corded steel, but he waited for her command.

"Now," she said. "Now, you may come."

Tim drove into her with a frantic energy and quickly exploded. He dropped his face to the hollow of her neck, his breathing hard and ragged. His fisted fingers relaxed and rested on her shoulders. She raised her hand to rub his back the way she used to. But she stopped. That kind of touch was too intimate, too personal, and he had not yet earned it. Instead, she lowered to her knees and took him in her mouth for another round.

When he finally regained his breath, he braced both of his hands beside her head and looked into her eyes. Now that her itch was gone, she felt bored and ready to leave.

"Stay the night," he said. "We'll talk at breakfast."

The air around them cooled and, half dressed, she realized how vulnerable she was now. "I can't. I have to go. I need to be there when Mrs. Reed wakes up."

"What's the deal with you two?"

"She needs a friend." She traced a circle around the center of his chest over his heart. "And you know, I can be a very good friend."

He traced his finger along her chin. "Sleep here."

"Better I go now."

He arched a dark brow. "You mean while it's dark and no one can see you leave."

"It's not that."

"It's always that way with us." Frustration coated the words. "We've been at this since high school, and you still won't tell anyone about us." He captured a strand of her hair, wrapping it softly around his hand. "I want more."

His voice annoyed her. "Nothing happens until I say it does, lover. But I know of a way you can earn a few points that might sway me."

# CHAPTER SEVENTEEN

*Tuesday, October 10, 11:25 P.M.*

When Jake arrived at Rudy's, he was dog tired but had heard from Rick that Georgia had landed a slot onstage at the last minute. As much as he needed to work, to sleep, he couldn't resist seeing her sing.

The bar was crowded and most hovered close to the stage where Georgia held the mic close to her mouth and sang Faith Hill's "Breathe." As her voice echoed through the room, energy moved through him, tightening around his heart like a fist. What the hell was it about her that got under his skin?

She leaned into the mic, closed her eyes, and her voice summoned sadness, loss, and frustration from the song. She could hit all the high and low notes with perfect pitch, but it was the emotion she so freely injected into each note that grabbed her audience and held them tight. Emotions he'd kept long locked in a very secure place burned in the center of his chest and coaxed feelings he'd not had since Boston.

"She's so good," KC said as he dried a tumbler with a bar towel. "Hard to take your eyes off her."

Jake turned, surprised to be caught staring. "She's great." He reached for the half-full glass of ice water and took a long drink, astonished that his throat was so dry.

"I'm puzzled someone hasn't snapped her up," KC said, a teasing note woven around the words.

"She's mean as a snake," Jake said, setting down his glass harder than he anticipated. "Pretty to look at and nice to listen to, but don't get too close. She'll bite your head off."

KC laughed as he carefully stacked the glasses next to a dozen others. "That's what keeps it interesting, don't you think? That's what I loved about my late wife. So nice and kind to many, but she kept me on my toes. She never minced words when she was pissed at me."

"How long were you married?" His gaze followed a drip of water down the side of the chilled glass.

"Twenty-five years."

"That's something."

KC's eyes dulled a fraction. "Sounds like a long time, but now it just seems like a blink."

Jake had been engaged to Alice less than two months. They'd planned a spring wedding. That moment went by so fast there were days he wondered if it were real. "Life goes so fast. It's over before you know it."

"Yeah." KC set the bar glass down as Georgia finished her song. "So you gonna nut up and ask her out?"

Jake carefully pushed his glass a few inches away. "Who?"

KC snorted a laugh. "Don't bullshit me, son. You know who."

Jake shrugged, deciding he'd rather play dumb than out his feelings for Georgia Morgan and suffer her wrath. "As soon as I get my tetanus shot."

KC laughed. "Pussy."

Jake grinned. The old man was right. Applause roaring in the room, Jake watched as Georgia seated her mic into the stand and turned toward the band. She paused to thank the other singer, who had stepped aside so she could sing a set, and the guitarist before climbing off the stage.

Several folks from the crowd rushed to Georgia as she exited the stage. She tossed back a lock of that red hair that she allowed to tumble free while she sang and smiled. At first glance, the smile looked electric, warm, and welcoming. But as he studied her face, he could see her jaw was set just a fraction and her shoulders stiff. Whatever emotions flowed so freely while she sang were now shut off, no different than twisting the spigot of a water faucet.

KC filled an iced glass with diet soda and lemon and handed it to Georgia as she approached the bar. Jake watched as long fingers with neatly short, unpolished nails raised the glass to her lips. As she drank, his gaze settled on the slim line of her pale neck.

She set the glass down on the bar. "That was fun. Thank Fancy again for letting me sit in on her band. I appreciate the time."

KC raised a glass toward Fancy as she took center stage. She returned a smile, as if understanding the small favor she granted would earn more stage time at Rudy's. "She was glad to do it. She likes you as much as the customers."

Georgia traced her finger down the line of moisture on the side of her glass. "Is Carrie working tonight?"

KC frowned. "Called in sick."

"Do you believe her?"

"Sounded like she had a cold."

Shaking her head, she dug her phone out of her back pocket and dialed Carrie's number. The woman answered on the second ring.

"Carrie," she said. "It's Georgia. I hear you have a cold." She listened, nodding her head. "You sound rough. Head all stopped up?"

Jake listened, not interfering, but ready to act if Georgia asked.

She drummed her fingers on the bar. "I can bring you some soup? And I promise I won't make it myself."

Laughter crackled through the line. "Okay. See you soon? Great."

Georgia ended the call. "Sounds legit."

KC nodded. "Good. I'll keep an eye out."

"Thanks."

"Everything all right?" Jake asked.

She faced him. "Sounds like it."

"Let me know if it's not," he said. "I can pay him a visit. Send a car by their house."

The offer touched her. "No thanks, but I'll keep it in mind." Shaking off the worry, she shifted the conversation. Nodding toward the stage, she asked, "So what did you think?"

Jake kept his gaze on her eyes, as if resisting the tug of instinct to follow the long line of her neck down to the very end of the V-neck. "The singing wasn't half bad. You got pipes."

"You. Got. Pipes." An auburn brow arched. "I pour my soul into that song and all you can say is 'you got pipes'?"

He liked the irritation humming in her voice. Liked the spark of challenge in her emerald gaze. "It was pretty good."

"It was great," she countered. "It was the best I've sung in a long time."

"So what you're saying is that you've been half-assing it until I showed up? I'm flattered, Georgia."

KC barked out a laugh and moved down the bar as if he wanted to be free of the blast zone.

"No, that's not what I'm saying."

A faint scent of perfume wafted around her. He'd not smelled the scent on her before. He liked it.

"Then what're you saying, Georgia?"

She lifted her glass to her lips. "Let's say everything clicked tonight."

"Why's that?" he asked.

She settled on the bar stool next to him, her posture a little less stiff. She was comfortable around him. She stifled a yawn and rolled her head from side to side much like her brother Rick did when he was tired. "So what did Marlowe say about the picture?"

Ah, they were back to the job. Always the safest thing to discuss. "He didn't recognize the guy."

Bracelets jangled as she ran her fingers through her hair. He saw the fatigue humming below the frustration. "I've been trying to track Amber down to ask, but Mrs. Reed says she's out and not answering her cell."

"You think this guy in Austin was the one sending the texts to Amber?"

"Could be."

"Why is he attracted to this type of girl?"

A bead of sweat trickled down her temple and he was so damn tempted to brush it away, but thought better of it. "I stopped trying to figure out what makes these guys tick. I just lock them up."

As she sipped her soda, she shifted and the spotlight dangling above the bar caught the coppery curls of her hair as well as the dark circles under her eyes. She stifled a yawn.

"When's the last time you slept?" His voice sounded concerned.

"I had a good night's sleep."

"This week?"

"A couple of nights ago." She raised her glass, smiling. "I'm good for a solid night's sleep at least once a week."

"You're the Energizer Bunny."

"Something like that."

Jake dug a ten-dollar bill from his pocket and tossed it on the bar. "I'm headed home. I need a few hours of sleep before I hit it hard in the morning."

She rolled her head from side to side. "I'm doing the same if I can get up off this stool. I dread the drive across town."

"I'm three blocks from here. You're welcome to my spare room."

A sly smile tipped the edges of her lips. "Nice try, Bishop."

"I'm too tired to be smooth. I'm offering the bed in my spare room. I need sleep. You need sleep. My house is blocks from here, not fifteen miles away like your apartment."

Eyes narrowing, she studied him as if she was waiting for the punch line. "So is this a new tactic for you?"

He leaned toward her a fraction. "If I wanted you in my bed, I'd just straight up ask. I don't need a gimmick to get a woman in my bed."

Her eyes warmed before they cooled. "I've heard."

He made no apologies for the number of women he'd slept with in the past. He was single and he liked sex without commitment. But since Georgia, the attention he paid the other women had been more for show. "You coming or not, Morgan? I'm really tired and I got to be going."

She tapped an index finger against the side of her glass as if ticking through the pros and cons of taking him up on his offer. "I hate it when you sound so logical."

He dug his keys out. "Leave your car in KC's lot. You can drive with me."

"I'm sleeping in the spare room."

"That is what I offered."

She bit her bottom lip and then stood as if coming to a decision. "I've got to get my purse from the back."

"Hurry up. I need shut-eye."

He watched her walk away, wondering how he was going to sleep at all tonight knowing she was in the room across from his.

"So what's going on between you two?" KC asked.

Jake dug his keys out of his pocket. "I offered a room for the night. My place is a hell of a lot closer than hers."

KC shook his head. "So you do like her."

"I do."

KC leaned forward, his gnarled right hand clench-ing the bar rag. "I know she's an adult. And she'd skin me alive if she heard me asking, but you're not going to break her heart, are you?"

His gaze scanned the bar, always watching, always expecting trouble. "No, but she might break my heart."

"That's not my problem."

"Stop worrying." He straightened, realizing he was speaking to Buddy Morgan's stand-in. "I've offered her a place to sleep for the night."

KC scratched the back of his bald head. "I didn't think she liked you that well."

"How much does she have to like me to sleep in the spare room?"

KC shook his head. "That I don't know."

Jake was laughing when Georgia appeared with her purse, jacket, and a small go-bag that he knew held the clothes she'd wear to the office tomorrow.

Georgia glanced at KC. "If you tell any of my broth-ers, I'll tell everyone I know that you're a secret scout for the top record producers in Nashville."

Jake didn't know much about music but knew that kind of rumor was enough to bring every wannabe singer flocking to the bar. KC wouldn't be able to walk down the street without someone trying to shove a publicity photo or demo in his hand.

"Hey, no reason to get that nasty," KC said, glanc-ing from side to side as if he was afraid she might al-ready have started a vicious rumor. "Your secret is safe with me."

She winked and blew him a kiss. "And your secret is safe with me, Record Man."

With KC groaning as he smiled, Jake followed her out the back of the bar and down the long narrow hallway to the back door and the small parking lot that KC kept for singers and the few lucky ones he happened to be fond of at the time.

Jake unlocked the car, and as tempted as he was to open her door, held back as she tossed her bag in the backseat and then slid into the passenger seat.

Behind the wheel he turned over the engine as she reached for the radio and changed his jazz station to a country-western station.

"Don't change the setting on my radio, Morgan. Took me a while to get it just right."

"I haven't changed anything. Just picked a better station." She settled back in her seat and seconds later leaned her head back and closed her eyes.

He drove, enjoying having her at his side. It felt right having her close. He sure as hell did not know what that meant but he accepted that whatever was happening now was taking them in the right direction.

Ten minutes later, he parked in front of his house located in the Germantown section of Nashville. It was small but had been fully renovated. His pop was a hell of a craftsman and had even driven to Nashville to build the cabinets in the spare room as a housewarming gift. Though Jake could hold his own with most carpenters, thanks to a half dozen summers working for his old man, he wasn't an artisan like him.

When he'd first moved to Nashville, the days in patrol were long and hard, but even after an hour or so of lifting weights in the gym, he had been full of energy he couldn't shake. So when he'd come home, he'd spend a couple of more hours knocking out walls or painting until he was too tired to remember Boston.

"We're here," he said as he shut off the engine.

She opened her eyes, shaking sleep from her head and straightened. She glanced toward the house and hesitated. Laughing, he reached in the backseat for her bag and met her on the other side of the car. He moved toward the front door, lit by a strong halo of light from an overhead bulb and opened the door. A flip of the switch and the inside appeared.

She set her purse down, allowing her gaze to wander the open living, dining, and kitchen area. It held a large leather couch flanked by two club chairs, a large coffee table with sports magazines and a couple of remotes. Of course, the large television screen set in the corner. The walls were painted a light brown to match the central carpet picked out by a gal he had dated a couple of years ago.

The place was neat and organized.

"Wow, Bishop. Nice digs."

"You sound surprised."

"I am. You've got style." Amazement threaded around the words.

"And you were expecting what?"

"A cave. Bearskins. Pizza boxes. Beer cans."

Ignoring a framed Boston Bruins jersey, she moved to a fireplace mantel where he had a few pictures of his family. She reached for a framed photo of Jake and three men who must be his brothers standing behind his parents at their home in South Boston. "When was this taken?"

"Last summer. We all met in New York to celebrate my parents' fortieth wedding anniversary."

She glanced at him and then the photo. "You all look like your father."

That prompted a laugh. "Don't tell that to my mom. She takes great pride in her four boys looking like her side of the family."

She studied the picture a second time. "Nope. No traces of her."

"My younger brothers do have her Irish temper. And they all three drive Pops nuts."

"What do they do?"

"They work in my father's construction company."

"So you're the outlier. The lone cop."

"You could say that." This close, he was tempted to reach out and brush back a lock of stray red hair. But he had promised to remain hands off, and he always stood by his word. He moved to a closet where he kept blankets and a pillow.

"Who's this woman with you?" she asked holding up a picture. "She's pretty."

His breath hitched when he saw her holding the silver frame. As he crossed to her, he released the breath and looked at the picture. The image featured a much younger version of himself with his arm proudly around a tall brunette. "That's Alice. We were engaged."

"KC said you had someone back in Boston."

He squinted. "You were talking to KC about me?"

She shrugged and replaced the picture. "I wasn't asking. It just kinda came up."

"What did he tell you?"

"Basically you left to protect your family. That true?"

"It is. I haven't been back to Boston since."

She straightened the picture so it faced out. "It's nice you keep her picture and her memory alive."

For a moment they stood inches from each other, the energy snapping between them before he cleared his throat. "Give me a second, and I'll put these blankets and sheets on the bed."

"I can do that."

He brushed her aside. "I can do it. Restroom is down the hall on the left."

She saluted and moved down the hallway. He glanced over his shoulder and watched the sway of her hips, wondering why the hell he had brought her here. It was going to be one long night.

By the time she emerged from the bathroom, he had made the bed up for her in the spare room. She glanced and smiled. "Thanks."

"Sure." Again, another moment arrived where he could touch her. But he didn't. "Sleep. I've got an early call in the morning. See you then."

She tucked a curl behind her ear. "Thanks, Jake. There's a star in heaven with your name on it."

"Yeah. A pretty damn big one."

\* \* \*

When Georgia heard Jake close his door, she shrugged off her jeans and slipped off her bra from under her shirt. She slid under the sheets and clicked off the lights. Her sore body, desperate for rest, all but sighed as she relaxed into the sheets.

But as she lay in the darkness and watched the shadows play and dance across the ceiling, sleep hovered just out of her reach. She wanted sleep, willed it to come, but it clearly was not ready for her.

She thought about Jake in his room. A room where he had had countless women. She shifted on the mattress, rolling to her left side, then back to her back, and then back on her left side. She listened as his purposeful steps moved around the room and she imagined him stripping off his shirt and laying it carefully over the back of a straight back chair in the corner. She bet he never tossed his clothes on the floor, or if he did in the heat of the moment, they never stayed there long. He was always meticulous. Careful.

When the light clicked off in Jake's room, she imagined him sliding into the center of his king-size bed. Seconds ticked past. The silence grew. When it was clear they'd not have sex, she allowed the breath she held to flutter over her lips.

Knowing he was so close offered a comfort she did not enjoy very often. Soon she'd awake. Soon she'd worry.

But for now, sleep.


Dalton Marlowe was on the phone the better part of the evening since the detective had left his house. Seeing the picture of the man in Austin, Texas, solidified in his mind that Amber had found another pawn to do her work. She could be so seductive and make a man do just about anything.

"Damn it. I'm so sorry I ever brought her into our lives, Mike."

Mike had been a good kid before Amber. He'd not been the smartest guy, but he listened and was easy enough to handle. Life had been good. And then Amber had shown up with her secrets and wagged her tight little ass in front of him, knowing he would want a taste.

He dragged a hand over his head. God help him, but the sex between them had been so good. That first time she'd come to him had been in a small hotel bar. She had swept her hair up, a black dress hugged her curves, and extra makeup made her appear older. He'd taken her up to his room and she'd slid off her dress, which pooled around her high-heeled feet. She'd been wearing only lace panties. She had let him fuck her three times before she'd whispered her secret in his ear.

Now, as he sat in the dimly lit parking lot of the bar, he thought about what it would take to control that little slut. Like a cockroach, she was hard to destroy.

He checked his Rolex and confirmed it was after two. The bar's parking lot was nearly empty and he could see inside that the staff was wrapping up. She'd be out soon.

When Tracy Ryder came out at two-ten she was alone, moving easily across the lot in three-inch high-heeled shoes. Her short skirt hugged trim legs that still got noticed. When she was younger, she was pure candy. The instant she first walked up to him and smiled, he was as hard as a pike. For months, he was so damn hot for her. When he wasn't fucking her in the city apartment far from his wife, he dreamed about fucking her. In those days, he could barely think.

In that sleek apartment, she rode him and moaned his name as if possessed. And then his wife had hired a detective who snapped pictures of him and Tracy in the hotel room. How the hell his wife discovered the affair, he would never know. When confronted with the pictures, she raised her voice and broke down into tears. She did not beg. She did not plead. She gave him a choice: break it off immediately or get out of the marriage and lose the money and all rights to their unborn child.

Even with the ultimatum looming over his head like the sword of Damocles, he hesitated, resenting that this plain, cold woman controlled his life. But his wife's money trumped the sex. Without it, he was nothing.

Shit.

He could only blame his lapse in judgment on youth and stupidity, especially as he now watched Tracy Ryder crossing the parking lot. A taut figure now sagged a little under a short miniskirt and a low-cut top. Once blond hair was now dyed a harsher and more unnatural white. And the wrinkles around her mouth were deep from years of smoking.

Whereas Tracy had been easy to handle, Amber had not. Christ, if he'd known what trouble Amber was going to cause, he might have just killed her himself right then and there in that hotel room.

As Tracy fumbled for her keys, he got out of the car and crossed the lot toward her. The chill in the night air quickened his step. The crunch of his shoes against gravel had her turning, eyes narrowing and her hand slid into her purse. No doubt those long red-tipped fingers were curled around the trigger of a gun.

"Tracy."

Her head cocked at the sound of her name. For a moment, she stared at him before she recognized him. "Dalton Marlowe."

Her wrinkled skin and brittle blond hair turned his stomach. "Where's Amber?"

A lift of the chin hinted to her disappointment, but Tracy had always been quick to recover. "At the Reed house, I suppose. She's been there since she got out of the hospital."

"What does she want? Why is she back?"

She moistened her lips, smiling at the discomfort seasoning his tone. "Amber? Who knows what Amber wants? But she won't let go until she gets it."

He flexed tense fingers. Laughter from a couple crossing the dark lot toward their car kept him from closing the gap between them and slapping her face. "I want to talk to Amber."

Bone thin shoulders shrugged. "I thought you paid her a visit in the hospital?"

"There were too many people around for us to have a proper conversation."

"God only knows what you'll do to her."

He tipped back his head, the irony of all this jabbing him. "Why should you care what I'd do to her when you never gave her any thought? You only cared about yourself?"

Painted eyes narrowed. "Fuck you."

"I did, and I'm still paying dearly for it." He tugged at the edges of his hand-tailored jacket. He was wasting his time with Tracy. The woman had no idea what her daughter was capable of doing. "If you see Amber, tell her I want to talk. She knows how to find me."

She sniffed, shaking her head slowly. "What's in it for me?"

The couple had vanished, leaving the two of them alone. He moved fast, snatching her thin arm in his meaty fingers. He tightened, squeezing until he saw the pain in her blue gaze. "Tell Amber to call me, Tracy, or I promise I'll bury you so deep, the cops will never find your bones."


Hal arrived home ten minutes after two, his head spinning from too much bourbon and beer. He fumbled with his keys, dropped them and cursed. "Goddamn lock. Carrie, you bitch!" This time she had locked him out. Bet that lady cop was filling her head with lies and trouble.

He groped for the keys, staggered, and stabbed the key into the lock. Inside, the house was dark and quiet. He fumbled for the light switch, pawing his hand down the wall until he felt it. With a click, a dumpy little room came into view. It summed up his life. Shitty.

"Carrie, where the fuck are you?" His voice was garbled and slurred. "Get your ass out here and cook me something to eat. I'm hungry."

He knew she was supposed to work tonight, but last call at Rudy's was one a.m. She should be home, and that damn kid should have been fed and asleep. "Carrie!"

He stumbled forward toward the kitchen, getting more pissed with each step. When he found that dumb bitch he was gonna knock some sense into her.

A light in the hallway went on and he turned to find her standing in the hallway. She wore jeans, a T-shirt, and a jean jacket. She'd tied up her hair and had scrubbed all the makeup off her face, revealing a dark bruise on her cheek. For an instant, guilt jabbed his gut, but he quickly shoved it aside. He hadn't wanted to hit her, but she made him. She always knew how to push his buttons.

"Get me something to eat," he shouted.

"I wanted to tell you face to face, Hal. I'm leaving with the baby."

"What did you say?"

"I'm leaving."

His temper flared hot. "And where the hell are you going?"

"I have a place to stay."

"That cop woman."

She swallowed. "It doesn't matter. I'm already gone."

"Like hell you are." He advanced toward her with fist raised. His mind was in such a fog of anger, frustration, and booze that he barely remembered the next half hour. It was a blur of Carrie's cries, bone-crushing hits, and blood.

When she fell to the floor and he finally stepped back breathless, the adrenaline that had rushed through him vanished like water down a drain. His vision cleared and for the first time since he'd arrived home, he saw Carrie. Really saw her.

Carrie. His Carrie. The woman he loved was lying facedown in front of the stove, her face beaten so badly he couldn't recognize her.

He stumbled back, slipping in the blood and nearly falling backwards. He looked down at his bloodied hands and cried, "Holy shit! What have I done?"

In the other room, he heard the baby's cries. His mind shut off and there was no more thinking as he moved to a drawer in a small table and removed a revolver. He put it in his mouth. The hammer dropped and the gun fired. Hal was dead before he hit the floor.

# CHAPTER EIGHTEEN

*Wednesday, October 11, 6:00 A.M.*

Georgia's sleep hadn't been light, but deep and so dark that it had been devoid of images or worry. Out like a light. As if pushing up from the depths of the ocean, she rose toward the light and burst to the surface.

Her eyes fluttering open, she was greeted by the sound of rushing water. A shower. Wherever she was, she wasn't alone.

She didn't instantly recognize her surroundings. She sat up and shoved a lock of hair from her eyes as she searched baseball pictures. Smoothing her hands over the hand-sewn quilt, she smiled when she remembered. Jake Bishop's house.

She slid her legs over the side of the bed and, running her tongue over her teeth, hurried to the second bathroom where towels waited. She dug a toothbrush from her travel bag and brushed her teeth, turned on the shower, and shut the bathroom door. After peeing, she got into the shower and washed away the lingering fatigue as well as the scents of Rudy's bar, which clung to the strands of her hair.

She soaped her entire body and washed her hair and by the time she stepped out of the shower, she felt . . . human. It took another few minutes before she put on clean clothes and combed her hair.

Emerging from the steam of the bathroom, the scent of coffee welcomed her. Jake stood with his broad back to her, staring out at the first hints of sunrise. Bread warmed in a state-of-the-art toaster.

"Good morning," he said. Without turning to look at her he poured her a cup of coffee and then splashed in a bit of milk along with some sugar as she liked it. When he turned, he looked rested, clean-shaven, and curious as he studied her. "Sleep well?"

She accepted the cup. "Honestly, it's the best I've slept in a while. Thanks for letting me crash."

"Anytime. No reservations needed."

She sipped the coffee savoring the taste and the warmth. "Thanks."

The toaster dinged and popped out its bread. He set both slices on a plate, buttered them, and placed them in front of her.

"Five star, Bishop."

"Aim to please." He popped more bread into the toaster.

She bit into the toast, which quieted her restless stomach. By the time he'd buttered his bread, she'd gobbled hers up. "Hit the spot."

"Good."

He was the perfect host and gentleman as he took

her empty plate, rinsed it, and set it in the dishwasher alongside his. "You got a full day?"

"I don't have to be in until eight." His spicy aftershave tugged at her.

"Good, you've got a few hours. Feel free to hang out here. Front door locks behind you."

"I'll need a ride back to Rudy's to get my car for work. Can you take me?"

"Sure." He tossed her a smile. "I'm headed to the Reeds' residence this morning. Time to talk to Amber again."

"Right."

Such the gentleman. No flirting, touching, or bantering. Nada. Zilch.

When he moved out of the kitchen to the side table drawer where he locked up his gun, she realized he was going to do exactly what he said. He was going to leave. Not touch her.

She smoothed her hands over her thighs. "Amber won't be up for hours."

"I'll run by the office. I want to read over the files again before I talk to her."

She set her cup down and moved toward him. "Why haven't you made a pass at me?"

Calmly and with no hint of emotion, his gaze rose. "Because I said I wouldn't. I don't lie, especially to friends."

She nibbled her bottom lip. "You always keep your promises?"

His gaze trailed over her, absorbing all the details. "I do."

She moved closer, not touching him but close enough that the energy of his body mingled with her own. Her fingers curled into fists, as if she stood on the banks of a deep lake, ready to take the plunge.

A muscle pulsed in the side of his jaw. "What are you doing?"

Consciously, she unfurled her fingers. Time to take the plunge. She took his hand in hers, caressing his calloused palm with her thumb. "You can't figure it out?"

A wry smile softened his stern features, but he made no move to touch her. "You've called me a hound dog more times than I can count."

"I know." She turned his palm over and traced the long lifeline.

His hand tightened around hers.

"Maybe, I'm rethinking my opinion of you."

He watched her so closely. "How so?"

Damn, he was really going to make her work for this. "I'd like to get to know you better." The words rasped as if they'd been wrenched from her throat. She stepped to within inches of him. "That okay?"

His hand rose up to gently trace the line of her jaw. "I think that might be acceptable."

He tugged her toward him, cupping his hand at the base of her spine. His chest felt hard under the smooth starched fabric of his shirt. His hand slid to her bottom, pushing her against his erection. She wriggled closer against him, savoring the fact that he wanted her so much, and pressed her lips to his.

He tasted warm and salty. Kissing him sent a thrill through every nerve in her body. She wrapped her arms around his neck and rose up on tiptoe and teased his lips open with her tongue.

A growl rumbled in his chest as he squeezed her bottom. "You're trouble."

"I like to think so." Her hand slid down his chest to his belt buckle. Without breaking the kiss, she unfastened his belt and reached the band of his boxers, suddenly feeling an urgency to have him inside her.

Jake tugged her shirt free of her waistband and slid his hand up her chest to her breasts. Rough fingers deftly pushed away the bra's cotton fabric and teased the tip of her nipple until it was rock hard and aching. She moaned, unashamed and so horny she really thought she just might explode.

"You like it?" he whispered against her ear.

"A lot."

"What do you want from me, Georgia?"

"I want this."

"Is this all you want?" Tension rippled through corded muscles.

Embarrassed by her emotions, she tried to slide her hand lower, but he manacled his fingers around her wrist.

"What do you want?" he demanded.

Frustration boiled inside her veins. She'd denied herself this kind of pleasure for so long and now the dam was bursting and desire was flooding all around her. "I want you."

He released her hand. "I've wanted this since I saw you onstage at Rudy's six months ago."

Her fingers moved below the waistband, wrapping around him. "I didn't think you noticed. You never said a word to me."

"I noticed." The intensity in his eyes darkened as she began to stroke. "You were singing 'Breathe,' like last night."

Pleased, she whispered, "Now every time I sing that song, I'll be thinking about this."

"Good. Because I'll be thinking the same thing." He ground out the words, drawing away from her as if he couldn't take the sweet torture any longer.

He pulled her to the bedroom and pushed her down on smoothed sheets. She tugged her shirt off, tossed it aside, and then reached for the clasps of her bra nestled between her breasts. Cool air brushed her nipples as she shrugged off the undergarment and watched him yank the knot in his tie free and unfasten the buttons of his shirt. He tossed his shirt onto the floor next to hers. The morning light peeked through the closed slats of window shutters, and cut across his wide muscled chest. A gold chain and a ring hung around his neck. Tattooed on his right bicep was a bold Celtic cross made of thorny vines. Woven between the barbs were the words *Honor, Family, Justice*.

Seconds after she wriggled out of her pants, he climbed on top of her and settled between her hips.

He reached into the nightstand for a condom and with practiced efficiency slid it on as she watched with growing need.

When he pushed inside of her, she was so tight. Groaning her name, he braced one hand on the bed while the other slid up her flat belly to her naked breast as her body molded and stretched.

When he began to move, her heart pounded against her throat. She allowed her hands to move over his muscled back. She squeezed. Raised her hips.

"God, I've wanted this," he said, his breath hot against her ear.

Tougher emotions came easy to her, but the tender ones left her feeling vulnerable, exposed, so she rarely spoke them aloud.

When she didn't speak, he asked softly, "Do you want me?"

"Yes," she whispered.

"Louder. And I want you to look at me when you say you want me as much as I want you."

She opened her eyes and stared into the depths of his gaze. "Just you. I want just you."

He kissed her on the lips, pushing his tongue into her mouth as he began to thrust faster and faster. She allowed the walls to drop and she could feel every bit of sensation that this moment offered. She wanted to make this last and to savor the build, but the need pushed her too fast. Before she knew it, her nerves lit on fire.

In the next instant, Jake came in a nerve-splintering moment.

He collapsed against her, his heart thudding against her chest and his breath warm against the crook of her neck. "Damn."

She smoothed her hand up his back to his wide shoulders. "Wow."

Jake rose up on his elbow and brushed the hair from her face. He kissed her gently on the lips. "I could get used to this."

*Out of the frying pan and into the fire.*

# CHAPTER NINETEEN

Jake didn't expect this morning. Loved it. Would not trade it. And was already wondering where this would take him.

She kissed him good-bye in the car and he cupped his hand behind her head, holding her close for an extra beat. Unspoken words danced between them but when he started to speak, she broke in.

"Don't say anything to my brothers."

His fingers brushed a curl from her face. Kissed her on the lips, wishing he could be inside her again. "So you gonna keep me a secret?"

"Not forever." She shook her head. "Better it came from me. I tell my brothers so they don't kill you."

He twisted the soft curl between his fingers and playfully said, "Your brothers don't scare me."

"Really?" She rolled her eyes. "When I think of all the potential boyfriends they've chased off."

"Sounds like they did me a favor."

"You might change that tune once you really get to know me."

He kissed her on the lips. "What are you going to say?"

"I've no idea."

"If you need backup, just call."

"They can be tough, but so am I." She kissed him quickly and reached for the door handle.

He grabbed her hand in his. "I don't like secrets, Georgia."

"Who does?" she asked.

Before he could argue, she leaned forward and kissed him on the lips, allowing her touch to linger. He reached for her arm, but she moved just out of reach, made a quick excuse about work, and slid out of the car. She left him sitting and watching as she got into her car. He remained where he was until her tail lights vanished around the corner.

Tapping his finger on the steering wheel, he drove to the office and picked up Rick. His partner slid into the passenger seat, a cup of coffee in hand.

Jake started driving. "You called ahead to the Reeds' house?"

"I did. I spoke to Emma Reed and she said Amber is up and dressed. She's expecting us."

"Great."

Rick tossed him a sideways glance. "You look different."

"Good night's sleep, I guess."

A grin crept along his lips. "Jenna and I had a good night's rest as well. What's this one's name?"

"You know I don't share." Jake kept his gaze on the road, his last few words with Georgia turning over and over.

"Right."

Fifteen minutes later they parked at the top of a circular driveway in front of the Reeds' home. Two story, the house had a wide front porch that stretched the length of the house, solid square columns supporting a second-floor balcony, and a gray slate roof. A well-manicured lawn surrounded the five thousand square foot home that had a European flair.

They climbed the long curved front steps and rang the bell. Seconds later, footsteps sounded in the hallway and the door opened to Mrs. Reed. She was dressed in crisp slacks, a white sweater top, and her hair was pulled into a low ponytail. A gold cross dangled around her neck.

"Officers. Please come in. Amber is on the sunporch."

Jake stepped inside, allowing his attention to roam into a side parlor where a painting of Bethany hung above the fireplace. In the portrait, she was about sixteen and wore a white dress. Her hands were folded in her lap and around her neck hung the same gold pendant found at the crime scene.

"We had that picture done when she just started St. Vincent. We were so proud of her."

"I've heard only good things about her," he said.

Her smile was a mixture of pride and pain. "Thank you for that. I know she wasn't popular at school, but I always believed she would grow out of all that and blossom into a beautiful young woman."

"I've no doubt she did just that."

Mrs. Reed's breath caught and without another word she moved down the carpeted hallway. The detectives followed.

Amber sat on the sunporch in a beam of sunshine. Her blond hair flowed around her shoulders and her small pale face was tipped toward the sun. She wore upscale yoga pants and a sweatshirt that he knew put someone back a couple of hundred dollars. On her feet were top of the line flip-flops. She had a pedicure to match the manicure. She was dressed in black at the funeral and had looked sleek and sexy. But here, she looked smaller, more passive, and even vulnerable.

"Amber, you remember Detectives Bishop and Morgan," Mrs. Reed said.

She rose, smiled like the perfect lady of the house. "Of course."

"How's your head?" Jake asked.

She raised fingertips to her forehead. "Much better. Stitches come out in a couple of days, but I've been getting headaches."

"Poor thing has had to rest," Mrs. Reed said. "I've been trying to get her to go back to the doctor but she won't listen to me."

"I'm fine," Amber said.

"I asked the duty sergeant about any leads on your attacker, but so far, nothing."

"He came, struck, and was gone before I could really react."

Mrs. Reed laid a hand on Amber's shoulder. "I've told her she needs to be more careful. It's not wise for her to always be out alone, especially at night."

Amber laid her hand over Mrs. Reed's and smiled.

To look at the two, it was a mother and daughter moment.

While Rick stood, Jake sat across from Amber on a blue-and-white flowered couch. His tendency was to lean forward and hold constant eye contact but keep his body at ease.

"I put Bethany's and Elisa Spence's cases into ViCAP. It popped on a similar case in Austin, Texas. A convenience store security camera picked up a person of interest who looks like the same man who trailed Elisa. Do you recognize him?" He removed the photo from his pocket and handed it to Mrs. Reed.

She accepted it and, for a moment, held it without studying it. Then, she pulled in a deep breath, dropped her gaze to the picture. For a long time she did not say anything and then she shook her head very slowly. "I don't know him, at least I don't think I do."

"Do you think he killed this Elisa Spence girl?" Amber asked.

"I don't have any forensic data to tie him to the case right now, but he is a person of interest."

Amber took the photo from Mrs. Reed and studied it again. "He's attractive. Makes sense a girl would be attracted to him."

"As soon as we find him and get him to talk, we'll figure it all out."

"You're different from the other detectives I dealt with," Amber said, fingering the edges of her sweatshirt. "Not all police can see through the killer's eyes like you."

"Don't know about that," Jake said with a grin. "But I'm very stubborn and don't give up easily."

She folded long lean hands and settled them on her

lap. "I wonder if he was some kind of stalker. I was in the paper so much five years ago. Maybe he followed me to Texas."

"Why do you say that?"

She moved back toward her chair and carefully sat down. "The texts and Georgia brought me back to Nashville. And now this guy that was in Texas like me is here. Circumstances just don't line up like that."

"They usually don't." Jake shifted, tugging his jacket forward. "Tell me about your relationship with Mike."

The shift in conversation caused her to pause and shift gears. She rubbed her temple. "Mrs. Reed, would you get me a glass of water and an aspirin."

"Of course, dear. I'll be right back."

When she was gone from the room, Amber said, "Mike was my friend. We hung out a lot. It started with me helping him with school. He was a great athlete, but he wasn't book smart. I helped." She sighed. "I even did some of his work for him. I wrote several of his college application essays as well. Honestly, he'd have not gotten as far as he had if not for me."

"His father knew about this?"

"He turned a blind eye. A couple of times he even slipped me a couple of hundred bucks. I tried to give it back, but he refused it. Told me to keep his boy on the straight and narrow."

"Dalton admitted to sleeping with you when you were very young," Rick said.

The color drained from her face and she glanced back to see if Mrs. Reed had heard. "He told you that?"

"He admitted to a sexual relationship."

Tears moistened her eyes. "I was barely sixteen. He told me if I wanted the scholarship to the school that a smart girl like me would know the cost."

"He held the scholarship for sex."

A tear fell and she swiped it away. "I didn't want to do it, but I needed a school like St. Vincent to get me out of my life. I was headed down my mom's path and that scared me to death."

Dalton and Amber had both confessed to a sexual relationship. She'd definitely been underage and now there was a question of coercion. "Did you tell your mother?"

"God, no. I didn't tell anyone for a long time. I was so ashamed. Eventually, Mike and I became close at school and I told him. Which I regretted almost immediately. Dalton and Mike had a strained relationship, but after that it was openly aggressive."

"Which explains why he doesn't like you?"

"Yes. He would hate for anyone to know he seduced an underage girl multiple times."

Her explanation didn't jibe with Marlowe's reaction to the affair. His body language had exhibited deep shame, not anger. "How long did the affair last?"

She glanced over her shoulder to make sure Mrs. Reed was still out of earshot. "It was just a few times."

"How long are you planning to stay in Nashville?"

"Not much longer. Mrs. Reed is great, but I can't keep living here. It's not fair to her. And I've got my job and apartment back in Dallas."

"And you'll put all this behind you again?"

"I came back to get answers. And now it looks like we have them. You have Bethany and Mike. And soon, the killer."

"We don't have him yet."

Her eyes sharpened. "I have confidence in you, detective. You won't need me to find the man in the photograph. It sounds like he's your killer."

"It does sound like that," Jake said.

Mrs. Reed entered the room with a glass of water and a couple of aspirins. She gave both to Amber, smiling as the young woman swallowed the pills and chased them with a gulp of water.

A sigh shuddered over her lips. "Thank you, detective."

"For what?"

"For working this case. For five years Mrs. Reed, Mr. Marlowe and I have suffered. And now we have answers."

Her expressions were flawless. Nothing raised red flags. Nothing. "Have you had any more of your memory return?"

Her brow wrinkled. "The nurse in the hospital said I was having a dream. That I mentioned Mike. But I don't remember anything."

"A dream?"

She raised her gaze to his and smiled. "Just a dream of Mike running in the woods."

"He say anything?"

"Nothing. I've struggled to remember, but the more I reach for it the faster it fades."

Jake imagined her dropping a thin trail of bread

crumbs hoping he'd follow. As much as she smiled, as much as she said the right things, he tried to picture her losing her temper.

Jake waited on the line as the secretary connected him to the CEO of Davis Marketing, where Amber Ryder worked in Dallas. He pulled onto I-40 and was headed east back toward Nashville. "Harvey Davis."

"This is Detective Jake Bishop. I'm with the Nashville Police Department."

"Yes, sir. What can I do for you?"

"I'm calling about an employee of yours. Amber Ryder."

Silence crackled for a second. "She's on leave right now. Had a family emergency."

"Yes, sir. She's here in Nashville."

"Is she in some kind of trouble?"

"Why would she be in trouble?"

Another pause. "No reason. Why the call?"

"Tell me what you know about Amber."

He cleared his throat. "What do you want to know?"

"She's tied to an old case. Just doing my due diligence. What can you tell me about her?"

Silence crackled. "Smart as a whip. We hired her part time in our accounting department while she was in college. We offered her a full-time job a couple of months ago."

"What does she do?"

"She works closely with our accounting director and assists with the company books."

Jake had the sense the man was guarding his words closely. "She's just out of college and it sounds like she has a lot of responsibility."

"Like I said, she's smart. She's saved us thousands of dollars. She has taken very aggressive postures that she's certain she can defend against an IRS audit. Nothing intimidates her."

"She gets along well with everyone?"

A pause. "For the most part. She's tough. Doesn't mince words. That doesn't always sit well with everyone." A subtle tension vibrated around the words.

He sensed more below the surface. "She's not been in any kind of trouble?"

Hesitation. "None. Detective, why are you calling?"

"She's a material witness in a cold case."

"I heard she got mixed up in something in high school."

"What did you hear?"

"Two kids vanished. One was her friend and the other her boyfriend. She was found badly injured."

He wrote the word *boyfriend* on a clean page in a small notebook he carried. The teacher at the high school suggested Amber and Mike were dating, yet Amber had denied it. "She ever talk about it?"

"No. It came up when we did the background check during the interview process. I did ask her about it, but she only answered with a yes or no. I got the sense it was still a sensitive topic for her."

"Anything else you can tell me about her?"

"I'm only qualified to talk about her as an employee. I'm unfamiliar with her private life."

Jake tapped the tip of his pen on the paper. "Well, sir, thank you for your time."

"Sure thing. Did Amber say if she's coming back to Dallas?"

"She gave me the impression she was returning."

A long pause. "Great."

He placed the phone in its case on his hip. "Interesting."

"How so?" Rick asked.

"Can't put my finger on it. Based on what he said, he liked her and her work." He leaned back in his chair. "It's the unspoken between-the-lines message that always catch my ear."

"And that would be?"

"Don't quite know yet." He had run a police background check on her to see if anything popped. Nothing had.

So what was bothering him about her?


Amber paced the bright sunporch, her nerves drawn tight. She picked up her cell phone and redialed the number she'd already called five times.

Mrs. Reed had left the house shortly after the cops to run errands. There was a maid floating around the Reed house somewhere so she was mindful as the phone on the other end of the line rang five and then six times and kicked into voice mail.

"Where the hell are you?" she whispered into the receiver. Frustrated, she tapped the phone gently against her thigh as she paced. Tim promised to answer the phone whenever she called, but he let the last two calls go to voice mail.

She raised the phone, preparing to redial. "Don't do

this to me. Us. You said you'd be there. You promised you wouldn't let me down."

She dialed the number again and listened as it rang and rang. No answer this time sent her temper rising and her thoughts in a different direction. If she could not rely on Tim, she could always find another man. She was good at finding men.

# CHAPTER TWENTY

*Wednesday, October 11, 3:00 P.M.*

Searching surveillance footage was meticulous and mind numbing but a necessary task that couldn't be overlooked. Jake had amassed footage from ten different cameras lined up along the coffee shop's street, as well as a couple of side and back streets. Each picked up a different angle and provided a piece of the puzzle that made up Elisa's last days.

A dry cleaners shop down the street had a camera that faced east away from the shop. He didn't expect to see much, but on the day Elisa vanished, the camera picked up a partial shot of a red truck headed toward the shop. The truck stopped at a traffic light before moving along with traffic. He backed up the tape and froze the screen at the moment when the camera caught the best view of the driver. The footage was grainy but he could make out that the driver was a bearded male with dark hair and a muscular build. Just like Scott. And the man in Austin.

Jake checked the date stamp. This was ten minutes

before Elisa had left the shop for the last time. He printed off the picture.

He continued to move through the footage frame by frame searching for glimpses of Scott Murphy as well as the man from Austin. There was a thin woman with long black hair who stood across the street. She wore large dark sunglasses and a big coat that covered her frame. She stood at the dress shop window across the street seemingly staring into the store. He froze the frame and realized her head was tilted up, almost as if she was studying the reflection in the glass. He watched the woman linger and then move down the street out of the frame.

He reviewed the tape again, but the woman never approached Elisa, nor did she speak to the man.

The next few hours were spent reviewing more footage with no hits. His neck and back ached and he needed a shot of caffeine as he popped in the next DVD from a women's dress shop.

He fast-forwarded to the time he knew Elisa was on the street and slowly scrolled through the footage. Twenty-nine seconds into the section he spotted Elisa moving down the street, coffee in hand. Fifteen seconds after her, the woman appeared and then, seconds later, the bearded man.

The man paused and appeared to be looking at something in the window and then, glancing in Elisa's direction, he began walking again.

DNA had been collected from Elisa's body but it would take weeks at best to get the results. Was Elisa an unexpected diversion? Was she simply his type?

And Bethany? The girl in Texas? For whatever reason, this guy liked killing smart women.

"So what the hell is it with you?" he muttered. "Why girls like that?"

"People will think you're insane if you keep talking to yourself." Georgia's words were glib but the undertone drifting beneath telegraphed nervous energy.

The sound of her voice had him smiling and turning. As much as he wanted to rise and pull her to him, he kept his emotions in check. He leaned back in his chair, allowing his gaze to move over her. "I found the guy following Elisa."

"Really?" Interest cut through the nervous edge that had sharpened her tone.

He tapped his finger on the screenshot he'd just printed. "Have a look."

She moved close, but not so close that their bodies touched. She smelled of his favorite soap. He liked that she wore his scent.

Nodding, she rested hands on her hips. "Damn. Good hunting."

"The needle is always there if you're willing to toss a lot of hay."

"So why's he in Nashville?"

"I've been asking myself that question." He could almost smell an arrest coming.

Georgia's cell buzzed with a text and she glanced down at the display. "KC is calling."

"More stage time."

"Let's hope."

"I love to watch you sing. I get so damn hard."

She leaned down and kissed him. "I'll be sure to let you know when I'm onstage."

He cupped his hand behind her head, deepening the kiss. "We're going to have a real date. One that involves those high heels."

"Count on it."


Georgia was in her office when she called KC back minutes later. He picked up on the first ring. "KC, what's going on?"

"Georgia, I'm worried about Carrie. She didn't come in to work last night and I've called her cell a dozen times and she didn't pick up."

Worry darkened her light mood. "I thought she had a cold."

"I'm not buying her cold story anymore. Can you go over there? I know you're at work."

"Sure, that's fine." She moved toward her desk and pulled her purse from her bottom drawer. "Call the police, and I will meet them there."

"She was talking about leaving him," he said.

"What?"

"After Hal came at you in the parking lot something in Carrie shifted."

An abused spouse was at most risk when they were leaving. Abusers, sensing a loss of control, often struck out more violently than ever to regain control. "On my way. Text me her address."

Second doubts hounded her as she drove across town to the small three-room house. Jesus, she was so afraid of showing weakness that she pushed Hal hard when he'd confronted her in the parking lot. Had she had a hand in pushing him over the edge?

Her worst fears were confirmed when she pulled up and saw three marked cars, lights flashing, and the yellow crime scene tape strung by the first responders.

She bolted out of her car and rushed up to a uniformed cop, quickly showing him her identification. "What the hell happened?"

"Looks like a murder/suicide."

A baby's cry cut through the chaos and she realized a uniformed officer was cradling Carrie's baby, trying to calm her cries. "The woman who lives here works at Rudy's bar. Her name is Carrie Jacobs."

"That fits the name on the driver's license I found in a purse by a suitcase. It looks like she was going to leave him."

"Her boyfriend is Hal West."

"That also fits. He appears to have died of a single gunshot wound to the head."

Tears burned the back of her throat. Had she caused this?

"It's a holy mess in there," the officer said.

"And the baby?"

"Neighbors heard the baby crying and called 911. She was found in her crib, very upset but physically fine."

She crossed to the young officer jostling the crying baby. She knew next to nothing about babies but figured she knew more than this rookie did. She reached out and he gladly handed her the child. She nestled it close and began to rock her body as she'd once seen her mother do with a neighbor's child. She spoke softly to the child until she settled. "Oh, baby Sara, I am so sorry. I should have made your mommy listen to me sooner."

"Young female is in the kitchen," the second officer said. "She's been beaten to death. A male is in the living room with a single gunshot in the mouth."

Invisible fingers clenched around her heart as she thought about her birth mother, Annie, who had been beaten when she was only days old. Instinctively, she made sure the baby's face wasn't smothered under the blanket. She smiled at the child. "It's okay, baby. It's okay."

"We've a call into social services and are trying to track down family."

"Okay."

The forensic van arrived and Brad got out. As he moved to the back of the van to suit up, an unmarked black SUV arrived and Deke and Rick got out. Her brothers strode to her. Both appeared taken aback by the image of her holding an infant.

"Deke," she said.

His face softened with concern. She could barely hold back tears as she recapped what had happened.

Georgia looked at Rick. "If you can take the baby, I'll suit up and go inside."

Immediately, Rick reached out for the child. "Yeah, sure, of course."

"You're not going inside," Deke said. "If you knew the victim, then you need to be out here and let Brad and another tech work the scene."

"I can put aside my feelings. I can do this."

"No. I wouldn't let another officer in this situation go in there and I'm not letting you go. Stand down."

Sadness cut and sliced her. "I kept telling her to leave the guy. He's been putting bruises on her for months."

"You didn't cause this, Georgia," Deke said.

She ran a trembling hand over her head. "I pushed her too hard. Every time I saw, her I pushed. I never know when to stop pushing. I'm always pushing. Goddamn it!"

Jake closed the door behind him, rattling keys in his hand as Georgia stood in the foyer of his house. She had called him from the crime scene, shaken and so upset he could guess at the tears threatening to overtake her. He told her to come by his place and where to find the spare key. He would be right over.

Her hair was damp from a shower and she wore only a towel. She'd called him thirty minutes ago. The murder scene was processed and she needed to see him.

Slowly, she dropped her towel to the ground, moving toward him. She didn't smile. Didn't flirt.

Instead, she closed the gap between them, wrapped her arms around his neck, and pressing her naked body against his, kissed him on the mouth. He banded his arms around her, pulling her close. Whatever emotion she couldn't express with words, her body conveyed. The unspoken need reached out to him and connected.

His body throbbed hard against her as she reached for his jacket and slid it off his shoulders. He kissed her on the milky pale skin at the nape of her neck and savored the soft moan in the back of her throat. "Do you want to talk about it?"

She shook her head. "No. Not one word. Or I'm leaving."

He unclipped his gun and locked it in the entryway table. When he looked back at her and saw the raw yearning in her eyes he nearly lost control. God, he wanted her.

He smoothed back her damp hair spiraling in ringlets and draping over her shoulders. He kissed her shoulder and then the top of her breast. They would talk later, but right now, he wanted to be inside her so badly he didn't dare risk losing her to unwanted talk.

He unfastened his pants and pulled his shirt free. Her hands, desperate and needy, slid up his torso as he unbuttoned his shirt. She pushed it off his shoulders and kissed him. He cupped her breast. Squeezed until she moaned.

He shed the rest of his clothes and ran his hand up her flat belly over the curve of her breast. She closed her mouth and swallowed. "Bedroom, now."

Taking her by the hand, he pulled her to his bedroom and sat on the edge of his bed. She lowered to her knees in front of him and smoothed her hand up his muscled legs. When she leaned over and put her mouth on him, he arched back, moaning her name. She seemed to crave anything at this moment that would bring her pleasure and erase the murder scene.

He cupped her shoulders and guided her onto the bed. She scooted up on the pillows and laid back as he straddled her. She reached for him.

"No," he said.

Frustration darkened her gaze. "No?"

"Slow and easy, baby. We're gonna enjoy this." He would touch and kiss every part of her body and chase away, at least for a little while, all the evil she'd witnessed today.

"I can enjoy fast."

He shook his head. "You'll like slow better."

"But—"

"Do you want me to stop?" He kissed the hollow between her breasts.

"No." The word escaped on a growl.

"Then, slow it is."

She moved her hand down his body, but he captured and kissed it before lowering his mouth to her neck. He pulsed hard against her and she wiggled as if the emotions were so powerful that they scraped against the underside of her skin.

"You're a sadist," she said.

He laughed. "Yes, I am."

"Don't men want it fast?"

"Sometimes." He kissed her neck. "Sometimes, not."

He moved his hand over her flat belly and she sucked in a breath. He circled his fingers over her belly button and then deliberately moved his hand lower. When he pushed his hand into her folds, she whimpered. "I'm not going to make it much longer."

He chuckled. "We'll find out."


Tim parked almost a half mile away from Dalton Marlowe's house to ensure that no one saw him on the property. With darkness around him, he worked his way through the wooded backyards until he reached the fence circling the large green backyard.

In the far back right corner there was a gap in the fence that offered just enough space between two iron slats through which his body could squeeze. He and

Mike had used it too many times to count when they snuck in and out of the house. That dumbass Mike was always in some kind of trouble with his old man and grounded so they'd resorted to sneaking. Mike had never cared about rules or restrictions. He came and went as he pleased.

Sucking in a breath, he wedged through the iron rods. In the last five years, his body had thickened with muscle, forcing him to push harder. Iron scraped over the buttons of his shirt.

Once inside the fence, he tugged his shirt back into place, taking time to make sure it was neatly tucked into his pants. He jogged across the manicured lawn to the back door. It was five minutes after midnight.

Now standing on the back porch, he stared at the brick mansion that had been such a big part of his teen years. Five years had passed since he'd last stood here. So much had changed since then. Mike and Bethany were dead. He'd followed Amber to Texas and now back to Nashville. He'd grown up. Gotten smarter. And yet this place was exactly as he remembered it. The gardener still trimmed the hedges in a straight line, flower boxes remained filled with the same kind of red flowers, and the grass was as thick and lush as a flawless green carpet.

Everything changed and yet nothing changed.

He considered testing the basement window with the faulty latch. Had his old man fixed it? Mike used that window often to sneak out of the house. His mother and father's excessive restrictions and her unending pressure for him to be perfect always sent him running.

Mike really had been a pussy. He'd been a spoiled

brat who had it all handed to him on a silver platter, but he'd never been satisfied. Always wanted more.

A week after Mike's mom died, they lifted a few bottles of bourbon from Marlowe's study and snuck through the fence. They ended up along the banks of the Cumberland River, sitting on the riverbank and tossing stones into the rushing waters. Amber had joined them. She'd hugged him and then kissed Mike on the lips. While Mike's eyes were closed, she looked at him, staring, teasing. He was jealous, angry that such a great girl wasted her time on a moron like Mike. His family didn't have the Marlowes' wealth, but his prospects were so much brighter.

As they drank more and more, Mike started to talk about his mom. She forbade him ever to see Amber again. She called her white trash. Mike's eyes went vacant as he said with no hint of emotion, "I shoved her hard and she crumbled like a rag doll." He explained with cold precision how she staggered back and lost her footing at the top of the stairs and fell down the entire staircase. The three of them sat in silence, digesting the weight of his words.

Later, the doctors would say Mrs. Marlowe's advanced stage of cancer killed her, but it was the fall that shattered her remaining strength and ended her life. Both Mike and his father mourned her passing in public. They wept openly at the funeral. They made donations in her name. They kept her portrait hanging in the study. And both were glad she was gone.

He pressed his finger on the back doorbell. As bell chimes echoed in the house, he pulled a clean handkerchief from his coat pocket and wiped the doorbell button clean. Lights clicked on inside. Fast, determine footsteps approached. By the sound of it, the old man wasn't happy about the interruption.

Good.

A small flutter of doubt dug into his gut as the latch on the other side scraped free and passcode numbers dinged as they were punched into the pad.

He straightened just a fraction as the door jerked open to Dalton Marlowe's frowning face. An instant passed as the old man stood and stared. Like the house, he was the same. The hair was still black but streaked with gray, the frown lines still bracketed his mouth, and his dark eyes were always searching for the next threat. Fit, he still favored nice clothes and even wore his wedding band. Mr. Marlowe understood the importance of appearances.

Tim grinned. "Mr. M. How's it going?"

Mr. Marlowe blinked. The anger that always buzzed behind his gaze softened. "Tim. What are you doing here?"

He removed a silver flask from his pocket. "I thought we could drink a toast to Mike."

Mr. Marlowe stepped aside, a sad smile easing the lines in his face. "Come on in, son. It's good to see you."

The door closed behind Tim. Mr. Marlowe clamped a hand on Tim's shoulder and then pulled him into a hug. "Thanks for coming by."

"Sure thing, Mr. M. The funeral was nice."

"Mrs. Reed planned it. She's good at that kind of thing, and I knew she'd do a fine job so I let her."

"I'm surprised you joined forces with her. I didn't think you were friends."

"I didn't want to, but the cops convinced me. They were hoping Mike's killer might have shown."

Cops by nature were slow moving, but even the dull witted got it right occasionally. "I bet they're watching the house now."

"They are. A patrol car drives by every fifteen minutes. I'm not sure what good it will do, but that's what I pay taxes for."

They moved down a carpeted hallway into the brightly lit kitchen. Smooth gray granite countertops glistened beneath custom-made cherry cabinets. Stainless-steel appliances glistened in the glow of pendant lights over a wide island sporting a large handblown glass bowl filled with oranges. "Can I get you something to eat?"

Tim twisted off the top of his flask. "Oh, you don't have to do that."

"I'd like to. You and Mike were best friends and having you here is a little like having him at home." Marlowe hugged Tim again, holding him close as if the old man actually meant it, which of course, he didn't. The old man might be hugging him now, but he was an evil son of a bitch. He used everyone. Mike said so, but more importantly, Amber said so.

Tim patted Mr. Marlowe on the back, willing to play the surrogate son. A sigh shuddered from Mr. Marlowe as he stepped back and tugged the cuffs of his hand-tailored shirt.

Tim drank from the flask and then handed it to Marlowe who also took a pull. "To Mike."

"To Mike."

Tim supposed this would be the time he felt a twinge of guilt, but there was none. "Weird to see you sitting next to Amber at the funeral."

Mr. Marlowe stepped back as if stung, the hard lines of his face deepening. "That woman is poison. She's a liar."

Tim bristled as anger stirred and burned under his skin. How dare this animal speak about Amber? "I talked to her briefly at the funeral. She sounds like she's doing well. She likes Texas."

He folded his arms. "Don't believe it for a minute. She's back here for a reason."

"She was kind to me."

"Don't kid yourself." Marlowe seemed to catch himself and shook off the rising tide of fury. "Look, I don't want to talk about her. I want to visit with you. It's been too long. Let me make you a sandwich."

"I'd like that."

As Marlowe turned to the refrigerator to dig out deli meats, bread, and condiments, Tim's gaze roamed the kitchen, letting it settle on the framed pictures of Mike on the wall behind a long farmhouse table. All were black and white and framed in sleek mahogany frames. "What's with the pictures? They're new."

"I had them done about two years after Mike . . . left. A reminder, I guess. I wanted to remember that times were once good between us."

Mr. Marlowe retrieved a plate from the cabinet and laid two slices of bread on it. "You still like spicy mustard?"

Tim took another drink from the flask, replaced the cap, and stuck it back in his pocket. He settled on a bar stool in front of the large island. He was careful not to touch anything. "Yeah, you have a good memory."

Mr. Marlowe carefully made the sandwich, set it on

a plate, and pushed it toward him before turning back to the refrigerator to dig out a couple of beers.

Tim had rehearsed this moment since Amber had come to him days ago. He forgot how much he loved her, how much he wanted her. When she was in his arms after they made love, he told her she could count on him. He would protect her this time. He loved her. But as she stared up at him with large liquid eyes, he saw the unspoken doubt. She didn't think he had the stones to stand by her. She didn't think she could count on him. But he would prove his love and devotion.

The old man twisted the top off his beer and carefully set the top on the counter. He opened another beer for himself and held it up. "Happy Birthday to Mike. Big twenty-three today."

Tim clinked his bottle against Mr. Marlowe's and drank. The beer was smooth and cold.

Mr. Marlowe moved to a cabinet and found a bag of chips. He scooped out a handful and placed it on the plate next to the sandwich. "She's going to get away with it."

"Who?"

"Amber. She killed my boy and that girl. I don't know how she did it, but she did. And she'll walk away as if none of this ever happened."

The sandwich tasted good. He took a second bite. "You think Amber killed Mike?"

"I know she did." The old man was quiet for a long moment as he drank his beer.

Tim liked the beer. It was top-notch like everything else in this house.

The old man was content to watch him eat his sandwich as he drank his beer. "How is work at the law firm?"

"It's great. I can't thank you enough for giving me the reference. I know it made a difference."

"Good." A half grin tugged his lip. "Glad to see you finally cut that hair. Pretty damn long the last time I saw you."

Tim rubbed his hand over his shorn hair. "My walk on the wild side."

Marlowe's smile froze. "You spent time in Texas, didn't you?"

"Sure." Tim balled up his napkin and tossed it on his plate.

"The cops showed me a picture of a guy in Austin. I didn't recognize him until now."

"Really?"

Marlowe looked at him, his gaze hardening as if the final piece of the puzzle clicked into place.

Tim smiled and reached in his pocket for latex gloves. "Amber told me what you did to her."

Color drained from Marlowe's face. "What?"

Dropping his hands below the counter, he tugged on the gloves. "She told me what you made her do."

He took a step back, the softness hardening to cold steel. "I don't know what she's saying, but she's a liar."

"No, she's not. I know her. Love her. Believe her."

Marlowe's eyes sparked with a fire Tim had not seen in years. "What the hell are you talking about?"

"When the cops find out what you did to Amber, you'll be ruined."

"You wouldn't do that."

"I would."

"I can crush you without breaking a sweat, kid. Don't ever think you can threaten me. One call and they can dig into your past and find out if you're the guy they are looking for in Austin."

He laughed.

"I will destroy Amber and take you down with her if you get in my way."

Tim's good humor vanished. He had known rage. Killed. But never had the anger been so hot and sharp. He shifted his grip around the neck of the beer bottle as if it were a club. Moving with a swiftness he'd learned on the football field, he raised the bottle and lunged across the kitchen island, cracking the glass against the side of the old man's skull.

Shock replaced that know-it-all smugness and King Marlowe staggered. Satisfaction burned in Tim, egging on his temper.

*Kill him!*

Tim's brain morphed from thinking to primal as he moved fast, scrambling around the island and landing hard blows with the bottle on the old man's face. Marlowe staggered and fell back to the floor. A look of panic and disbelief swept over the old gray eyes.

Tim reached in his pocket and pulled out a clear plastic bag. With a snap he opened it and straddled Mr. Marlowe. He pulled it over the bloodied head and twisted the ends shut, cutting off his air flow. Tim settled his weight on Marlowe's chest and held the bag in place as his victim struggled for air. Several minutes passed until finally, Marlowe's eyes rolled back in his head and Tim was certain he was dead.

Tim removed the bag and checked for a pulse. There was none. Satisfied, he poured out the remaining beer in the sink. He dumped both bottles in his plastic bag as well as the remains of the sandwich. He turned on the hot water tap and when steam rose from the now hot water, he washed the plate and dried it with a paper towel, which he used to wipe down the counter.

As he backed away, his heart still thundered in his chest. He stared at the body, noting how death had robbed all the fire and bravado.

His temper cooled. And with clearer eyes, he now realized he was finally worthy of Amber.

# CHAPTER TWENTY-ONE

*Thursday, October 12, 9:00 A.M.*

Jake and Rick drove past a collection of news vans and through the front gates of Mr. Marlowe's driveway. Jake parked at the top of the driveway behind five squad cars and the forensic vans that were crammed in the front of the circular drive. Officers stood at the ready just outside the yellow crime scene tape that blocked off the front entrance and wafted in a gentle breeze.

Out of the car, Jake and Rick strode up to a young female uniformed officer who stood at the base of the stairs. She was tall with a runner's lean frame and wore her hair tied back in a tight bun at the base of her neck. Her uniform was crisp, sharp, and her shoes polished. Her name badge read GRIMES.

Jake and Rick paused. "We received a call about a half hour ago. Can you fill us in?"

Officer Grimes shifted her stance. "I received a call this morning that the housekeeper discovered a possible homicide. Two units were dispatched, and when I arrived, the housekeeper met me on the front steps.

She said Mr. Dalton Marlowe is dead. I found him in the kitchen expired from a combination of head trauma and possibly asphyxiation."

Rick rested his hands on his belt. "Did the housekeeper see anything while she was in the house?"

"No. As soon as she saw Mr. Marlowe, she ran outside."

Jake glanced up the stairs to a small camera posted above and to the right of the front door. "Security cameras working?"

"The hard drive in the library has been removed."

Jake studied the perimeter of the property lined with tall cypress trees that hugged a black wrought-iron fence. "Someone who visited this house often would know how to sneak onto the property, past the patrols, and would know where the camera recorders were kept." His first thought was Amber Ryder, who'd spent a great deal of time in the house.

The officer nodded. "We've two officers searching the perimeter now."

Jake and Rick thanked Officer Grimes, who logged them into the crime scene, before donning black latex gloves and ducking under the yellow crime scene tape. They climbed the brick front staircase and stepped into the foyer.

More cops milled in a study to the right and he heard several talking in the back of the house. Murder in this kind of neighborhood made the rich nervous and politicians worried so cops showed in force.

They moved through the house toward the kitchen where they found Georgia photographing the body. She glanced up, and for a split second locked eyes with Jake, before she glanced back down at the body. After they made love, she kissed him, and as she dressed, told him she was headed to KC to talk to him about Carrie's funeral. She had no family so there was no one to make arrangements or take care of the baby. She said Rick planned a call to Social Services to determine what arrangements had been made for the baby.

He knew she blamed herself for what happened.

Having her this close and not being able to touch her frustrated him. He missed her warmth, her softness cradled against him.

Georgia now glanced in the viewfinder of her digital camera and then, confirming she had the right shot, looked up at her brother. "He was hit in the head several times with a blunt object. My guess is he fell and then the killer asphyxiated him judging by the bruising and scratches around his neck. The killer likely used a plastic bag."

"So our killer was strong?" Jake asked.

"I would say so although Mr. Marlowe would have been incapacitated by the head injury."

"This fact would likely rule out Amber."

"I agree," she said. "He also was savvy, or so he thought. He took the time to wash a plate and wipe down the counter." She sniffed. "And I smell the faint odor of beer. A beer bottle would certainly stun a man."

"Did you find any bottles?"

"No. I looked in the trash both in and outside of the house and I found nothing. He's smart enough to know if he touched either, his DNA would be all over the bottles."

"A shared beer. No signs of forced entry. Sounds like this guy was a friend. Marlowe knew his killer.

Liked him enough to share a beer," Rick said. "That would not have been Amber Ryder."

"The killer," she said pointing down the hallway, "might have washed his hands, but there are faint traces of blood on the hallway carpet. He hit Marlowe and picked up a little blood splatter on his shoes. He left trace amounts along the way to the office where the security camera hard drive was hidden. He removed the hard drive."

"The average killer usually doesn't put this kind of thought into a crime," Rick said.

Georgia smirked. "He left something behind. I haven't found it yet, but it's here."

Jake moved toward the body, knelt, and studied the brutally beaten face. "What the hell set him off?"

Rick leaned against the counter. "Yesterday was the eleventh. Mike's birthday. Maybe that had something to do with it."

Jake tightened his jaw. "That's the kind of detail a friend of the family would remember." He thought about the head injury on the side of Marlowe's head. "I'm guessing a tall, strong guy. Like Tim."

Rick shook his head. "Why the hell would a guy like Tim throw his life away by killing Dalton Marlowe?"

"He and Mike knew each other in high school. Tim made it clear he didn't like him," Jake said. "We need to find out more about Tim and Mike and their relationship. And I'd bet money Amber plays into this somehow."

"Where's the housekeeper?" Rick asked.

"She's in the living room," Georgia said. "Very shook up."

"Thanks, Georgia," Jake said.

She nodded, turning back to her job as if they were simply two coworkers working a crime scene.

Jake and Rick moved to the living room where he found the petite Hispanic woman holding a rosary rocking back and forth in a chair. Her dark hair was peppered with white and the skin around her eyes lined. "Ma'am, I'm Detective Jake Bishop. This is my partner, Detective Rick Morgan. Can we get you a glass of water?"

"No water for me, but thank you."

"We'd like to ask you a few questions. Are you up for that?" Jake asked.

"Yes."

He sat across from her in a sleek leather club chair and kept his voice low and even as he asked, "What's your name?"

"Maria Torres." She looked up at him, mumbled a prayer, and fingered a delicate gold cross around her neck. "I never seen a dead body before."

"It's not easy, I know." He pulled a notebook and pen from his breast pocket. "What time did you find Mr. Marlowe?"

"Just after seven. I come every morning at six to make Mr. Marlowe his breakfast."

"You don't live on the property."

"No. I got my own place that I share with my daughter, Rosa. But if there's a party and I have to stay late, there's an apartment over the garage."

"How old is Rosa?" Jake's tone was easy, conversational and anyone listening at this moment would have thought he was talking to a friend.

Her eyes flickered with pride. "She's twenty-one. She's in school. Very smart."

"How long have you been working for Mr. Marlowe?"

"Since my Rosa was one year old."

"So you knew the late Mrs. Marlowe?"

"I did. She was a lovely woman. Very sweet. Intelligent. She used to buy treats for my Rosa."

"You must have known Mike Marlowe?"

Her expression grew guarded as if an old habit of hiding secrets kicked into play. "Yes. I knew him."

"What can you tell me about the boy?"

She glanced toward the kitchen almost as if she feared Marlowe was standing there listening. She sat straighter and mumbled another prayer.

"He can't hear anymore," Jake said with an assuring smile. "You can speak freely."

She crossed herself. "I knew Mike since he was a baby. He was a hard boy to take care of. Always getting into trouble. Always looking for something that would bring him pleasure no matter what he hurt."

"How old was Mike when his mother died?" Jake asked.

"He was fifteen. It was a sad day for everyone in the house. We all wept for the lovely lady."

"I understand she was sick."

"*Sí.* With the cancer. But it was the fall that killed her."

"One of the teachers at Mike's school mentioned the fall."

"Mr. Marlowe didn't want anyone to know about it. He said it would do no good."

"Were you here when it happened?"

"I was in the kitchen. I heard her arguing with Mike, and then I heard her fall. I found her at the bottom of the main staircase."

"Where was Mike?"

"Hurrying down the stairs toward his mother. He said she lost her footing. Said it was an accident." A long breath shuddered between her teeth. "She passed two days later. She never woke up."

Jake glanced at Rick whose stark expression telegraphed what Jake thought. Mike had been at the top of the stairs before his mother fell. They had argued. Had it been an accident or had he pushed her?

"What was it like for Mike after she died?"

"He was hard to deal with before, but after she died, he was impossible. He and his father fought all the time. He was running wild, drinking, and sneaking out of the house. His girlfriend was here whenever Mr. Marlowe wasn't."

"Amber Ryder?"

"Yes. Mike adored her."

"What did you think of her?" Jake asked.

"Very pretty. Polite. But . . ."

"But what?"

"Always watching."

"She was a poor kid and this is a rich man's house." As a teen, Jake went into nice houses with his dad on summer construction jobs. Hundred-year-old brick mansions on Beacon Hill that made his Southie row house look no better than a toolshed. He remembered being in awe as well as jealous.

She slid the cross back and forth on the gold chain

while she spoke. "It was more than that. Yes, there have always been pretty things in this house, but she was most fascinated by the pictures."

"What kind of pictures?"

"Of the family. She especially liked the pictures of Mr. Marlowe holding Mike when he was a baby." She shook her head. "In the pictures, he looked like such a sweet baby." She crossed herself. "My Rosa said Amber was always flirting with the boys whenever Mike was not around. Rosa would see them all at football games and parties. Amber she said could make any boy do whatever she wanted. Rosa called her a witch. Mike was bewitched. Always sneaking out of the house to see her."

Rick rested his hands on his belt. "How did he sneak out of the house?"

"There's a window in the basement. He didn't think I knew, but I did. He used to sneak out of it when he was a teenager. He would also bring in his friends that way."

He imagined the tall wrought-iron fence that circled the property. "What about the fence around the house?"

"There's a small gap in the corner behind the cypresses. It's hidden, but a few know about it."

"Can you show me the basement?"

"Yes." She rose and, turning her face from the kitchen, made the sign of the cross before moving toward a side staircase. She switched on a light and descended the carpeted staircase. Jake's parents had a basement but it wasn't the kind of place anyone wanted to spend time. Dark and dank, it had a low ceiling and poor lighting. No one went down there unless it was to do laundry or store something for the season.

This basement had tall ceilings, richly paneled walls, and spot lighting that lit a collection of photographic images of shadowed outlines of a naked woman. The furniture was sleek, elegant. One hell of a space.

The maid moved past the kitchenette area where a small window looked out over the side of the yard. She tested the lock. It worked. "When Mike snuck out, this was always unlatched until he returned."

As she stepped back, Jake moved toward the window. It was small, but big enough for a man to squeeze through if his build was slight. Like Tim. But the killer had not used the window.

Tim had come through the back door and he left the same way. "You said the gap in the fence is where?"

"On the north side of the fence behind the cypresses."

"Thank you, Mrs. Torres. Why don't you go upstairs? I'll call you if I need anything else."

She crossed herself. "Yes, thank you."

Jake and Rick followed and found Georgia bagging the victim's hands. "Georgia, can you have a look at the fence out back? There's a gap."

"Sure." She rose and grabbed her fingerprinting kit.

The three walked out the back door. The air was cool but the sun bright. Jake moved to the north corner of the yard and pushed through the trees, holding the branches back for Georgia and Rick. The gap hadn't been apparent until now.

"You think he came in that way?" she asked.

"I do."

"Well, the killer was good about not leaving prints in the house, but let's see if he was as smart when he wedged through the fence."

"Why kill the old man? What's to be gained?" Rick asked as Georgia dusted for prints.

"Maybe Amber cast a spell on our buddy Tim," Jake said.

Rick nodded. "Maybe."

"What do you think about what the housekeeper said about Amber?"

"Amber comes from an economically and emotionally challenged family. It's logical to attach to a family like the Marlowes who, on the outside, appear close and functional. She sleeps with Mike, thinking she can make this family her own. Father sees her as a gold digger. Father and son fight. A not so original story." Rick shifted his stance as if his hip had tensed.

"But Amber likes the boys. Likes to flirt. What if she flirted with Tim and she caught him in her spell like she caught Mike?"

"If you want to go that route, then if Tim is capable of killing Mike's father, he's capable of killing Mike and Bethany," said Rick.

"He's got an alibi for Elisa's time of death. And Amber says she didn't know Elisa," said Jake.

"If not for Elisa, we'd never have found Bethany and Mike's bodies."

"Why kill Bethany?" Jake asked.

"Wrong place. Wrong time."

"Maybe."

"Let's say Amber's fall five years ago really was an accident," Jake said. "She's too messed up for Tim to carry her out of the woods. She tells him not to worry. She can claim amnesia to cover for Tim and no one will ever know he was in the woods."

"Or she really doesn't remember," Rick countered. "We can have all the theories in the world, but until we can prove it, any decent defense attorney will rip our theories to shreds."

"We need to find Tim."

Georgia whistled and held up a white piece of print paper with a dark thumbprint. "Jake, was it you that said forensic science was too slow?"

"You have a print."

"You bet I do."


After Tim left through the back fence, with the evidence of his crime in the plastic bag, he drove to a neighborhood in Nashville's east side. He drove his old four-door car, knowing it would blend and easily be forgotten by anyone who happened to see it. After he made the drop, the adrenaline pumping through his veins vanished. Exhausted, he found a quiet street in an area near the university. He closed his eyes, planning to sleep for only a few minutes.

When he awoke to sunlight, he realized he had slept for hours. Damn! He needed to see Amber and tell her what he'd done. Show her he could be trusted.

He drove to the Reeds' neighborhood and waited until he saw Mrs. Reed leave for an early morning exercise class and then he hurried to the back door. He knocked hard and seconds later heard the clip of her footsteps on the other side of the door.

The door swung open and Amber stood before him. This close to her now, smelling the soft scent of her perfume, the desires that never, ever were satisfied, churned.

He'd always loved her. Always loved the smell of her freshly washed hair, the way she painted her nails a faint pink, the feel of her soft skin rubbing against him. The person before him wasn't the girl he'd adored in high school, but a woman. She wore slim black pants and a white sweater that hugged her breasts. Her shoulder-length hair was neatly styled, her makeup expertly applied and her earlobes sparkling with diamond earrings.

If anything, he wanted her more than ever. "Amber."

"Tim," she said. "I've been calling you."

"I heard your messages. I had a job to do before we could talk. Can I come in?"

She stepped aside, curious but also annoyed.

He closed the door and clicked the deadbolt in place, searching for signs of anyone else in the house. "Is there anyone else in the house?"

"No, we're alone."

"Good." He cupped her face in his hands and kissed her hard on the lips. She tasted sweet, soft. As he deepened the kiss, she wrapped her arms around him, nestling close.

He tugged her shirt free of her waistband, but as his hand slid up her flat belly, she broke the kiss and stepped back. "We talk first."

He moved forward, reaching out to take her again in his arms, but she sidestepped him. "The sooner you talk, the sooner we play."

She raised a manicured hand to run a finger along the beads of a pearl necklace around her neck. She studied the dark stains on his shirt. "I'm waiting?"

"I went to see Dalton Marlowe," he said.

"Why?"

His gaze was drawn to her hands that just days ago had been wrapped around him. "I know who he is to you."

Her brow furrowed. "What do you know?"

Shaking his head, he couldn't articulate the words that still tasted foul. "It doesn't matter."

She saw past his stony gaze. "I've been calling and calling you, but you never answered."

Everything always made sense when she spoke. She made complicated simple, but when he thought of losing her, the world spun out of control. He liked that about her. Hated it about her. "I had to see him. It was time to take care of him once and for all."

Her eyebrows knitted. "What happened? Did you fight?"

"I hit him."

Her chin lifted as if the scene with Dalton played in front of her. "You hit him. How badly is he hurt?"

"I knocked him down and then I wrapped a plastic bag around his head. I killed him."

Her face paled and she stepped back, shaking her head as she raised her fingertips to her mouth. "You killed him! Jesus, Tim, how did it get so out of control?"

"I wasn't out of control. I knew exactly what I was doing. I know how hard it was for you to face him, and that you could never do what I did, so I took care of it. I was protecting you."

He took her soft hands in his and pulled her closer to him. Her expensive perfume wafted around him and he grew so hard. Without thinking, he backed her up until she was pressed against the wall. His hand went to the waistband of her pants. "Marlowe was the one that pushed for this investigation to reopen. Now that he's gone, it will die."

She grabbed his hand. "Tim, stop. We can't do this. Not now. Not here!"

He yanked hard at the waistband button and it popped, falling to the tiled floor. "You need to know you can count on me."

"Tim, stop." She pushed hard against his chest. "I know I can count on you."

He pushed down her pants to her knees and reached for his own zipper. "I would do anything for you. Because I love you. We're two sides of the same coin."

Her body stilled and her resistance melted. Sensually, she stepped out of her pants. "You've been there for me so many times."

Tim cupped her taut ass, not wanting anything else now other than to drive deep inside her. "We're the same person."

She raised steady hands to his face and held it. "I see that, now."

He looked at her beautiful face. "I said I'd take care of you, and I will."

"Did anyone see you leave the house?"

"No. I left through the back door and went out the gap in the fence just like I did when we were kids. But the maid will be there by now. She'll have found him."

"Okay."

"It'll be fine. They'll never trace it back to me."

She kissed him. "We can't do this here. Mrs. Reed will be home soon. She can't catch you here."

His breathing was ragged and labored as his thoughts zeroed in on one thing—having Amber. "Where then?"

She ran her fingers through his hair. "Let's get a motel room. Meet me at the Middle Motel."

"When?"

"Go now. I'll be minutes behind you."

Reluctantly, he stepped back and fixed his pants. "You sound like my Amber again. Thinking."

She tugged her pants over her hips and zipped them. "Yes, I'm always one step ahead."

He kissed her.

"Hurry," she breathed against his lips. "Wait for me. I'll be there later this afternoon and we'll have hours to be with each other."

He leaned forward, grabbed her arms, and kissed her hard on the lips. She leaned into the kiss, allowing him to taste her and explore the inside of her mouth. There was so much promise in her touch. She was his soul mate.

She pulled back, moistening her lips. "Go on and go. I'll call you soon."

"I love you, Amber."

She smiled. "I love you, Tim."

Twelve hours passed before Georgia left the Marlowe house. She and Brad had spent the entire time collecting, documenting, sketching, and photographing trace evidence and fingerprints. She had pulled a very clear thumbprint from the back fence as well as an index fingerprint. They would be processed and analyzed when they got back to the lab.

When she arrived at the lab it was close to eight o'clock at night. Fatigue tightened the muscles in her back and legs. Her stomach grumbled as she realized she'd not eaten since last night.

Brad pushed through the lab door with evidence boxes in his hands. "This is the last of it. I'm locking it up and will start processing first thing in the morning."

"Thanks, Brad."

He rubbed his hand over his chin that was covered in dark stubble. "Tell me you aren't staying tonight."

"No. I'll head home." She'd not spoken to Jake since she'd seen him at the Marlowe crime scene. As much as she wanted to see him now, she needed time to think.

Grabbing her phone, she dialed KC's number. He picked up on the second ring. In the background, she could hear muffled music and she imagined him in his back office with a pile of paperwork in front of him on an old desk he'd used when he worked homicide. "Hi, Georgia."

"I'm checking in about the arrangements for Carrie. Sorry I haven't called today. There was a crime scene."

"I know, kid. I know the job has to come first."

She pressed tired fingers to her forehead. "Where's the baby?"

"Jenna has her."

"Jenna? My sister-in-law?"

"Your brother Rick got Social Services on the phone. He talked to them for at least an hour and convinced them to let Jenna and him keep the baby for now."

A sudden rush of tears welled in her eyes. "That's what Buddy did for me."

"He sure as hell did. I remember when your old man

was on the phone talking to the social workers for you. He was a force to be reckoned with. Rick was the same way today."

"I didn't know they wanted children."

"You know Rick. He plays his cards close to his vest."

The stress that had coiled around her spine since she'd seen the baby crying released. She glanced at the clock. "It's too late to call and check on them tonight."

"All the arrangements for the baby came together only a few hours ago. Rick said he'd call you in the morning and give you an update."

A tear snaked down her cheek and she swiped it away. "That works for me."

"You okay, kid?"

"I keep thinking about Carrie. How could a man who says he loves the mother of his child do that to her?"

"You and I both know shit happens on the streets that make no sense. Evil is evil."

"But she was the mother of his child. How could a father do that to his daughter?"

"Like I said, evil is evil."

To argue this was pointless. KC was right. "Thanks for all you've done."

"You sound dead on your feet."

"I'm fine."

His old chair squeaked and she imagined him leaning forward in it. "Go home and sleep. You'll be no good to anyone tied up in knots and exhausted."

"I will. Thanks."

"Promise?"

"I promise."

She hung up the phone and stretched her head from side to side. Buddy had gone to the mat for her when she was too little to defend herself. Rick would do the same for Sara. He would protect that kid with his life.

And yet some fathers turned on their children. Her own birth father, a married man Annie had loved, had denied her. Hal denied Sara her mother.

Closing her eyes, her mind suddenly tripped to Amber. There was no father in her life.

Not in the picture . . .

What if he had been around?

What if . . .

She moved to her computer and turned it on. When it was up and running, she went to the database of DNA samples and on a hunch printed out Amber's, Mike's, and Dalton Marlowe's all taken five years ago.

The printer hummed out the documents as she hovered and waited, her heart thumping in her chest. When she had the printouts, she laid them on the large light table and looked at each one. She compared the size of the sixteen genetic markers.

She paired Dalton's with Mike's and could clearly see that the boy had inherited distinct markers from his father. Drawing in a breath, she lined up Amber's results. It took less than a beat for her to see the truth. No one had seen it before. No one.

Dalton Marlowe was Amber's biological father and Mike's half sister.

She stepped back from the table, stunned. Not only by the connection, but what it also implied about the relationship Amber had shared with her brother and her father. Did she know?

Her phone rang, startling her. A glance at the display set her nerves on end. "Amber?"

"Georgia!" Amber's panicked voice reached through the phone line.

"Amber, what's wrong?" She pushed a strand of hair from her eyes, doing her best to keep her cool and not tip her hand.

"It's Tim."

"What about him?"

"He says he knows what happened in the woods."

# CHAPTER TWENTY-TWO

*Thursday, October 12, 10:00 P.M.*

Georgia's fatigue burned off in a blink as she stepped away from the light table in her lab. It was as if Amber sensed Georgia had connected these critical DNA clues. "How could Tim know what happened in the woods?"

"He said he was there and knows details. He has always known. He told me to meet me at the Middle Motel. Room 116."

"Dalton Marlowe is dead."

"What?" The word rushed over the line. "How could Dalton be dead?"

"He was murdered."

"Did Tim do it?"

"We don't know yet." Georgia rose and slid her feet into her shoes. "Okay. Where are you?"

"I'm at the motel now. I can see him inside pacing in front of the window."

"Don't go in and talk to him until the police arrive."

"I've got to find out what happened in the woods,

Georgia. It has haunted me. If the cops show, he won't talk to anyone and I might not ever find out."

Whatever Amber's relationship was to Marlowe and his son didn't mean that Tim wasn't a real threat to her now. "Wait for me."

"Just hurry. I'll wait for you outside the room." Panic chased the words out in a rush.

Georgia rang off and tied her shoelaces before she called Jake. He answered on the third ring. "Jake Bishop."

His voice was rough like gravel, heavy with fatigue. He and Rick would have been working nonstop on the Marlowe case and she wondered if he'd even gotten enough time to eat something. "Amber called me."

"When?"

"Just now." She recapped her call about Amber's fear of Tim. "I'm headed over there."

"Georgia, don't engage her or Tim." His tone sharpened, reached out as if trying to grab hold of her. "Wait until Rick and I can get there."

"Where are you?" Georgia pulled her messy ponytail free of the hair band and combed her fingers through her hair.

"We're ten to twenty minutes out." In the background, she heard Rick mutter a curse.

"I'll see you there."

"Don't engage." In the background, Rick said, "Listen to him, Georgia."

"Jake, I pulled DNA for Marlowe and Amber. They're father and daughter."

His answer was a muttered curse. "Okay. We'll deal

with that in due order. Now, we've got to get Tim secured."

She moved toward her desk where she kept a gun locked in the bottom drawer. She fished out her keys from her purse, unlocked the drawer, and removed the gun. "I won't engage. Unless I have to."

She ended the call to his curses. Shoving the phone in her back pocket, she rushed to her car. The moon hung high in the sky. The air was cool and crisp. This late there was little traffic and the drive went quickly.

Georgia spotted Amber's car nosed in a spot next to room 116. She scanned the lot for Jake and Rick's vehicle and seeing no sign of it knew she'd act alone if forced. She sat for several minutes before she saw the curtains flutter.

Room 116 had a large picture window now covered with a thick curtain. The curtains fluttered once and then twice more as if someone had peeked out of it.

"Damn it." The gun holster now resting on her hip, she dug out her cell as she got out of the car. Dialing Jake, he answered on the first ring. "I see only Amber's car. I don't see her or Tim, but the window curtain in the room is moving. Someone is in the room."

"Do not go in that room, Georgia," Jake growled. "I've got uniforms on the way."

"What if he's in the room alone with her? You and I both know he could have killed Marlowe. It'll take only a few seconds to incapacitate and then kill her." She'd not been there for Carrie. She'd not been able to save her. "Tell the uniforms to come in without sirens. I don't want to spook this guy."

"Understood. I am minutes—seconds—out. Wait."

Impatience clawed at her gut. "Jesus, she could be already dead."

"Stay put!"

As she edged closer to the motel room, she heard the *pop, pop, pop* of gunfire. "Damn it."

"What?"

"Shots fired. I have to go in."

"No!"

Phone clutched in her hand, she unholstered her gun and raced toward the door, the blood in her veins pumping so hard that she couldn't hear Jake's shouted warnings.

Standing to the side of the door, she held her gun close as she reached out and pounded on the door. "Tim Taylor!"

In all the years working in the forensic field she had never fired her weapon outside of a firing range. And though she was trained for moments like this, no amount of practice could really prepare her.

Silence echoed from the room. One. Two. Three.

"Amber! Amber, it's Georgia!"

"Georgia!" Amber screamed. "Help me! I've shot Tim."

She reached for the door handle and turned it, allowing the door to swing open as she waited for any kind of return fire. Over the sound of her own pounding heart she heard Amber's weeping, desperate and frightened.

She drew in a breath as she adjusted her hold on the gun and turned to go into the room. Blue lights behind her flashed as Jake and Rick pulled up in their unmarked car. Both men were out of the car in seconds, guns drawn.

Jake paused and looked at her, unvarnished fear burning in his gaze as it swept over her. Signaling for her to stay, he moved past her into the motel room as several marked cars pulled into the lot.

As Amber cried in the middle of the room, she held a gun in her hand that now pointed at the ground. Her face had paled to a bloodless white and when she raised her gaze, it was filled with fear. Tim lay on the floor, facedown, his arms splayed out.

"Put the gun down," Jake ordered. "Put the gun down!"

Amber glanced at the gun as if she forgot she were holding it and slowly released her grip and the gun fell to the floor.

Jake quickly picked it up and checked the chamber for a round. "What happened here?"

"He started talking about the woods almost immediately," Amber said softly. "He said he killed Bethany and Mike and was going to kill me just like he killed Marlowe. I grabbed the gun. It went off."

"Tim confessed to killing Dalton Marlowe?" Jake asked.

"Yes." She pressed her hand to the darkening bruise on her cheek. "I freaked out and he came at me. I told him to stop. I told him I didn't want to shoot him."

Jake turned Tim over and they all saw the bright red bloom of blood in the center of his chest. The bullet had exited out his back.

Pressing fingers to the man's neck, Jake shook his head. "There's a heartbeat, but barely."

Rick reached for his cell and punched in numbers. "This is Detective Rick Morgan. I need an ambulance."

As he rattled off the address, Georgia holstered her gun and stood ready as Jake grabbed a towel from the bathroom and moved to Tim's chest and pressed it firmly onto the wound.

"He's really alive?" Amber asked.

"Barely," Rick said.

Georgia knelt beside Jake. "What can I do?"

"Help me press this towel onto his chest."

Tim's face had turned a deathly white and she feared it would be only minutes at most before he bled out.

Amber hovered over Tim, her expression blank. "He's alive?"

Jake, not answering this time, tipped Tim's head back and opened his airway. "Very shallow breathing." He checked his pulse again. "Faint heartbeat."

The towel had turned a blood-soaked red as Georgia continued to apply pressure. A faint gurgling sound echoed from Tim's mouth. At least one of the lungs had been hit. Blood would also be pooling inside the body and lungs. He was drowning.

In the distance an ambulance wailed, growing closer and closer with each minute. Amber lowered her face to her hands and began to weep. "I didn't want to shoot him, but he wouldn't stop. Why didn't he stop?"

"Where did you get the gun?" Jake asked.

"It was Tim's. He brought it."

"How did you get the gun from him?"

"I don't really know. He said he was going to rape

me first and then track down Mrs. Reed. I didn't fight him, and I waited until he set the gun down to undo my blouse. It distracted him long enough for me to grab the gun and shoot. I just wanted him to stop." She looked down at the near lifeless body. "I didn't mean to hurt him. I just wanted him to stop."

Red lights of the ambulance flashed on the walls of the motel room, casting an eerie glow. The rescue crews rattled a gurney carrying equipment through the open door, unpacking as they went.

"I need this room cleared," a paramedic ordered.

Rick took Amber by the arm as Jake spoke to the paramedic, who nodded and said he'd take over.

As the paramedic took Georgia's place, she rose, her hands now red with blood. Jake grabbed a small towel from the bathroom and wiped her hands and his own clean as they moved outside.

Georgia moved past Tim as one member of the rescue crew started an IV and the other swapped the towel for a pad of clean gauze.

She stepped outside. The chill touched her sweat-soaked skin and along with the adrenaline dump sent a shiver through her body.

"Are you all right?" Jake asked.

"I'm fine. Do what you need to do."

He hugged her and then she moved toward her car where she kept a clean blanket along with MREs, a change of clothes, and shoes in the trunk. She raised the lid and pulled out a blanket, which she wrapped around her shoulders.

Turning, she saw Rick speaking to a limp Amber. The woman looked devastated. Jake along with Georgia moved closer, needing to hear and better understand her story.

"Why did you call Georgia?" Jake asked.

Amber smoothed her hands over her head. "I don't know. She's the closest person I have to a friend since I came back to Nashville. And I knew Tim might be trouble. I thought she could help."

"Why not call the cops?" Jake challenged. "They would have been better equipped to help you."

She shook her head. "Like I said when I was mugged, I hated the way the cops grilled me five years ago. None of them believed me. They wouldn't listen. I didn't want to do that again."

Jake glanced at the blood smeared on his shirt. "But you called Georgia."

"I called a friend," she said.

"Why'd you leave the Reeds' house?" Jake's questions were clipped and quick. He fired the questions like bullets so she didn't have time to fabricate.

"Tim called me. Offered to tell me about the woods." She touched her fingertips to her lips and turned her face from the body as if it pained her to look at it. "He said he needed to tell me the truth, but I didn't trust the way he sounded."

"His chest has a center mass wound, Amber. You aimed to kill."

"I didn't," she said, her eyes watering. "I shot to stop him. I didn't want him dead."

"Why did he need your help?"

Fresh tears glistened in her eyes. "He said he'd done something horrible."

"What did he tell you?"

She pressed trembling fingertips to her temple. "He said he killed Mr. Marlowe."

"Someone did," Jake said.

Amber drew in a deep breath as if to slow down Jake's rapid-fire questioning.

"How did Tim find you?"

"He's been following me since I came back to Nashville."

"Why didn't you tell us this originally?"

"I panicked. I thought you wouldn't believe me. I thought none of you trusted me."

Jake rubbed his chin darkened with stubble.

Georgia glanced back into the motel room where paramedics were trying to resuscitate Tim. Too much about all this bothered her, but she couldn't articulate it.

She hurried to her trunk and grabbed a camera. As the rescue crews worked on Tim, she stood out of their way. From the threshold she began to take pictures of the room. What was wrong with this? Amber's explanation made sense, but something didn't fit. She couldn't see it. Couldn't put it into words. But her gut gnawed when a crime scene didn't match the witness's accounts.

Three more marked cars had appeared and now filled the parking lot near the ambulance. Lights flashed as uniformed officers got out of their vehicles, hands on their guns.

The paramedics had run an IV into Tim's arm and had packed his wound and put an oxygen bag on his face. As Jake hovered close, they loaded Tim onto a stretcher and locked it into the raised position. As one paramedic squeezed the bag over his nose and held up the IV, the other pushed the stretcher.

Tears spilled down Amber's face as Tim was wheeled past. "Is he really alive?"

"Barely," one paramedic said.

Tim was loaded in the ambulance and the paramedic climbed into the back beside him and closed the door. The other paramedic ran to the driver's seat, and seconds later, the siren wailed and the ambulance left as a uniformed officer moved toward the scene with a roll of yellow crime scene tape.

As more marked cars arrived, Georgia indicated the areas she wanted marked off. Though she was tempted to process the scene, she held back. She was now a part of this investigation and her involvement could be misconstrued as a conflict of interest later in court.

Jake's focus shifted from the ambulance to Georgia's tired face as she moved toward him. "Are you all right?"

"Yeah. As many crime scenes as I've processed, I've never been involved with one. Now I seem to be linked to two."

"Why do you think Amber called you?"

"I guess it's like she said, she feels I've been a friend to her. I took her to the hospital after she was mugged."

He pinched the bridge of his nose. "Do you buy her story?"

"I don't know." She stared into the open door of the motel room. They stood in silence for a moment. Taking it all in. "Thanks for coming to my rescue."

He shook his head as if he hadn't been worried. "Figured I'd keep the motel guests safe from you. You're not always the best marksman."

"I hit the target when it counts."

"Eventually."

Feeling heat rise in her cheeks under his gaze, she glanced toward her brother who escorted a frowning Amber toward the squad car.

"I told you my story," Amber said, twisting to look up at him.

"You can tell us again at the station," Rick said.

"Am I being arrested?" she asked.

"Questioned."

Her eyes narrowed. "I want an attorney."

"Why?" Jake asked, approaching. "You're not being detained, just questioned."

She swiped a strand of blond hair from her eyes. "I remember how it went the last time. I want an attorney."

"I haven't arrested you."

She shook her head as fresh tears fell down her cheeks. "I don't care. I'm not saying a word without an attorney."

"You have one you can call?"

She folded her arms over her chest. "Rachel Wainwright."

Jake's head cocked. "The wife of the chief of homicide?"

"She's a defense attorney. One of the best and she takes on people who can't pay."

"You've done some homework."

She swiped away a tear, her gaze chilling. "I wasn't coming back to this town ill prepared."

Amber had invoked her right to counsel and there was little Jake could do but call Rachel Wainwright.

Defense attorney Rachel Wainwright arrived at the Nashville Homicide Department an hour later. Her low heels clicked on the tile floor as her long legs made up the distance under the glow of a fluorescent light. She received the call from Detective Jake Bishop that a woman he was holding for questioning was refusing to answer questions without an attorney present. She quickly ran a comb through her short dark hair and changed into dark slacks and a black V-neck sweater.

She didn't like approaching a case cold but she'd get up to speed quickly. She picked up a visitor badge at the front desk and made her way to a double mirror that looked into a holding room where Jake Bishop and Rick Morgan sat opposite a slender blonde, who could only be described as angelic. Whereas the lighting made most look sallow, her skin glowed a faint pink. She wasn't handcuffed. Sitting in front of her was a half-eaten sandwich and a can of diet soda. She'd not lived in Nashville when Amber Ryder had found herself in trouble five years ago and could only imagine the fear running through a teenaged girl's mind when confronted with questions from an army of cops and reporters.

Rachel knocked on the door, then opened it. Jake and Rick stood.

Jake politely nodded. "Rachel, thanks for coming."

She acknowledged Jake and Rick, but shifted her attention to the blonde. "Amber Ryder?"

The pale woman rose. "That's right."

"I'm Rachel Wainwright. I understand you need an attorney?"

She looked up with blue eyes as pale as a clear lake. "Yes. Thank you so much for coming."

Rachel liked and respected Jake and Rick, but she was here as a defense attorney and not as a friend of the family. "Gentlemen, if you will give me some privacy with my client."

Jake glanced at Amber, who stared up at him with wide, worried eyes.

Amber shook her head. "They can stay. I've nothing to hide, but I want an attorney present. You've heard about my past with the law."

"Bits and pieces," Rachel said. Most of what she heard had been from her husband, Deke Morgan. And as much as she loved that man, he was a cop first and she often did not completely share his view of the police.

Jake's phone buzzed and he glanced at the screen before frowning. "It's the hospital. Would you excuse me?"

"Sure," Rachel said. He ducked out of the room.

Rachel motioned for Amber to sit and she took the chair across from her. "Is there anything you need?"

Amber tugged at the hem of her sleeve. "I want to see Mrs. Reed. She'll be worried about me."

Rachel looked up at Rick. "Detective?"

His stance stiffened just a fraction. "I can call her."

Amber flexed her fingers. "I don't want her to hear my story from a cop. I want her to hear it from me. She needs to see me and know I'm innocent."

"Why not your mother?" Rick asked.

Amber looked at Rachel with watery eyes. "My mother can't help. Is it so unreasonable for me to see Mrs. Reed?"

Rachel tapped short plain fingernails on the table. "Detective? It's not an unreasonable request."

Rick frowned, but before he could answer, the door opened to a scowling Jake.

"That was the hospital," Jake said.

"How is Tim?" Amber asked.

"Still alive," Jake said. "A miracle, considering the injuries, but he's in surgery right now."

"So he's going to live?" Amber's tentative smile beamed hope and worry.

Jake slid his hands into his pockets. "Docs say he's a tough guy. It could go either way."

She lowered her face to her hands. A sigh shuddered through her before she looked up, eyes red-rimmed and tearing. "I never meant to hurt him."

Rachel pulled out a legal pad and pen. "Detectives, I need a moment with my client."

"Sure," Jake said.

When the door closed behind them, Rachel looked at Amber. "Tell me what happened." Amber recounted her story, starting with Tim calling and asking her to meet him at the motel.

The story was tight. Made sense.

Rachel had defended her share of the guilty. She never judged, believing in every person's right to a fair trial. Some of her guilty clients had been bad liars. Some had been very skilled. Over the last few years she had developed a knack for ferreting them out. She needed to know fast where she stood with a client's defense. Every citizen in Nashville would be following this case.

But with Amber, she couldn't get a read. Everything about the woman spoke of truth. The mannerisms. The inflection in her voice. Even the way she looked at Rachel as she spoke. All signs of telling the truth.

But a very small twist in her gut belied the body language and the words. The woman could be hiding something, but that didn't mean she had intended to shoot Tim. Hiding one secret didn't mean she was guilty of another. She couldn't pinpoint what Amber held back, but there was something. The trick now was to figure out what her client was hiding.

# CHAPTER TWENTY-THREE

*Friday, October 13, 12:30 A.M*

Georgia accepted a cup of coffee from Jake as the two stood outside the interview room while Rachel talked to Amber. "Have you been able to get ahold of Mrs. Reed?"

"No," Jake said. "She's not answering her cell and she's not at her home. Which does not make sense given the time. We're looking for her."

She dug her fingernail into the side of the Styrofoam. "Do you think Amber knew she was Marlowe's kid when they slept together?"

"Says a lot about her if she did." Jake shook his head. "No wonder the guy looked like he could jump out of his skin when he was close to her."

She glanced into her cup. "So how bad is Tim?"

"Pretty bad," he said sipping his coffee.

"On a scale of one to ten."

"Ten being dead?"

"Yeah, sure."

He stared over the brim of his cup. "He's a ten."

"What?" A frown furrowed her brow. "How long have you known?"

"He died at the scene. The IV and the ambulance were all theater. I didn't tell you because you had to buy into it completely so I could sell it to Amber."

There had never been any hint of Jake's deception until this moment. "So you just basically told a huge fat lie."

He grimaced as if she'd insulted him. "A little white lie in my book. And when it's a homicide investigation, all bets are off."

She glanced toward her brother who looked perfectly content as he read a text on his phone. "Rick, did you know?" she asked

Without glancing up, he typed a message. "Pleading the Fifth."

"Damn it." She punched her brother in the arm. "What are you two trying to accomplish?"

"If Amber shot Tim in self-defense as she said, then she'll continue to be glad he's alive," Jake said. "All her lying and the reports of promiscuity could be a result of her relationship with Dalton.

"But if she meant to shoot Tim, then she'll be worried he will discredit her story. He might just tell us that he helped her kill Mike and Bethany five years ago. He might know something about Elisa. He has an alibi for her death, but he knows a lot more than we do. She's going to be really worried about him talking to us."

Georgia dealt in forensic facts. She collected data. Analyzed data. She was black and white. And all this was too very gray for her. "And if she didn't mean to shoot him?"

"Then she'll go on as an innocent woman would, and we will tell her the bad news in a day or two. She's smart and if she held to her amnesia story for five years, she's not going to be easy to crack."

Rick rose. "I'm going to walk the halls and call Jenna. I want to check on the baby."

"How's she doing?" In the chaos of the day she'd forgotten about the child.

Rick grinned. "She's doing really well. Jenna is in love."

"Carrie had no family," Georgia said.

"I know. I've got Rachel looking into it all."

She cocked her head. "Does that mean you're going to keep Sara?"

"We sure are going to try. The Big House hasn't been the same since you were there to terrorize it." The Big House had belonged to their parents and all during her childhood had been filled with laughter, the scent of her mother's cooking, and occasionally her own tantrums.

When Rick left, Georgia's gaze nailed Jake. "You don't play fair."

"No, I don't," he said with no hint of apology. He leaned closer and said, "But I have been more than fair with you."

She glanced around, half expecting to see Rick or Deke, before she wrapped her arms around his neck. "You're such a brave little solider for dealing with me."

"I'll have it no other way." He rested his hands on her hips. A muscle twitched in his jaw. "You scared the hell out of me today."

She folded her arms. "I was doing my job."

"Don't give me that. You took a reckless chance." He shoved out a breath as if he caught himself doing what he'd promised he would not.

"I thought you liked my independence."

"You're great on the job, and we all know you're a badass who can take care of business. But it's not a sin to need someone else every so often."

She shifted uncomfortably. "I don't know what to say."

His gaze darkened with disappointment. "Life is too damn short. Stop trying to muscle it alone."

She moved out of his embrace, stepping back a step. "Ah, where's the fun if there's no challenge?"

Before he could respond, Rick returned to the room and held up a picture of Jenna holding the baby. "I thought you might like to see this."

Georgia smiled. "Very nice, Daddy."

He clicked off the phone. "Don't get ahead of yourself. Any word from Rachel or Amber?"

Jake turned his attention from Georgia. "Waiting on Rachel. She's still talking to her client."

"You really think Tim wanted to hurt Amber?" Rick asked.

"I don't know."

"So what do we do now?" Georgia asked, her voice more hoarse than she expected.

Jake took a sip of coffee. "I'll be doing a little asking around about Tim for the next few hours, and then I'm going to turn Amber loose and see what she does."

\* \* \*

Jake and Rick arrived at St. Vincent school just before seven. The campus was just beginning to stir, and the principal's office was open. Jake called the principal and asked if Mrs. Garfield would be willing to talk to them again. She agreed.

They found Principal Byrd and Mrs. Garfield in the front office alone, drinking coffee. When the detectives entered, the two educators set down their cups and moved to the counter where several yellowed files were stacked.

"Thank you for seeing us," Jake said.

Mrs. Garfield shook her head. "We were so sorry to hear about Tim and Amber. What a terrible thing."

"Yes, ma'am," Jake said.

Principal Byrd opened the first file. "We were thinking about your questions about Amber and Tim and if there was a connection between them in high school. I asked Mrs. Garfield to pull all the photos taken for the yearbooks the years those four were here."

She thumbed through the photos. "I was the faculty advisor for the yearbook for several years and all the students brought their candid stills to me so I could consider them for the yearbook. To encourage the children to take pictures, we gave out weekly prizes for the best photo. You can imagine with most of the children having cameras on their phones how many pictures we got." She adjusted her glasses and grinned. "Not all of them were ready for primetime if you know what I mean. A tad racy."

Jake grinned. "High school never really changes."

"No, it doesn't," she said. "Regardless, after you called the principal, I spent this morning going through photos specifically looking for Amber, Tim, Bethany, and Mike. As it turned out, I'd pulled many of Bethany and Mike because we'd decided to do a tribute page to them in this year's edition."

She lifted a stack and laid them out much like a casino deals cards. "They are in chronological order, starting with freshman year, which as you can see is mostly pictures of Tim and Mike. They both played football and it was natural that they be photographed more."

Jake surveyed the pictures, noting the two boys looked clean cut and all-American. In several photos, Tim had his arm around Mike and the two, wearing football jerseys, were laughing. There was only one candid of Bethany. She was in the campus garden planting flowers, smiling shyly up at the camera. As he stared at the young girl he thought about the bones laid out in the cold, damp cave. It took a twisted kind of evil to hurt someone that innocent.

"There are a few pictures of Amber beginning junior year. Most of them are on the sidelines at the football games in the fall." She tapped one. "Amber is standing behind the cheerleaders here, and if you look closely, you'll see Mr. Marlowe off to her right."

Jake studied the picture of Daddy Marlowe. "He's glaring at her."

"Yes, he is," she said. "Looking at this I remember once crossing the parking lot to my car one evening and I saw the two of them talking. He wasn't touching her, but the way he leaned forward was aggressive. Angry even."

Knowing what he knew now about their relationship, his resentment made sense. He'd slept with Amber. Thought he was having an affair with a cute young girl and then he finds out she is his underage daughter. "When was she accepted to the school?"

The principal reached for a pad filled with notes. "She was accepted only about a week before the start of school. Last-minute add-ons are not the norm, so I looked up her file. Dalton Marlowe expedited her application."

Had she blackmailed him into getting her a spot in the school? It would explain much of his behavior.

Mrs. Garfield picked up the remaining junior year pictures and laid them out. "As you can see, more pictures of Mike and Amber. She's with him a lot of time at lunch, in the hallways, at the school play, and by the football field. They are clearly a couple."

"What about Tim?"

"Not so many pictures of him. And the ones we have, he's not with Mike much, and if he is, he's not smiling." She picked up the third stack. "There are quite a few candids of Amber and Bethany. Amber seems to be involved in the clubs. She and Mike are still caught on film together in the spring but not as much. And," she said, flipping more pictures, "she's with Tim a few times."

The photos were taken from the bleachers and shooting down on Tim and Amber who are standing so close they are touching. She is touching his chest and his hand is cupping her bottom. Amber's hair was dark and long in high school, but even then, she had a dark, smoky, seductive look that would have made every boy at that school look twice and dream of having her.

However, what really struck him was Tim's appearance. Long hair. Beard. He didn't look anything like the young conservative man on the rise. He looked like the guy in Texas who was a person of interest in the murder investigation.

Rick exchanged a glance with Jake. "When was that picture taken?"

"The spring of their junior year," Mrs. Garfield said. "Their ill-fated trip was six months later."

"Do you know much about Tim's family?" Jake asked.

"Old Nashville family," Principal Byrd said. "Father passed away a couple of years ago and mother travels a great deal. It was always assumed, according to his guidance counselor's records, that he would go to law school."

Mrs. Garfield showed them one last junior year picture. It was of Amber and Mike. But in the background Tim was glaring at them both. His expression looked dark and angry.

Jake tapped the image with his finger. "If looks could kill."

Georgia's cell rang minutes after she entered her apartment after a long night at the police station. She'd dropped her bag and was staring into an empty refrigerator as she fished the cell out of her back pocket. Her front doorbell rang and she moved toward the door and opened it without much thought.

She found herself face to face with Amber, who stood there holding a tissue to her nose. Her watery eyes were wide and bloodshot and her nose red as if she'd been crying.

Tension chilled Georgia's skin. "Amber?"

Amber sniffed, dabbing her nose. "I didn't know what else to do. Where to go."

She gripped the door. "I thought you were going back to Mrs. Reed's house. You said you wanted to see her."

"I did go back to her house and she's not there. I don't know where she is and I'm in a panic."

Jake had released Amber during the early morning hours as he'd promised. Now was the big test. Was she a victim or a killer? "Where is your mother?"

"I don't know. She should have gotten home by now."

She stepped aside, allowing the woman to enter. Had she found out about Tim? "Come in. Would you like some coffee?"

"I'm fine. I'm exhausted." A sigh shuddered through her. "I just needed a place to catch my breath. And to figure out my next move."

"Next move?" Georgia closed the door. So why was she here? "Have a seat."

Amber settled on the couch, leaning back and studying her for a moment. "Rachel was able to convince them to release me. She took me to see Mrs. Reed. I searched the whole house for her and when I couldn't find her, I got a cab here."

Nothing she said sounded wrong. But she always had a good explanation. "Are you sure you don't want something to eat? Maybe a bagel?"

"That would be great. I'm starving."

She moved to the refrigerator and pulled out a couple of bottled waters. She twisted off the top of one and handed it to Amber. From the freezer she removed frozen bagels and placed them in the microwave. "How's Tim?"

"Detective Bishop said he was improving." She sipped, drinking for several seconds. "I called the hospital on the way over here, but they won't release any information. They can only give out information to family. His mother was always in Europe this time of year, so I'm guessing they're trying to find her now."

"That's standard with hospitals. It's against the law for them to release confidential patient information."

Shaking her head, she closed her eyes for a moment. "I never thought that life would repeat itself and I'd be back in this damn town defending myself again. I only came back here to find answers."

Georgia watched Amber twist a thread on the hem of her shirt around her finger and tighten it until the tip of her finger turned red. "You shot Tim in self-defense and the cops will piece it together. Jake and Rick are fair and smart and they'll get to the bottom of this."

She rubbed her fingers against the darkening bruise on her cheek. "Tim is crazy. He was obsessed with me in high school. Obsessed. I was with Mike and he hated it. Several times I caught him standing outside my bedroom window."

"Was he always like that?"

"He always ran hot and cold. Very loving one minute and then furious the next. Mike wasn't the best guy in the world, but I liked him a lot. And I wanted to be with him despite what his father had done to me."

Did she know about her paternity? Georgia eased into the chair across from Amber. "Did Tim tell you what happened in the woods?"

"He said he found me with Mike and he shot him. Bethany heard the shot and came running. When she did, he shot at her, but the gun jammed so he hit her with a rock and then stabbed her. He said I freaked out and started running. I must have slipped on wet leaves as I was running down the trail. Fell and hit my head and broke my arm. He thought I was dead. He panicked and ran."

"He just left you."

"That's what he said."

"He went to a lot of trouble to hide Bethany and Mike's bodies. Walled them up. Hung up Bethany's pendant as a kind of grave marker."

"I don't pretend to understand the mind of a madman."

"Did you tell Detective Bishop?"

"I told him, but he didn't believe me. I don't think any of them believe me."

She smoothed her hand over the table. "He said that?"

"Yes."

Jake hadn't believed Amber from the very beginning. But he hadn't tipped his hand to her. He was too smart to let Amber know his true thoughts.

"You need to make him believe I didn't mean to shoot Tim," she said. "You're my only friend."

"And Mrs. Reed."

"She's old. Fragile."

"What about Rachel? She's your attorney."

"I don't know her. Not like I know you."

Fingers of fear crept around Georgia's neck. She rose. "I need to call Detective Bishop. We need to talk to him together."

Amber hurried after her, grabbing her arm. "Do you really think you can convince him?"

Georgia glanced down at her arm, tugging it from Amber's embrace. "It couldn't hurt to try."

She reached for her cell and dialed. His phone went to voice mail and she left him a message, telling him he needed to come to her place. Amber was here. She needed his help.

"Maybe he will let me in to see Tim. If I can see Tim, I might be able to get him to confess."

"I don't think they'll let you see Tim until he recovers from surgery."

"I didn't think so." She shook her head. "If I can get to someone with authority in the hospital, I can make them understand."

Georgia had no doubt that Amber could persuade just about anyone of anything. She had a look and a way about her that reached out and made you notice her. "I know about Mr. Marlowe."

Amber shook her head. "What do you know? He forced me to have sex. Is that what you know?"

"He's your father."

She winced as if she'd been slapped. "He wasn't a father to me! Not ever."

"But he's your biological father. We ran yours, Mike's and Dalton's DNA from five years ago. You all share the same markers."

Amber flinched. "That's not true!"

Georgia had the sense she was now playing poker with a master. She used words, facts, and injuries like playing cards; always careful to reveal only the cards she wanted seen. "It's true. And you know it."

Amber turned from her, dropping her head. For a moment her shoulders shook as if she were weeping. And then she turned, pointing the barrel of a gun at Georgia.

Her heart skittered and then stilled as she forced her mind to calm and think. "What's that for?"

"You're smart. How did you make that connection? My mom doesn't even know that I know."

"More importantly, how did you find out?"

"Letters stowed in the attic. Letters from Dalton to Mom telling her they were done and the enclosed check was all she was going to receive from him." Amber shook her head. "And the crazy part to me was that she accepted what he gave her and walked away. Walked away from all that money. She knew he would kill her if she leaked the truth or tried to blackmail him."

"How long have you known?"

"The summer before my junior year. I went to him and scoped him out in a hotel bar. I could always make myself look a little older and with a fake ID and a slinky dress the bartenders looked the other way."

"You were just a kid."

"Like I said, I'm good." She brushed a wisp of hair from her eyes. "And he had a thing for young girls. You know the first time I sat next to him at a bar he looked at me with such lean hungry eyes."

"You seduced him."

"I did. Three times. And I taped each hook-up.

When I showed it to him at first he didn't look that worried. He even laughed. Then I called him 'Daddy.' I thought he was going to stroke out. That was a real family moment."

"Did you kill Bethany and Mike?"

"I did," she said leaning forward as if she were sharing a great secret. "And I hid their beautiful damn bodies so well I knew they'd never be discovered if I didn't give you a really big clue. Enter Elisa's stinking dead body."

"Why her?"

A sigh shuddered through her. "You could tell by looking at her that she thought she was smarter than everyone. So much better than the rest of us. But all it takes is a little attention and girls like that melt. I paid a good-looking guy to flirt with her in the coffee shop, but when it became clear he wasn't doing it for her, I approached her."

"You planted Elisa's backpack in Scott Murphy's motel room."

She looked pleased. "Very smart. All I had to do was promise him more money and he came running. While he was getting his fix, I dropped off the backpack. Too easy. Coaxing Elisa into the woods was also so easy. See old Scott wasn't getting the job done so I had to seduce her myself. She was ripe for the picking."

"You were the one in the woods with her?"

"Yep." She laughed. "Hell, what is it with smart girls? They are so dumb in the real world. Take Bethany. Coaxing her into the woods took little effort. The trick is to know which buttons to push."

"Bethany? You were never her friend."

"Not exactly true. I liked hanging around her mother. Liked feeling pampered. It was a first for me. Bethany, as smart as she was never appreciated what she had."

A cold realization shot through her mind. "Where is Mrs. Reed?"

"She's where she wants to be."

"What does that mean?"

"She's with Bethany," she whispered.

"What did you do to her?"

"Nothing she didn't really want."

Georgia had seen the aftermath of evil at crime scenes. She'd testified against monsters in courts of law. But those monsters were always cleaned up and coiffed by attorneys and rarely spoke. This was the very first time evil stood so close. "What do you want from me?"

"I need you to call that hospital so I can see Tim. I need to know if the fool is ever going to wake up." Amber winked as if Georgia was now willing to play along. "You know they'll talk to you."

Georgia pulled her phone from her back pocket. But instead of dialing, asked, "When you fell in the woods, Tim was there with you, wasn't he?"

"He freaked out. Started crying. I could barely see for the pain, but I told him not to worry. I said I could fake amnesia. I would never tell on him. He swore he would never tell. We'd have been fine if not for you re-opening the case. He did fine five years ago because I took all the heat. He even came to Texas occasionally to play with me a little. But as loyal as he thinks he is, he couldn't stand up to real pressure from the cops. I couldn't trust he could remain strong."

"When did you decide to kill him?"

"When he told me he killed Dalton." She laughed. "He killed my daddy and I just couldn't let that stand. Again, he was easy to manipulate. To lure. To kill."

"So if Tim dies, then what?"

"Then you die and then I find myself a real good attorney and stake a claim to Daddy's money." She waved the gun. "Come to think of it, you actually did me a favor. Dalton couldn't have declared Mike legally dead in a couple more years and knowing how much he loved that dumb kid he might not ever have done it. Everyone knows the money went to Dalton. I was going to blackmail him, but now I can simply inherit it all as his sole heir."

"You won't get away with this."

She rolled her eyes. "I did it once, and I'll do it again."

"What are you going to do if Tim lives and he talks?"

"He won't live. He can't. Won't." She motioned to the phone. "Now start dialing, bitch."

Georgia left a message with Jake. "He's going to come here."

"I'm counting on stud paying us a visit. If you're good, I'll let you watch."


Jake had expected Amber to go to the hospital after he released her. He put a tail on her and they reported that she went to the Reed house, lingered there for a while, and then left.

And then he got the call from Deke that Scott Murphy had been arrested. He was a perfect match to the sketch Jenna had drawn and had been found in a crack house.

"The guy swears he didn't kill Elisa," Deke said. "He said he was paid three hundred bucks to hang out with Elisa and follow her around."

"Did he say who paid him?"

"A woman."

"Who looks just like Amber?"

"That's correct," Deke said.

"I want to talk to him, but first I have to track down Amber. She never went to the hospital." His phone beeped. "I've got a call coming in from Georgia."

"Call me back."

Jake played back her message. "Shit. Amber is with Georgia. She must have slipped the surveillance team."

"What the hell does she want with Georgia?" Rick asked.

"I don't know." Anger burned in his gut. "But we're going to her place now. Based on this message, Amber's been there ten minutes at least."

"Drive."

Jake wove in and out of traffic, covering the five miles to Georgia's apartment in record time.

Guns drawn, Jake and Rick raced up the stairs, quickly and quietly. Rick remained on the top stair while Jake crept closer to the door where he heard Georgia arguing with Amber. Her words were short, clipped, and angry.

He couldn't tell where they were positioned in the room. Breaking in the door now might be the wrong call, but if he hesitated, Amber would certainly kill her.

Jake held his gun tightly and softly knocked on the

door, hiding his concern. "Georgia, it's Jake. I've news on Tim."

Seconds passed and then he heard the turn of the deadbolt. The door opened to only Georgia. One look at her pale, strained features and he knew Amber was close. "So how's Tim?" she asked, her voice even as if they were having a normal conversation.

"He's awake," he said, forcing a grin. "We hope to take his statement early this afternoon."

The door swung open a little wider and he saw Amber standing to the side, a gun in her hand. It was pointed at Georgia's back.

"Come inside, sugar," Amber ordered. "Close the door. This is a private party."

His hands at his sides, he moved inside, but didn't lock the door, aware that Rick would follow. "Tim is talking, Amber."

Amber recovered from her shock, backing up. "Really? And what's Tim saying?"

The pictures from the high school told the story. "That you two have been an item since high school. He's always had a thing for you. He visited you in Texas. And when you came back to town, you two hooked up again."

Amber's smile wavered. "That's not true. He would never talk to you about me."

"You said it yourself," Georgia said. "You didn't think he was strong enough to resist the heat if questioned. Jake, did he tell you how he and Amber killed Bethany and Mike?"

"He told the whole story." Frowning, he jabbed his thumb behind him. "I don't think he knew about the other guy."

"What other guy?"

"Scott Murphy. The guy you had flirted with in the coffee shop. I bet when I tell him you two were sleeping together, he'll really tell all."

"You're lying. I never slept with that guy."

"Yeah, but that's not what I'm going to tell Tim. Matter of time before he rolls over on you."

"Tim won't talk."

Footsteps sounded on the stairs, catching Amber's attention for a split second. As Jake reached for his gun, Georgia shoved Amber backward, recovered, and raised the gun in an instant.

Jake fired a double tap into her chest while Georgia stayed crouched. She staggered just a split second, greenlighting Jake to put one last round into her head.

Rick shoved through the door and Jake kicked the gun out of reach should Amber still be alive.

"Backup is on the way," Rick said.

Jake calmly holstered his weapon and knelt beside her body. He searched for a pulse to confirm death, not that it would have mattered. The twisted bitch was dead.

Relief shot through his body, as he rose, turned to Georgia and helped her up. He wrapped his arms around her and she relaxed against him with a shudder. "Are you all right?"

"Just great."

He held her close. Listening, but not quite sure what to say next.

"She's insane," she breathed. "She said Mrs. Reed is with Bethany."

"We'll have to do a search of her house." He pressed his lips close to her ear, and his gruff voice was only loud enough for her to hear. "Why'd she come after you?"

"She was trying to figure out if Tim were alive or not."

"Shit."

A tremor shuddered through her body. "She thought she actually had a shot at Dalton's money now that she was his only surviving child."

"Damn." Jake tightened his hold around Georgia's small frame. "I love you."

She clutched the fabric of his jacket. "Say it louder. I don't think Rick heard you."

Rick closed his phone, tucked it in his pocket. "Something I should be aware of?"

She remained close to Jake, not bothering to move away. "Rick, Jake and I are dating."

Rick stilled. "Say again?"

"It's serious." She could feel Jake's gaze burning into her, but she couldn't tell if this pronouncement pleased him or not.

Rick cleared his throat. "How long?"

"Not long."

Rick clenched his jaw, clearly chewing on words he wasn't sure should be spoken. "You were never good at keeping secrets as a kid, Georgia."

She remained close enough to Jake to feel his body heat. "No. I'm still not too good at it."

Rick looked at Jake. "Break her heart and you know what happens next."

Jake didn't blink. "What if she breaks my heart?"

Rick shook his head. "Then that's your tough luck for getting involved with a Morgan. It's a one-way street."

"Roger that."

Rick drew in a breath. "I need a walk."

When he was gone, Georgia met Jake's gaze. "That out in the open enough for you?"

He kissed her full on the lips, hovering close when he spoke. "It's a start."

# EPILOGUE

*Three months later*

The Morgan clan had arrived in force.

Georgia, Deke and his wife, Rachel, Alex and his new wife, Leah, all stood in the judge's chambers and watched as Rick and Jenna held baby Sara. They watched the judge sign the final adoption papers. "That makes it official. You may now officially welcome Sara Adele Morgan into the clan."

Rick leaned over and kissed Jenna whose eyes filled with tears that spilled down her face.

Georgia swallowed hard and softly clapped. She would love this baby as if it were her own flesh and blood. "Another Morgan girl to terrorize the clan. I like it."

Jenna smiled at Georgia. "Baby Sara kinda looks like you."

Georgia glanced at the baby. "Yeah, I think she has my nose."

KC and Georgia had arranged a small funeral for Carrie. A search revealed no relatives who would take the baby, leaving an open path for Rick and Jenna to talk with Social Services.

Alex, tall, lean, and normally very reserved to the point of cold, wrapped his arm around Leah as the two walked up to Georgia and smiled. "Where's Jake?"

"He's in criminal court. Had to testify. He said he'd catch up shortly."

She and Jake had attended Alex and Leah's wedding on Christmas Eve, and though her brothers were still getting used to the idea of the two of them as a couple, they accepted him for the time being.

Deke wrapped his arm around Georgia. "Baby Sara reminds me of you. Buddy called you a small tornado the day he and Mom signed your adoption papers. I think Sara is your match."

She never realized how much emotion must have infused the moment her parents made her an official Morgan. They didn't speak about it often, but now she realized when they did, why her mother always grew a little misty-eyed. "I will gladly hand over the mantle as the youngest, most troublesome Morgan."

"Not troublesome," Deke said. "More like a spit-fire."

Sara would have questions about Carrie along the way, and Georgia would be on hand to share the stories she remembered of the shy girl who always had a smile.

The Morgans all made their way into the marbled hallway where Jake stood, his hands in his pockets. He smiled when he saw Georgia and crossed to kiss her. No more hiding from them. They were a couple.

"Is it official?" Jake asked Rick.

Jenna beamed as she adjusted the baby's pink bow on her head. "Signed and sealed."

"That's good." He wrapped his arm tighter around Georgia. "She's a lucky baby to have you."

Jenna shook her head. "We're the lucky ones."

Georgia's chest tightened with emotions she really couldn't put into words.

As if sensing this, Jake hugged her closer. And in a voice only loud enough for her to hear, said, "You doing all right?"

Tears threatened as Rick, Jenna, and Sara stood beside the judge and posed for pictures. "Sure, why not?"

"You have that look," he said.

This morning, she'd woken up in his arms, feeling safer than she had in a long time. For weeks, she'd woken up from nightmares featuring Amber standing over her bed. "What look?"

"The faraway worried kind."

"I'm fine."

It had taken Jake and Rick weeks to untangle the webs Amber had spun. They'd traveled to Austin where they had learned that Amber and Tim had hunted and killed a girl just as they had Elisa, Bethany, and Mike.

Amber truly was a woman with no conscience. A sociopath. From the moment she learned that Dalton Marlowe was her father, she set out to completely destroy him. Bethany's death had been collateral damage. She'd been in the woods that day. Wrong place. Wrong time. No witnesses. It had been almost the perfect crime. Until Georgia had placed the call to Amber telling her the case was reopened.

Suddenly, the satisfaction Amber had enjoyed knowing how she'd hurt Marlowe by taking his son, vanished. Her hatred drove her back to Nashville to finish what she'd started.

However, when she had run into Mrs. Reed, she found herself falling back into an old pattern, allowing the woman to mother her. Amber had lied to Georgia about Mrs. Reed. She'd not killed the woman but drugged her and left her in her room. Whether she had an affection for the woman or simply still considered her useful, no one would ever know.

Jake threaded his fingers through hers, warming her skin. His touch reminded her of how alive those hands could make her feel. "So, you got any other cold cases you want to stir up?"

She laughed. "You know me. Never a dull moment."

He kissed her on the lips. "God help us all."